# SAPPHIRE SPRING

# Also from Christopher Rice and C. Travis Rice

**C. Travis Rice**
SAPPHIRE SUNSET: A Sapphire Cove Novel
SAPPHIRE SPRING: A Sapphire Cove Novel

**Thrillers**
A DENSITY OF SOULS
THE SNOW GARDEN
LIGHT BEFORE DAY
BLIND FALL
THE MOONLIT EARTH

**Supernatural Thrillers**
THE HEAVENS RISE
THE VINES
BONE MUSIC: A Burning Grill Thriller
BLOOD ECHO: A Burning Girl Thriller
BLOOD VICTORY: A Burning Girl Thriller
DECIMATE

**Paranormal Romance**
THE FLAME: A Desire Exchange Novella
THE SURRENDER GATE: A Desire Exchange Novel
KISS THE FLAME: A Desire Exchange Novella

**Contemporary Romance**
DANCE OF DESIRE
DESIRE & ICE: A MacKenzie Family Novella

**With Anne Rice**
RAMSES THE DAMNED: THE PASSION OF CLEOPATRA
RAMSES THE DAMNED: THE REIGN OF OSIRIS

# SAPPHIRE SPRING

## Sapphire Cove

### Christopher Rice
### Writing As
# C. Travis Rice

BLUE
BOX
PRESS

Sapphire Spring
By Christopher Rice writing as C. Travis Rice

Copyright 2022 Christopher Rice
ISBN: 978-1-957568-03-4

Published by Blue Box Press, an imprint of Evil Eye Concepts, Incorporated

# Acknowledgments from the Author

A huge thank you, as always, to the amazing team at Blue Box Press for being the perfect home for this series. Liz Berry, Jillian Stein, and M.J. Rose, along with the amazing Kim Guidroz, Kasi Alexander, and Asha Hossain. A big shout out to the amazing Jenn Watson at Social Butterfly.

The first Sapphire Cove novel was written during lockdown, and it was the escape I desperately needed from the difficult years of 2020 and 2021. As soon as I was able, I headed down to Orange County to learn more about the real-world resorts that have inspired these pages. A big thank you to Jenna Jiampietro, the guest relations manager at Montage Laguna Beach, for giving me an amazing backstage tour, and the resort's former security director Chadwick Pohle.

One of the many perks of being best friends with the amazingly talented writer Eric Shaw Quinn is that he is also a genius at plotting and story development. He gave this one a transformative read and I'll be forever grateful for it. A reminder that we have a weekly podcast called "TDPS Presents CHRISTOPHER & ERIC" which you can find on your podcast platform of choice or at www.TheDinnerPartyShow.com. You should also read his *Write Murder* mystery series because it's as funny as he is.

# Author's Note

I am deeply indebted to the following Iranian-Americans who generously shared their lived experience of Persian culture and gave this novel such thoughtful and sensitive reads. Kian Maleki, Navid Nakhjavani, and the lovely and talented Tara Grammy, one of the finest actresses at work today, thank you for helping me bring Naser Kazemi's story to life.

*Sapphire Spring* is a romance novel that deals explicitly with issues of high school bullying, addiction and sexual abuse.

# 1

Naser Kazemi had spent most of his adult life trying to get rich people to rein in their spendthrift ways, and so he'd learned, long ago, the best strategy for getting an A-type personality to do what you wanted them to do—never, under any circumstances, tell them what to do.

As a CPA, he'd encircled his clients with facts and figures that corralled them onto a better, more prudent path.

As the newly hired controller for Sapphire Cove, the person responsible for maintaining the resort's bottom line, his successes had involved alternatives over admonishments.

His proudest moment since taking the job three months before was the colorful PDF he'd submitted to the hotel's general manager outlining how the resort could afford better landslide insurance if they reduced the insane amount of money the man was spending on in-room toiletries and the custom-made glass bottles they came in. The presentation had worked its intended effect, even if several of the gruesome landslide photos he'd included had caused his boss to cry out as if he'd been struck. Naser had remained unfazed. Connor Harcourt, Sapphire Cove's general manager, had also been his best friend since their freshman year of college. Naser was no stranger to the expressive flourishes the man made when he didn't get his way.

In the end, numbers couldn't be argued with—arrange them in the right order, and they could make a hard truth easier to swallow, but the truth was still there, impervious to bullying, threats, or displays of emotion. That's why they'd always been Naser's first love.

But sometimes when it came to men like his best friend— successful, determined, wealthy, and entitled men—only an outright threat would do, and that's why, when he found Connor in a huddle with the hotel's executive chef and pastry chef fifteen minutes after Connor was supposed to have left on his first vacation since taking the reins of the resort, Naser gripped him by one bicep and whispered into his ear, "If you don't leave in the next thirty seconds, I'm going to show everyone who works here the coffee cake footage."

Connor's round blue eyes blazed. "You wouldn't dare."

Naser would totally dare, and they both knew it. It was perfect blackmail material. That's why it still occupied a special folder on Naser's phone.

In it, a pajamas-clad Connor screamed louder than the smoke alarm in the kitchen of their college apartment as he hurled glass after glass of water at their smoke-billowing microwave. Today, Connor Harcourt was a successful former events planner who'd saved his family's resort from ruin the year before. Back then, he'd been a child of such privilege he'd grown up with his own personal chef. Which was why, shortly after moving in with Naser, he'd set a coffee cake to reheat for five minutes, reducing it to a charred, ember-studded husk and filling their apartment with acrid, yellow smoke. In the wake of the incident, and in the interest of keeping their apartment from burning down, he'd insisted on giving Connor several classes in kitchen procedures.

Suddenly, the two men had departed the resort's massive kitchen, making a serpentine path through the tide of bleary-eyed guests who were crossing Sapphire Cove's marble-floored lobby in search of the breakfast buffet. As agreed, Jonas Jacobs, the resort's special events director, and Gloria Alvarez, its assistant general manager, fell into step behind them. Jonas wheeled the suitcase Connor had abandoned in his office when he'd shown up earlier that morning after assuring everyone, including his fiancé, he wouldn't make it in to work that day.

"Don't forget the contractors are coming tomorrow to measure for the new fitness center."

"On it." Gloria's voice made Connor jump. He realized he was being corralled out the front door of his own resort by not just one, but three of his senior staff.

"And the organizers for the arborist conference have called twice to complain about the vegan menu for their awards dinner, so don't—"

"They're my ten o'clock," Jonas responded.

The four of them stepped through the automatic doors and into the hotel's motor court, which was largely shaded by a vine-threaded pergola. The vine was a luscious morning glory. It required almost constant pruning, but its deep blue blossoms were a nod to the hotel's name. Over Naser's objections, Connor had insisted it was worth the expense.

On the other side of the gurgling French fountain, Logan Murdoch sat behind the wheel of his cherry red pick-up truck. When Sapphire Cove's tallest and most muscular staff member was on duty as the hotel's security director, he typically wore a blue blazer, khakis, and a white dress shirt. But today was the start of his and Connor's first vacation in a year and a half, which was why he sported a T-shirt bearing the logo of his father's kickboxing gym.

At the sight of his fiancé spreading his arms in a gesture of *Didn't we talk about this, babe?*, Connor spun and planted a finger gently on the center of Naser's chest. "And you! Don't freak out about your sister's event on Friday."

"I'm not freaking out."

"You're not now, but you'll probably start as soon as I leave."

"I'm fine, Connor."

"And Pari's event will be too. Jonas is more than capable of handling her. We have a very clear contract. And I gave her a ton of discounts and a room for the night, so she should be happy as a clam."

"How do we know when a clam is happy again?" Naser asked.

"Nas!"

"You didn't have to do all that, Connor."

"Of course I did. I granted your sister lifetime diva status when I was nineteen."

"Another mistake. Your chariot awaits."

"You know, Logan and I could always wait to leave until Sunday. I'm pretty good at handling Pari."

"You buy her things and get her drunk. It's not exactly three-dimensional chess. Go, Connor. You've earned a break." Connor went to take the handle of his suitcase when a thought seized Naser, and he seized Connor's arm. "And Blondie, know this. If you and Logan pick a site that involves camping or a long hike, I will unleash a plague of locusts on the ceremony."

Connor and Logan's weeklong road trip to the Pacific Northwest was also a location scouting trip for their wedding. Both men loved the ocean, but they worked day in and day out in a sunny paradise, so they'd decided to host their destination wedding in a sweater-friendly setting where the beaches were more suited to the type of dramatic, moody walks made by the characters on the British television shows Connor and Naser liked to binge watch. The last time they'd discussed it, Connor's heart had been set on Cannon Beach, where a dramatic haystack rock sat just offshore. Logan seemed on board, but mostly because *The Goonies* had been filmed there, and he'd been obsessed with the movie as a kid.

"Nas, please. My idea of roughing it is a patio brunch without an umbrella."

"You're also very much in love, and Logan's capable of convincing you to go outside your comfort zone now and then." Naser grabbed the lapels of Connor's blazer and pulled them nose to nose. "Don't let him. The rest of us need climate control and a roof over our heads if it rains."

His best friend kissed him on the cheek, then accepted the handle of his suitcase from Jonas. "We already have to watch World War II documentaries every night before bed. I'm as far outside my comfort zone as I can go." He stepped off the curb and started for Logan's gleaming truck. "Goodbye, everyone. Don't destroy my hotel. I spent way too much time saving it."

"We all did, sweetheart," Gloria called after him.

When Logan stepped from the truck to help Connor with his bag, Naser thought the two men might be about to have words about Connor's tardiness. Instead, Logan enfolded his fiancé in his powerful arms and kissed him on the forehead.

Gloria let out the kind of sigh little girls make over puppies.

Naser felt a pang of jealousy. He was happy for Connor, truly, but he'd be lying if he didn't admit he longed for someone to look at him the way Logan Murdoch looked at his best friend. How he was supposed to meet that special someone was anyone's guess. He rarely left the house for anything other than work, and he'd pretty much given up on dating apps since they all coughed up a never-ending stream of problematic white boys who demanded he abandon his power-bottom status to conform to their vaguely racist role-play fantasies of being dominated by a terrorist or sheik.

Breathing a sigh of relief, Naser turned to face his compatriots.

Gloria, an ample-framed woman, had pulled her hair back at the crown, letting her black curls cascade on both sides. As always, she wore the placid half-smile known to hotel managers the world over, a smile that said, *I will do my best to accommodate even the most absurd request and pretend to accommodate the ones too absurd to accommodate.*

Jonas Jacobs, on the other hand—responsible for charming clients into forking over their life savings on weddings with high probabilities of ending in divorce—was smirking at him. Jonas had decided to go bald earlier that year, but he still maintained his precisely sculpted goatee beard. He was the only Black department head at Sapphire Cove and had been for years, a fact Connor had been trying to change with more diverse hiring practices. As always, his perfectly tailored dark suit was some subtle shade between navy and black, and he sported an ironed pocket square to match his tie—today they were purple. The devilish glint in his hazel eyes suggested he was aware of the agenda Naser planned to pursue now that Connor and Logan were gone.

"Well, isn't this wonderful!" Naser declared.

"That eager to see them go, huh?" Gloria asked.

Naser spread his arms and gave them a bright smile. "For the first time in its history, the keys to Sapphire Cove have been handed to three proud people of color. And all it took was for one white boy to drive away in a truck."

"Two white boys, actually," Jonas said. "And if only that was all diversity took, darling."

Gloria tittered. "Also, I certainly don't mean to step on this milestone moment for the hotel, but *I'm* actually in charge of Sapphire Cove, being that I'm the assistant general manager."

Jonas cleared his throat. "Don't overthink this, Gloria. Nas is just trying to butter us up so we'll help him destroy his sister."

Naser raised a warning finger. "We're not going to destroy my sister. We're just going to destroy her event so that it doesn't destroy the hotel."

"You know, Nas, I've been working with her for a few months now, and I have to say your sister is a very impressive and successful young woman. Perhaps you should—"

"My sister once hired a troupe of unlicensed fire eaters to perform inside a thatched roof hut for one of her promo events, and they set fire to the hut and a bar table."

"Fire eaters need a license?" Gloria asked.

"And you, Jonas, just because you're older and way taller than me doesn't mean you have a right to lecture me on my own family."

Jonas shrugged. "Come now, Nas. Everyone who works here is taller than you."

"Gentlemen, please." Gloria waited until she saw she had their attention. "Now I don't want to throw gasoline on the fire here. Or fire eater, I should say. But we got some calls late last night that might be related to the event, and I thought we should discuss."

Dread froze the pit of Naser's stomach. "What kind of calls?"

Gloria sighed. "Look, I try to be as culturally sensitive as I can be given that my family's from Honduras and I've spent most of my career here being called That Nice Mexican Lady"—Gloria mimed air quotes that could punch through concrete—"but what's a googoosh?"

Naser's breath left him in a thin wheeze. His hands went to his face before he could still them. Not because Gloria had made some terrible faux pas—because he could see where this was headed, and it ended with him and his sister wrestling each other into Sapphire Cove's pool as they called each other bad words in Persian.

"Oh God," he heard Gloria say. "Did I step in it?"

"Googoosh is a she," Jonas said.

Gloria winced. "Oh, so I'm off to a great start. Sorry."

Naser moaned into his palms. "Why are we getting calls about Googoosh?"

"People are asking if it's true and how much tickets are going to be."

"Oh my God!" Naser moaned into his palms.

"Am I allowed to ask who Googoosh is?" Gloria asked.

"The most famous Iranian pop star in history," Jonas answered. "She's the Celine Dion of pre-Revolutionary Iran. Basically, if you want to see a room full of Iranian Americans scream with joy, tell them Googoosh is about to perform."

Gloria clapped her hands together. "And she's coming to Sapphire Cove? How wonderful!"

Nasser dropped his hands from his face. "It's not wonderful! Googoosh can sell out an arena!"

"All right, well, Dolphin Ballroom's open Friday," Jonas said.

"No, you guys aren't getting it," Naser said. "Googoosh is not performing at the launch of my sister's new handbag line. Pari's just telling everyone that so she can beef up attendance. But for us, that means all of Persian Orange County and Persian LA and possibly Persian Chicago and New York will be clogging this motor court on Friday night, wanting to know where the damn Googoosh concert is."

Jonas curved an arm around Naser's shoulders. "I thought you preferred Iranian American.''

"Persian is one less word, and I have a lot to get out right now.''

"All right, well,'' Jonas said, "let's look at it this way. If she fails to produce Googoosh as promised, the guests might filter into the other spaces, and it'll be a banner night for Camilla's and the bar. But I figure this is probably a misunderstanding.''

Naser gripped Jonas's elbows and tried to level him with an expression that conveyed a galaxy of disappointment and worry. "And I am begging you, Jonas, *begging* you—do not give my sister the benefit of the doubt about anything ever.''

Suddenly Gloria was staring past them with a wide-eyed look that suggested Godzilla had strolled into the motor court and was looking around for a place to sit. Naser spun. A Mack truck with a tarp-enclosed cargo bay coated in decades' worth of concrete dust lumbered in between the idling sports cars and luxury SUVs.

Gloria made a beeline for the open window on the driver's side. Naser and Jonas followed. "Gentlemen, no offense, but we have a service entrance for a reason,'' she called up to the truck's driver.

"Sorry, it's our first time here.'' The driver leaned slightly out of his window, revealing more of his hairy and paint-splotched left arm. "We're here to take down the pergola.''

"I'm sorry, the *what?*'' Gloria asked.

"The pergola, you know. On your pool deck.''

"Oh, dear,'' Jonas said. Naser spun to face him. Jonas shook his head, expression suddenly grave. "Your sister asked if she could tent the pool deck, and I told her no because there was a pergola in the way.''

"And now she's getting it out of the way.'' Naser spread his hands and grinned. "What an amazing young businesswoman she is. We should all be more appreciative.''

Chastened, Jonas bowed his head.

"Who sent you?'' Gloria called up to the driver.

"Some fashion designer lady.''

"Oh, dear,'' Jonas muttered.

Naser spun toward the driver's side of the truck. "What's in the back of your truck, sir?''

"Jackhammers. What do you think? We going to play twenty questions or can I get to work?''

"None of the above, Prince Charming,'' Gloria answered.

As Gloria began giving the driver instructions on how to leave,

Naser grabbed Jonas by the shoulder and steered them toward the lobby doors. "Is this just a misunderstanding too?"

"Where are we going?" Jonas asked.

"Your office. To do the worst thing ever, but it has to be done."

"What?"

"We're going to call my sister on the phone."

# 2

By his first year of college, Mason Worther had discovered the key to waking up after a night of hard partying. Before you expose your eyes to sunlight, first establish if you're in your own bed.

Years later, he was putting that time-tested strategy to use again. For the fifth time this month. Or was it the sixth? He wasn't sure.

Careful not to poke his head above the covers, he groped for the nightstand drawer and found the clues he needed to pinpoint his location: the box of condoms he'd picked up the week prior—freshly opened, which might explain the weight in the bed next to him—and the little mirror he'd snorted lines off the night before—and too many damn nights before that. At least he'd put the thing away, a sign his most recent house party hadn't been a total catastrophe, even if he couldn't remember much of it. Even if his head and stomach said otherwise.

*It's Thursday,* he thought. *Who has a rager on a Wednesday night?*

Mason Worther did, apparently.

After another few minutes of drifting in and out of nauseated sleep, he pulled the comforter down over his face, squinted at the palatial, sun-filled master suite of his beachfront home, and said a prayer of thanks he hadn't burned the place down during the night. Or early that morning.

Not only had he forgotten to pull the drapes, but the sliding deck doors were also open to the balcony and its view of bright blue Pacific stretching to the horizon. The sound of crashing waves filled the room. Seagulls cawed outside. A woman played at the surf's edge with her two toddler-aged kids. Like most of the houses lining Capistrano Beach,

Mason's didn't have much of a yard. Just a concrete patio with a hot tub that dead-ended right at the sand. The ocean was his yard, and his dad paid a premium for it.

Anyone else who woke up to this view would probably be grateful, happy. Blissed out, even.

But he was miserable. Again.

Miserable and hung over. His favorite combo, apparently.

And if the sun wasn't blinding enough, the carpet was bright white, the walls were bright white where they weren't glass, the fixtures all polished chrome. Maybe if he hadn't let that friend of Chadwick's design the place, he'd have a comfortable home. The guy snorted Adderall for breakfast and made every home he touched look like a supervillain's lair. He was all about clean, open spaces, which meant most of the things Mason needed to live were stuffed in two hidden closets downstairs that erupted like clown cars whenever he opened them.

Mason struggled to remember the night before, pulling up a tape loop of memories dulled and melted by Balvenie and blow.

The *vroom vroom* of Chadwick Brody's new Maserati tearing down the little private road toward Mason's house. Pretending to listen to some big speech about the new laser peel tech his best friend was rolling out at his dermatology practice this year as the guy chopped up the first fat white lines of the evening, but as with most of the speeches that Chadwick made after first entering Mason's house, it ended abruptly with Chadwick throwing open the doors in Mason's wet bar and shouting, "Where the fuck is your gin, bro?"

Fast forward to jumbled footage of more blow inhaled off the glass coffee table downstairs—the one held up by a giant brown seashell that still sometimes scared him first thing in the morning because he kept mistaking it for a sleeping dog—with the girls Chadwick brought, because Chadwick always brought girls, talking a mile a minute about whether Paris was cooler than London even though Mason had never been to Paris. Just London, and it was on a business trip with his dad, and he'd never made the train for Paris like he'd planned to. But for some reason admitting that to a bunch of swimsuit models he didn't know had seemed as embarrassing as admitting his house belonged to his dad.

Sometime around then, Benny—or was it Barry? Chadwick was always switching drug dealers!—showed up after Chadwick declared they were running low on party favors. And that's when Mason realized how late it was, that another casual get-together had turned into a sleep-stealing coke fest. Realized, with a sinking feeling, that tomorrow—meaning today—was a workday, and it would probably be shot. Worse, the drugs were wearing off, and all he wanted to do was start up again to avoid the come-down, but that could mean he either went for another three hours or another three days. Lately, there was no telling where the wall was.

And that's when his memories faded to black.

There was a shift in the comforter next to him. He heard what must have been a leg sliding to the floor. Then a man sat up in bed, and Mason's heart turned to ice. It wasn't the first time he'd come out of a blackout in bed with a guy, but no way could he have hooked up with another dude in front of Chadwick and his crew. Not without fires being started and blood being shed.

Buck naked, the guy stood up, revealing a perfectly sculpted, brown-skinned ass that left Mason wishing he could remember what he'd done to it. His guest started for a pair of white briefs that were draped across the back of one of the bedroom's giant chairs. The chairs were big and soft and on a swivel base so you could take in the view or turn to watch the flat screen on the side wall. They were not the place you tossed your underwear if you were just tucking yourself in for some shut-eye in a buddy's bed. The underwear had been thrown there, probably by Mason. After he'd taken it off with his teeth.

"Sleep good?" the guy asked. He turned and gave Mason a smile that didn't look remotely drowsy or hung over. Mason tried to stay focused on the guy's handsome face—a vaguely familiar face—and not the hefty cock and hairless balls he was tucking inside his underwear.

Mason groaned, waggling one hand in the air. The stranger gave him a polite smile, then started the hunt for the rest of his clothes.

"Uhm, you want to take a shower or something?" Mason asked.

"No, I'm good. I'll just call an Uber."

The guy found his plain white T-shirt and pulled it on, then smiled and headed for Mason's side of the bed.

Mason braced for a recitation of all the crazy shit they'd done together the night before, planning to nod his way through it then ask for the guy's number just so the handsome stranger wouldn't ask for his. He'd never call him, of course. That's how he always played it when he shared a bed with a man. No strings attached. No follow-up either. He had a reputation to protect. *A reputation, yeah, right. As the lackey to a dad who's also my boss, a dad who makes Mike Pence look LGBT friendly.*

The guy was standing over him now, smiling. Mason smiled back.

"I need to get paid, babe," his guest finally said.

"Oh."

A rush of memories came pouring back. Mason alone in the bathroom as his guests argued their way out the front door downstairs, his finger hovering over the ad on the Buddy Rent app. Marco or maybe Mario. Mason wasn't sure, just that whatever name he went by, it probably wasn't real. A blow job so good it had Mason's head plastered to the pillows as he gasped and choked for air.

"Yeah, sorry. Don't mean to make this awkward. But it was going to be two hours, and then you wanted an overnight, so...that's more."

"Oh," Mason said again. "How much more?"

"A thousand."

"A thousand more, or like—"

"Just a thousand."

*Kill me now.* "Gotcha. You take checks?"

The guy reached into a designer backpack resting against Mason's nightstand and removed an honest-to-God credit card reader.

"Bank cards work," he said brightly. "You can write me off as a consultant. That's what everyone else does."

Mason nodded, got to his feet, and started a search for his discarded jeans, hoping like hell his wallet was still in the back pocket. If he had to search the entire house for it, the mood would go from awkward to awful. He found his balled-up briefs and tugged them on. A few feet away, his crumpled jeans were lying on the carpet right inside the open deck doors. When he crouched down to pull the wallet free of the back pocket, his stomach lurched. Just as he tried to catch his breath, he looked up and saw the mother playing with the kids down on the sand was his next-door neighbor, Shirley Baxter, which meant the toddlers nearby were her grandkids. A former soap star, she'd taken such good care of herself and had so much excellent work done, it was hard to tell she was in her late sixties when you saw her up close—much less from a distance. He lifted a hand to wave. The furious look she gave him told him his party—a party he could barely remember—had kept her up half the night.

Only then did he remember he was barely dressed, and with a strange guy in his bedroom, to boot. He yanked the drapes closed before Shirley could read the scene in more detail.

One swipe later, his guest was putting his credit card reader back into his backpack. The guy nodded and started for the door.

At the threshold, the escort paused and looked back.

"And hey, I hope you and Naser figure things out."

Adrenaline coursed through him, plating his sour stomach with something that felt like ice. "I'm... What?"

"Sorry. I just...you were pretty upset."

"I talked to you about Naser Kazemi?"

Since Mason and his buddies had deliberately mispronounced the guy's name throughout high school—turning the s into a z—Mason took care to pronounce it correctly now, putting the emphasis on the *ah* sound in the first syllable and pronouncing the second like *air* with an *s* attached.

"You didn't say his last name, but yeah, it sounded like you guys had history or something. And apparently, he's got beautiful eyes." When the guy saw the expression on Mason's face, he grimaced. "Hey, don't worry about it. It's all confidential. That's how this works. So, you know, if you see me training a client in the park or something, mum's the word, all right?"

"Sure thing," Mason croaked.

Then Mason was listening to the guy's footsteps rattle the glass and steel staircase to the first floor.

Head spinning, Mason bent over, grabbed his knees, and tried to breathe as deeply as he could.

Had he actually hired a male escort to come over within minutes of Chadwick being in his house? Had Chadwick seen the guy? He should text him just to be sure, but his stomach rolled at the thought. A knot of shame and guilt twisted his gut whenever Naser Kazemi's beautiful face strobed across his mind. And now he'd cried about him to an escort he didn't remember hiring?

A few minutes later, he was in the shower, the water just below scalding. Typically on hangover mornings, he took pleasure from the sight of his chiseled, gym-perfect body, as if the finely honed perfection of his outer shell was proof that everything underneath was more healthy than it felt. Lately, it was starting to feel like the opposite was true. The shell, no matter how sculpted, was in danger of cracking and falling away, revealing the pulsing mass of vices and fears that was Mason Worther's life.

*Get your shit together, Mason. If you want your life to be a giant party, at least make it a fun party.*

# 3

Because his position hadn't existed up until three months ago, Naser worked out of a small, windowless room that had previously been storage for the events department. It shared an interior hallway with Jonas's office and an employees-only bathroom. Most employees didn't know the bathroom existed—a relief, considering the plumbing was in Naser's side wall.

Jonas's office, on the other hand, was palatial by comparison, a time capsule of how the hotel used to look before a recent renovation had taken it in a more spare, flat white and Dale Chihuly-inspired direction. So it was there, amidst the Louis XIV furniture and atop the thick Oriental rug, that Naser and Jonas decided to face the dragon that was Pari Kazemi. On speakerphone.

"Are we ready?" Naser asked.

"No time like the present." Looking suitably chastened, Jonas sank into his giant desk chair and folded his hands across his lap. On the wall behind his head were pencil sketches and vintage photographs of the hotel from throughout history.

Naser hit the speakerphone's button and dialed his sister's number. After a few rings, the room was filled by the gentle, melodic voice Pari Kazemi only used on her voicemail.

"This is Pari Kazemi. I'm unable to take your call at present because I am fully engaged in the act of creation."

"Oh, Jesus Christ," Naser moaned.

"Before you share your thoughts with me today, I'd like to gift you with a verse from Rumi."

Naser's eyes rolled back into his head. He flounced down into the chair in front of Jonas's desk.

"Little brothers should be seen and not heard, especially if they have chosen to live lives free of daring as mediocre number crunchers whose sole purpose is to interfere with outpourings of genius from their older and more talented siblings."

Jonas frowned. "This isn't Rumi."

"This isn't her voicemail. Pari, knock it off and tell us why you sent jack—"

Pari's imitation of a voicemail beep sounded more like a possession scene from a Blumhouse film.

Then she hung up on them.

Naser shot to his feet, craving a pillow to punch. Instead, he headed to the window, hoping the view of the hotel's southern side lawn would calm him. Outside, a wall of interlocking Draco palms rose between the grass and the downhill slope of rooftops that were the hotel's private villas. Some of Sapphire Cove's pre-renovation drapes framed the window—thick and dusty pink and puddling on the carpeted floor, a pleasant throwback to all the events Naser had attended here in college when he was just Connor's best friend. Now he wanted to gather them in both hands and scream into them.

A few deep breaths later, Naser said, "I don't want to be one of those people who calls everyone I disagree with a narcissist, but my sister is a narcissist."

Jonas rose and fetched himself a bottle of water from his mini-fridge. "Perhaps. The world has so many."

He offered Naser a bottle, which he reluctantly accepted. Naser craved something stronger, but it was barely past nine in the morning, so he gulped the Arrowhead on offer. "How can you be so calm about this?"

"Well, she's not my sister." Jonas returned to his chair.

"She sent jackhammers to the hotel."

"And Gloria sent them away."

"She knows I work here. She should be more respectful."

"Nas, our boss, who happens to be your best friend, just told you he doesn't have any concerns about her event. I have...a few, but..." Naser glared at him. Jonas sighed and threw up his hands. "She has something called an elevator clause in her contract. It means that she doesn't have a strict cap on her headcount, but we're not on the hook to provide food and drinks for the extra guests if we don't have it on hand."

"So she could put this Googoosh rumor out there and a hundred people could show up and there's nothing we could do?"

"Not quite. There's a fire marshal limit on the pool deck."

"What is it?"

Jonas cleared his throat and looked to his lap. "Five hundred."

Naser let out a ghostly sounding wail and rested his head against the nearest wall. "This was supposed to be a fifty-person cocktail party. She always does this!"

"Nas, do you care to tell me what this is really about? Events aren't your department, and you're close to stroking out about this."

"Insurance is my department, and my sister has a tendency to set fire to things."

"True, but we're well covered."

"My family is also my department, no matter how much I try to get fired." Jonas gave him a steady look, a look that had inspired Naser to make his fair share of personal disclosures since they'd started working together. "It's rude. She should be more respectful of where I work. Why is she having the event here anyway? She had to know I'd be breathing down her neck."

"Maybe Connor's discounts sealed the deal. Listen, Nas, the elevator clause is a self-negating thing we build into contracts so that we don't have to be jerks about crowd control. If she doesn't pay for booze for the extra guests, the extra guests will leave. It's that simple."

"And if she sneaks in booze from an outside vendor?"

Jonas rolled his head from side to side, unspoken words buzzing in his throat. "Well, that would be a violation of her contract."

Naser grinned. "And we could shut her down over it?"

"A prospect I don't think you should relish quite so much. But if you're determined to, let's discuss why."

Naser threw himself down into the chair again, this time hard enough to make the joints squeak. He crossed his arms tightly over his chest. "Venture a guess, since you're so determined to therapize me."

"Well, with the caveat that *therapize* is not a word, I'd say you're afraid other people here are going to judge you for your sister's behavior. And that raises a lot of uncomfortable feelings because, as you've mentioned on a few occasions, you weren't exactly drowning in friends back in high school."

Naser flinched at the truth of it.

Jonas's gaze didn't waver.

The man was sophisticated in ways Naser found both comforting and intimidating, depending on what mood he was in, and right now, Naser was in a lousy one. Jonas was also gay but had never made one peep about his dating life or hooking up with someone, only to mention once that he was single and "without prospects," as he'd phrased it. Maybe Jonas was a private person, or maybe his self-discipline resulted in a firm boundary between the personal and the professional. Or maybe he was just infinitely more mature than Naser. He was two decades older, after all. Whatever the case, they'd become closer over the few months they'd worked together, but their conversations felt decidedly one way. Simply put, Jonas was better at delivering insight about others than revealing any about himself.

"High school was a long time ago," Naser finally answered.

The air between them cooled. With a small nod, Jonas moved a stack of file folders to the side on his desk and made a show of opening one. "And clearly you'd rather not discuss it."

"You know, you're not exactly forthcoming about your own past, Mr. Jacobs."

Jonas opened a file and began flipping pages. "I have a degree in comparative literature from Georgetown. I was at the Four Seasons in DC before I came here. And before that, I worked for a while in—"

Naser had heard these statistics rattled off many times before. "Corporate America. Yeah, I know, but you never mention which corporations."

Jonas looked up suddenly, leveling Naser with a gaze that looked both vaguely amused and parental. "I apologize if the high school comment was too far."

"You know, all the corporate America line does is inspire rumors about you anyway."

Jonas returned his attention to his file. "Is that so?"

"Yeah, the latest is you had a relationship with a closeted sports star and had to sign an NDA."

"Well, I do love my Baltimore Ravens. Honestly. What an exciting life I lead in other people's minds."

Naser got to his feet. "Well, I'll go back to *my* department again. Focus on what *I* do for the hotel. Clearly I can't rise to the esteemed level of elegance and professionalism that's on display here in the office of Jonas Jacobs."

Jonas flipped contract pages. "I am not taking this bait."

Naser had just gripped the doorknob when guilt seized him. Jonas was his second closest work friend after Connor, and all the man had done was show concern. In response, Naser had deflected the topic onto Jonas's mystery-shrouded past. That was shitty, and he needed to make it right. When he turned, he saw Jonas look up from his desk expectantly.

"I was bullied."

Jonas straightened, nodding.

"Like every day. By these three guys. These three hot, rich, football-playing white guys."

Even as he tried to make them dim, the names strobed through his mind in bright red lights.

*Chadwick Brody.*

*Tim Malbec.*

*Mason Worther.*

He tried to blot out the images of their adolescent physical perfection that had emblazoned themselves on his mind, his painful sense memories of their leering stares and sharp, sudden shoves, moves that had blended desire and menace into a combination that still haunted him, still warped the edges of his fantasies in ways he sometimes tried to flatten with both hands.

Jonas leaned back in his chair. "Was it racial?"

Naser shook his head. "It was about the way I walked, mostly. They called me Prancer. That was one of the nicer things."

Jonas nodded with understanding.

"Anyway, college, meeting Connor, that was the first time I had friends. Felt like I belonged. Now friends and work are intertwined and... I guess you're right. The idea of my sister doing something that might reflect badly on me here is making me a little jumpy."

"Connor adores you, and I think you're a delight. A somewhat ornery and obsessive-compulsive delight, but a delight nonetheless. Nothing Pari does on Friday night will change that."

"Thank you, and I guess I know that, but I'm having trouble *feeling* that."

Jonas nodded. "We'll work the event together, you and I. You can keep an eye on her, and I can keep an eye on you and make sure you don't get too…jumpy. Deal?"

Naser nodded. "I'm sorry about prying into your past."

Jonas shrugged, returning his attention to his file.

"Although, if you really did spend your post-college years getting railed by a hot NFL player, I'm not that sorry."

"Be gone, child. I have work to do."

# 4

Fully dressed, spritzed with cologne, and fortified by a protein shake and a couple swallows of hangover-easing Corona he'd managed not to throw up, Mason was ready for work.

He was already two hours late, and he hadn't yet left the house.

At his former gig up in LA, his preferred office wear had been lightweight Italian dress pants and white linen shirts. But at Worther Properties, any outfit that wasn't composed of solid, primary colors and brass buckles typically inspired a homophobic comment from his dad, so today, Mason was dressed in khakis and a navy blue cotton dress shirt that felt scratchy and uncomfortable.

He was backing his silver Ferrari Roma out of his driveway and onto his private, gated street when there was a tap on the window next to him.

Mason jumped and saw Shirley Baxter standing next to his car. As always, her floral sundress exposed her lean, freckled arms, and her flame red hair was tied back in a ponytail.

He made his best *I'm in a hurry* gesture and she made her best finger-twirling *roll the window down right now, I'm thirty years older than you* gesture. There'd be no escaping her, he realized. She was retired, lived right next door, and sat on the board of the homeowners' association that governed this private drive. She was also what his late Aunt Mary would call "a tough old broad" and his dad would call something that could get a man kneed in the groin.

As soon as he rolled the window down, she said, "Really?"

"I'm sorry. It won't happen again."

"You said that the last five times, Mason."

"We'll keep the music down next time."

"And the screaming, and the people having sex on the beach, and the fist fight on the patio, I'm assuming because someone was mad about the people who had sex on the beach."

*Fist fight? Jesus Christ!*

He fought an urge to check his own fists for bruises. Shirley seemed to notice. He expected more anger. Concern entered her expression, and she leaned forward slightly. "I'm not a nun, all right, Mason? I used to tie one on back in my day. But three in the morning? In the middle of the week? Come on. That's out of control."

"Look, I said it won't happen again, all right?"

Shirley straightened, glancing in both directions as if she thought someone might be spying on them. It wasn't likely. Most folks had already left for work. Whatever she was about to say must be a real secret. When she leaned in close, Mason was startled by the sympathy in her expression.

"Mason, there was a time in my life when the party got out of control, too. If you want, I can tell you how I got back on the beam." She let this sit. His brain was still foggy, and he was having trouble sorting out her implication. "I can *help* you if you want."

Her earlier irritation with him was preferable to this pity.

"Tell you what, ma'am. Help me by staying on your side of the property line, and I'll stay on mine."

She recoiled, tongue making a lump under her upper lip, nodding as if some suspicion of hers had been confirmed.

He'd just made a mess for himself. He could feel it.

She was all business now. "Eleven p.m. on weeknights, one a.m. on the weekends. Anything later than that, I'm going to the homeowners' board."

Mason rolled his eyes. "Fine."

She tapped the roof of his car before she stepped back. "Don't make me pull my bitch routine on you, Mason Worther. I lasted in soaps for thirty years, and the one producer who tried to put his hands on me ended up with broken fingers."

As he watched her walk off, he felt a guilt so powerful it edged on shame.

In the beginning, she'd been nothing but nice to him. On the day he'd moved in, she'd knocked on his back door with a gift basket and an offer of coffee on her patio, and his first thought had been, *What's the catch, lady*? Maybe because he'd never really had a mom, and his dad was a cross between John Wayne and a king cobra.

And now, even though it felt childish and stupid and beneath him, he was revving the engine as loud as he could before he backed out of his driveway.

If there was one area of his life where Mason currently excelled, it was hiding hangovers at the office.

He arrived at the Irvine headquarters of Worther Properties with barely five minutes to spare before the design meeting for Vistana's spec house. The morning staff meeting he'd missed altogether. The firm had two major developments on deck—one a stone's throw from their office, the other farther south in North San Diego County. Vistana and Escansedo were both McMansion-filled, gated subdivisions-to-be, with Spanglish-sounding names meant to evoke that special magic of people wealthy enough to build a multimillion-dollar house inside a wildfire zone. But Vistana was much closer to building out its first homesites, so their model homes were up for design review first.

By the time he was headed back to his office, there was still no sign of his father.

With a nod, he told his new assistant—the one his father had transferred to Mason's desk after she'd asked his dad not to curse at her—she was free to grab a long lunch out of the office.

Once his door was shut again, he managed his first deep breath since that morning.

His office had a nice western view over the 405 Freeway to the first scrub-dappled mounds of the coastal hills. There wasn't room for a sofa or love seat, so he pushed his desk chair against the wall and curled up into the fetal position on the carpet behind his desk, tucking his chair's lumbar pillow under his head. He'd nodded off a few seconds earlier when he was roused by the sound of his door opening. Figuring it was just a coworker who wouldn't see him behind his desk, he held his breath and stayed statue still.

A second later, high-heeled footsteps punched the carpet toward him.

"Seriously?"

The only voice he would've wanted to hear less was his father's.

"Why are you here, Fareena?" Mason asked.

"We need to talk."

"Aren't you the one who said we're not dating?"

"Correct. We *were* sleeping together, but we're not doing that anymore either. Oh my God. Get up, Mason. This is ridiculous. It's the middle of the day."

Mason pulled himself to his feet with one hand on the edge of his desk. "I had a party last night."

"You have a party every night." Fareena rolled her eyes and settled confidently into the chair across from his desk as if they were about to talk business.

Her ink black shoulder-length hair looked freshly flat ironed. When she crossed her shapely legs, Mason was pleasantly reminded of all the time he'd spent between them. She always dressed like she was about to board a private jet for Paris and was one of the few women he knew who found a way to work faux fur into all of her warm-weather outfits. Some women had shoe collections; Fareena had a knee-high boot collection consisting of some of the finest imported leathers one could buy. Her parents had thwarted her plans to become a fashion model right out of high school by forcing her to take a job at the family's real estate agency. She'd gotten back at them by becoming the top earner and outperforming all three of her older brothers four years running.

"You know, I talk to my therapist about you," she said.

"I'm that good, huh?"

"It's not a compliment."

"I guess you don't want to grab lunch then."

"We need to talk about the incident." Fareena cleared her throat and placed her hands over her top knee.

"I said I'd pay for it. What's the problem?"

"Do you even remember what you broke?" she asked.

"Just that you said it was really expensive."

"I said that the next day."

"You take checks?" Mason opened his desk drawer.

"I don't want your check," she said.

"I'm good for it, babe." Mason grinned.

"Your dad's good for it."

"Low blow, sweetheart. Last time I checked, you were working at a family firm too."

"And I've managed not to sleep on the floor since I started. And don't call me sweetheart, Johnnie Walker."

"You know, usually when we go at each other like this, we'd end up going *at* each other, if you know what I mean."

"I know what you mean," she said, "and no thanks. That's like, no thanks forever."

"Am I really that bad?" Mason gave her his best pouty face.

She went stiff and quiet, which is what Fareena always did when she was fighting emotions she didn't like. "You're not bad, Mason. I'm just tired of waiting for that moment in between your third drink, when you're all sweet and sexy, and your fifth, when you get…messy."

"What did I break?" Mason asked.

"My mother's favorite vase. You were reliving a moment of high school football glory, and you decided to spike it."

Mason tried not to wince as shame coursed through him. "Cash, then?"

"No. I need you to attend an event with me on Friday."

"So we're not dating and we're not sleeping together anymore. But you want me to go on a date with you this weekend."

"It's not a date." Fareena stood. "You are accompanying me to an event, and once we're there, I'll tell you what I need from you. That's how you'll make it up to me." Fareena placed her hands on her hips and tapped both sets of manicured nails twice against the fabric of her pants, her typical gesture for *This meeting is adjourned.*

"Three-ways aren't usually my thing, but I'm open."

"We had a three-way, Mason. A long one."

"With Thalia?"

Fareena leaned over his desk and dropped her voice to a whisper. "With Michael."

"Your gay friend," Mason whispered.

"Michael isn't gay. He's bi. Like *you.*"

Mason's pulse roared in his ears. If he wasn't already feeling the spins, he might have stormed out of his office right there, but instead he felt pinned to his chair by the ferocity of Fareena's stare. "It's the twenty-first century, Mason. Have you ever thought that maybe you judge yourself more harshly than anyone else?"

"Have you met my father?" Mason growled.

Fareena nodded and held up her hands in a gesture of surrender. "Fair enough," she whispered. "Your secrets are safe with me."

"And Michael?"

"You left him very satisfied. Don't worry."

But he was worried. And he'd stay worried. Probably until he could get home and put some more hair on the dog.

"Is he going to be there on Friday?" Mason asked.

"He's not. But don't worry. It'll be fun. It's a party."

"Okay. Should I pick you up or—"

"Yeah, nice try. I don't let Messy Mason drive me."

"So that's your nickname for me?"

"Sweetie." Fareena braced her hands against the edge of the desk and leaned forward. "It's *everyone's* nickname for you."

"Where should I meet you then?"

"Sapphire Cove, eight o'clock, at the valet stand."

"I thought that place went under."

"Old news. They're fine. My friend's brother works there. See you then." Fareena headed for the door. "Just look presentable. And rich. That's all that matters. Try to be reasonably sober, and let me do the talking."

"To who? This is about a vase. By the way, even though we're doing like an in-kind trade here, what's the price tag I'm settling?"

One foot out the door, Fareena said, "You're investing twenty thousand dollars in my friend's clothing line."

"*Say what?*"

Fareena froze, staring at him over one shoulder. "What happened to *I'm good for it, babe?*"

"That friggin' vase was not worth twenty grand."

Fareena's eyes blazed. She turned and drew the door shut behind her with a decisive click, the anger coming off her in waves strong enough to press Mason back against his desk chair.

"That *friggin'* vase was one of two of my mother's prized possessions she was able to smuggle out of Iran when the Shah's regime fell. It was in her family for generations. She hid it under the floorboards of the car my father drove to the Turkish border where the guards tore through her things and confiscated all of her jewelry, including her *wedding ring*. When she found out that vase was broken, Mason, she wept as hard as she did when she had to leave her country. I don't care if she bought it at a souvenir stand on Newport Beach, *I* decide how much my mother's tears are worth. Not you."

Every response Mason tried to marshal died inside his chest. He'd tried them all before, in foolish defense of his ever-lengthening list of drunken fuck-ups.

"Tell you what." Fareena fished her phone out of her purse. "Why don't I call my mother and tell her who broke her precious heirloom, and then she can hash it out with your dad directly? How does that sound?"

"Like blackmail," he grumbled.

"Does it? Because it's called accountability." She started dialing.

Mason extended one hand. Fareena lowered her phone in response. "What's the designer's name?"

"You're squaring a debt here. This isn't about whether or not you like her work."

"Fareena, come on."

"Pari Kazemi."

Suddenly it felt as if every bone in Mason's body had turned to lead. Apparently, he did a bad job of keeping his emotions from his face because Fareena winced. But she still held her phone in one hand, ready to make good on her threat.

"Does she have a brother?" he asked.

"Nas, yeah. Why. You know him?" Her brow furrowed in disbelief.

Guilt and shame reached critical mass inside of him. Here was Fareena, living proof his blackout antics were spinning out of control. And she'd brought a name into his office. A name that suddenly and viscerally connected him to the shitbag he'd been in high school. A name he'd apparently spoken in his haunted dreams the night before. The walls, it seemed, were closing in on him, and there was no pushing back without breaking both arms.

Maybe Naser and his sister weren't close and there'd be no chance of running into the guy at the event.

But Fareena had just said her friend's brother worked at Sapphire Cove. That had to mean Nas.

He had no choice but to see the situation in a new way—as an opportunity.

An opportunity to kill two birds with one stone, and maybe walk away feeling better than he had on most mornings since he'd been forced to move back home after drinking his way out of a plum gig in LA.

Mason nodded and raised his hands in a gesture of defeat. "Deal."

Looking skeptical, she seemed to gauge his sincerity with cold eyes. Having seen what she needed to see, she dropped her phone back into her purse.

"See you Friday."

When she was gone, part of his stomachache seemed to have left with her.

Was it just the excitement of having a goal, a project, a sudden plan?

Twenty thousand dollars was a lot of money, but maybe he could negotiate a different figure if he stayed sober like she asked, put his best foot forward. And maybe he could make things right with Fareena and Naser at the same time. Two birds with one stone and all that.

And then, maybe, he'd stop whispering Naser's name in his sleep.

Or maybe he wanted to see Naser again for a very different reason.

## Eleven Years Ago

*Mason wasn't a liar.*

*Omissions, he believed, didn't count as lies, so if the price of being one of the most popular guys in high school meant keeping your mouth shut about how much you wanted to kiss another guy, then so be it. But on this particular morning, Mason's pants might as well have been on fire.*

*He'd straight-up lied to his two favorite running backs. There was no way around it.*

*The workout he was currently putting them through hadn't come from the pages of* Men's Fitness. *And no, Hugh Jackman hadn't used it to get Wolverine's abs. The truth was, Mason had designed the frenzied intervals himself in hopes of distracting and exhausting his partners in crime before the bell rang for first period. So far, it was working like a charm. A charm bathed in sweat.*

*Both guys had torn through the first few sets of push-up burpees in record time. But they were losing momentum now, their cheeks flaming red, their biceps flushed and bulging.*

*Nearby, Mason paced, not too far from where he'd thrown the winning pass against the Tustin High Ramblers the Friday before. He was pretending to time them on his stopwatch, but really he was counting the minutes until school started. If the guys didn't bail before then, Naser Kazemi would make it safely to class, having been spared the usual bullying their crew gave him every morning.*

*And since everything they'd done to Naser for years now was basically Mason's fault, it was the least he could do.*

*On the guy's first day at Laguna Mesa High, Mason had sidled up to him in the hallway, instantly drawn by the sassy swing in his walk, the scent of his elegant cologne—way nicer than the Axe Body Spray most of the guys at their school spritzed themselves with—and his first glimpse of the guy's beautiful brown eyes. For an instant, he thought he'd be able to curve an arm around the little dude's shoulders and play the whole thing off as a friendly hello to the transfer student. But when he saw the stunned looks Chadwick and Tim were giving him, he realized how badly he'd messed up and used that same arm to steer the new kid headfirst into the nearest empty locker.*

*From then on, they were off and running. Knocking Naser into walls, tearing his backpack off his shoulder and tossing it yards down the hallway before he could react. One time, Chadwick banged the shit out of the guy's PE lock while he was showering, leaving it so mangled there was no way he could open the locker and get to his clothes. Then he'd stolen the towels from the locker room, giving Naser no choice but to strike out in search of help, naked as the day he was born. But somehow, their target had managed not to expose himself to the other students that day, which had disappointed Mason's buddies to no end.*

*And what had Mason done to stop it? Not much. As usual.*

*While he always tried to keep their antics from escalating to dangerous levels, he hadn't done squat to dial it down, terrified that if he spoke up, his two best friends would realize what had really happened on Naser's first day was a total loss of no-homo composure triggered by feelings Mason didn't want to name, feelings that terrified him more than the prospect of losing a championship game.*

*Still, the flutter in his chest Naser Kazemi gave him didn't mean he was into guys.*

*At least that's what he told himself every night as he looked for sleep on the ceiling of his bedroom. Hell, when Susie Hollingsworth's parents had gone on that trip last summer, he'd spent a whole weekend with her doing stuff that would have made her parents weep, and he'd enjoyed every minute. If Susie wasn't lying, he'd been pretty good at most of it too. He was a ladies' man, for sure.*

*So Naser made his pulse race. So what? It didn't mean he was a guys' man too.*

*The whole thing was easy enough to explain. Naser Kazemi was pretty, and pretty was something girls were, and so the parts of Naser that turned Mason on were the parts that reminded Mason of a girl.*

*Enough said.*

*Then, just a few months earlier, Naser had decided to grow a mustache, a mustache that had filled Mason's head with thoughts of what it would be like to kiss someone who had one. Thoughts that made the sides of his face tingle and his neck get hot.*

*Way more than enough said, and in a frightened voice in Mason's head that not even a few beers stolen from his dad's stash could quiet.*

*"How many more, dude?" Chadwick asked, breathless.*

*"Twenty," Mason lied.*

*"You're just trying to wear our asses out because you like us sweaty," Tim shouted.*

*"Or you've been running like you've got bricks on your feet and I'm trying to lighten you up."*

*Chadwick added a jump to the end of his burpee, which vaulted him about eight feet into the air. At the top, he flipped Mason the bird. The funny thing about Chadwick was that his facial expression looked the same no matter what he was doing—his eyes were always wide and staring, full lips always parted as if he were either struggling to breathe or planning to take off running on his muscular legs at any second. Tim Malbec had the same constantly tensed energy, except his chest and shoulder muscles had Chadwick beat, and his narrow eyes and small, thin-lipped mouth made him look reserved and vaguely suspicious of everything.*

*It was easier for Mason to think of his best friends' bodies in these clinical terms given the widespread consensus they were three of the hottest guys in school. Not just easier. Given how often the three of them jerked off together, it was also safer. For Mason.*

*Chadwick suddenly popped to his feet without performing the push-up that was supposed to mark his every contact with the ground. "Shit! We're gonna miss Prancer!"*

*It was the nickname they'd given Naser, inspired by the swing in his walk. Both guys ran for the sidelines where their windbreakers were draped over the chain link fence. Mason's grand plan, he realized, was about to hit the skids.*

*"We're not done. You promised!"*

*"We can finish your wussy workout later, QB," Chadwick said. "They're doing some kinda scale model thing in Ms. Guidroz's class today first period, and Prancer's one of her little favorites. I want to see him try to balance the thing on his head while I yank his shorts up his ass." Chadwick stuck his tongue out and leered as he punched his arms into his windbreaker's sleeves, which, Mason thought, was a pretty weird way to talk about the butt of someone you didn't like.*

*Crap. How did Chadwick know about Naser's project? Was he secretly following Naser too?*

*Mason had known for days, after he'd spied on the guy from behind a shelf in the whisper section of the library and heard him excitedly telling some of his friends about the scale model of the ancient Persian city of Persepolis he was building for Ms. Guidroz's visual arts unit, knowing the whole time that if his buddies saw him carrying something like that on campus, they'd do whatever they could to make him drop it.*

*"Come on, guys. We're rank. We gotta shower." Mason chased his best friends*

*past the bleachers and toward the main building.*

*"We've got time," Tim called back. "First period's in twenty, and the dork always shows up early."*

*"Dude, let it go. Just this one day."*

*Chadwick stopped and spun. "Why? What are you, Ms. Buckner all of a sudden?" Buckner was the hippie-dippy guidance counselor they all made fun of but then secretly cried to whenever shit hit the fan. But for the manly men of Laguna Mesa High, a comparison to her was a worse insult than being called a homo.*

*"Look at it this way, Mason." Ever the mediator, Tim approached. "The guy's always looking at our dicks. Every time we touch him, we probably take the edge off and keep him from fagging out on Coach Harris and getting expelled or something. It's basically a public service, what we do."*

*"Zactly." Leering, Chadwick rapped the center of Mason's chest with the back of his hand, then took off, leaving Mason no choice but to pursue.*

"Traffic jam or toilet bowl?"

His father's voice jerked him back to the present.

Mason turned from his office window.

People always said he was the spitting image of his dad. They were both tall, big-boned, Nordic-looking blonds. The main difference between them now was his father's trimmed mustache. The one time Mason had dared to call it a porn 'stache, his dad hadn't even cracked a smile. Folks who didn't know them that well had branded them the Vikings, an inappropriate nickname if there ever was one, given it implied a greater degree of cooperation between them than they'd ever been able to achieve.

"Excuse me?"

"Your excuse for being late." Pete Worther stepped inside the office door he'd opened without knocking. He didn't bother to close it behind him, probably so whoever was outside could hear the verbal abuse he was about to hurl at his son. "You going to give me some bullshit about getting stuck in traffic or were you bent over a toilet bowl again?"

"Alarm didn't go off."

"Get a better alarm, dumbass. You missed the staff meeting."

"I made the design meeting."

"Like I give a shit. I didn't spend decades building this company so I can babysit staff meetings. That's your job. Now that you're back."

*Came crawling back,* his father had been close to saying. But every now and then, even he showed some restraint.

"I apologize."

Pete nodded. "I'm trying to care, promise."

"Let me know how that goes."

Even at this subtle dig, Pete's eyes flashed with anger.

Pete Worther was a man whose every breath, step, and move was defined by anger, and for most of his life Mason had been the target of it. His father had never raised a hand to him in his life, but the man knew how to bruise with words.

"Stop being late or you can give me my house back."

"You told me I had to live in the beach house."

"I told you I wasn't going to let a new employee with a known drinking problem commute two hours from LA each day. The beach house is a perk."

Mason nodded.

Pete gave him a once-over. "You wore those pants to the design team meeting?"

Mason nodded.

"Brave choice. Team's got a bunch of cocksuckers on it. Don't want to give them the wrong idea."

With that, Pete Worther was gone, leaving Mason with a racing heart and a fantasy of grabbing the man by the back of the neck and hurling him headfirst into the nearest wall, a fantasy he'd been nursing for as long as he could remember.

# 5

When she saw Naser and Jonas approaching her across Sapphire Cove's pool deck, Pari Kazemi threw her arms skyward and cried, "Naser-*joon*, brother of mine, how nice of you to dress like something other than the manager of a drug store!"

"Why would that be a problem?" Naser asked. "You love drugs."

She clutched Naser's shoulders, her manicured nails pressing into the fabric of his suit like daggers poised to shred. He was lucky his sister didn't design men's suits. Otherwise, she would have forced him to wear one of her own colorful creations. He figured the radiant smile and air kisses she was gracing him with were for Jonas's benefit. The man had matched him step for step, poised to make good on his promise to ensure the Kazemi siblings didn't start clawing each other's eyes out in the minutes before Pari's event started.

"Any reason you didn't return any of my text messages?" Naser smiled back.

"The party isn't going to plan itself."

"My messages were about the party," Naser said.

Wearing a smile that looked more like a grimace, Pari started brushing at Naser's shoulders as if there were dust bunnies clinging to his suit. Which there weren't because Naser always took a lint roller to himself several times before leaving the house, no matter the outfit. Which Pari knew because she always made fun of him over it. Which is what he figured she was doing now. "I know, but sometimes you say you want to talk about one thing and then I respond and it's six hundred other things, and because I run my own business, I have other things to do than to take ten pages of ever-changing directions from my *adorable* little brother."

She pinched his cheek. Hard.

In Persian, Naser said, "Pinch my cheek again and I will—"

She started responding in Persian before he could finish the sentence. "I can place both hands around your throat and squeeze and then we can—"

"English, *please,* my dears!" If there was such a thing as a polite shout, Jonas had achieved it. He'd made Naser promise to keep the conversation in a language he could understand. Otherwise he wouldn't be able to intervene before trouble struck. "How's prep going so far, Ms. Kazemi?"

"Call her Pari," Naser grumbled.

As his sister launched into a dramatic yet self-effacing monologue about all the drama that had allegedly gone into transporting the equipment needed for tonight's event, Naser searched the pool deck without moving an inch. No sign of the mannequins that were supposed to display the new handbags. But no blatant contract violations or evidence of hidden circus animals either. Instead, he saw hotel staff setting up high-top bistro tables and bars and a gorgeous sunset primed to explode into a fiery symphony of pink and orange, right around the time Pari's first guests arrived.

There wasn't a trace of the Bliss Network's giant gold B, a logo that had been attached to almost everything Pari had done for three years now. The home shopping network in question had given a huge push to Pari's most recent creation earlier that year, a cross between a scarf and a shawl designed to flatter full-figured women. The *shal,* as she'd called it, was made of lustrous fabric that wrapped around the back of a person's neck, leaving much of the shoulders exposed before plunging toward their mid-section. Its two wide fabric flaps were lined with hidden buttons that allowed the person to cover as much of their stomach as they liked. The number of buttons, Pari insisted, were about giving women options, something she said was too often missing from women's fashion. But it was her use of bold color and intricate geometric designs that made them a standout.

Their mother, on the other hand, had taken great exception to the fact that its name, *shal,* was the Persian word for shawl. In her view, this was a problem because what Pari had designed was not, in fact, a shawl. How would Americans feel, Mahin Kazemi had asked, if a foreign company launched a new brand of bicycle and called it a *car?* Whenever she was confronted with this linguistic logic, Pari would erupt with a fiery tirade on how she didn't need her hospital administrator mother lecturing her on the intricacies of fashion marketing, and that's when Naser would slip away to text Connor about nonsense so he could take his mind off the yelling in the other room.

If the Bliss Network wasn't involved in tonight's event, maybe Pari had decided their specifications for the party weren't up to her exacting standards.

Which meant she'd paid for it out of pocket with money she didn't have.

At least no one was trying to demolish anything.

As always, his sister was a lovely vision. Her long black hair was swept into a stylish updo, and the ample curves of her body shimmered in a lace and tulle sheer-top gown beaded in hypnotic, spiraling designs. She was glowing, and it wasn't just her foundation. It also wasn't a good sign. Pari always glowed right before she started fires.

It would be easier, Naser thought, to allow his sister her assorted moments of being the center of attention if she didn't spend every day acting like the center of the universe. But whenever she was in high-diva mode, clutching at nonexistent pearls as she told tale after tale of her triumphs against a misunderstanding universe that had yet to recognize her talent and genius to her satisfaction, Naser felt like he was going to grind his back teeth to dust.

"So," Naser finally said, "Googoosh."

"Oh, I know," Pari gasped, eyes wide. "Isn't that crazy? People think she's coming!"

"Crazy," Naser said. "So it's just a rumor then?"

"I don't know. Maybe she saw my interview on BBC Persia."

Pari's BBC Persia interview, while flattering, had only been three minutes long. Four years ago. But she'd been bringing it up continuously ever since, so in her mind it probably seemed much longer.

"The rumor isn't just that she's attending, Pari, it's that she's performing."

His sister let out a small cry that sounded like she'd rehearsed it in the mirror every night for three years. "That would be so amazing. Can we get a microphone just in case?"

Jonas cleared his throat. "Unfortunately, the mics and sound systems we have on hand are for speaking events, not musical performances.

You'd need a mixer board for that."

"Oh, well. That is disappointing."

Naser took a step toward her. Pari, as always, held her ground. "I'm not sure it'll come close to the disappointment your guests will feel if they show up for a Googoosh concert and find out she's not actually coming. And since you are my dearest and only sister, I figured out a pretty effective way to save you from that level of embarrassment."

Pari swallowed and pursed her lips. "Did you now?"

"Yes. I've talked it over with Jonas, and here's what the hotel's going to offer you, which I think is pretty generous given the misunderstanding with the jackhammers earlier in the week—"

"Jackhammers?" With a furrowed brow, his sister shook her head and looked between them both. "I don't know anything about jackhammers."

"—we're going to station some of our security team at your check-in table, and they're going to let each person know individually that Googoosh is *not* performing. That way their disappointment won't disrupt the party."

She wasn't gritting her teeth, but the hand she'd brought to her throat to indicate fake surprise was now clutching her neck. In the silence that followed, a seagull cawed. A giant heating lamp was rolled across the deck behind Pari by its base. The whole time, Naser expected his sister to hurl him into the pool by one ear. And she might have if Jonas hadn't been there. Instead, she screwed a polite smile onto her face and lowered her hand from her throat. "I'm not sure that's necessary, Nas."

"It is, though," Naser said. "So it's what we're going to do."

"Connor and I should talk. Just in case."

"Connor's on vacation. Jonas and I are in charge tonight."

Pari slipped into Persian. "Vacation? He's not coming? Tell him he's no longer one of my official gays."

"Now about that Persian," Jonas interjected.

"I'm sure he'll miss the membership benefits greatly." When Naser answered in Persian, Jonas threw up his hands and sighed.

"Connor and I have a relationship you don't understand, so I'd like to hear what he has to say about—"

In English, Naser said, "All right, *look*, Diane von Worstenberg—"

Jonas clamped a hand on Naser's shoulder and stepped between them. "You know, I think we covered everything we need to cover for now. Ms. Kazemi, we'll be back to check in now and then to make sure everything's going smoothly. And if you need us, you can text my cell, or I'm sure you can text Naser. He'll be with me the whole night."

"Thank you, Jonas," Pari said sweetly. "I'll text *you* if you don't mind. Sometimes when I text Nas, the response is too long for me to get through before bed."

With that, Pari turned and headed in the direction of one of the assembled minibars where a server was setting out bottles.

"Turn around," Jonas said softly, "and let's go to my office. We can be more effective from there."

"She started the Googoosh rumor. I know she did."

Behind them, Pari cried to everyone and no one, "How come I'm the only Persian girl whose gay brother *isn't* fun?"

Naser was preparing to turn around and show his sister just how goddamn fun he could be when Jonas turned him again with one powerful hand and steered them back inside.

# 6

Mason spent most of the hours leading up to Friday night rehearsing scenarios for his reunion with Naser Kazemi.

In his favorite, he took Naser's hand in a firm and confident grip, stared right into his eyes with sober sincerity, and assured him in his most confident voice, "I've never felt right about the way we treated you. If I had it all to do over again…"

And that's where the daydream fizzled and died. Because the way he wanted to finish that sentence didn't exactly jibe with the Hallmark tone of his opening line.

The truth was, if he had to do high school over again, he would have tried his best to get Naser naked in a janitor's closet, see those beautiful brown eyes up close, and find out if a bright sheen came into them when his body was played like an instrument.

*If I had it all to do over again, I would have been better to you.*

Those were the words he'd settled on by Friday evening, once he was showered, dressed, and ready to call the Uber.

So far, the buildup to Pari Kazemi's event had given him a sense of purpose and what felt like a tenuous—if temporary—sobriety. A drink, he'd promised himself, would be his reward once the apology had been made.

A text from Chadwick Thursday afternoon had confirmed Mason hadn't flashed his bi side in front of his best friend Wednesday night. Or if he had, Chadwick had been too wasted to remember.

That evening, he'd shrugged off the man's offer of a trip to their buddy Lenny Victor's house in Newport Beach. Lenny was a trust fund baby who collected drones, swimsuit models, and enough cocaine to keep most of the OC up and chatting for days on end. A short visit to his house could turn into a thirty-six-hour black hole that ended with him and Chadwick trying to make their way home from a stranger's house in Malibu, two hours north, while trying not to throw up.

Mason had also avoided his nightly bottle of wine before bed and woke up Friday morning clear-eyed and ready for a bruising workout at the gym before work.

So when Chadwick's picture lit up the display of Mason's phone a few minutes before Mason had planned to summon an Uber, he was tempted to ignore the call, afraid any contact with his oldest and most reckless friend would throw him off his game. But old habits die hard even when they don't come in bottles.

"That thing I told you about," Chadwick said, "I'm going to need it earlier than I thought."

"What thing?"

"Aw, fuck, dude. How bad did you black out Wednesday?"

"Decisively."

"You looked like you were hearing me. Anyway, some woman's making a complaint 'cause I fired her, and she says I went to her house and threatened her. And it was a night I was at your place, so I just need you to give a statement that I was with you. That's all. It's just some bullshit."

Gooseflesh prickled on the back of his neck. Chadwick was crudely specific when he wanted something and frustratingly vague when he was freaked out. This felt like a dangerous mix of both. "A statement? To the police?"

"No, just my lawyer."

"An affidavit."

Which, despite Chadwick's casual tone, was a more serious and binding document than a statement to the police.

"Yeah, right. Whatever. Something Latin."

"What night was it?" Mason asked.

When Chadwick didn't answer with the date, a clear, small voice in Mason's head said, *He's lying.*

Rumors had always swirled about Chadwick's practice—that his nurses, all female, were short on experience and long on good looks for a reason. And then there were the anonymous *Yelp* reviews claiming to be from patients who said he'd offered them discounted treatments in exchange for sex. He'd loudly claim they were planted by his competitors, and he was always on the verge of getting them taken down. But together with Chadwick's general attitude toward women, the stubbornness of these rumors had always fed dark, unspoken suspicions in Mason's mind.

"Jesus, really?" Chadwick finally asked. "Now you sound like my fucking lawyer. I don't remember what night it was. Just that I was with you."

"All right, well, if this is a legal thing, then obviously she's given a date. So find out what date she gave and then give it to me so I can…you know, cover you."

Had he just offered to lie for his best friend?

Or had his careful, if halting, wording suggested he would never do such a thing? The long silence implied neither one of them was quite sure.

"Cool, cool," Chadwick said. "I'll get it and I'll, uh, you know, get it to you. Listen, I gotta go. Starla's coming over, and that girl can suck the chrome off a trailer hitch and she's the sex before you eat kind, so…"

"Cool."

"I'll text you later and see if you want to hang. What's this party you're doing again?"

"Just a work thing," Mason lied.

Then the line was dead.

He couldn't mention the name Kazemi to his best friend—Chadwick would freak and make Mason's shot at a redemption mission all about him. Maybe say a bunch of shit that made it clear he was way closer to being the guy he'd been in high school than Mason was.

Come to think of it, after almost forty-eight hours of having a clear and sober head, Mason had never been more aware of all the things he couldn't tell his supposedly best friend.

Worse, the dark cloud that had always hung over their friendship looked poised to burst. This had always been Mason's fear—that one of them would eventually take the party too far, demand some form of rescue from the other they couldn't quite give. But he'd figured the event in question would be some split-second, drunken accident neither of them saw coming.

This was different, something that had started in Chadwick's workplace. Something that might involve weeks', maybe months' worth of meetings with lawyers.

Months of Mason being asked to lie.

He was halfway upstairs to his bedroom before he realized his hands were shaking.

When he opened his medicine cabinet and took out the bottle of Xanax Chadwick had prescribed for him, he shook two blue pills into his palm as if they were aspirin.

They were preferable to a drink, he told himself, and if anything, they'd calm him down enough that he'd be able to articulate the right apology to Naser. Relaxed, he'd probably do a better job of charming his sister too.

At this point, Fareena was a lost cause.

But as the pills made their painful way down his throat on an inadequate swallow of water, he knew he'd made a terrible mistake.

Again.

## 7

An hour after its start time, Pari's event was one hundred people over its headcount, and Naser and Jonas were circulating slowly through the crowd like parent chaperones at a junior high dance. Persian pop music poured from the speaker towers on all sides of the pool deck. But it wasn't Googoosh. It sounded like a dance remix of a tune by Jamshid, whose throaty and haunting voice always reminded Naser of his father. And that, he realized, might be part of why he was so stressed out this evening. Pari's work embraced their Iranian heritage at every turn, and the results always brought a complicated mix of feelings to a simmer inside Naser's soul.

Jonas gripped Naser's shoulder. "Let's make separate circuits and see what we can see, and then we'll meet back here in a few minutes and debrief. Remember, take no action without talking to me first, my little warrior. Deal?"

It was a concession to a crowd that had grown so thick he and Jonas could only scope out the entire party by splitting up. Naser nodded. In a second, Jonas was lost in the press of bodies.

One of the wine stations was already empty, the tuxedoed server clearing its empty bottles. And yet none of the surrounding guests seemed to be hurting for a glass.

That's when he focused on an aspect of the party that had initially bothered him for an entirely different reason. Fortune-tellers. Four of them. They weren't being played by women of color, at least, which somewhat offset the troubling stereotype. Underneath the flowing, beaded, and wildly overdone costumes, each one glowered like a budding Karen three seconds away from calling the manager.

Also, who hired *four* fortune-tellers for a single party? Were they running a special?

And why was the turnover at their tables so high?

Either they weren't very good at their jobs or their fortunes were incredibly concise.

*In the coming year, be sure to avoid men named Bob. That'll be five hundred dollars. Have a nice evening.*

He headed for the nearest fortune-teller's table, cutting off a few guests before they could take a seat. He dropped down into the folding chair with a loud *thunk.*

"Want to know the future, kid?" she asked with all the enthusiasm of a basset hound.

"I'm not a kid."

"Sorry. You're just small, I guess. How old are you?"

"There's an age requirement for fortune-telling?"

She rolled her eyes. "Hold out your hand."

Naser complied, expecting her to pretend to read his palm. Meanwhile, he extended both feet underneath the table in search of contraband, and sure enough, the toes of his dress shoes collided with something hard. Something that clinked. Something that sounded like glass bottles.

"Where's your ticket?" the woman said.

"I need a ticket for fortune-telling?"

"Honestly. Like I need this tonight. This costume makes me smell like a fucking chemical fire."

"You're a very profane fortune-teller, you know that?"

"Report me to the fortune-tellers' board. Red or white?"

*"I knew it!"*

"Easy on the shouting. I just work here."

"You *don't* work here, and that's the problem because you're not a fortune-teller"—Naser bent to one side and flipped up the tablecloth, revealing a case of red and white wine bottles and stacks of wine glasses exactly like the ones used by the hotel's catering department—"you're a bartender! From an outside vendor!"

"Try answered an ad on Craigslist and found out about this stupid costume when I showed up. All I do is pour, all right? So what is it, little man? Red or white?"

Thrilled to have finally uncovered his sister's grand deception, Naser sprung to his feet. That's when a gown slapped him in the face. At first, he assumed Pari had witnessed his detective work and was now determined to beat him to death with one of the display dresses that had yet to make an appearance. But when he stumbled backward, he saw the fabric that had smacked him was still spinning through the air. Not spinning. Whirling. Because it belonged to one of several whirling dervishes who'd just erupted into their dance on different parts of the pool deck. A light smattering of applause broke out, and then some of it continued as folks clapped along to the beat of the music. The dervishes didn't wear the unadorned robes of their Zoroastrian forebears, but their movements were beautifully coordinated. As they all started twirling in the same direction, the guests parted around them. After a minute or two, they'd converged at the end of the massive swimming pool furthest from the hotel.

They weren't just a performance piece, Naser realized, they were crowd control.

Jonas appeared next to him.

"Who's going to tell her whirling dervishes were about reaching a mystical state where you renounced worldly possessions? Their gowns are almost always monochromatic. These guys look like flying color wheels."

"Oh, I'm sure you will," Jonas said.

"Not a chance. She's the *queen* of Persian culture."

"You'll find a way to slip it in, I'm sure," Jonas said. "More importantly, while perhaps a bit dangerous given the crowd size, whirling dervishes are not, technically, a violation of her contract."

"But the fortune-tellers are," Naser growled.

After he explained the devious plot his sister had concocted using smuggled liquor and drink cards, Jonas nodded. "Wow. Your sister's good."

"Traitor."

"Hush, now. The show's starting."

A spotlight shot down out of the heavens, illuminating the dervishes' real accomplishment—they'd cleared a stage area where the entire party could see it. As for the spotlight, Naser looked to the roof of the hotel's lobby and saw two dark shadows crouching on either side of the blinding white blaze.

The crowd erupted in more cheers. Naser looked in the direction heads were turning and saw something emerging from the entrance to

Camilla's he didn't have a name for yet. It was terrifyingly tall, and there was something very large and shiny on top of it. As the stilt walker passed them, Naser realized the giant shiny crown rising from the person's head was actually a chandelier.

"Maybe that's why she wanted a tent," Jonas said, "so she could hang chandeliers."

"So she put them on stilt walkers instead."

"Like I said, your sister's good."

"And like I said, you're a traitor."

One stilt walker was followed by another, and another. Three more appeared from the service alley that ran along the northern wall of the hotel, connecting some maintenance offices with a back entrance to the pool deck. All told, six stilt walkers now framed the whirling dervishes, the shimmering light cast by their chandelier crowns glittering on the dervishes' multicolored gowns.

Naser had to admit, the amazing display showed off his sister's formidable talent. And he saw now why she'd wanted the chandeliers. The effects their lights made on the spinning fabric was dazzling, like sunlight sparkling off a rushing river.

But they weren't just any chandeliers. They were thick and round. Their concentric circles of long dangling crystals tapered gradually, each one a close replica of the chandeliers inside the Shah Cheragh mosque in Shiraz. When he realized this, he felt a tug in his chest.

Suddenly he was twelve years old again, sitting next to his father on the sofa as the man leafed through picture books of his homeland, a mixture of wonder and longing in his voice as he described the landmarks within. Waxing rhapsodic about Shiraz, the city where he'd been born. Its sights and splendors, how it was the final resting place of Hafez, one of the greatest Persian poets in history. His father was not a religious man, but the shimmering, jeweled walls and ceiling of Shah Cheragh, the mirrored mosque, as it was often called, brought tears to his eyes. "Someday I will take you there, Naser-*joon*," he'd made the mistake of saying one evening. "And we will stand there bathed in all that light."

In that exact moment, his mother had appeared in the kitchen doorway, eyes blazing. Drawn by the anger and fear in her expression, Naser's father slid the picture book onto Naser's lap then followed his wife into the kitchen. Naser had tried not to eavesdrop, but the anger in his mother's tone added volume to their frenzied whispers. Persian, for the most part, was a languid and melodic language, but that night, the

words between his parents flew. At first, his father defended himself—
they were not political refugees like so many of their friends. They had
not worked in the Shah's government. His father had done his military
service before they'd left. They could return if they wanted. They still had
their Iranian passports. Getting Naser and Pari into the country for a
short visit might be no trouble. That's when his mother's anger had boiled
over, her voice rising above a whisper. "*Pesareto bebin. Mibini kiyeh. Mibini
chejuri ra mireh, chejuri harf mizane. In nemitune bere be Iran. Midooni ke nemitune
bere.*"

*Don't translate*, he'd told himself, *you don't want to know, so just don't*—
But in the end, he couldn't help himself.

*Look at your son. Look at who he is. Look at the way he walks. A man like
him cannot go there. You know this.*

A man like him...

He knew exactly what she'd meant. Twelve years old and already too
obviously gay to return to his homeland without bringing shame upon
their family. His mother, who had never said a word to him about his
walk or manner of speaking, was convinced her Iranian elders would
recoil from him. His hand flipped the picture book closed as if it
contained pictures of gruesome crime scenes. He was mounting the steps
and bound for his room before the tears could come. The way he talked
and walked was why the other kids made fun of him at school. Now it
was the reason he could never see the land of his ancestors.

And his family's reason as well.

That was the last time his father ever mentioned Shiraz or the
mirrored mosque. A few years later he was gone, felled by a sudden heart
attack when Naser was a freshman in high school.

Applause jerked him back to the present.

The whirling dervishes were taking a bow. The spotlight died, but the
chandeliers still glowed in the tiki torch glow. Then the pool deck was
swept by the familiar opening strands of a song that transported Naser
back in time again. And he wasn't alone—the lilting windpipe sounds, the
rush of warm and energetic strings, they both brought cries of nostalgic
joy from so many around him. To Naser, they brought a tightness to his
chest. Brought more memories of being a young boy as his father and
mother danced around the living room together to this very music, Pari
nipping at their heels like an excited puppy, his parents reveling in the
soaring and beautiful lyrics of a love song they shared with an Iran they
claimed was no more. An Iran Naser might never know. And so Naser

had buried himself in his book or his schoolwork or a family budget as the other members of his family danced to the music of Googoosh.

Now he could feel Jonas's eyes on him, trying, no doubt, to interpret his strange blend of emotions.

The spotlight reappeared. A gorgeous woman clad in one of his sister's shimmering gowns stepped into its halo. Her radiant locks of lustrous platinum hair looked intimately familiar, and that was how a live performance of Googoosh's classic tune *"Man Amadeh-Am"* filled the pool deck.

Sort of.

"Googoosh?" Jonas asked.

"Try Navid Ahmadi. We dated in college."

Jonas nodded. "A drag queen, I see."

"The only Iranian one she knows."

The crowd had figured it out, too, but rather than protesting, many were clapping and singing along. It helped that Navid's performance was spot on, complete with the gentle air kisses and beatific smiles Googoosh always gave her sellout crowds. When it was done, there was an uproarious round of applause, and then models—meaning Pari's LA actor friends who needed work—began cat walking the handbags.

Which were not what Naser was expecting. Their lines were so sinuous they looked almost like extensions of the models' bodies, and the brilliant colors and intricate geometric designs reminded him of panels from the Shahnameh, the Persian Book of Kings. Some were covered in bejeweled floral designs so intricate they almost looked like dark mosaics. All in all, it was a much bolder statement than the *shal*, and Pari had paired them with older dresses from her collection. Simple, monochromatic dresses. Dresses into which she'd tried again and again to inject Persian design influences only to be told by her handlers at the Bliss Network that her instincts were *too bold*, which was white people code for *too foreign*.

As Naser watched, he could see the full extent of what Pari had done. By ensuring the handbags molded with the body, she'd essentially added the very color and culture she'd been bullied out of including in the dresses years before when she first brought them to market.

His sister remained one of the most determined people he'd ever met, and as usual, this left him both frightened and impressed.

As applause broke out all around them, Naser studied the crowd.

On the other side of a pool sparkling with floating, floral-rimmed candles, a tall, blond, insanely gorgeous man leaned against one of the bistro tables, wine glass in hand.

Naser's breath left him in a single, loud huff.

It couldn't be him. No way.

He blinked, figuring the vision would vanish. That the painful childhood memories unleashed by his sister's fashion show had opened a door in his head to painful high school memories as well.

Then Mason Worther ran one hand back through his silky blond hair. His signature move, even back then. In high school, whenever someone mentioned Mason in conversation, they usually imitated him running one hand back through his hair like a model in a L'Oréal commercial. And he still did it, apparently. He was doing it right now.

Because he was here.

And suddenly Naser was sixteen years old again.

**Eleven Years Ago**

*The day he was due to present his model of Persepolis to Ms. Guidroz's history class, Naser's mother insisted on driving him to school. She claimed it was because her SUV had a bigger cargo bay than the Camry he'd inherited from Pari before she'd gone off to design school, and she was right. But Naser figured a different, less charitable agenda lay just beneath the surface of her offer of assistance.*

*She didn't trust him to present Persian culture without her firm guidance, and if he didn't watch it, she'd try to escort him to class where she'd loudly correct any historical errors in his presentation from the back of the room. That would be the most embarrassing thing ever. And given how badly high school had gone so far, that was saying something.*

*"You are sure you don't want me to walk with you to class." Like so many of his mother's supposed questions, it was hard to hear the question mark at the end.*

*Ever since his father had died, she'd kept her hair short. Her father had loved her hair long and thick and black. Her refusal to grow it out again was a testament to her grief. If her husband was not around to enjoy her lustrous locks, then no one would, not even her.*

*"I'm fine, Maman."*

*But he wasn't fine. Ever since he'd completed the first miniature lamassu, he'd dreaded this moment, knowing that getting the model safely to class would be harder than any aspect of building it. He could already hear the shouts of his tormentors, as if they were ghosting through the Googoosh song his mother was playing on the radio.*

*Chadwick, Tim, and Mason had doubled their aggression these past few months. After he'd transferred sophomore year, they'd forced him into the occasional locker, but it was always quick and efficient—mostly gay slurs coughed under their breath whenever he tried to answer a question in class. Junior year they'd moved on to harder shoves and shoulder knocks. The locker stuffings had become more aggressive, with some half-assed attempts by Chadwick Brody to jam the door shut from outside. Like the Laguna Mesa Golden Boys felt the need to prove their manliness as they neared manhood, and Naser's sanity had become their proving grounds. In response, he'd started jumping a fence at the back of campus so he could avoid a morning walk through the central courtyard. But no way could he employ that strategy with a delicate model in his arms.*

*He'd debated giving the project less than half his usual effort, just so he wouldn't have to bring something he was proud of somewhere it wouldn't be safe.*

*Laguna Mesa High was not a place Naser Kazemi brought things he didn't want broken. But even though he wasn't the bravest kid in town, the idea offended him.*

*Persepolis, he'd decided, was worth the risk.*

*The school's parking lot came into view. His heart started to race.*

*"Maman, turn off Googoosh."*

*His mother's typical sound of frustration resembled a bird-like caw. "This is not Googoosh. This is Ramesh. You need to know your Persian music. That's why I play it."*

*"Not near school. You promised. You picked the one high school in Orange County that has, like, no Persian kids. It's all white supremacists and Koreans."*

*Naser felt instantly guilty when his mother's face fell. "Be friends with the Koreans then."*

*"I am."*

*There was a sad silence. "It is close to my work, Naser-joon."*

*"I know, Maman. I'm sorry."*

*And moving closer to work had been a priority after his father had died and she'd assumed responsibility for getting Naser to school before he was of driving age.*

*As she turned into the school's front parking lot, his mother lowered the volume slightly.*

*Eyes to the pavement, Naser stepped from the SUV. He heard his mother unlock the cargo door.*

*"Naser."*

*Startled, he turned to her. He was grateful she was still behind the wheel. Was it concern he saw in her eyes? The prospect she might know anything about the bullying twisted his gut into several more painful knots than had been there the second before.*

*"You are sure you don't want my help."*

*"I've got it, Maman."*

*She nodded.*

*Then he was hoisting the model from the cargo bay.*

*In the few seconds he was forced to balance it in one arm and close the cargo door with the other, he was convinced he'd get knocked from behind by one of his brawny tormentors. But the next thing he knew, he was headed up the front walk toward Laguna Mesa's drab stucco main building, heads turning to study his handiwork—the sprawling ancient Persian city in its glory days, before it had been savagely torched by Alexander the Great. No one was muttering the word* fag *under their breath, and most of the looks seemed impressed. Maybe those were good signs.*

*Then he reached the main courtyard. It was packed with students sitting in their morning cliques on the concrete benches and tables. If Ms. Guidroz's class hadn't been first period, he might never have done the model to begin with. No way would he have been able to protect it for even half a school day.*

*The door to safety was in sight. He could see Ms. Guidroz inside, clearing the wipe-off board with long sweeps of her arm that barely jostled her always-perfectly-in-place pixie cut. If he could just make it another few yards...*

*Then he heard them. Chadwick and Tim were in the lead, hair tousled and sweat matted, faces flushed from recent exertion, wearing their team windbreakers, barreling down the nearest set of steps, moving with the speed that had made them varsity athletes by their sophomore year.*

*"Praaaaaaaaaaaannnnnnnnnncer!" Chadwick Brody always yelled the nickname with a terrifying blend of fury and delight.*

*Naser froze, his hands gripping the edges of his model so tightly his knuckles and wrists started to burn.*

*He thought about running the rest of the way, but that would also risk sending the model to the concrete.*

*Then there was another high-pitched yowl. This one didn't form a word.*

*At the base of the steps, Chadwick and Tim froze and turned just in time to see Mason Worther crash to the concrete. The impact looked bone rattling, like someone had picked him up and dropped him from a great height. Mason's breath left him in a strained wheeze. Bystanders winced and brought hands to their faces.*

*Mason Worther, star quarterback, had wiped out—hard.*

*A part of Naser told him he should take a moment to enjoy this, the idea that the universe had knocked Mason on his ass before he could screw up Naser's day—again.*

*Then he realized what the universe had also done. The prospect of their star quarterback being badly injured had so terrified Chadwick and Tim they'd forgotten about Naser altogether and rushed to Mason's side.*

*Naser started moving.*

*A few seconds later, he'd pushed the door to Ms. Guidroz's classroom shut with his back, and his favorite teacher was taking the model from his hands with an indulgent smile that told him she knew what had just transpired outside but didn't want to embarrass him by bringing it up.*

"Nas!"

Not Prancer this time, but his actual name.

Suddenly he was enfolded in Mason Worther's big, grown-up arms as the man's wine breath doused him from a great height.

It had all happened so fast—the realization that not only was Mason at the party, but he was also Fareena's date. Then he'd frozen up like he had in Laguna Mesa's courtyard that day as Fareena had pulled Mason around the end of the pool toward him by one hand.

And now Mason Worther's arms were around him.

And there could be only one explanation.

Mason Worther was very drunk.

Which didn't change the fact that he was still obnoxiously hot.

Ten years after graduation, the guy looked like a *True Blood*-era Alexander Skarsgård, his tailored suit hugging a muscular body he'd never stopped working on. And yeah, chances were he'd stayed a cornsilk blond thanks to a good colorist, but he'd grown into his height, and his blue eyes blazed in the light of the surrounding tiki torches. That neck Naser had fantasized about gripping with both hands as Mason drove into him with rageful abandon was even thicker and more muscular now. And the man stared at him with the same wide-eyed openness he'd used on him back in school. Looks like these had always been bait, Naser was sure—designed to draw him in so Mason and his friends could treat him like a rag doll deserving of ridicule.

"How you doing, buddy?" Mason boomed.

"Well," Fareena said, "you two know each other, it seems."

"Damn right. Laguna Mesa Panthers. Leave 'em on the field in pieces, right, Nas?"

One arm wrapped around Naser's shoulders, Mason pulled back and raised his other fist. Mason Worther, the guy who'd torn his backpack off him more times than he could count, was expecting Naser to greet him with a fist bump.

He returned the fist bump weakly. "Or in lockers."

Mason cackled.

Fareena looked from one to the other as if they'd both grown additional heads. "You played sports in high school, Nas?"

"Is dread a sport?"

Mason went to ruffle Naser's hair and encountered a solid plate of hair product that would have had him wiping his hand with a napkin if he'd been more sober. "Hey, listen, we loved Nas. I mean, look at those eyes. How could you not love those eyes?" The *s* on the end of *eyes* lasted longer than it should have.

"What happened to relatively sober, Mason?" Fareena asked.

"One glass of wine. That's all."

Fareena pointed a manicured nail at him. "*This* is not one glass of wine."

Mason shrugged, as if to say, *Women, amIrite?*

He glared back at him, but what he was thinking was, *Did Mason Worther just compliment my eyes?*

"All right, all right," Mason slurred. "It's true. We did kinda give Naser some shit in high school. I mean, just a liitttllle"—Mason raised his thumb and forefinger as if he were indicating the world's tiniest penis— "just a little shit, right?"

"Actually, more like a whoooollle"—Naser spread his hands as if indicating a giant loaf of still-baking bread, which forced Mason to drop his arm from Naser's shoulders and take an unsteady step backward—"lot of shit. Like a whole, whole football field of shit." He kept spreading his hands until his arms were thrown open wide. "I mean just year after year after *year* of shit."

Fareena gripped one of Mason's shoulders to keep him from stumbling into the swimming pool behind him. "Before this exchange drowns me in class, may I ask how we're defining *shit* here?"

Mason sputtered and waved a hand through the air in front of him. "Oh, you know. Just guy stuff. Right? Just guys being guys. And stupid. You know, stupid guys. Right, Nas?"

Maybe if he hadn't looked to Naser for confirmation, for unearned split-second forgiveness, Naser could have held his tongue and let it slide. But Mason Worther was as smug and arrogant and good looking as he'd been back then. And Naser wasn't a scared teenager anymore.

"Yeah, *guy stuff*. Like when you and your buddies used an anonymous email account to write a letter to the assistant baseball coach—who was a huge homophobe, by the way—and you pretended to be me and professed my sexually explicit love for him. Even though I was a minor and not out of the closet yet. That was an amazing piece of guy stuff that resulted in so many *amazing* conversations with my mom. And the school."

Mason's mouth snapped shut. His labored breaths caused his chest to rise and fall. His crew had never been held responsible for that little stunt, but this stunned reaction was all the confirmation Naser needed.

Fareena's professional mask cracked down the middle. "Jesus Christ, Mason."

The guy swallowed and squinted as if Naser and Fareena were flickering in and out of existence before his glassy eyes.

Then he cleared his throat. It seemed like an attempt to gather himself, but the sound was so stuttering and weak it only made clear how wasted Mason Worther was.

"What can I say? I'm a piece of shit." He shrugged as if the fact was too obvious to occasion comment. "And like all pieces of shit, I should be flushed. So I'm going to head out. You and I can settle our thing later, Fareena. But for now, Mason Worther's just gonna—"

Mason was underwater before he could finish the sentence. He'd turned and walked right into the pool.

The splash wasn't big enough to draw much attention.

In an instant, Naser and Fareena were slack-jawed, watching the man they'd just been talking to swim toward the pool's opposite end, ducking under floating candles as he went. He'd only break the surface for a second or two, like he thought he was invisible when submerged.

Jonas, who'd been conferring with security near the entrance to the restaurant, raced in the direction of Mason's most likely destination.

Suddenly Naser was doused in Fareena's elegant perfume. Her arms were around him. He returned the hug as best he could, but his head was spinning. Maybe because he felt like he'd just stumbled out of a time machine. "I am *so* sorry, Nas. He asked if Pari had a brother, but I had no idea."

"Are you guys dating?"

She rolled her eyes. "No. God, no. We *were* fucking, but that's been over for a week. He owes me money, and I thought I'd have him pay off the debt by investing in Pari's line."

"Why does Pari need investors?"

Fareena's eyes glazed over, and she sipped wine. "Oh, you know, she's just trying to raise some side money for some projects outside of her comfort zone."

"How does Bliss Network feel about that?"

Fareena sipped more wine. "They're figuring it out."

On the other side of the pool, Jonas, along with J.T. and Keoni from the security team, were swaddling Naser's high school bully in towels they'd swiped from the cabanas. As they led him inside, Jonas looked back, met Naser's stare, and opened his arm in a clear gesture of *What just happened with this guy?*

"Seriously, this is terrible, Nas. What can I do?"

"Why did he keep touching me?"

She shrugged. "Because he's drunk. He's kind of *always* drunk. I mean, the dick was really good, so I overlooked it for a while. Until it turned whiskey on me. But anyway…sorry." She rubbed between his shoulder blades with aggressive tenderness. "You don't want to hear about Mason Worther's dick."

This wasn't entirely true, so Naser kept his mouth shut.

Just then someone trilled Fareena's name from across the pool deck. It was Pari.

Fareena smiled and waved, then she turned to Naser. "I'll just tell her the investor didn't show. Don't worry. But let me go talk to her for a sec and make sure she didn't notice any of this mess. I feel like *shit*."

Then she was gone, and Naser was staring at the spot where Jonas and two security agents had helped Mason rise from the pool like a beardless Poseidon who'd been dressed by Tom Ford.

He told himself it wasn't his problem. It wasn't even his job. His goal had been to contain his sister's excesses, and in that, his only margin of success was that the hotel around them wasn't on fire. But the night was still fairly young. Mason Worther was a blast from the past he didn't want or need. Jonas hadn't asked for his help.

If all that was true, why was he rounding one end of the pool, approaching the open space where the retractable walls of glass had turned part of the indoor restaurant into the party area? He studied what he could see of the lobby and paced a little, nodding and smiling at guests he knew, but mostly looking for any sign of Jonas. Or Mason. Or the security guys who'd helped him from the pool.

He was about to head off in the direction of Fareena and his sister when his phone buzzed. It was a text from Jonas.

> **Do you happen to know this
> tall, drunk fellow? We could
> use an assist.**

That was all it took to send him into the lobby. The janitor mopping up the wet trail Mason had left across the marble floor told Naser they'd taken the swimmer to the events office, which bothered Naser deeply. Despite his tiny office, he treasured the little private pocket of Sapphire Cove he and Jonas shared. Mason's presence there felt like a violation. That said, escorting him to the management offices would have meant letting him drip over a long expanse of carpet, so Naser couldn't fault Jonas for the call.

The group he was looking for had gathered inside the employees-only corridor. Minus one. Mason Worther. The two security guys hovering outside Naser's closed office door were a study in contrasts— Keoni was a giant Pacific Islander who carried himself like an NFL player, and J.T. was a pasty white boy with a twangy Southern accent and the calculated musculature of someone whose last job had involved having sex on camera. Which it had.

"Sorry, but you guys were talking so I thought maybe you could help," Jonas whispered, tugging Naser into his office.

"We went to high school together." He tried to keep it from sounding like the loaded statement it was and succeeded.

"Think you can get him to sign this?" Jonas handed him a clipboard holding some papers.

"Where is he?" Naser asked.

"Your office."

"Dripping all over everything? Thanks, Jonas!"

Jonas recoiled. "He finished toweling off in the bathroom and then we gave him some hotel merch to change into. He's not wet, I promise."

"Sorry, I didn't mean to..."

"No, I'm sorry. I saw you guys talking and thought you were friends. Don't worry about it. I'll have him sign the release myself."

"No, it's fine."

"Is it?"

Before Jonas could ask twice, Naser was knocking on his own door, Keoni and J.T. parting on either side of him like the Red Sea.

Mason told him to come in.

Naser obeyed, pulling the door shut behind him, realizing, too late, he was suddenly alone with a spectacularly shirtless Mason Worther, who was looking at him with one eye as he pulled a pair of hotel-branded sweatpants up over his very bare ass. Of course, he'd ditched his underwear. They were soaked, and Sapphire Cove didn't sell any. He'd run his hands through his thick wet hair, and now he looked less like a party accident and more like a fashion model preparing for a beachside photo shoot.

"You told me—" Naser turned, grabbed the knob. "I'll come back."

"It's fine."

Mason turned, the sweatpants leaving little to the imagination.

*Wow. No wonder Fareena had trouble letting him go.*

He pulled a hotel bathrobe off the back of Naser's chair and put it on like it was a trench coat.

"Is this your office?" Mason asked.

"Uh huh. So no major injuries? You didn't break anything? Didn't hit your head?"

Mason shook the head in question.

Naser handed him the clipboard. "Okay. Then sign this, please."

Without asking what he was about to put his name on, Mason signed the paper and handed the clipboard back. He missed Naser's hand by about a foot. When he went to adjust, embarrassment flashed in his eyes. Then he sank into Naser's desk chair like his bones suddenly weighed tons. Naser checked the signature. It was about six inches above the signature line, but it was legible.

"I guess I should get out of here." But instead of moving, Mason leaned back. The flaps of his robe fell open, revealing one pink nipple Naser imagined sucking on until Mason gasped in pain, then sucking harder until his own mouth hurt from the effort. "Hey…" Mason tried to sit up and turn around at the same time. It didn't quite happen. Behind him, his wet clothes rested in a loose pile on a badly folded towel, presumably the one he'd used to dry off. At least they were on the carpet and not atop one of Naser's precious few cabinets. "Can you… Can you just…"

"Your phone?" Naser asked.

"Yeah."

He moved to the pile, crouched down, and extracted Mason's water-droplet beaded iPhone from the soggy mess. It still glowed. Mr. Worther, son of a wealthy real estate developer, had the newest and most waterproof model. When Naser turned, he saw his former tormentor was now resting his head and arms atop Naser's desk calendar, one eye slitted. "Can you get me an Uber?" he muttered.

"Can you sit up so we can unlock—"

"Sevensixtwonine," Mason slurred, eyes closed.

Naser had tapped in the code before realizing the man had just given him a piece of incredibly personal information he might never have shared while sober.

"Mason?"

No response. Mason Worther had just passed out on his desk.

And then the office door flew open, and a wall of spicy perfume hit them both. "Get up!" Fareena shouted.

When Mason didn't respond, she slapped one hand against the side of the desk. Her target jumped. "Now, Mason! Up and *out*. I can't believe this. You promised me."

Mason tried to sit up straight, but he was bobbing and weaving like he'd been unconscious for hours. Like he'd forgotten Naser was standing right behind him.

Naser's thoughts were racing, but it was mostly just one thought, over and over again. *Seven six two nine. Seven six two nine. Seven six two nine.*

Fareena adjusted Mason's robe to ensure he didn't expose himself to the lobby. "Seriously, I'm so sorry about this, Nas. I flagged down a cab out front, and they're going to take him home. Thank God he didn't drive."

Naser just nodded.

And then they were gone.

And Naser was all alone.

With Mason Worther's unlocked phone.

# 8

Holding the raw materials of Mason Worther's personal life in his sweating hands, Naser sat at his desk, plotting his revenge.

What lay ahead, he reasoned, didn't require him to surrender his moral code.

Entirely.

The goal was clear.

He wasn't out to invade Mason Worther's privacy. Or steal anything from him. What he wanted was a little justice. A leveling of the scales. To that end, he was content to pursue payback for just one incident in particular, the one he'd brought up on the pool deck moments before. In Naser's view, it towered over the many others by virtue of how it had arrayed a host of unwilling participants against him.

He gave himself over to painful memories, figuring they would focus and embolden him.

Saw Coach Harris's sculpted features trembling with red-faced anger as he held a sheet of paper in one hand he'd sharpened into a dagger with three precise folds, heard him spitting out words like inappropriate and outrageous and disgusting. Even though Naser hadn't written it, the email had made him feel as if someone had reached inside of him and pried loose secrets he'd been storing behind walls of brick and mortar. Sure, Coach Harris had played a role in his most secret jerk-off fantasies, but never in his life would he have shared those fantasies with anyone, especially their source.

Mortifying meetings followed. With the principal, the guidance counselor, and an increasingly rageful coach who acted as if a reserved sixteen-year-old social outcast with few friends outside of Math Club had tried to fondle him in the shower.

For years, Mahin Kazemi had managed the surgical labs of some of the best and most arrogant neurosurgeons in Southern California. High school administrators proved no match for her. When the threat of expulsion was raised against her son, she turned into mother lion, bringing in samples of Naser's writing and slapping them down on the principal's desk so he could see the awkward phrasing and long, run-on sentences in the email bore no resemblance to her son's eloquent essays. And the school produced no evidence connecting the anonymous Hotmail account to Naser, either.

Victory, when it came, proved bittersweet. In the end, the school caved. Talk of firm discipline was dropped, and Coach Harris ended up with a slap on the wrist for directly confronting a student over sensitive and sexually explicit material. But nobody ever asked Naser who he thought sent the letter, and Naser never bothered to share his suspicions. Mason Worther, Chadwick Brody, and Tim Malbec were far too central to the success of Laguna Mesa's beloved sports teams to be brought down with anything other than incontrovertible proof.

Then, a few days after the matter was settled, someone had slid a pamphlet for a gay conversion therapy clinic inside Naser's locker.

But he'd known instantly it wasn't his regular tormentors. Coach Harris was the culprit. He'd been sure of it. The man's well-known homophobia was exactly why Mason and company had used him for their plot.

The memories worked their intended effect.

Years later, Naser's fingers were trembling with rage.

He opened the text messages app on Mason's phone.

His plan was to send Mason's special, emotional, coming-out message far and wide. Then the son of a bitch would be forced to deal with the resulting explosion the second he woke with a splitting hangover. Back in high school, word of Naser's supposed love letter to Coach Harris had torn throughout the school. Nothing short of widespread humiliation would square the debt.

Then a text popped up on the screen.

> **Too busy sucking dick to answer my emails???**

The sender's name was Pete, but his address book entry had no last name.

Another text followed it.

> **How many times have I told u we don't get wknds in our biz? U want fun Fridays go wait tables like those faggots you went to UCLA with.**

"Jesus." The second text didn't feel like a joke. It felt angry, and the homophobia in it was more biting and explicit. It also carried a whiff of authority. The phrase *our business* suggested this Pete guy was a supervisor or employer.

He opened the thread containing Pete's other messages. It was long. Very long. And every single one was just as hostile. Nagging, repetitive reminders of work tasks, nitpicking criticisms of Mason's behavior in the office—everything from the way he walked to the clothes he wore—most of which began with hateful rhetorical questions.

> **You too dumb to figure this out on your own?**

> **Do you need sign language on proposal formatting? You wrote this like you were getting dragged behind a truck.**

Who was this Pete, and why hadn't Mason murdered him before now? Naser turned to his computer. A few keystrokes later, he was looking at the stylish website for WORTHER PROPERTIES. It featured slideshows of sparkling McMansions with tiled roofs and glittering swimming pools spread out across dry rolling hills set aflame by California sunsets. And there, under the ABOUT US page, was a studio photograph of Mason Worther and a similar-looking and similarly coiffed Nordic tower of muscle who was about twice his age. And the older man's name was Pete.

*Oh my God. This monster is his dad?*

A dad who seemed incapable of addressing his grown son without employing a profane description of a sex act between two men.

The more he scrolled through Pete Worther's texts, the worse it got. Maybe because it never let up. The man used gay slurs like most people used indefinite articles. And his son was on the receiving end of his abuse day after day after day.

*No wonder.*

Naser told himself to stop scrolling, told himself that if he kept reading, he'd lose his nerve. But now he was taking in all the passive, spineless responses from Mason. Never once did the guy snap back, and Mason's responses made clear they weren't just joking around. Again and again Mason apologized, rolled over, and promised to do a better job. The abuse kept coming, and Mason Worther just took it.

Just like Naser had back in high school.

Suddenly his revenge plot felt like a rope that would pull him headfirst into a soup of hatred and anger. He sucked in a deep breath and took stock of what he'd been poised to do. Shame bloomed deep in his gut. He'd been about to use the idea of sex between two men as a tool to smear, to destroy. To inflict pain. He wasn't a teenager anymore. He was a grown man. What kind of gay man would that have made him?

The message was clear, and it was for him. Naser needed this phone, and the glimpse it had given him into Mason Worther's tortured, drunken life, gone.

And there was only one way to do that.

Or so he thought.

He scrolled through the apps quickly, trying not to spy. But he was looking for anything that might give him Mason's address. He found something better. After a few seconds, he stopped swiping at an icon featuring a sloping roof that was meant to say *home*. The app was called DigiKey. Inside was a portal for the homeowners' association that included Mason's street and a home address Google Maps told him was smack in the middle of Capo Beach. The app also yielded a QR code he figured would get him through the gate. If he was met by a manned guardhouse instead, he'd simply hand the phone to the guard and be on his way. Easy peasy.

The entire drive there, at every red light, Naser was tempted to pick up Mason's phone and start swiping. Maybe peer into the guy's photo library, check for hookup apps that might suggest an undercurrent of truth to Pete Worther's hateful insults. With every second he resisted the urge, he felt prouder of himself.

A little way south of Sapphire Cove, Capo Beach was considered prime real estate in a county awash in it—a row of mismatched two- and three-story houses that fronted right on the sand. But Naser had always thought a strong enough rain could bring down the giant cliff that sat right behind it, crushing all those multimillion-dollar boxes into dust.

The app worked just as he expected. As the gate arm swung upward, he pulled his Volvo XC40 onto Mason Worther's private street. There were no streetlights, so the reflection from his dashboard was making it hard to see the addresses. He powered the passenger side windows down to get a better view. Cool ocean air filled the interior of his mini-SUV. A puddle of warm light fell across the street one house ahead. If Google Maps hadn't steered him wrong, it was coming from Mason's home.

The closer he got, the more he could see of the house—a bland concrete box with a spacious alleyway between it and the house to the north, which was under heavy construction. The garage was wide open and empty, save for a few high-ticket items. What looked like a jet ski underneath a plastic tarp, and then a set of skis for the water and the snow, both leaning against the wall. Only one of everything. A storehouse of bachelor treasures left open to the shadowy night.

*Oh, dear God, no. Tell me he didn't take off driving somewhere.*

From where he'd stopped the car, Naser could see a back door to the house inside the garage standing open by several inches. The light from beyond was dim. He waited for someone to emerge, but with every passing minute, it felt more and more like he was studying the evidence of a rapid abandonment. A drunken one. He parked his Volvo against the fence on the opposite side of the street and saw the dark railroad tracks that lay on the other side. Mason's phone in hand, he hurried into the garage. Even though he could easily step through the back door, he knocked on the inside of it twice, three times, then four times and loud. No answer.

"Mason?" It felt silly, ridiculous even, to be calling out his former bully's name with what sounded like neighborly concern. "Mason. I have your phone." There. He'd said it. It was almost like a confession. And he was sure it would bring the man stumbling toward him if he'd heard it.

Apparently, he hadn't, because there was no response.

He pulled the door open with one hand and slowly ascended a set of blond wood steps that put him in a gleaming, empty kitchen defined by *American Psycho* minimalism. It was open to the vast living room, with a central island covered in white marble and silver fixtures. The range was so big it could feed a party twice the size of any this spacious house could accommodate. The rest of the house was so white he was willing to bet Mason probably banned even closed bottles of red wine.

"Mason?"

No answer. He set the phone down on the counter. The little thud it made against the marble was the cue that he needed.

*You've done your job. Depart the devil's lair.*

But he couldn't move. There was still cause for concern, he told himself. If he had knowledge that someone as drunk as Mason was on the road currently, did he have an obligation to report it? Should he establish that Mason was actually gone? Was it worth the risk? Mason might shoot him if he drunkenly mistook him for an intruder. He seemed like the type to own more than one gun.

Naser wandered into the living room and right up to the seashell-supported glass coffee table. A large shadow was visible beyond the walls of glass looking out onto the night-dark ocean. Dim golden light came from both ends. It was a car. A nice one by the looks of its curvilinear shape. The headlights were off, but the parking lights glowed. And it was farther out on the sand than any car should be.

He opened the house's back door and started toward it. In January, the night winds right by the water were strong and chilly, but the Ferrari's top was down. Where he sat slumped to one side in the driver's seat, Mason's blond hair blew in the wind.

*"Mason!"*

Not a peep, not a stir. Naser ran. Sand filled his shoes, but he didn't care. The wrongness of the scene before him had swept aside all rules and boundaries. Mason Worther, it seemed, had tried to drive himself straight into the ocean, and that could only mean one thing.

Had he been trying to drown?

Naser yanked open the driver's side door. Mason jerked sideways.

He'd been resting one arm against it, and with the support gone, he was suddenly groaning and trying to right himself. He'd changed into a T-shirt and jeans, but he was barefoot, which might partly explain his lousy driving.

*Fine, he's alive. I should go.*

Instead, Naser surveyed the beach. He must have missed it when he drove past the alley, but somehow Mason's Ferrari had traveled between his house and the one north and managed to drive all the way out onto the sand without drawing anyone's attention. Probably because his northern neighbor was swaddled in scaffolding and billowing plastic tarps. Then Naser looked to the house just to the south.

Mason had been noticed after all. A lone figure stood on the second-floor balcony, floral print robe billowing in the wind even as she held the tie at her waist. The woman's flame red ponytail looked poised to spill loose from her scrunchie. Large potted plants filled most of the space around her, their leaves dancing in the wind. An empty hammock swayed beneath glittering strands of string lights, and the light pushing through the glass was honey colored and warm. By contrast to her welcoming abode, Mason's lair looked like a spaceship that had fallen out of a wormhole and landed on the sand next to it.

Naser felt a pressure against his fingers and jumped.

Mason had reached out through the shadows and taken his hand.

*He's touching me. Again.*

"Nas." The nickname turned into a long, low moan. "Nas is heeerrrreee."

"Okay. Let's get you inside, Formula One."

The giant man's considerable weight shifted onto Naser's shoulders the minute he got him to his feet, and suddenly it felt like their walk back to the house would take hours.

"I'msorreNas."

"Were you trying to hurt yourself, Mason?"

"Wannasaysorrree." Mason stumbled forward, and they almost went down together until Naser planted his legs firmly in the sand and bent slightly at the waist.

"Uh huh. Let's get you inside."

"I was..." Mason cleared his throat, then let loose several hacking coughs. "I was gonna go back... Back to hotel... Tell you I'm sorrreeee."

So he wasn't trying to drown himself.

Had he really been planning to drive back to Sapphire Cove and apologize? In his condition, that idea would have been as dangerous as driving straight into the surf.

They'd reached the back door before Naser could answer. Mounting the floating metal staircase to the second floor was easier than crossing the sand, so long as Naser didn't look down. The stairs had no risers, and it was a clear drop straight through to the house's foyer below. Then suddenly they'd stumbled together into a sprawling master suite where a heavy set of ripple-fold drapes had been pushed back, revealing an open deck door offering a sweeping view of the beach they'd just crossed. The bedside lamps were still on, casting a gentle glow across the plush, cream-colored carpet. He guided Mason to the edge of his bed, sat him down on the side, and took a step back.

"Sorree," Mason slurred.

*Get out,* Naser thought, *get out now.*

"For what?" Naser asked.

And then suddenly Mason had taken his hand, and the next thing Naser knew, the silky comforter was rising up all around him and Mason Worther's weight and brawn was pressing into him, and then the tips of their noses were touching and Mason was gently gripping Naser's wrists as he spread his arms out on either side of his head.

*Mason Worther is on me. I am under Mason Worther. What the hell is happening?*

He didn't feel pinned down, exactly. Just enfolded in a big, sloppy embrace. Any illusion that Mason might have deliriously mistaken Naser for someone else vanished when he found himself looking up into the man's big blue eyes. The guy gently chewed his bottom lip as if their sudden proximity had sobered him up a little. Naser thought he should say something, but he was thunderously unsure of what it should be.

*Get off me.*

*Kiss me.*

*Wreck my ass, trash.*

All three seemed equally likely to trip off his tongue. So he decided to say nothing.

Mason spoke first. "Reason I alwayssss pushed you into lockers is 'cause... Is 'cause I wanted to fuck you against them."

Naser felt his mouth open in shock and his cheeks tense in a way that told him his eyes had gone saucer wide. That's when Mason kissed him.

Naser felt knocked out of his flesh, as if the thought *Mason Worther is kissing me* was so big it crowded everything else from his body, including his soul. Then the unrestrained, deliciously messy power of Mason's kisses drew him back inside his skin. The hunger coming from Mason pulled something from Naser he couldn't contain, something that was tangled all through his sexuality, a sexuality that had been shaped by the mind games wielded against him by men like the one kissing him now.

A riot of voices in his head screamed at him. They sounded like his mom, like Connor. Like anyone who'd ever cared about him. Mason Worther was a bully. Who cared if his father had turned him into one? More importantly, he was drunk. Blackout drunk, from the looks of it. Naser should stop, run, and forget. In exactly that order.

Instead, he was writhing against Mason's rhythmic pressure, trying to match the man's serpentine moves with his own. Another few seconds of this, and a familiar switch would be flicked, and Naser would loop his legs around Mason's lower back, grinding his erection into Mason's crotch. If Mason was experienced enough with men to read the signs, he would know what it meant—that everything inside of Naser was relaxing, opening, melting, and that Naser had started to imagine what it would feel like to be filled with Mason's cock. And that meant he was craving it.

It was coming. It was close. That sense that every inch of his body would soon give way to the hungry and willful spinelessness of submission, a submission that had always been central to his desire.

One of his legs, he realized, was hovering in the air above Mason's lower back.

*Oh, shit.*

He straightened it instead and forced it to the comforter.

When Mason felt him stiffen, he went still, pulling back. He studied Naser with slitted eyes, but his lips were still puckered. They could resume kissing the second Naser gave the word, his face seemed to say.

"You're drunk." Naser had meant it as a whisper. Instead the words came out at full voice.

As if he'd been struck by a blow he could vaguely feel, Mason closed his eyes, then he rested his forehead against Naser's.

"I'm always drunk." He rolled sideways off Naser's body, but one giant arm stayed sprawled across Naser's chest.

Silence fell, silence except for the rush of the surf outside and the occasional clink of the windblown drapes knocking against their steel curtain rod. For a while, Naser just lay there. He was sober as a stone, but his head was spinning. His world, his history, his sense of who he had been and where he'd come from, had been tilted on its axis. Mason

Worther had just admitted he'd fantasized about having sex with him even as he bullied him. Part of him had suspected that might be true, and another part of him thought it was a tired cliché queer men used to console themselves about past abuse.

It didn't exactly warm the heart, but it did melt some assumptions about Naser's history.

And Mason Worther's.

A thing that was not supposed to happen had happened, and now there was no telling what would happen next. And Naser could still taste that thing on his lips and feel the aftereffect of it like a velvet coating on his skin.

And across his chest.

He studied Mason's hand and fought an insane urge to bring the man's fingers to his lips and kiss them and won. When he turned his head, Mason's face was close to his, full and insanely kissable lips puffed against a pillowcase that probably cost more than Naser's car note. His breaths were slow and even.

Naser slid out from under Mason's arm.

In the kitchen, he took the phone off the counter, carried it up to Mason's bedroom, and set it on the nightstand. The man still hadn't moved an inch. This time, Naser backed slowly away from the bed, unable to take his eyes off the fallen giant. But his feet felt heavy. Was he passing up a deliriously hot opportunity? To spend the night snuggled up against Mason Worther's big, hard body? Yes. Because Mason Worther was both wasted and possibly sexually confused. Which meant the morning after would be a nightmare for them both. For Naser, it could be downright dangerous.

Downstairs, he studied the Ferarri's distant shadow and decided that sports car extraction wasn't part of the services he'd offered that evening. When he turned to go, an animalistic growl swept in through the open back door—some ludicrous sports car, he was sure, and it had pulled to a stop outside the garage.

A door popped shut, and footsteps scraped concrete.

"Whose fuckin' Volvo is that?"

He knew that voice. Had heard it croon *"Praaaaaaaaaancer"* more times than he could count.

Chadwick Brody.

A white-hot bolt of terror shot up his spine.

Naser started sweating from places he'd never sweated from before.

A full-body stress reaction of the kind he hadn't experienced since high school.

Memories pelted him. His nostrils flared with the turned-up soil smell that had always blanketed Laguna Mesa's football field. The dirt under the bleachers scraped his knees again as shame clogged his throat. Running into Mason that night had been disturbing. Running into Chadwick Brody was out of the fucking question, a minefield of memories he'd tried to keep buried for years.

Naser panicked. His planned method of escape was about to be Chadwick's entry point.

Heart racing, he hurried for the front door. Heard more voices outside, mostly female, clearly waiting for Chadwick's return. They'd spot him if he left.

As he heard Chadwick's footsteps enter the kitchen, he grabbed for a door handle nearby, ducked inside, and drew the door shut, holding the handle in place even as his palm greased it with sweat. The upper part of the door was slatted, but their angle was so sharp there was no seeing through them. The slats were probably meant for ventilation. Sensing space in the shadows behind him, he figured he'd stepped into the laundry room.

Chadwick's footsteps rattled the stairs to the second floor, accompanied by the high-heel clacks of his date. "Mason, you beautiful blond son of a bitch! Get up! This is Carmen, and she wants to be your first bestest friend. Naked."

So Mason Worther was still close with this bastard? Then Mason Worther was still trash.

He could hear Chadwick's shouts as he tried and failed to rouse Mason, followed by the complaints of Chadwick's female companion that the guy wasn't waking up and they should leave.

"He's breathing though, right?" Chadwick posed the question as if they were checking on a dog. "Yeah, he's still breathing. *Mason,* quit being a fucking pussy and get up!"

A few more attempts, each met with silence. After a complaint from the woman Naser couldn't make out, Chadwick unleashed a stream of profanity. Her abrupt silence suggested he'd directed it at her.

The stairs rattled again. Heart in his throat, he held on to the door handle as if the door would come free of its hinges the second he let go.

He half expected Chadwick to pause in the foyer, scenting Naser like a dog.

But a few seconds later, he and his date were gone.

Then Chadwick's car roared like a dragon and wheeled off into the night, probably awakening everyone on Capo Beach who'd gone to bed early.

As silence fell, Naser started to shake all over, a tremor that emanated from his bones. Chadwick's departure had done little more than release the dam of tension that had held Naser's panic in place, and now it threatened to drown him in a single wave.

He took a deep breath through his nostrils and was about to let it out in a long, comforting exhale when he tried to turn the handle and found it was locked.

The door was locked.

From the other side.

And on this side, the handle held a keyhole.

Cursing under his breath, Naser found a light switch on the wall next to him. He'd been right—this was a laundry room. And on the lower portion of the door, he saw fading scratches that didn't reach any higher than the knob. So that's why the handle was the reverse of what he would have expected. Someone, possibly Mason, had kept a dog in here at some point. A dog that must have excelled at escaping its crate.

He went for his pocket and realized that in his rush to return Mason's phone, he'd left his own in his car.

"*Mason!*" There was so much panic in his voice, he felt instantly ashamed of his cry. He rattled the door loud enough to rival Chadwick Brody's sports car.

Silence greeted him.

He was trapped.

He was being punished by the universe for the dangerous, voyeuristic curiosity that had led him to bring Mason's phone to his house. He could have just called Fareena. Or taken Mason's phone to the lost and found and been done with it. But no, he had to see how the bastard lived.

And the whole scene was dreadfully familiar to the one he'd often used to shield and comfort himself back in high school. As a teenager, when the pain of each day had become too much, Naser would put an extra layer of walls between his mother and the sound of his nocturnal tears by sinking to the floor of his bedroom closet and wrapping his arms around his knees. On a regular basis, he'd gone to sleep there, waking in the morning curled into a ball on the carpeted floor. He sank to the same position now, as if old scars had programmed the habit into his joints.

Would the tears come now?

The reunion with Mason might have been manageable.

The sudden forced proximity to Chadwick Brody had been a nightmare come true.

Mason had been bad back then. Chadwick had been worse. Way worse.

He knew he should get up, search the room. Look for a hidden key.

But the exhaustion that followed the adrenaline dump of panic had seized him. It was paralyzing, but compared to the terror of moments before, it was also a comfort. All he wanted to do was breathe again. Slowly. Carefully. He managed a few good ones before he passed out cold.

# 9

When Mason woke, feeling like a spike had been driven through his temples, he was sprawled atop the covers.

What had happened to his suit and tie? He was in jeans and an old fraternity T-shirt he couldn't remember putting on, surrounded by his familiar pillows and satin bedspread. He rolled onto his back. The sun hit his face like a bucket of cold water. He'd stupidly left the drapes open, the headache-inducing signature of yet another bender. Now his eyes felt like they were about to burst from his sockets.

Muscles got stronger the more you traumatized them at the gym. Shouldn't the same thing be true of hangovers? Shouldn't your body get better at handling them over time?

*No. They're getting worse because I'm getting worse.*

The comforter around him was blanketed in a cologne he didn't recognize, but when he sat up, he saw his bed was sex worker-free.

To keep his head from throbbing, he took the stairs slowly and carefully. It was no use. Halfway down, even the most careful steps proved nauseating, so he gave up and descended the rest of the way full speed, one hand to his forehead, already fantasizing about aspirin and a beer.

At the base of the stairs, the unfamiliar cologne hit him with its strongest wave yet. It was coming from the laundry room. He unlocked it and pulled the handle. For a while, he stood there blinking, trying to convince himself he wasn't hallucinating. Naser Kazemi—an older, brawnier, more bearded version of him—was asleep atop a pile of

Mason's dirty laundry he'd formed into a pallet on the exposed concrete floor.

But even in sleep, with his hands folded delicately against his chest, he looked like he was deep in thought. And wasn't that always the combination that had done things to Mason's insides—Naser's strutting, sassy energy mixed with a seriousness that made him seem wise beyond his years? It's what had inspired the nickname his buddies had said with derision, but which Mason had always used with a fair amount of repressed desire.

*Prancer.*

Naser's eyes fluttered open, and Mason found himself studying dark eyelashes he longed to feel against his cheeks, his chest.

"I brought your phone." Naser rose to his feet, fighting a yawn.

He'd left his phone with Naser. Had he had a conversation with Naser? His palms and neck were suddenly sweat slick, but he did his best to play it cool. "And then you decided to catch some Zs?"

"I took a wrong turn. The door was a surprise. Did you have a dog or something?"

"Yeah, it was more than I could handle."

Naser's brow furrowed. "What did you do with it?"

"I drowned it. What do you think I did? I found another home for it. I'm not a monster."

Naser glared at him as if it were up for debate, and could Mason really blame him?

Their stare-off continued as Mason groped for something to say, something that might capture some essence of the apology he'd planned to make the night before. Had he made one? Had he even tried? But all he could think was, *Don't barf in front of Naser.*

"Mason?"

"Yeah."

"May I leave your laundry room now?"

"There's a key inside the AC vent."

"Okay, well, next time I get trapped in here, I'll be sure to be three feet taller."

Mason stepped aside, and Naser moved past him swiftly, head bowed and avoiding eye contact just like he'd always done in high school.

When they reached the kitchen, Naser made a beeline for the back door. Even though everything about this situation was awkward to the point of being nuts, the thought of Naser leaving quickly and without another word made Mason want to reach out for the guy.

"Naser!"

His guest spun, eyebrows rising. "So you do know how to pronounce my name."

"Um, listen..."

Naser listened. Unfortunately, Mason couldn't manage to say anything.

"What's the last thing you remember about last night?" Naser finally asked.

"The Uber."

"You came home in a cab."

Mason looked to the tile floor. "The Uber on the way there."

"Oh. Wow."

"Look, just don't judge me, all right? I know I need to rein it in a little."

"A little?"

"A lot, maybe."

"Don't judge you. Okay. So don't make a mean nickname for you and hurl it at you every time I see you. Don't shove you and steal things from you and call you slurs. That kind of thing?"

"Part of the reason I was there last night was to apologize to you. Fareena said the name, and I put two and two together and..." Mason made a hand gesture for *etc.* that made him feel like a bobble head. If only he could sit down. But he felt like he should do this standing.

Naser crossed his arms over his chest. "Okay. Well, you didn't. Apologize, I mean."

Mason opened the door to the fridge. "You want something to drink?"

"You clearly do."

"Is that a no?"

"Is this an apology?"

"Well, you don't really seem receptive to one right now, so I figured I wouldn't bother."

"I see. So I'm supposed to make this easier for you."

"I mean it was over a decade ago, right? I don't know. Maybe lighten up a little bit." He could hear squealing brakes in his head. He wasn't sure exactly how one was supposed to do this, but he was pretty sure this wasn't it. The sight of a frosty beer bottle inches from his hand banished all other thoughts. Mason pulled out the Corona and popped the cap off against the edge of the counter with the side of one fist. The first swallow swept through him with comforting strength. Then he saw the stony, startled expression of the man a few feet away. Mason had done this very thing so many times it was routine, but Naser's silent reaction drove home the reality of it. Not out of bed ten minutes and already hitting the sauce.

He had a problem, a serious problem.

Suddenly, the bottle felt scalding to the touch. He set it on the counter.

"Is this how you lighten up?" Naser asked. "Corona in the morning?"

"Isn't everyone kind of a dick in high school?"

"So the apology has become a justification."

"I did try to keep them under control, you know."

Dark eyebrows rose, his upper lip crooked in tandem. He wasn't sneering at him, but he wanted to, that was clear. "How?" Naser finally asked.

"I made a rule. No racist stuff."

Naser's face turned to stone. "Oh, excellent. I'll get you a cookie."

Mason wanted to die. Again. "I guess I shouldn't ask for credit for that."

"You most certainly should not."

"I'm not who I used to be is what I'm saying."

Naser lowered his eyes. "I'm going to go. Enjoy your breakfast. It's better with a lime."

"Nas, please."

Naser spun. "Don't call me that. My family calls me that. My friends call me that."

Mason held up his hands. "I'm trying here."

"If this is the best you can do, maybe take a break." Naser started to leave again.

"You know, you're really being hostile and aggressive, and I'm just trying to—"

Naser spun. "Okay, reality check, Brené Brown. I don't owe you anything. I didn't track you down. I didn't stalk you at your sister's event and then fall in the pool drunk. And I didn't ask for an apology. Even a lousy one. Because I don't want to talk about any of this. Ever."

"You did bring my phone back. I mean, you could have had Fareena do it."

"You'll be lucky if Fareena ever wants to lay eyes on you again."

"Define luck. Have you dated Fareena? I felt like a purse with a penis."

"You don't exactly seem like a great catch right now."

Mason slugged from his beer and toasted Naser with the bottle. "Good thing I'm not trying to get caught."

"Well, there's a lot you're running from, that's for sure."

"You know, Nas—excuse me, *Naser*. I've got an idea. Just say it. Say it all. Say everything you've wanted to say to me for years. Get it out of your system."

"Three years of being bullied and abused because of who you are and what you can't change doesn't leave your system in five minutes because some privileged white boy has decided he wants to offload his guilt to improve his hangover."

If Mason's wits had been more about him, if he hadn't been as hung over as New Orleans the day after Mardi Gras, he might have managed a response to this. But all he could think—all he could *feel*—was that he'd helped build the anger that filled his kitchen now. And the discovery that Naser's wounds were still this raw after ten years drove home the need for an apology while simultaneously making it harder for Mason to articulate one.

"I'm still investing in your sister's line."

Naser threw up his hands. "My sister doesn't need investors. She's backed by a massive home shopping network. Fareena was just busting your balls."

"Still investing."

"You're *stalking*, and I'm not going to make this easier for you."

"I didn't ask you to."

"You were."

"I stopped. I'm stopping. So…let me have it. Say what you've wanted to say since…then."

"Then?"

"High school."

Naser bowed his head and sucked in a deep breath that caused his upper back to rise and fall. He shook his head, which suggested he was dismissing his first words, his first response. *Not a good sign*, Mason thought.

"I'll tell you this. I haven't wanted to say it for ten years, but I've wanted to say it since last night. In your drunken stupor, you told me the reason you used to shove me against all those lockers is because you wanted to fuck me against them. And I think you said it because you think it makes it better. But it doesn't, Mason Worther. It makes it worse. It makes everything you did feel like a betrayal, and it makes you a hypocrite on top of a bully. I'm a numbers guy, not a therapist. But something tells me if you were really different from who you were back then, if you could accept who you really are, you wouldn't be drinking a beer first thing in the morning after a blackout."

Mason felt as if every gasp of oxygen had been pressed from him by a giant hand. How was it possible for someone half his size to have so much power over him? Words, he was reminded, were so much more powerful than brute force when they were aligned with hard truths. First came the initial shame of realizing how much he'd revealed to Naser while drunk, then came the leveling insight of Naser's assessment. He told himself to stay silent, but his defenses had already coiled.

"Guess we're not gonna fuck then."

Naser raised his head and took a step back, and Mason would be lying if he didn't admit he was satisfied by the man's sudden breathlessness. It looked as if Naser had never expected Mason to express a desire for him while sober. "No," Naser finally said. "Because I have something I didn't back in school."

"Herpes?"

Naser rolled his eyes. "Self-esteem."

"Overrated, especially when you find out how good I am in bed."

"The parts you can stay awake for at least."

And with that, Naser was gone.

When he took the beer bottle in his hand again, his hand shook.

When his vision blurred, he told himself it was the hangover making a mess of his emotions.

He knew better.

It was the shame of being seen—for who he was now, for who he'd been then.

He'd always thought there was an overwhelming complexity to his life that justified his drinking. Always figured that someday he might sit down with a therapist to sort through it all, but right now he didn't have the time. He was too busy trying to put a career together, showing up late for work and going on benders with a best friend he couldn't stand to be around when he was sober.

The complexity had been replaced by cold, hard simplicity that had landed like a body blow.

He was a closeted bisexual who drank to douse the pain of his double life, and for most of his high school career, he'd abused the classmate he'd desired more than any other.

Why pay hundreds of dollars an hour to some nodding psychiatrist to learn what he already knew? Especially when Naser Kazemi had delivered up this hard truth with a few well-chosen sentences.

Why cry over it?

But that's what he was doing, and as much as he was trying to will his hand to his mouth, he couldn't bring himself to lift the bottle off the counter. When he looked to the frothy amber liquid, he saw Naser's wide-eyed shock at the sight of him drinking first thing in the morning. And when he tried to look around him for comfort—at the minimalist, gleaming surfaces of this designer-perfect beachfront house that was his and not his—he felt like a man living inside the shell of someone else's life to avoid dealing with his own.

*I can't do this anymore.*

The voice in his head sounded as clear as Naser's had sounded moments before, but with more fatigue than anger.

He heard fluid gurgling down the drain before he realized what he'd done. He'd upended the Corona bottle and was emptying it down the drain, a possibly fruitless gesture given how much liquor was in the house. But it felt like a start.

His six-figure car parked out on the sand in full view of his neighbors, Naser Kazemi storming out of his house on a tide of all-too accurate accusations, the revelation that he'd spilled secrets about himself in a blackout—it was all too much to escape, too much to run from.

What if, this time, he didn't run?

If he showered before what he wanted to do next, he might lose his nerve, so he brushed his teeth, applied some deodorant, and threw on a fresh T-shirt. Then he was passing through his back door and walking across the sand toward his neighbor's house. As was her habit, Shirley Baxter was sitting on her tiny back patio with a cup of coffee and her iPad, shaded from the sun by a giant straw hat and sunglasses so big they could double as roller rinks.

"Morning, neighbor," she said as he approached. "Fun road trip last night? Mexico's that way, you know." She pointed south down the coast.

Then she saw the expression on Mason's face and sat up slowly, as if she were being approached by an unfriendly-looking dog.

When he reached the edge of her patio, his feet froze and his throat closed.

Sensing the tumult of emotions in him, Shirley removed her sunglasses, freckled face a mask of concern.

"You said you could…"

"Mason?"

"You said you could help me," he finally managed.

Understanding dawning in her expression, Shirley stood like a soldier being called to rise by the first bars of the national anthem.

# 10

Sure, Naser had more self-esteem than he'd had back in high school, but that didn't mean turning down a porny hate fuck with his former bully on the man's gleaming kitchen counter hadn't left him embarrassingly hard on the ride home. That his best consolation came from imagining the extent to which Mason's hangover breath would have killed the mood wasn't exactly a sign his aforementioned self-esteem was working at full capacity.

Yet.

He closed his front door behind him and sighed.

The cinnamon potpourri on the console table comforted him. He'd come to associate the pleasant odor with the sweet relief of returning home after a long period of being reluctantly social. He was an introvert by nature, better in small groups. Happiest during little dinner parties with his closest friends. But his greatest pleasure in life was looking up and realizing he'd passed several hours reading a good book alone in his townhouse and he had nowhere else he needed to be. A counselor he'd seen in college had told him it was the result of being from a large family where he'd always felt the need to conform. Butch it up. Play it straight. As if those things had ever been possible.

He was Prancer, after all.

And now he was razor wire tense and beset by dark and twisted fantasies of Mason's body pressing down against his. The guy's dirty laundry hadn't made the most comfortable bed, so maybe a nap—or several—were in order. But first, he had to deal with the jittery half-aroused state he'd been in ever since leaving Mason's house.

He headed upstairs to his bedroom.

A few years back, Naser had decided his penchant for pain in the bedroom might be something worth treating, the warning signs of a tilt toward self-abuse that could turn into a cutting habit if he didn't watch it. Connor had accused him of performing shame-based Internet therapy on himself, so Naser had decided to see a real therapist who wasn't composed of *Wikipedia* entries and alarmist blog posts from dubious sources.

Dr. Kelley, whose crystal and dream catcher-filled office made him feel instantly at home, had been more of a listener than a diagnoser. But at first, he couldn't decide if she was holding her tongue because she had a gentle soul, or if she was waiting for him to hang himself. For weeks, she'd sat attentively as he'd poured out his self-judgments. How he liked it when his partners squeezed him a little too hard, slapped him enough to sting. How he felt a rush of almost euphoric pleasure when a man closed his hands around his throat. And how he feared these kinks had all been installed in him by his former bullies, and that alone was a reason he should be more vanilla in the bedroom.

The whole time, he'd been sure she was gently formulating some terrible diagnosis she planned to hit him with at the right moment. *Masochista pathologis homosexualis* or whatever. Instead, one day she'd simply rested her pen on her notepad and said, "Honey, maybe the only thing wrong with the fact that you like some salt with your sugar is that you think there's something wrong with a little salt."

In other words, if he wanted to bite down on his arm while spearing himself with huge dildos in the shower, what was the harm? So long as he didn't draw blood or get an infection.

But there was no denying that Mason Worther, or some archetypal version of him, played a starring role in the fantasies that swirled through his head during Naser's solo shower sessions. They were a revolving wardrobe of bargain-basement porn scenes: the angry cop who used his cock to let you know how fast you'd been going; the cold, laser-focused doctor who demanded Naser submit to extensive physical examinations for his own good; the demanding daddy of a boss who punished workplace infractions with a swift open hand on Naser's bare ass. But underneath the costume, these remote, hyper-masculine figures of authority and power and privilege, whose desire lashed out at Naser in the form of frenzied assaults that made his balls ache, were all some version of Mason.

Engaging in one of those fantasies now might purge the man from his system.

Or it might make this mind fuck of a twenty-four hours last even longer.

For a while, Naser sat on the edge of his bed, favorite dildo resting on his lap, trying to decide the best course of action.

Then his phone rang.

It was Gloria Alvarez, which couldn't be good, given today was Naser's day off.

"Tell me she didn't burn down the hotel," he said by way of greeting.

"Not yet. But she is smoking on her balcony, and we've had some complaints from other guests."

"I'll call her right now."

"And Nas…"

"Yeah?"

"Jonas said you had to leave the party last night to deal with some guy you knew who got too drunk?"

*That's one way of putting it,* he thought. And note to file—he owed Jonas an apology, both for being short with him about putting Mason in his office and leaving the event without explanation.

"So I thought you should know. During tear-down, your sister was crying. Hard. Jonas said he practically had to carry her up to her room."

"Why?"

"I'm not exactly sure, but before she lost it, she was apparently telling most of her staff goodbye."

Naser shot up from the bed, the dildo dropping to the carpet and rolling. *"Goodbye? What?"*

Even as he voiced the question, a dark suspicion started to form in his mind. The signs had been staring him in the face, but he'd been too distracted by his fear that his sister would make trouble for him in his workplace, and then Mason's explosive arrival.

The absence of the Bliss Network's logo at the event.

The need for discounts from Connor.

The frostiness in Fareena's eyes when she talked about possible investors.

The fact that she'd brought a potential investor to begin with.

"I'm on my way."

"Sounds wise," Gloria answered softly.

# 11

Mason had braced himself for a rapid-fire interrogation as soon as he'd asked for his neighbor's help. The kind you'd see on a reality show about addiction, or a sad movie about his life. What was his plan? Did he have a therapist? Was he going to rehab? He didn't have any of those answers, and he hadn't been asked to provide them, because as soon as he'd asked for help, Shirley had headed across the sand toward his house, looking back once to make sure he was following.

Then they were standing inside Mason's kitchen as she helped herself to his coffee maker and began brewing a pot without asking him if he wanted any. She wanted some, apparently, and that was a sign she didn't plan to leave anytime soon.

While they waited for the coffee to percolate, she turned to his fridge and began removing the bottles of beer, followed by the bottles of white wine. Then she opened the freezer and removed three bottles of vodka. She didn't blink at the amount.

"So we can either throw this all out or give it away to the neighbors," she said brightly, hands on her hips. "Do you know Susan and Phil a few doors down? They're having a party next weekend. They might take it."

"I guess you don't have a use for it."

"I do not." Shirley smiled. "I haven't had a drink in forty years."

"Impressive."

"Is this all the liquor in the house?"

"Yes." Mason felt a butterfly's flutter inside his chest.

"Are you lying to me?"

The butterfly turned into a wasp that stung his heart. "Yes."

He expected Shirley to yell at him. Instead, she smiled bigger and said, "Good. Let's get to work. Show me all your hiding places."

"Do you do this professionally?"

"I don't make money off this, no. Should we start in the bedroom or the garage?"

"What about the coffee?"

Shirley smiled again. "I set it to keep warm."

Feeling as if his bones had turned molten, Mason said, "The wet bar's right here."

He popped open the glass doors and began setting the mostly empty bottles onto the counter. She searched under the kitchen sink, found a stack of flattened brown paper grocery delivery bags he'd been meaning to recycle, and began unfolding them one at a time. Then she started filling them with bottles.

For a while, the two of them worked in silence, neither one acknowledging the oddness and abruptness of what they were doing. It didn't take long. Soon the bags were so full the bottoms would tear if they lifted them off the counter.

Then he took her to the bedroom. From the top shelf of his closet, he removed three full bottles of Absolut, and from the nightstand, a silver-plated flask full of the same, which he emptied into the bathroom sink while she watched. They carried them to the kitchen, and he fell silent. She gave him a look that was calm, knowing, unimpressed, a look that said, *I know we're not done.* So he took her to the garage. There, tucked into a niche behind the water heater and wrapped in a packing blanket, he extracted six more bottles of Absolut and three six-packs of Corona, like an earthquake emergency kit for a booze hound. Shirley seemed unfazed. She collected the bottles dutifully and without comment.

They returned to the kitchen. The insane amount of liquor spread out on Mason's bar counter was testament enough to the problem that had defined his life for years now. But this time when he felt shame, he also felt a tug of release at the end. A sense of hope. He was quitting, after all. He'd said it out loud.

Made a promise not just to himself, but to his nosy next-door neighbor.

But wow. It was going to be a lot to quit.

And still Shirley was looking at him. No judgment. Just persistence.

"Should we visit your medicine cabinet?" she asked.

*Jesus, she was good.*

"I'm antidepressant free at the current time."

"Cute, sweetie, but I'm not talking about daily medications prescribed by medical professionals. I'm talking about the other stuff."

"Other stuff?" Mason asked.

"You know, stuff you talked your way into but didn't really need. Old pain meds you've been hoarding since some procedure a year ago. Other people's prescriptions they gave you because you gave them that charming smile of yours."

Shirley Baxter, it seemed, had done this before.

Mason grinned. "You think I'm charming?"

"A smile and a man are two different things. Let's have a look."

She patted him on the shoulder and headed past him for the stairs. And just like that, they were standing in his bathroom as Shirley opened the medicine cabinet. A day before, this would have seemed like an outrageous violation. Now it felt essential for his survival. She found the Xanax immediately, read the label, and held it out for him to see. "Have you been diagnosed with anxiety disorder?"

He shook his head.

She read the bottle's label again. "Is this Dr. Brody a psychiatrist?"

He shook his head again.

"What kind of doctor are they?"

"He's a dermatologist."

One eyebrow went up, and she nodded. "So a skin doctor prescribed you a powerful, take-as-needed antianxiety medication. You've got pretty great skin. Why so nervous about it?"

A day before, he would have kept his mouth shut or found a redirect, but it felt like telling the truth, or just a little bit more of the truth than he usually did in a moment like this, might save him from another miserable and hungover morning, another long march of shame back to a temporary sobriety he'd soon obliterate. He wanted something different, and so it seemed like his only choice in this moment was to do something different.

"It's Chadwick."

Shirley nodded. "Your friend with the Maserati and the yelling?"

Mason nodded.

"Do you take it every day?" she asked.

He shook his head. "Just when…"

"When what?"

"When I'm trying not to drink too much."

"So you use these as a replacement for alcohol?"

The lie he wanted to tell rose inside of him like a column of magma. But something about the patient gaze of the woman in front of him plugged the volcano. "Sometimes *with* alcohol."

"Which could be fatal." Shirley opened the bottle, turned, and upended it into the toilet. Then she hit flush. The sky-blue pills spun before they vanished. In his mind, he heard them singing *Bye, Bye, Bye* by NSYNC. Was it his mental illness or his sanity swirling down the drain? Only time would tell. And if he'd lost his mind, she'd have to deal with the consequences. She lived right next door. He followed her downstairs.

She gestured to the bottle-filled bags on the counter. "Obviously this is going to take me several trips."

She started transferring the grocery bags into the cardboard box they'd found in the garage. Throughout this entire ritual, it had seemed as if nothing he had done had offended her or surprised her. Like she had seen it all before. Was she a plant? Had his dad moved her in next door so she could spring on him in a moment like this? That couldn't be true. His dad didn't care about him that much.

"You're coming to lunch with me and some friends today."

"Today? Really? I mean, I'm not exactly at my best."

"Two hours to clean up. How's that sound?"

"Wow. Okay. Um... Shirley, seriously. I'm a mess. Why would you want to introduce me to your friends *today*?"

She looked him dead in the eye. "Because they're the kind of friends you need, Mason."

To his surprise, she managed to hoist the entire box off the counter with both hands and hardly a wince.

Boy, she was strong for her age. "Get the back door for me."

He complied, and she stepped out into blazing morning sunlight that drove knives through his eye sockets. Halfway across his patio, she turned and winked. "Oh, and Mason, you might want to go take care of your car."

She headed off in the direction of her house, leaving Mason to wonder what in God's name he'd just done.

# 12

"Not today, tiny demon."

It had taken seven knocks to get Pari to come to the door and even then, she'd done so right as Naser had been preparing to open it with his universal key. Hair in a wrap, generous curves hugged by a sarong of her own design, eyes hidden behind sunglasses, everything about Pari looked beachy and casual save for her perfect coating of dark fuchsia lipstick.

"I'm here about the smoking," Naser lied.

He was there because he feared his sister's business was in trouble, but with someone of Pari's ego, he knew he'd have to sneak up on the topic gently.

She sighed, turned from the door, and granted him entrance with a weak hand wave. Every room at Sapphire Cove had an ocean view, but Connor had given her one of the best, a fourth-floor deluxe king with a sitting area, spacious balcony, and a view south down the coast.

"Whatever. I put it out hours ago. Some guy yelled at me from another balcony. He was all like, 'What do you think this is, 1986?' And I was like, 'Would you prefer it was weed, 'cause that's what the rest of California smells like now.'"

He followed her through the open sliding glass door. She settled into the lounger next to a half-empty mimosa in a champagne flute. "I know this is about the party. Can you yell at me tomorrow? I'm tired."

Naser leaned against the balcony's concrete wall. "That makes two of us."

"Yes, I know. I'm so exhausting."

"It's not you, Pari. It's not always about you."

Instead of anger, he saw puzzlement on his sister's face. "What happened?"

"I ran into someone from my past."

"What past, Naser? You barely leave the house."

He sank into the empty chair next to the lounger. "I know you think my life is boring because I'm not driving up to some Hollywood premiere every week, but I actually do go places and do things."

"No. I just think you want *my* life to be boring."

"I want your life to have a budget. There's a difference."

Pari took a hard slug of mimosa. "You're mad about the fortune-tellers."

"And you never care if I'm mad, so what does it matter?"

She nodded as if she was considering this, then an uncomfortable silence fell. Uncomfortable, Naser realized, because his sister seemed on the verge of making a candid admission. Possibly a vulnerable one. And that's not how they worked with each other. For most of their lives, they'd addressed each other in boastful declarations and outright threats. He had as much of a part in that dynamic as she did, but the older he got, the more he wanted it to change. "Connor gave me a million discounts, and I still came up short. So when it came to the wine, I had to get creative."

"That's all?"

Pari sighed and slouched. "Maman didn't come."

"Is that what the Googoosh thing was about, trying to get her to come?" He figured it was probably about trying to draw all the potential wealthy Persian investors in Orange County, but he kept this to himself.

She shrugged. "It wasn't the only thing. I thought Sapphire Cove would help. And you, Naser-*joon*. Why do you think I practically bankrupted myself to have the party here? She adores you, and now that you work here, this place is all about you in her mind."

"Well, sorry I wasn't enough of a draw."

"Oh, that's not it, and you know it. She and Baba both. You were always their perfect child. Persepolis. The model you made. For school. Remember it?"

Naser's skin crawled. "Junior year. Yeah, it's coming up a lot lately."

"She knew you were being bullied. She called me five times that morning. She thought the other kids at school would break it. I had to stop her from following you to class that day."

He was stunned. He'd spent that morning assuming his mother had wanted to horn in on his presentation when the truth was she'd been as afraid of his walk to class as he'd been. Even today, he'd never told her about the bullying. After his father had died, he'd been determined to be strong for his family in the only way he knew how. Crunching numbers, planning, advising, warning.

Or, as his sister put it, nagging.

If he couldn't be the best little boy in the hallways and on the playing fields of Laguna Mesa High, he'd have to score his touchdowns with Quicken. He'd put a foundation under his grief-stricken family the only way he knew how.

To hide how stunned he was by this revelation, he said, "Persepolis turned out fine."

"Of course, it did." She smiled bitterly. "You have always been absolutely and terribly perfect."

"Oh, yeah. That's why the kids at school called me Prancer. Because they thought I was perfect. Come on."

"Fuck those kids. I'm talking about your family, the people that matter."

"So am I. It took all the strength I had in the world to come out to her, and she just stopped trying to marry me off to a woman last year."

Pari shrugged. "Bah. Consider yourself lucky you're not constantly being suffocated by the marriage traditions of our Persian mother."

"I don't." His abrupt tone clearly startled her. She studied him as if waiting for another little eruption. "I don't feel lucky that my mother has never once asked me if I'm even dating anyone."

"But that's just it, Naser. You don't tell her when you are. Because you're afraid if you do, you'll stop being the favorite. With her, you being gay, it's all abstract. Something she knows but never sees. Because you never show her what it looks like. So you keep your head down, and the two of you go after me because I'm the perfect target. Big, loud Pari with her big dreams and her messy, complicated business. I bring you closer together. Just admit it already."

"What happened with the Bliss Network? Where was their logo last night?"

Pari shrugged and looked away before he could see the flash of pain in her eyes. "Same story. I was too bold. Too Persian. Too me."

Naser reached into his pocket for his sunglasses and slid them on. He tried to be casual about it, but he was in a rush to hide whatever emotion his eyes might betray. His sister had lost her only distributor, her only marketing platform outside her own social media channels, and that very morning he'd callously blown off a potential investment offer from a guy who lived in a multimillion-dollar beach house and felt Catholic-level guilt whenever he heard the last name Kazemi.

What had he done?

Was it her fault for not telling him or his fault for not seeing it earlier?

Maybe a little of both.

Pari finally broke the tense silence. "I'm tired, Naser."

"Of what?" He hoped she didn't mean him.

"Of this business. I'm tired of fighting day in and day out for an inch of ground only to lose five the next day. I'm tired of scrolling through Instagram and seeing famous designers post inspirational memes about staying true to yourself and your vision, only to be slapped back as soon as I'm true to mine. I'm tired of the pats on the heads from Beverly Hills Persians who thank me for trying to preserve our culture but won't pony up a dime to help me actually do it.

"Ever since Bliss dropped me, I've been thinking of what it would be like to have a normal life. Maybe a pension. A union. Some HR person I can go to when a man puts his hands on me after an investor dinner. Maybe move back here to the OC. Marry a nice Persian doctor. Be like you and Mom. Then I remember the contempt you both have for me, and it feels like I have no options at all."

Naser rolled his eyes.

"Don't you roll your eyes at me!" she barked.

"You do the negative self-talk, Pari. I'll handle my eyes, okay?"

"See? Contempt!"

"Disagreement is not contempt, and concern is not a *lack* of love. It's the opposite. And if you think anything other than Maman and I love you, it's the mimosa talking."

Pari drank more of it as if she needed to be sure.

Naser forced himself to say it before he could think it twice. "No promises, but I might be able to put something together for you."

Pari shook her head. "Uh uh. No way. I'm not taking your money, Naser. There're too many things you don't understand about my business."

"It won't be my money."

"Don't even think about asking Maman. She's already said she'll never invest."

"Not her, either."

"Then who?"

"Like I said, no promises. What kind of timeframe are you looking at before…" He couldn't finish this sentence with the words *you go broke.*

Pari took a long inhale that raised her bare shoulders, then looked out to sea. "I'll have to close down my workshop in LA next month because I won't be able to make rent. Callie says she'll stay on as long as she can without pay, but she's got a baby on the way. Everyone else, I…"

Pari's jaw quivered, and the next thing Naser knew, his sister's words had been lost to her tears. She bowed her head as she cried into one fist.

They rarely hugged, so Naser pulled his chair close to her lounger and reached out for the hand she wasn't holding to her mouth. To his surprise, she let him take it and didn't resist when he gripped it firmly. "I talk a lot of shit, but I'm not ready to quit," she finally croaked. "Still, last night, I threw it like it was my goodbye party just in case. That's why I wanted Maman there."

"It's not goodbye. Not yet."

Pari lifted her head and removed her sunglasses, letting him see her tears—her vulnerability—for the first time in he couldn't remember how long.

"Okay, well you're not alone. I made some connections last night. But Fareena's big investor didn't show, apparently."

Naser's stomach roiled. "I'll see what I can do."

"Thank you, Naser-*joon*," she whispered.

Then he went inside to call down and order his sister another mimosa.

# 13

The Ferrari was in better shape than he'd feared, but backing it out of the sand took several minutes and didn't do much for his pounding headache.

In the shower, the throbbing in his temples lessened, but it didn't abate. Cranking the water to near scalding helped. He managed not to throw up as he got dressed, which seemed like a victory, but every few minutes, he had to sit and breathe for a while, and all told, it took him about an hour to put on blue jeans and a polo shirt.

Once he was dressed, he returned to the kitchen. The coffee mug Shirley had poured for him was still sitting on the glass table. It was cold now, so he popped it in the microwave, set the timer for thirty seconds, and lost himself in thought as he watched it spin. No matter what happened, coffee would always have a different association for him now. It would remind him of Shirley Baxter's unexpected kindness and maternal patience.

Maybe that's why, when it was done heating up, he actually drank most of it.

At two hours on the dot, he heard three short beeps of a car horn outside. He screwed on an Anaheim Ducks baseball cap he'd never worn anywhere but the gym and popped on a pair of sunglasses, hoping both would work together to hide his hungover state. Then he went outside to find Shirley Baxter smiling and waving at him behind the wheel of her white Tesla Model S. She'd blown out her hair, put on a full face of makeup, and changed into a white silk blouse that matched her car.

She drove considerably, given his condition, but his head still spun whenever she took a corner. "Where we eating?" he finally asked, even though the thought of food made his stomach lurch.

"We're stopping off somewhere else first."

He knew better than to ask where. He had the sense that if you gave yourself over to the care of a woman like Shirley, there was no doing it halfway.

When she turned into the crowded parking lot of a cliffside park in Laguna Beach, he was struck by a terrifying three-word thought—children's birthday party. He braced himself for screaming eight-year-olds, figuring it was a fitting punishment for all the loud parties to which he'd subjected the woman next to him.

Then he saw the knot of smokers standing outside the little sloped-roof public building he and Shirley were headed toward and realized this would be a grown-up affair. Possibly a rough one given the tattoo sleeves on some of the smokers. Then they were inside the building, a drab community room with stunning views of the sparkling, blue ocean through its floor-to-ceiling windows and a coffee smell so strong it might have knocked him on his ass even if he wasn't hung over.

And that's when he knew.

Knew even before he saw the scroll hanging from one wall that had the twelve steps written on it. Knew good and well what she'd rooked him into, and his first thought was, *Aw, Jesus H. Christ, lady.*

But a kind of shock set in, super powered by exhaustion, and suddenly Shirley was introducing him to people and they were all pumping his hand with enough energy to send him a little off-balance. And even though this was an honest-to-God AA meeting, they all seemed happier than he'd been in years. And they all knew Shirley well. Because this was her thing, apparently. This was why she knew how to clean out the secret stashes and medicine cabinets of guys on the verge of an overdose or a fatal car crash.

Suddenly they were all settling into a large circle of chairs. Someone placed a paper plate on his lap that had three big sugary doughnuts on it. "Sugar's gonna be your friend for a while," they said. But by the time Mason could thank them or see them, the person was gone, Shirley was sitting next to him, and he was scarfing down a doughnut as everyone got quiet.

Someone read something, then someone else read something else. It felt and sounded vaguely churchy. There were a few mentions of God that made him flinch. But he also heard phrases like *the only requirement for membership is a desire to stop drinking* and *we have no dues or membership fees*, both of which threw a wrench in his suspicions that someone was going to hit him up for a donation. But if it was expensive to hang out here, most of the crowd didn't look like they could afford it. Diverse barely came close to describing the group. The outfits suggested a variety of economic backgrounds. Some folks looked fresh from prison. Others looked like they'd just rolled in from the yacht club. And they were all doing something in turn, Mason realized with a jolt. Each one of them was saying their name, and something else right after.

A label.

A brand.

A diagnosis of sorts.

An admission.

Then the whole group said their name right back.

To his terror, Mason realized it would soon be his turn.

By the time his abductor spoke up, Mason's heart wasn't just racing—it was thundering in his chest like it might explode. The rush of adrenaline sweeping him was so powerful it made his hangover seem like a distant memory.

"I'm Shirley and I'm an alcoholic."

"*Hi, Shirley!*" the group roared with deafening good cheer.

And then all eyes were on Mason.

His throat closed up.

He stared back at the faces staring at him. Looked for judgment or disapproval. A reason to leave, an excuse to run.

Instead he saw a gallery of sympathy and understanding, some fear that matched his own, probably from other newbies like himself. And when his vision of them misted, a few of them nodded encouragingly.

"I'm Mason and I'm..." His throat closed up again the way it had when he'd first asked Shirley for help that morning.

When he tried to suck a breath in through his nose, tears spilled down his face, and he felt himself gnawing angrily on his lower lip. "I'm Mason and I'm..."

Shirley's hand came to rest gently on his back and rubbed.

"I'm Mason and I'm a..."

When the word *alcoholic* finally came from him, it was so wrenched by the sob that accompanied it, he was sure they couldn't understand him. He buried his face in his hands as he shuddered. It felt like the first good cry he'd had since he was a little boy. He was sure they'd ask him to leave.

Just step outside to get a hold of himself.

Instead, they said, "Hi, Mason," in a confident chorus, then they applauded his courage.

By the following evening, Shirley had taken him to six different meetings, all with different crowds and different flavors.

This wasn't the AA he'd seen in movies, with its grim basements, lazily spinning fans, and broken ex-cons. These were people living at full tilt, without the obstructions of hangovers and missing time and paralyzing shame. They were bright-eyed and social and full of energy. And they ate sweets almost constantly. The names and phone numbers came fast and furious and from too many different types of people for him to dismiss them as come-ons. A few pelted him with questions he didn't know how to answer. Did he have a sponsor? A home group? How much time did he have? That's when Shirley would politely butt in and tell everyone he was a newcomer.

At one of the meetings, the lead speaker talked about something they called the eighth and ninth steps. Each time he'd mentioned them, Mason had looked to where they were written on a scroll hanging from the wall behind the speaker's chair.

**8. Made a list of all persons we had harmed, and became willing to make amends to them all.**

**9. Made direct amends to such people wherever possible, except when to do so would injure them or others.**

*Direct amends.*

It sounded intense, and the speaker's story had confirmed it.

The man had abandoned his kids when they were five and six. When he cleaned up his act and tried to make contact, his ex-wife had forgiven him without letting him back in, and that was her right and always would be, he'd said. Getting better meant being better, he'd assured them. Doing better. Day by day, minute by minute.

And he was trying to be a better parent to his adult children. First, he'd made them aware that he was alive and sober and ready for whatever relationship they wanted. Then, little by little, they'd opened up to him again. Tested him, given him chances to fail. To bail. Instead, he showed up early and stayed late and called first to see what he could bring.

In short, the guy had done the exact opposite of the fumbling, half-assed apology Mason had tried to give Naser Kazemi on Saturday morning.

Now, hangover-free, he and Shirley made their way down a trail on the San Onofre bluffs through the deep orange light of dusk, the rugged mountains of Camp Pendleton rising to their right just beyond Interstate 5 and the glittering surf roaring toward the base of the bluffs off to their left. It had been over twenty-four hours since he'd crossed the sand between his house and Shirley's, twenty-four hours since he'd purged his home of every drop of liquor. But it felt like it had been a week, at least.

This rugged stretch of coast just over the San Diego county line was one of his favorite places to walk and think, but up until now, hardly anybody in his life had known this. It was too isolated for dates, and after a few visits Chadwick had dismissed it as being too devoid of women in bikinis. Bringing Shirley here felt like sharing a secret.

The night before she'd invited some sober folks over to their house for a late-night card game where Mason was clearly the guest of honor. When the clock passed two a.m. and nobody had made a move to leave, he realized what they'd done. They'd kept him occupied until the bars and liquor stores closed.

"You gonna stand watch over me again tonight?" he asked.

"Yeah, I think it's time for you to handle last call on your own. But I am right next door and just a phone call away."

"Seriously? You'd be cool with me waking you up in the middle of the night just because I was having a freak-out."

"Mason Worther, you're either the luckiest son of a bitch or the unluckiest. You have a retired sober woman living next door to you during your moment of clarity. You will not be able to escape recovery no matter how hard you try."

"Seriously, though? The middle of the night."

Shirley shrugged and studied the sunset. It bathed her freckled face in dark pink light that made her squint and smile at the same time.

"Oh, I get it." Mason nodded and followed her gaze.

"What?"

"You *have* to do this. It's like a requirement for membership type thing."

"Haven't you heard? The only requirement for membership is a—"

"Desire to stop drinking. Yeah, I got that part. But the service thing sounds pretty important too."

"I give what I was given when I came in. That's how it works. And no offense, but it's a reminder."

"Of what?"

Shirley looked him dead in the eye. "What you're going through right now, yesterday morning, I don't want to have to go through that again myself. Ever again. I didn't quit drinking to become a saint, Mason. I quit because I was miserable. If it didn't look like you were in the same boat, I'm not sure I would have gone to all this trouble."

He appreciated the honesty, even if it did sting a little bit. And he had her to thank for the fact that he didn't feel as miserable as he'd felt the day before. Instead, he felt a strange kind of elation. He'd heard another word bantered around at the meetings, but with a positive tilt he'd never given to it before—surrender. He'd stopped fighting the idea that he could someday drink like a normal person, and the result was a combination of relief and hope. All those hours spent on hangovers and cover stories and getting wasted could be spent on something else.

"Thank you," he said, "for the trouble."

"It wasn't trouble. Not really."

They fell silent, studying the sea for a while. "We really do live in paradise, don't we?"

"When it's not on fire, yeah." He grinned.

She laughed, and they fell silent again.

Before he could think twice about what he wanted to say next, he gave voice to it. For the past day and a half, thinking aloud had proven essential to his newfound health. "I want to become a better man. I mean, that's what it's about, isn't it? You stay sober by being a better man."

"Or person."

"Person, right. Sorry."

"In some sense. But don't try for sainthood on your second day. Take things one day at a time. Do the things that will make you feel better about who you are. Be the person you want to have dinner with. Stand in line with. Work with. Visualize that person, and then do your best to be that person, bit by bit."

"Sounds simple."

"It isn't. It's gradual, though. One day at a time. Bite-sized pieces."

"Bite-sized pieces," he said, but in his head, he was already thinking about which piece he planned to bite off first.

# 14

Forty-eight hours without a drink or a pill had left Mason Worther flushed with the kind of energy he usually felt after a long run. But that was only one reason why he was straightening up the break room at the office Monday morning.

"You doing speed now, son?"

He turned from the counter where he'd been sorting the different sweeteners into several ceramic bowls he'd brought from home. His dad blocked the doorway behind him, wearing pressed Ralph Lauren and a suspicious scowl.

Shirley had told him to look for opportunities throughout his day to be of service. To shift his focus outward through a series of small and helpful acts and away from the potential anxieties of withdrawal. *Contributions to the stream of life,* she'd called them. She'd also told him not to shout his AA membership to the rafters until he got his footing and put a few weeks of sobriety together. And even then, he should only confide in the folks who absolutely needed to know and the people he might someday try to help the way Shirley was helping him.

"Just trying to contribute."

Despite the man's icy expression, with Pete Worther, an absence of profanity felt like a win, so Mason smiled before he could stop himself.

"Some little Middle Eastern dude's in your office. I don't recognize him. What's he doing here?"

A cocktail of excitement, arousal, and terror caused his heart to thunder. "I'll handle him."

"So you know him?"

He pushed past his father through the doorway. "I've got it, Dad."

"Guess this isn't work related."

"I'll handle him and get back to work. Promise."

He could feel his dad's eyes on his back as he hurried off, hoping the man was struck by the energetic sheen of his new sobriety and not the fear quickening his steps.

In Mason's office, Naser stood ramrod straight in front of the desk, holding a few stapled-together papers with a grip more tense than they required. Freshly showered and redolent of the cologne that had blanketed Mason's sheets Saturday morning, he'd styled his ink black hair to the same matinee idol perfection he'd sported throughout his high school years, the hairstyle that always made him look like someone dropped out of another time into their world of fades and buzz cuts—someone rare and special, classically beautiful. And then there were his tailored slacks that turned his ass into something Mason wanted to squeeze in both hands until Naser went swaybacked against him and moaned.

When Mason locked the door behind him, Naser smirked and nodded at the floor.

"What?"

"I'm not here to out you, Mason." He'd whispered the words for added effect.

"That's not... I'm just trying to give us a little privacy, okay? My dad's a difficult character."

"I know."

Mason sat down behind his desk. "How do you know my dad? He was just telling me he didn't recognize you."

Naser shook his head, looked to the floor. "It's uh, I..."

"His reputation precedes him, I guess. Please. Have a seat. I'm glad you came."

"I won't be here long. I've got to get to work." Naser set the papers in front of Mason and gestured for him to read. Mason skimmed, recognizing the bare bones of an investment agreement. Some of the language seemed boilerplate, and some of it seemed pure Naser. Once he had the gist of it, Mason set the contract down. "I thought your sister didn't need investors."

Naser smiled. "Far be it from me to deny a man a chance at redemption."

"As far as we are from Saturday morning, apparently. No offense, but this is one of the worst investment agreements I've ever seen, Naser. The rate of return is basically zero. And the dollar amounts and schedule are both blank."

Naser smiled and sank into the chair he'd declined a moment before. "The investor in question knows nothing about the fashion industry and has not expressed a desire to learn. In light of that, giving the investor any sort of creative control over the business in question would be a grievous mistake for all involved. Further, the investor's motives for investing lie far outside any concerns that could be considered...businesslike."

"The investor is sitting right here, and he doesn't remember making any of these statements. Also, I think it's cute that you start sentences with *further* out loud and not just in emails."

Naser raised one eyebrow. "The investor is known to have a spotty memory. And there are suggestions he has issues with reliability and consistency as well, so any proposed payment schedule should be...dramatically shortened."

"The investor has questions," Mason said.

Naser spread his hands in a welcoming gesture.

"Did you reconsider my offer because you got more info about the state of your sister's business after you left my house?"

"Are you bisexual?"

Mason flinched. Naser's stony expression said that had been his intention—and that his sister most certainly did need new investors. "How are those two questions related?"

"We're only sitting here because for three years you and your buddies subjected me to a form of sexual harassment that's still considered semi-acceptable in most secondary school settings."

Mason took a deep breath. The door was still closed. And locked.

"Yes. I'm bisexual."

Naser seemed startled by the direct answer. He nodded slowly, his tongue making a lump under his upper lip. As if this whole thing would have been easier for him if Mason had deflected or lied, and now he was having to reassess.

"So Fareena wasn't just busting my balls. Your sister really needs money, doesn't she?"

Naser smoothed invisible lint off the thighs of his slacks. "I knew you were bisexual," he muttered.

"Then why did you ask?"

"I don't know, maybe you were gay and closeted. But Fareena's Fareena. She's not going to waste time on a guy that doesn't have a genuine attraction to her."

"So I repeat, why did you—"

"Do your buddies know?" Naser was staring at him, eyes blazing with anger.

The question knocked Mason back in his chair an inch. "Tim's been dead five years."

Naser looked to the carpet. "I'm sorry."

"You don't need to be. He was terrible to you. The Coach Harris email was all his idea."

Naser drew a deep breath. "Thanks for letting me off the hook, I guess. How did he pass away?"

"Pills. He always said they were for a sports injury from USC, but he warmed the bench the whole time, so that story never made sense. I think he really liked pills. We're not sure if it was deliberate or if he overshot the mark. There wasn't a note, but his life wasn't in a great place."

Remembering those last few visits with Tim now that he was trying to get sober was more painful than he'd anticipated. Back then, Mason had thought he'd had his shit together, and by comparison to his old friend, who'd dropped out of college and was working odd handyman jobs for his uncle's contracting company, it had certainly seemed that way. He and Chadwick had even talked about hauling Tim into a rehab—over beers.

Naser nodded, and a silence fell. A silence that, like everything else between them, seemed to bend the laws of time.

"And Chadwick Brody?" Naser's voice was drawstring tight, but his gaze was steady and penetrating, full of the unspoken recognition that Chadwick had always been the worst out of the three.

"He's still around."

Naser was staring at him, waiting for him to say something further. Sensing, it seemed, that Mason's answer hadn't been complete or entirely truthful. But maybe expressing hesitation or shame around the topic of Chadwick was what Naser needed to see.

"And no, he doesn't know that I'm bi. And yes, if you were to walk out of here right now and share this information with the world, you could really screw up my already screwed-up life. Especially with the man down the hall."

"I'd never do that."

"I wouldn't blame you if you did."

For a second, Mason thought the guy might soften toward him.

"I know what it feels like to be outed before you're ready," Naser said. "I'd never inflict that on someone else."

"We didn't *out* you. Everything we did was wrong, but it wasn't like we knew for sure that you were gay."

"Yes, you did. You knew every time I looked at you. That's why you did it."

Was Naser admitting to having been as hot for Mason as Mason had been for him?

Maybe so, because Naser looked away before Mason did.

Mason picked up the contract. He did some quick math in his head, quick enough that he couldn't think too long and hard about the consequences of what he was about to do. He wrote down a figure, followed by a schedule, then he flipped to the signature page and signed his name. Pari Kazemi, he saw, had yet to add her own.

When he handed the contract back to Naser, the guy read Mason's additions and went stone still.

"A lump sum payment of one hundred grand on signing?" Naser sounded winded. Mason nodded. "You don't have to buy my silence, Mason."

"I'm not trying to buy anything. I'm trying to make this right."

Naser swallowed and looked to the paper again as if he thought his eyes were deceiving him. "Okay, well, obviously nothing's final until my sister countersigns."

"I'll be here if anyone has questions."

"Proof of funds would be nice."

"You saw the house."

Naser stood. "It's not your house. I did a title check."

Mason laughed breathily. "Well, you're good at your job. I can have proof of funds to you by the end of the week."

"Good. I'm not saying a word to her until after then. I don't want to get her hopes up."

Naser turned and headed for the door. Mason figured his speed was an effort to conceal any evidence of his gratitude.

"Naser."

He stopped, fingers resting on the knob. They both seemed frozen by knowledge that if Naser opened the door even a crack before they were done talking, he might let some of Mason's secrets spill out into the world.

"What was the worst thing we did?" Mason asked as gently as he could.

Mason prepared himself for another verbal strike. But when Naser turned to him, head slightly bowed, he saw the man was struggling to swim through a sea of painful memories, struggling to get his arms around one without drowning, and the twist in Mason's gut felt almost as bad as a hangover.

"Honestly, a few years ago I would have said the worst thing was that letter to Coach Harris. But in the end, it kind of worked out. Harris got a slap on the wrist for how he handled it, and a year later he was busted for dealing steroids to students and went to jail. But the thing you guys did to my PE locker that time, when you banged the lock to shit while I was in the shower so that I couldn't even get it to open, that was probably the worst.

"I was so afraid to walk across campus with no clothes on I missed a test. And I failed it. Because I wouldn't tell the teacher the truth. That I'd been so freaked out I hid in the locker room for three whole class periods until a janitor showed up. If I had to do it over again, I would have put on a stiff upper lip and—I don't know—held paper towels over myself or something. But I was fifteen, and I was ashamed of my body because I was afraid of what my body wanted. It's why I used to always shower after the other boys. And you guys knew all that, and that's why you did it."

"Three hours," Mason said suddenly.

"That's what I said."

"No. For three hours, the time you spent trapped in that locker room, I will do whatever you want, however you want, wherever you want."

Naser glanced at the door behind him. "I have to go to work."

"Not right now. We'll set a time. This weekend, maybe. How's Saturday?" Mason reached into his desk drawer and pulled out one of his business cards. "My cell's on there. Text me and I'll be there, and I'll do whatever you want for three hours."

Naser took the card as if he thought it might be hot to the touch. "Within reason, I take it."

"Your words, not mine." Mason's voice had gone husky before he could control it.

Naser shook his head. His mouth opened. He stared at the business card as if it were an invitation to scandal and ruin.

"One p.m.," Naser finally said. "I'll pick you up."

"One p.m.," Mason said.

Then Naser was gone, and Mason was smiling like an idiot at his desk.

# 15

"This is a most intriguing and complex situation, and all possibilities must be weighed."

Brow furrowed, lips pursed, Jonas Jacobs stirred his iced ginger tea. It was Sapphire Cove's signature drink, served in a tall, slender glass frosted with the hotel's logo. Typically, Naser and Jonas enjoyed a pitcher around lunchtime in their offices, not out on the pool deck. Senior staff were only permitted to take their meals in the hotel's public spaces when entertaining outside vendors and contractors. But Naser had obtained special permission from Gloria so he could treat Jonas to a nice meal—a make-good for being difficult around Pari's event and then abandoning him in the middle of it. They'd originally planned a Tuesday breakfast, but when Naser's car dealership called and asked him to move up his maintenance visit by one day, the change had allowed them to schedule a proper lunch on Wednesday.

Today was one of those rare instances when the morning marine layer had failed to burn off as the day wore on, obscuring the tops of the nearby hills and turning the usually blue ocean slate gray, allowing them to remove their sunglasses halfway through their chicken salads.

"Jonas, do you watch anything on television besides PBS?"

"BBC Select. So this drunken Scandinavian character has placed no parameters on the request whatsoever?"

"I said, 'Within reason, right?' and he said, 'Those are your words, not mine.'" He'd managed a pretty good Mason Worther impression, capturing a voice that turned suggestive and husky whenever it dropped below a certain volume.

"So ostensibly you could tie his wrists to the bed frame and flog him for three hours and you'd be within the bounds of your agreement."

Naser's fork froze halfway to his mouth. "Ostensibly. Sure. But I don't have much flogging experience."

"Much?"

"Any."

"I see. But you're uncomfortable with the idea of adding an intimate dimension to his offer."

"Yes."

"And that's why you didn't have depraved, slobbering sex with him on the floor of his office Monday morning?"

"*Slobbering?* Jonas Jacobs! I am stunned. You've never spoken to me this way before."

"We've never discussed our sex lives before."

"And we're not now. This is not about my sex life. I am not having sex with Mason Worther. It's a terrible idea. It would make me feel like a…I don't know, a sellout. Or, you know, some cliché of a queer man who's sexualized his oppressor. I can't get involved in all that. As you just said, it's too complicated."

"Come now, Mr. Kazemi. I'm not saying you should get *involved* with him. He sounds like a train wreck caused by a plane crash."

"Well, then what are you saying?"

"I'm saying you should have filthy, depraved, forget-your-name sex with him for three hours and then never speak to him again. That should square the debt quite nicely, don't you think?"

"Is that what you'd do in my situation?"

"We're not talking about me, mainly because my type isn't giant, frequently drunk white boys who look like they should be raiding English villages."

"Mason Worther is not *my type!*"

Naser dropped his eyes to his lap to hide the fact that, minus the drinking, Mason Worther was totally his type.

"Nas, where's your mom?" Gloria's voice made Naser jump. Suddenly, she was standing over the table, looking puzzled and concerned, sweet floral perfume coming off her in pleasantly distracting waves.

"What about my mom?"

"I saw her in the lobby a few minutes ago. I figured she was waiting for you. I thought she was joining you guys."

Naser looked to Jonas. "Go," he said with a wave of his hand. "Mothers trump all. But I might eat all the bread."

Naser promised he'd be back as soon as he figured out what was going on.

When he spotted his mother, she was slouched over the far corner of the front desk, giant sunglasses hiding most of her face, either content to be ignored by the two staff members working the reception desk or waiting on someone who'd already assisted her. She was dressed in one of her signature flowing black dresses, threaded with a bright scarf that almost matched the color of her hair, a heavily dyed page-boy cut of the kind Googoosh had helped popularize among Iranian women in the late sixties. Despite having a taste for designer labels, she had never gone out in public wearing one of her daughter's designs. Together with the giant sunglasses, the fact that she'd draped the scarf over her head suggested she was trying to go incognito. If only it hadn't been bright gold.

"Mom!"

Mahin Kazemi jumped and cried out. "What are you doing here?"

"I'm sorry, *I'm* the surprise? I work here."

"But your checkup, Naser-*joon*."

"It got moved. Wait. Did you think I wouldn't be here? What's going on, Mom?"

She drew him into a firm embrace. "No, no. I came to check on you. I was worried. How did the checkup go? Badly, I am afraid, because you are not telling me." She placed her hands against his cheeks to gauge his temperature.

"It was for my car, Mom. Why are you here?"

"I just told you. I was worried because I thought it was a doctor's appointment."

"Here you go, Ms. Kazemi," a bright voice announced next to them. It was Julie, the chipper new hire from reception, and she was holding a branded hotel bag with several items inside he couldn't make out through the opaque white plastic. "It was under the bed, just like you thought. Sorry. We're upgrading all the beds so there's no gap between the floor and the box spring, but you had one of the rooms we hadn't gotten to yet. Hi, Nas." Julie waved and departed, leaving the two of them in awkward silence.

His mother gazed into the bag as if she wanted to disappear into it.

"Is that Pari's stuff?" he asked.

"No, your sister has no taste in makeup. She wouldn't know what half of this is."

"Oh my God. Were you at the party on Friday?"

Mahin shushed him, took his arm, and steered him toward the lobby doors. Lowering her voice, she said, "I was, and I wasn't."

"Explain, please."

"I got a room over the pool. I watched from there. If I didn't like it, I didn't want her to see the look on my face."

He thought the chances were much higher his mother didn't want Pari to see the look on her face if she *did* like it, but that wasn't for him to say. "Did you...like it?"

Mahin shrugged, the same shrug she gave when she thought admitting an affection for something would make her look silly or weak. "Oh, what do I know? I have no style, apparently. Your sister, she goes, and she starts this whole business that's about Persian culture, and I try to tell her things and make suggestions and she dismisses me. She says, 'You just want everything to look like Farah Pahlavi, and all she did was dress like Jackie O.' She treats me like I'm this buffoon with no culture and no class, and meanwhile, everything she does is the whirling dervishes and the nonsense. She's making us look like clowns."

"She's talented, Mom, and she was devastated you weren't here."

"Your sister is devastated when her phone freezes up for five seconds. I was here. I just didn't tell her I was here so she wouldn't expect me to say something nice."

"Oh, Mom. Don't worry. I don't think she ever expects you to say something nice."

At the lobby doors, they stopped, and she turned to him. "Naser, please, my son. Don't lecture me about your sister. The last time I spent the day with her, I put together a little party. In Beverly Hills. You were busy. But I got all my richest Persian lady friends in one place so Pari could meet them and talk to them and get money from them. And what does she do? What does my beautiful daughter do? She brings a microphone and she lectures them for forty-five minutes about how they all wear black because America has pressured them into hiding their true Persian femininity. The diaspora must embrace color again, she yells as if it is a song and we are all protesting. I wanted to die, Naser-*joon*. I wanted to die right there where my daughter and all my friends could see. In the garden of my friend Shirin Farhani, who drives a Maybach and owns a lake."

"There's some truth to what she's saying, Mom."

"Bah. Who cares? Persian women in their sixties don't want to hear it from a girl who has never seen Tehran."

When they reached the entrance to the motor court, he saw her BMW was idling outside. She'd probably slipped the valet a twenty to keep it close.

She placed a hand to his cheek again. "You are doing okay, Naser-*joon*? You are not dying and not telling me?"

"Not that I'm aware of. But I'm an anxious enough person that if you put me alone in a room long enough, I'll probably decide otherwise."

"You are not anxious. You are very detailed and persistent. And you use these things to make money, which is the best thing we can do with our crazy. This is a good thing, Naser-*joon*."

He kissed her on the cheek. "Thank you, Maman."

"Your sister's crazy? It makes her no money, and she is always crying. Not a good thing. Tell me about the drunk man."

Naser's heart skipped a beat, and he coiled every muscle in his body to try to keep his reaction stuffed down. Had she witnessed the entire incident from the shadows of her balcony, swaddled in some heavy, hooded robe like a character out of *Game of Thrones*?

"What drunk man?"

"The one who put his arms around you and fell in the pool on Friday."

"Oh, him. He was no one. Some guy Fareena was breaking up with."

But he wasn't seeing his mother's face now, he was seeing the look she'd given him across the front seat of her car that morning eleven years ago. Now, thanks to Pari's mimosa-loosened tongue, he knew how concerned his mother had been that day, knew she had some inkling of what he was being put through every day at school. And that made it even harder to say Mason's name.

"He hugged you like he knew you."

Naser wondered if this was the first time his mother had ever witnessed another man show affection for him that wasn't entirely friendly.

"He was drunk. That was all. We got him outta here."

If his mother knew he was lying, she didn't let on. He felt, once again, the familiar tension that always passed between them when they wandered too close to the topic of his sexuality. An awkward moment where he was never quite sure who wanted to broach the topic less—him or his mother. Pari's accusations on Saturday had stayed with him. Did he play a bigger role in placing that topic off limits than he was willing to accept?

She nodded, leaned forward, and kissed him on the cheek. "Work now, but dinner soon. Without your sister, or maybe she comes for only part of it. The part where we don't get to talk."

He nodded.

As soon as she was gone, he turned and almost ran smack into Jonas, who was holding a paper bag with Camilla's logo on it. "They needed the table, so I had them pack up your salad. I hope that's okay." He handed Naser the bag as he watched Mahin step inside her parked car and drive off, then he turned and gave Naser a knowing look. "Some guy Fareena was breaking up with?"

"Don't. I handle my mother the way I handle my mother."

"I see. I've got a call in ten. Should we continue our conversation this evening?"

"I think I've got a pretty good sense of where you stand, thank you, Jonas."

"Suit yourself." Jonas turned and headed across the lobby.

A thought gripped Naser. When he called out the man's name, he stopped, turned, and Naser closed the distance between them.

"Do me a favor and don't tell Connor anything about this if he calls and checks in. He's already texted me to ask how the party went, and I keep sending him a screen cap of the Dictionary dot com page for vacation."

"So you *don't* want your best friend to know about you and Mason?"

"There is no me and Mason. But Connor knows everything that happened to me in high school. In excruciating detail. If he finds out I'm spending time with Mason on Saturday, he might have opinions about it."

Jonas smiled and nodded. "And our closest friends should always be opinion free."

"Some of Connor's opinions turn into judgments."

"Perhaps. But I find that distinction often exists solely in the mind of the one being addressed, and usually because the other person's opinion has...hit home, shall we say."

"Jonas—"

The older man held up his hands in a gesture of surrender. "Relax. Your secret is safe with me. I have to say, I'm somewhat honored to be the only one who knows about this."

"Congratulations. Maybe someday you'll tell me at least one of the corporations you worked for."

"I would, but I'd have to kill ya." Jonas winked and walked off at a clip.

# 16

Up with the dawn, bare feet pounding the wet sand at the surf's edge, sweat pooling on his shirtless torso as the brisk winds worked to whisk it away—in one week's time, this had become Mason Worther's new morning ritual, a run at first light that made the long stretch of beach in front of his home feel like an exotic, unexplored world.

Followed by gallons of coffee. Caffeine had become his new drug of choice, along with early morning exercise.

And thoughts of Naser, who'd be here in a few hours. Which might explain why Mason's eyes had popped open before sunrise.

The AA folks had told him exercise was a great way to boost natural endorphins. They'd also promised that sugary candy was his most effective weapon against withdrawal. Occasionally, it made him laugh— running himself ragged along the sea only to shove fistfuls of M&Ms into his mouth as soon as he reached the kitchen. "Sobriety first, fad dieting later," Shirley had quipped when he'd pointed out the contradiction.

For the first time since college orientation, he felt like he was on the right path, making good choices and enjoying the benefits.

*I am healthy.*

*I am sober.*

*I am going to find out what expression Naser Kazemi makes right before he's kissed.*

He'd left his cell phone on the counter during his run. There was a text waiting for him.

From Chadwick. His gut clenched. This hour on a Saturday morning wasn't usually Chadwick's prime time. He'd sent a picture of a woman Mason didn't recognize. She was sleeping, and she was naked. And the only reason Mason knew this is because in one part of the frame Chadwick's hand drew back the comforter from her body. He'd deflected most of Chadwick's texts all week with tap backs and insincere LOLs, but this one was over the line.

Mason winced, fingers taping before he could stop them.

**Did that young lady give her consent for that photo?**

Mason had finished half a cup of coffee before the response came.

**Fag.**

Chadwick threw the term around all the time, always as an insult, and often at Mason. This time, it landed hard. Mason felt his jaw tense as he glared at the screen.

He mulled over a dozen different responses, ranging from the self-righteous to the confessional. In the end, he set the phone aside and started upstairs. Maybe not denying the label was honest enough. For now.

He was almost in the shower when he remembered Chadwick's strange request from a week ago. There'd been so much drama since, he'd forgotten entirely about the affidavit. It helped that Chadwick had never gotten back to him with the date in his former employee's complaint.

Which was odd.

Had he managed to smooth the whole thing over? Doubtful, given Chadwick's raging ego and his passing understanding of the legal system.

Or had he realized Mason wasn't going to lie for him?

If it was the latter, the realization wasn't enough to destroy their friendship, given the casual and jokey texts Chadwick had been sending all week. As he stood under the cleansing spray, Mason found that fact strangely disappointing.

A few hours later, Mason was dressed and sitting on Shirley's balcony for their regular one-on-one. They were taking turns reading paragraphs from the *Big Book of Alcoholics Anonymous*. So far, their morning sessions had been a wonderful chance to discover he wasn't alone when it came to twisted and self-deceptive ways of thinking about drinking. When his phone chimed with a text, he shot to his feet. "Be right back. Two seconds. Promise."

She sighed. He'd been distracted all morning, often losing his place in their readings, and twice she'd called him on it. Now he was racing through her textile- and ceramics-filled house toward the street outside.

His old fraternity brother Jake Donaldson was standing in front of Mason's garage door, next to the used blue Lexus sedan he'd emailed Mason pictures of the day before. After UCLA, Jake had gone into his dad's luxury car business, and he was currently shaking his bald head in what looked like numb denial over their rushed transaction.

"You're either out of your damn mind or going broke. Which is it, Worther?" They shared a half bear hug.

"Neither." Mason tapped the hood of his new car with his knuckles.

"Did you check your account? Funds should have landed yesterday."

"I did and they did and we're good." Mason yanked his key fob from his pocket and opened the garage door. They both watched with reverence as sunlight spread across the shiny silver exterior of his Ferrari Roma. *Former* Ferrari Roma. He'd already pulled the keys off his chain, and as Jake just kept shaking his head, Mason pressed them into one of his hands, forcing the man's reluctant fingers to close around them.

Jake entered the garage. "This is like the Beethoven's symphony of cars and you're replacing it with James Taylor."

"Nothing wrong with James Taylor."

"Look, if you've got kids on the way and you need a backseat, I can get you something way nicer than a sedan."

Mason didn't need something nicer. He needed the cash. He did the math again in his head because the totals pleased him. The Ferrari was still so new Jake was barely taking a markdown on it, and he'd had it checked for beach damage that week and it had come up clean. The Lexus sedan, on the other hand, was used. He was losing only $40,000 to the trade-in. That easily gave him the $100,000 he'd promised Naser he'd invest. On top of that, another $90,000 that was all his. Which meant, more specifically, not his dad's. By Worther family standards, it was hardly a fortune, but most people would kill for it. He planned to sock it away. It felt like the beginning of something. Real savings.

*Independence.*

"Seriously, dude. Remember Laurie Walsh, the econ major I dated?

She's working bankruptcy law now. I can call her if you're in trouble."

"I'm not in trouble. Priorities are changing, that's all."

"Howdy, gentlemen." Shirley's voice startled them both.

"Jake, this is my neighbor Shirley Baxter. Shirley, this is my friend Jake. He sells cars."

Shirley raised her eyebrows and gave Mason a once-over. "We're buying a car?"

Jake approached her with an outstretched hand, his eyes wide, his slack-jawed stare a sudden reminder that to the rest of the world Shirley Baxter was a celebrity. "Ma'am, it's so nice to meet you. My mom loved your show. She used to DVR every episode, and my dad would get pissed 'cause it was five days a week and they kept running out of space."

"That's very sweet of you, Jake." The tension around Shirley's eyes had Mason suppressing a laugh. Earlier that week, she'd joked about how most of the people who recognized her in public were the children of die-hard soap opera fans—die-hard soap opera fans who'd recently died of old age.

"All right." Mason clapped his old friend's back, and the guy made a dramatic show of setting the keys to the Lexus sedan into Mason's open palm.

Then Jake was behind the wheel of the Ferrari and starting the engine as Mason and Shirley backed slowly out of the open garage to watch his departure. He pulled even with them and rolled the window down. "Last chance, Worther. No take-backs. I'm already fielding calls about this beauty."

"Go with the Ferrari gods, my friend."

Mason gave a *start your engines* motion, then Jake shook his head and drove toward the guard gate, leaving the two of them in fresh silence slowly filled by the nearby rush of surf.

"So you're *selling* your car," she finally said.

"Buying and selling. Something sensible, smart. This is a good sober car, right?"

She walked a slow circle around the sedan, but she was mostly studying Mason. "A Lexus, *sensible?* Wow, sweetie. You are definitely a child of Newport Beach."

"Ouch."

"And if you're trying to impress this old high school friend you're seeing later, I'm not sure losing the Ferrari is the way to start."

"I'm not trying to impress anybody. That's the point."

"Ah, so there's a *point* to this meeting. What is it exactly? It's clearly on your mind."

Mason turned. He'd deliberately avoided giving Shirley any details about Naser's visit because he was sure she'd have opinions about it. And he'd be forced to listen because, so far, heeding her advice had been working well. But he was determined to follow through with his plan. In some sense, he'd come to see it as a reward for a week of sobriety and good works. Making things right with Naser by making Naser moan. The perfect blend—like M&Ms after exercise.

"We've got history, and I'm trying to clean things up. He seems open. You know, like a ninth step kind of thing."

He figured throwing out some AA speak might get him a win. Instead, Shirley nodded and studied the empty garage. "I see. Well, just remember the twelve steps are in order for a reason, and you've barely done any writing on one. Not saying you should have. I mean, you just started. But nine's a long way off, Mason. No need to rush."

"Can't hurt to do a little advance work then. Lay some groundwork."

"Yeah, well, you might want to talk to an unbiased third party about what you need to clean up first. You know, make sure you're laying the right groundwork."

If she was trying to put a torrid implication into the phrase, it didn't show in her expression. She seemed serious as a grave. Based on what he'd heard in a week's worth of meetings, the ninth step asked you to pay back money you'd stolen, give honest explanations to people you'd abandoned or slighted while trying to cover up the costs of your addictions. Even serve time for crimes you'd tried to walk away from. Sex with guys you bullied in high school hadn't been mentioned.

Yet.

But shouldn't Naser be the one to decide how Mason righted past wrongs?

"I'll take that under advisement," he said.

Shirley nodded and held up her hands in a gesture of surrender. "All right. We'll reschedule this morning, obviously. I've got to head to the grocery store and start prepping for dinner tonight. My daughter's bringing a new boyfriend I can't stand, so I need to serve something that'll make him chew all night while I do the talking."

"Spiritual," Mason said.

"Speaking of spiritual, be careful today. And remember, don't drink or take a pill or I'll kill you, sweetheart. See how that works? God bless and all that. And don't forget you took the cookie commitment at Sundown Sobriety this evening."

"It's in my calendar," he called after her.

With a wave, she turned and left him standing next to his new car.

A sensible car. *Sensiblish.* If you'd grown up in Newport Beach.

A car that meant sobriety.

Freedom.

And making Naser Kazemi happy.

A few hours later, Mason got a text on his phone from a number he didn't recognize.

**It's Nas. I'm outside.**

*Nas, is he letting me call him that finally?*

**Want to come in?**

**No.**

*So much for a thaw,* Mason thought.

Mason grabbed the printout of his bank statement off the counter and headed for the door.

Outside, Naser's Volvo idled.

When he slid into the passenger seat, Mason was startled by the stark contrast between their outfits.

Naser was dressed like he was ready to go for a jog on the beach—green gym shorts, a white T-shirt with a bright colorful logo for something called the Farhang Foundation, and white plastic-framed sunglasses that looked like the kind you'd drop in a beach bag without a second thought. Meanwhile, Mason looked ready to go yachting in Newport Harbor. Today was the first time in his life he'd ironed a polo shirt, and his jeans were some acid-washed designer crap Chadwick had forced them to buy at a boutique in LA with a name he couldn't pronounce and a clerk who'd looked eighteen but talked to them like they were both idiots.

"Good afternoon, Mr. Worther," Naser said with all the enthusiasm of a foghorn.

Mason smiled and handed Naser the bank statement that showed proof of funds.

Naser stared at it without removing his sunglasses. The tense set in his jaw suggested he hadn't expected Mason to deliver. Now that he had, Naser looked stuck. Finally, he nodded, and went to hand it back to him.

"You should probably hold on to that," Mason said.

Nodding again—nervously this time—Naser folded it up and placed it inside the armrest, then he went to take the car out of park and started to make a U-turn. "Where we going?" Mason asked.

"You'll see."

"Okay, one sec here." Mason reached out and gripped Naser's right arm. "Before we head out, a condition."

Naser slammed on the brakes. "*Now* we're going to do conditions? Are you backing out, Mr. Worther?"

"No. I want to be sure you're not going to lure me into some alley and have your friends come and beat the shit out of me or something."

"*My* friends don't beat the shit out of people."

Mason was tempted to defend himself, point out that his crew had never technically beat the shit out of Naser either. But he didn't plan to spend the next three hours justifying.

"It's just one condition, Nas."

He waited for Naser to correct him with his full name. He didn't.

"No alleys?" he asked.

"No broken bones," Mason answered.

"Fine. No broken bones."

Then Naser was driving again.

"So it's going to be a surprise?" Mason asked once they'd cleared his guard gate.

"Yep."

And with that single short word, Mason's libido, newly purged of the many depressants that had sometimes watered it down, exploded with fantasies of what was to come.

He saw them pulling up to a seedy, dirty motel. Naser throwing open the door to a room he'd prepared with a sling and a table full of sex toys.

Preferably to be used on Naser, since Mason had zero experience being on the bottom. Although the idea of Naser tying him down and meting out a slow and special punishment gave him a delicious thrill. One guy Mason had hooked up with a few times had talked about bath houses, which Mason had thought were a relic of a bygone era. But apparently LA still had a few, and guys shuffled in there at all hours for release. Did Orange County have one? Was Naser taking him to one now?

When Naser finally pulled into the parking lot of an Irvine strip mall anchored by a Starbucks and a Jamba Juice, Mason found himself looking for blacked-out windows and vague neon signage. Maybe some kind of secret all-male massage parlor where they were about to live out a public sex fantasy.

Naser parked, said, "Follow me, please," then stepped from the car without checking to make sure Mason had complied.

Paces from the entrance to their destination, Mason saw not blacked-out windows, but a giant rainbow logo painted under the words **OUTLIVE!** Beneath the rainbow was the phone number for something that billed itself as a Crisis & Suicide Prevention Hotline. His balls deflated a bit, and he got a cold, vaguely sick feeling in the pit of his stomach. The next thing he knew, they'd stepped into what looked like the carpeted waiting room of a doctor's office. The gaunt, elegantly dressed woman behind the desk got to her feet with a warm smile and began addressing Naser in a language he suspected was Persian. They talked for a minute. When Naser finally introduced the woman as Leila, she extended a slender hand and gave Mason a long, unreadable once-over.

"Welcome," she said. "I'm the director of operations for Outlive. Shall we start with a tour?"

"Sure." Naser started forward without waiting for Mason's response.

Mason was afraid any response he gave aloud would be a croak, so he nodded and attempted a polite smile.

And suddenly they were moving through the cramped warren of offices, two of which were closed off by glass doors painted with the words **QUIET PLEASE—Active Call Center**. Inside, telephone operators wearing telemarketer-sized headsets were either conducting calls or waiting for one to come in. And on a wipe-off board on one wall was a freshly written list of **Mental Health Professionals on Call** followed by the first initials, last names, and phone numbers of what Mason assumed were psychiatrists or counselors. The names had color coded abbreviations after them, and as Mason peered through the window, he saw a code key explaining what each meant. They were areas of expertise. *GI = gender identity. TI = trans issues. TRS = trauma specialists.* The list went on and on.

He felt breathless and sweaty, and not in the way he'd planned.

He was imagining being forced to sit and listen to recordings of panicked phone calls from young kids contemplating taking their life over who they were. Or sitting in a circle of chairs for three hours with bullying victims lecturing him on the impact of his behavior, like those apology tours celebrities went on after tweeting hateful trash. It would have been fitting, and maybe a far more appropriate amends than what he'd had in mind, but it wasn't exactly exciting.

Would they let him use the bathroom first?

Leila explained the functions of Outlive as if he were a potential donor, and maybe that's what Naser planned for him to be. The hotline was their reason for existence, but they also conducted outreaches for LGBTQIA youth throughout the Orange County area. But their central purpose, she explained, was finding effective ways to turn what was often a desperate outreach phone call into the first step on a path toward mental health support and, in some cases, physical safety for the caller. How could a cry in the dark become a stepping stone, was how she phrased it more than once.

Throughout it all, Mason nodded, but his face felt hot and his eyes dry, and he was feeling both called out and exposed. But nobody was talking about him. Not really. Not yet. Still, Naser's message was clear—how many of these panicked late-night calls were coming from kids battling their own versions of Mason, Chadwick, and Tim each day at school?

The tour ended in a crowded storage room where overstuffed cardboard boxes bulged.

"So this is where you'll be," Leila said, and Mason just nodded as if this made total sense, even though he had no idea what was planned for him next.

Naser was looking at him for the first time since the tour had started. He wore the drowsy smile of Winnie the Pooh cradling a honeypot.

"So, as I'm sure Naser told you, we generate a considerable amount of paperwork as you can see, and after a while, we need to destroy it. A lot of what's in here are from intake files for callers who got connected with care and then moved on. Then others made an initial contact but never followed up, and if we haven't heard from them after three years, we destroy the file for confidentiality reasons. And also because, to be frank, storage is pricey, and we're clearly running out of it." She gestured to a plastic folding table and chair he'd missed upon entering. A large black paper shredder sat on the floor next to it. "So that's what you'll be doing."

"For three hours." Naser grinned.

Mason grinned back. The truth was, he felt a surge of relief. So no lectures or painful listening tours. Just office work. He could survive office work. Even an overwhelmingly boring amount of it.

Suddenly Leila was extending a clipboard toward him. "Now, obviously you won't be seeing any names here because we do our best to keep our files confidential, but in case you do, this is a nondisclosure agreement I need you to sign. It just says you agree to keep the contents of everything you're destroying today absolutely confidential. A lot of the contents of the files are pretty personal. I hope that's okay."

"It'll be fine," Naser said. "He's really good at signing things."

Mason's smile hurt his face. He took the clipboard and started reading through the pages.

"All right, well, I'm manning reception while Crystal's at lunch. You guys let me know if you need anything." She was almost to the door when she stopped. "Oh, and Nas, just bring me the form once he signs it."

Naser nodded.

And suddenly they were alone together.

"Number two." Mason signed the form and handed Naser the clipboard.

"Number three, actually." Naser took the clipboard and checked the signature blank, which seemed a little officious. Was he concerned Mason had signed the form *Dick Hunt?* But they were his three hours, so Mason wasn't going to complain.

"What was number one then?"

"You had to sign a release form at the hotel saying you weren't injured after you went in the pool."

Mason felt a hot flush of embarrassment. "So where should we start?"

"We?"

"Sorry. Where should *I* start?"

"Doesn't matter. They're all going to the same place."

"Shredtown."

"Yep."

"It's not a bad place to hang out for a while. It's quiet. Private." Mason gave Naser a cockeyed grin meant to convey exactly what he'd like to do to him if Naser decided to close and lock the door behind him.

Naser shrugged. "I mean, it doesn't have chrome fixtures and ripple fold drapes, but you'll make do."

Mason hefted a box off one shelf and carried it over to the folding table, deliberately flexing his arms so his biceps would bulge invitingly inside his polo's tailored sleeves. He dropped the box with a grunt and removed the lid.

"So you just going to watch?" Mason asked.

"Oh, no. I've got errands to run." Naser held up his phone to show that he'd set a stopwatch timer for three hours. "But I'll check in with Leila to make sure everything's going well."

"To make sure I didn't jet, you mean."

"Your words, not mine. Happy shredding, Mr. Worther."

Trying to hide his disappointment, Mason nodded and swallowed. Naser tapped the phone's screen and held it up to show the countdown clock had started, then he was out the door, pulling it shut behind him as he wore a beaming grin. Then he was gone.

It was a strange feeling, this blend of humility and horniness. He wasn't used to being shot down by men or women. The truth was, it had probably happened a bunch recently. He just couldn't remember it. But now that he was sober, he could feel the rejection rippling across his skin, and it made him feel self-righteous and determined. And hungry. So fucking hungry. For Naser.

Mason ran his fingers over the tops of the files in the box he'd just opened, rustling the tops of the folders like stalks of wheat.

*Contributions to the stream of life,* he heard Shirley Baxter's voice say as he took a seat at the folding chair and went to work. But a more recent phrase echoed through his mind after it. *Cries in the dark.* His fingers tingled as if the files were giving off a strange energy—the pain of the callers whose experiences were documented within, but also the surging energy of their desire to get better, to not give in to the dark.

The room was musty and warm, and the AC was old and struggling. The dusty curtain a few feet away was covering a glass door to the parking lot in back, an easy escape should he try to take it.

A week ago, he'd decided not to run from the hard truths of his life.

Now he wanted to do nothing more.

Instead, he stayed put and started to shred.

# 17

Naser's errands consisted of running to his car, driving into the parking lot next door, finding a spot where he could see the entrance to Outlive, and responding to the insane number of texts from Connor that had come through during Mason's tour of the offices.

His best friend had sent an extensive photo thread of possible wedding locations, a sign that he and Logan were on the road and headed home. To any lodge or hotels that seemed perilously perched on the edges of ocean cliffs or isolated enough to be the scene of an Agatha Christie mystery, Naser gave a thumbs-down tap back. Mostly, he watched Outlive's front door, making sure Mason didn't leave.

An hour and several *Washington Post* articles later, it was time for a distracted stroll through the Spectrum mall, during which several check-in calls with Leila confirmed that not only had Mason continued working, he'd run next door to Starbucks and bought drinks for everyone on shift.

At three hours on the dot, Naser found Outlive's reception area empty, and the sound of laughter coming from down the hall.

In the storage room, Leila and Mason were chatting away over their coffee cups. Several shelves were empty. What remained of their former inhabitants had been reduced to a tower of empty cardboard boxes stacked next to the back door and several bulging, tied-up trash bags of shredded paper. On the floor at Mason's feet was a knee-high stack of papers that looked like they'd been pulled from file folders and collated. Why, he wasn't sure. When Mason saw Naser studying them, he stood up. "I pulled all the staples out so they'd be easier to feed into the shredder next Saturday."

"Are you coming back with him, Nas?" Leila asked.

"Coming back?"

Mason rested one hand against the folding table as if laying claim to his territory. "Next Saturday. I gotta finish the job."

"It's probably going to take more than just one more Saturday," Leila said.

"It'll take what it takes." Mason locked eyes with Naser. "Right?"

"I guess so." Naser swallowed.

Leila shook Mason's hand. "Well, if I had a gold star badge for office work, I'd pin it on you, Mr. Worther. But all I've got are flyers and office supplies. Can I interest you in a ballpoint pen? Maybe a legal pad?"

"He's not in it for the paper products." Naser held Mason's stare without wavering, trying to determine if it was satisfaction or a challenge in the man's eyes. But all Naser could think was, *Now what? Are we done?*

Apparently sensing the strange current of energy flowing between both men, Leila moved to Naser, kissed him on the cheek, and brought her mouth to his ear. *"Ta mitooni bokonesh."* Then she was gone.

"What did she say?" Mason asked.

"She thinks you're nice," Naser said.

Roughly translated, she'd said, *You can get it,* but no way was he repeating that to Mason.

"Little does she know." Mason grinned.

"Fair."

Naser had not, for the life of him, expected Mason to complete a full three hours.

Instead, he'd expected a phone call full of seduction and charm in which he tried to wiggle out of the last hour or two, setting the stage for another fiery argument, the kind Naser had been craving all morning. Arguing with Mason felt easier than having the guy flirt with him. Maybe the less Naser said now, the higher the chances Mason would punch the clock and they'd be done, and Naser would escape this experience unscathed. Without giving in to his burning desire to throw the lock on the door behind him, hit his knees, and take the bastard's cock down his throat right here, no matter the cost to his self-esteem.

Mason picked up his Starbucks cup and shook it in one hand. "I would have gotten you something, too, but I didn't know when you'd be back."

"We said three hours so..."

"Yeah, but I figured you'd come back before then."

"Figured?"

Mason gave him a lazy grin. "Hoped."

Naser wandered to the stack of pages. "What were they like? The files, I mean."

"Tough." Mason's smile faded. "Anonymous, like Leila said. But from what I saw, there are a lot of really shitty parents out there."

Suddenly, Naser was remembering those hateful texts from Pete Worther, figured Mason was remembering some version of them too. Then he noticed Mason staring at him, and his eyes shot to his. "Can I ask you something?" Naser nodded, frightened by Mason's grave look. "Did you ever call this place? You know, back when…"

Naser swallowed, but the hard lump at the back of his throat didn't go away. "Yes."

The silence felt thick, like the air after a fire.

"About us?" Mason finally asked.

Naser nodded, wondering if that would be enough. From the way Mason stared at him, it wasn't. "About you three. About a mother who could see what I was but didn't want to talk about it. About the fact that Coach Harris slipped a flyer for an ex-gay clinic into my locker after the whole email debacle…and I kept it."

"The flyer?"

Naser nodded. Another silence, this one heavier. Much more painful.

"Why did you keep it?" The sudden wet sheen in Mason's eyes suggested he knew.

Naser had never admitted this tidbit aloud to anyone, never shared with anyone the hours he'd spent reading and rereading its deceptive language, wondering if their supposed solution might have worked for him. If it would make him as happy as the models in the stock photographs looked. His thinking becoming more and more contorted and destructive as he read—a teacher had recommended it, after all, so maybe there'd been something to the idea. Something that would bring relief, something that would make it all stop. The whole thing, he could see now, had been its own form of suicidal ideation, a desire to destroy himself as a means of ending the harassment and the pain. Once he'd realized that, he'd picked up the phone and called the number on the Outlive poster he'd seen taped to the inside of the front window in his favorite coffee shop.

"It was either go there or call this place. At least that's how it felt. I made the right choice."

Mason's jaw quivered. He took in a long, slow breath that lifted his chest. "Definitely coming back next Saturday then. And however many others it takes to finish the job."

"I'm not sure I'm free next Saturday," Naser lied.

"You don't have to come. It's my job to finish. Although I'd love it if you did."

"Did what?"

"Come."

If the word was supposed to have a double meaning, Mason's serious expression didn't let on.

"You know, Mason, I'm not sure all of this was necessary. Honestly, most days, when I felt bad about high school all I had to do was remember the look on your face that day you tripped when you guys were trying to fuck up my model."

"I didn't trip, Nas."

Naser was stunned silent.

"I knew what day it was. I'd overheard you in the library. I knew you were making this big model of Persepolis, and I knew you'd do a great job of it, and I knew Chadwick and Tim would fuck it up if they saw it. All morning I'd been trying to distract them. I came up with the hardest interval workout I could think of and made them meet me early so we could do it on the field. But Chadwick knew about the model, too, and I had to get creative. So I took a flying leap so you could get to class before they got to you. I hurt my arm so badly I couldn't play the next three games. And we lost all three so…"

Naser was speechless.

Finally.

"At any rate, whether you come back with me next Saturday or not, I wanted you to know that. I didn't trip. I threw myself down the stairs."

Naser couldn't breathe.

When it came to their days at Laguna Mesa, letting go of even the slightest bit of anger toward Mason felt like it might drown him in overwhelming feelings.

"Nas?"

"Yes."

"Come back to my house."

"For what?"

"Dinner."

Naser frowned. "You can cook?"

"What, you're surprised?"

"I just figured you were the order in and eat out type."

"I've been known to order in for weeks at a time, but I also grill. You a vegetarian?"

"Hell, no."

Mason headed for the storeroom door. "All right, then. Let's go. We'll see if I've got everything you want. If not, I'll get it delivered."

"Mason, you've done your three hours. You're off the hook."

In the doorway, Mason stopped and turned. "I don't want to be off the hook."

Then he left, giving Naser no choice but to follow.

They barely said a word on the drive back to Mason's house.

Naser's heart was in his throat by the time they stepped through the front door, and as Mason set various butcher-wrapped cuts of meat out on the counter for him to inspect the labels, he heard his responses to the man's questions as if he were yards from his own body. Once they'd decided on which steaks to cook, Naser forgot their decision but was too embarrassed to check the labels again because it would reveal how nervous he was.

Mason handed him a bottle of sparkling water he'd apparently asked for, and then they were staring at each other. In Naser's condo, the surrounding appliances would have made hums and ticking sounds to fill the awkward silence, but in Mason Worther's beach house—in *Pete* Worther's beach house, he reminded himself—top dollar had purchased a whisper-quiet kitchen.

"It was pretty stuffy in that storage room. I'd like to shower."

"Sure. I'll wait down here."

"With you." Mason took a careful sip of his sparkling water, eyes locked on Naser's face. "I'd like to take a shower with you, Nas."

Naser's bottle froze halfway to his mouth. He could hear his pulse in his ears.

Mason had replaced the cocky swagger of last Saturday morning with a directness and intensity that made a hunger so powerful roar through Naser the skin on his throat got hot. But behind it was stark terror—terror that the minute Naser disrobed, Chadwick Brody would explode from a nearby closet, baseball bat swinging. That this was all a trick or a trap.

But Mason was walking toward him, slowly and carefully.

"Is that something you want?" Mason asked. "To take a shower with me?"

"I didn't work as hard as you. I'm not very dirty."

"I could fix that." Mason grinned.

"There he is."

"There *who* is?"

"The guy from Saturday morning."

"This guy's a lot more sober, and a lot more capable of…how did you put it? Staying awake during the act."

"So this isn't just about showering, is it?"

Mason took another step toward him. Gently, he grazed a finger along Naser's cheek, just above his beard. Naser's eyelids fluttered before he could stop himself. So much for keeping his cool.

"What do you want it to be about?" Mason's whisper was the husky, strained kind. The kind a man tries to place over his desire like a lid atop the raging boil of his appetite. "I've got a long list of all the things I've wanted to do to you since high school. And when I found you in my laundry room, it only got longer."

"You first then."

"I did go first. Almost a week ago tonight, apparently."

"But you didn't remember saying it."

"Doesn't mean it wasn't the truth."

"But even if it was the truth, that doesn't make it better that you—"

Mason shook his head. "I didn't say it did. I said I wanted to do what you want."

"And forgive me for thinking that you want me to hit my knees right here and take you down my throat because it'll make you feel less guilty about those days."

"That's a pretty vivid description for someone who's pretending to be averse to the idea."

"Pretending?"

Mason bowed his head and took a step back, raising his hands in a gesture of surrender. "Just dinner then. But if you don't mind, I'm gonna clean up."

Mason was almost to the stairs when a force more powerful than reason took control of Naser's voice.

"I want to watch."

Mason stopped and turned.

Naser wasn't sure he had the confidence to articulate further, but his next words came from him before he could stop himself. "You guys were exempt from P.E. because you played a sport, but the first two weeks you had to come to class for mandatory physical testing. And in the locker room, it was hard not to look at you. In the showers, it was worse. So if you really want to give me what I want, what I wanted back then, Mason Worther, you'll let me watch you shower. You'll let me really look at you without being afraid to."

Mason's blue eyes twinkled.

Then he pulled his polo shirt up over his head, revealing his sculpted torso. Naser's still-wary gaze traveled from the hard ridges of the man's obliques to the faint dirty-blond happy trail climbing from his flat stomach to the center of his rounded pecs. He let his gaze linger on those pink and cream-colored nipples he'd wanted to suck and nibble until they were bright red.

"Let's hit the showers," Mason said, and then Naser was listening to the man's footsteps rattling the stairs, every bit of resistance leaving him as he followed.

When Naser was halfway up the stairs, he saw Mason's white briefs lying crumpled on the floor at the top.

# 18

The bathroom, like the rest of the house, was all sharp angles and hard, shining surfaces. But the shower was a giant fish tank. Inside, a gloriously naked Mason Worther was on full, sudsy display. As Naser stepped into the gathering steam, Mason role-played the part of the oblivious, impossibly beautiful jock, eyes closed, head tilted back as he shampooed his hair while the spray sluiced down his torso.

Naser told himself to wait, to keep his eyes above the waist for at least the first minute or two, then reward himself with a glance south when resistance became torture.

Once again, he didn't listen to himself.

Mason Worther, it seemed, liked to be watched. His subtle performance was causing his cock to throb and rise above balls so perfectly sculpted Michelangelo probably used to dream about a set just like them. Naser felt himself fall back against the edge of the counter behind him. Allegedly his feet were touching the tile floor, but he couldn't feel them. His world was Mason. Mason Fucking Worther. Naked and exposed and sober and indulging Naser's debauched request.

The glass door started to fog up. When it swung open, Naser jumped. "Deal's a deal," Mason said with a smirk, and that's when Naser realized he'd opened the door so nothing would obscure Naser's view.

He'd dressed down that day to send the message he didn't care what Mason thought of his appearance, that everything this day was *totally casual and nonsexual, got it?* Now his baggy mesh gym shorts were doing nothing to hide an erection so painful it seemed ready to shred his briefs.

Mason wasn't helping. He was leaning against the shower's stone back wall, safely out of the spray as he soaped his chest and then the back of his neck. When he felt Naser's focus on his face, he lifted his head and gave him a seductive half-smile that made Naser feel both molten and airborne.

"Not fair," Naser said before he could stop himself.

"What?"

"I'd hoped you'd be small."

Mason cackled. "Worried you won't be able to take this—"

"*No.* I wanted you to have at least one physical flaw."

"I do. I'm a pale-skinned white boy, and that's never really done it for me."

Naser was too wound up to laugh.

Mason stepped back under the spray and rinsed himself off. When he turned to face Naser again, his cock was standing at full, porn star-perfect attention.

And there was that look, that long, lingering look that used to say, *I dare you to want me so we can punish you for it.* A look that used to fill young Naser with equal parts desire and dread before making him run for his life. Now it meant something else entirely. Maybe it had always meant something else entirely. Maybe it had always meant, *Come to me. Help me shatter who we fear we have to be.*

Naser couldn't look away this time, couldn't run. If he'd done either of those things, maybe Mason wouldn't have made his next move. The man stepped forward and gripped the edges of the door. "You gonna get your quarterback a towel, Nas?"

Naser's breath left him in a low, trembling hiss. With shaking hands, he picked up a fluffy bath towel from the pile atop the wooden stool inside the bathroom's sliding door. Heart hammering, Naser started toward Mason, who took a step out of the shower stall. He went to hand him the towel, but Mason turned his muscular back to him. A signal that made Naser suck a deep breath through his nostrils.

"You gonna towel me off?" Mason asked quietly.

Naser answered by wrapping the towel around Mason's back, the layer of fabric between him and the feel of Mason's damp skin feeling like a tortuous buffer of a thousand miles. He rubbed the towel down Mason's back, then sank to his knees so he could dry Mason's ass. He was fighting the urge to nip at one of the cheeks when Mason turned, and suddenly his throbbing cock was in Mason's face. Naser's vision spun, and he tried to suppress a throaty grunt but failed.

The juxtaposition of Mason's raging erection and the calm and casual expression on his face made Naser's throat close up for a second. He opened it with two quick swallows. "You like being looked at, don't you, Mason Worther?"

"If you're the one looking, Naser Kazemi."

Determined not to give in just yet, Naser toweled off Mason's shins, his ankles, and his big, beautiful, hair-dusted feet.

"I don't remember you getting this hard when I looked at you in the locker room."

"I had a lot of tricks for keeping it down."

"Oh, yeah? What were they?"

"Who cares?" Mason said. "I sure as hell don't need them now."

Naser toweled off his thighs.

Mason grinned. "You gonna touch your quarterback, Na—"

"Shut the fuck up," Naser whispered, then he swallowed Mason's cock down to the root.

"*Fuck,* Naser." Something between an exclamation and a groan. Despite his confidence, he sounded as full of delirious surprise as Naser was over the twists of fate that had brought them to this debauched moment. "Fuck, Naser. Goddamn."

He'd dreamed of this a thousand times. On his knees, worshiping Mason Worther's cock with frenzied abandon. But never once in his dreams had Mason tenderly run his hands through Naser's hair the way he was doing now. Never once had the man sounded stunned and grateful for the attention.

He'd meant to swallow Mason's length in one long, testing gulp. See how much of it he could take, calibrate his next ministrations. But one gulp turned into two, then three, each time pushing against the far limit of his gag reflex. His jaw ached from the delicious exertion of it, from the heady smell of bergamot-scented body wash spiced with fresh masculine musk. He pulled himself off it, gasping for breath. To keep his hands from shaking, he needed to focus. So far, it seemed to be working. But the second he loosened his grip on the base of Mason's warm shaft, his fingers trembled once more. He tightened his grip again as he tasted, licked, and suckled the head.

"Look at me," he heard Mason say. "Nas, look at me. Please."

Naser complied, gazing up the flushed, naked distance between them. But he didn't stop, couldn't stop, and when Mason smiled down at him and chewed his lower lip, Naser prayed every hot flash of his desire was evident in his eyes as he devoured Mason Worther with sloppy hunger fueled by years of frustrated desire. Then, suddenly Mason went tense with something that looked like panic. "Nas, *stop*."

Terrified, Naser pulled back.

Mason's spit-slick cock popped from his mouth and bounced. Fear speared Naser's chest, sending icy prickles across his shoulders.

A freak-out? Was that what this was? Had their role play turned Mason into a tortured teenager again in the blink of an eye?

No, that wasn't it. Mason was gripping the edge of the open shower door with one hand, chest rising and falling in short bursts. Was he hyperventilating? His teeth were gritted, his eyes screwed shut. Naser recognized the look immediately—a struggle for self-control.

*If he blows right now, I will sop up every drop. I will drink it like milk.* The other voice in his head telling him to get a hold of himself was quieter, much quieter. It was shouting a losing battle against another, louder voice. The one that told him Mason Worther had given birth to all of Naser's desires, and the second Naser had dropped to his knees before the man, he'd committed to drink from the source.

Still gasping, Mason managed a sheepish smile. "I'm sorry."

"A dick like this usually doesn't merit an apology."

Shoulders tensed and hunched forward, core flexed as if his abs alone could hold back a gushing eruption, Mason laughed, then sucked in a deep breath as if any display of amusement might cause him to gush.

Naser knew he should get to his feet. It was the least he could do to support Mason's effort at self-control. But he couldn't. Couldn't rise from the sight of Mason's spectacular nakedness, his teeth clenched tight to hold back the paralyzing pleasure Naser had called forth after only a few minutes of wild and blissful work. Naser went to place his hands on Mason's flexing, flushed quads, but at the first graze of his fingers, the man flinched and hissed, ticklish everywhere, it seemed. "Just another few seconds. Just another few."

Naser laughed.

"I dreamed about you," Mason whispered, by way of explanation.

"Dreamed about me?"

"I'd talk about you in my sleep, and I'd wake up with strangers and they'd say, 'Who's Naser?' Because I was dreaming about what it would be like to be with you. I used to dream about you looking up at me. Under me. Sucking me. So when you started to do it, I almost lost it. Sorry."

*Lies,* Naser thought. *They have to be lies.*

But Mason's body wasn't lying.

Naser stood and took a step backward, resting his butt against the counter behind him. Mason hadn't moved an inch, but his eyes stayed locked on Naser's, as if he could sense the man's disbelief and was prepared to explain himself further. Flushed and gasping but tensed with an energy that seemed feral, he was like a caged animal trying not to break his chain.

During sex, Naser typically went boneless. It was easier to let an aggressive top turn him into a plaything. He was used to being slapped, manhandled, spanked—all of which he'd ask for. Sometimes it scratched his biggest itch, but mostly it had just been an effective method for dealing with partners he didn't know very well and might never see again. He'd done plenty of willful, theatrical begging. But he wasn't used to being adored. He was tempted to say it wasn't his kink, but the truth was, he hadn't come across a man willing to offer it. But that's what Mason's words vibrated with now—adoration.

"You've never known the power you have over me," Mason whispered.

"You never asked me to use it."

"I've been asking for a week now."

"Yeah, well, maybe I didn't want to abuse my power."

"Maybe a little abuse is exactly what I deserve."

As Naser slowly closed the distance between them, Mason's eyes widened. His cock was at half-mast now, but for Mason Worther, half-mast would have been the height of a flagpole on another man.

Maybe he did what he did next to make his point, or maybe he just couldn't resist the delicious sight of Mason Worther's perfectly rounded balls. Naser gripped them, then squeezed, applying slow but building pressure, watching Mason's expression cross the temperature gauge from green to red.

"Nas," he gasped.

"Hurts?"

"No... Might come."

"Oh, you can hold off, Worther. You're a big, strong quarterback, remember? You can keep that load locked up nice and tight, golden boy.

You wouldn't want everyone to think you're some little pussy like that boy you and your friends chase all over school."

Mason bit his bottom lip. "I want to do a lot more than chase that boy," he growled.

"Yeah, well, you better be prepared for what you're going to have to do when you catch him."

"Oh, yeah?"

Naser nodded, alternating now between caressing the undersides of Mason's balls with his fingers and doing his best to seize his tightening sack in a suddenly painful grip that made Mason's nostrils flare. "Yeah, you and your bastard friends have messed him up good. Made him want certain things."

"Things like what?" Mason asked eagerly.

"Things that hurt," Naser whispered into Mason's ear.

A huge admission. One he'd made to only a handful of people in life. And here he was, making it to the man who'd installed the buttons, the triggers. The locker room role play, the tension of the hours before, it had all brought them to this point, where they could admit things in a dark whisper that would take months to confess over dinner. "I like a little pain. The kind you can turn on and off. You know, one tap for keep going, two taps for slow down, three for full stop."

Naser alternated painful grips and pleasurable strokes on Mason's balls, sending the man into a drowsy, nostrils-flaring fugue. *Sugar and salt.*

Mason nodded slowly, effecting the look of a good student even as the feelings coursing through him seemed ready to incapacitate him. "One tap for keep going, two for slow down, and three for full stop. Is that how it works with you, Naser?"

"Basically, yeah."

Silence now. It never occurred to Naser that this proposition might frighten Mason—that an invitation to indulge some playacting version of the beast he'd been in high school might run counter to his mission to make things right. But hesitation was one thing. Mason's epic hard-on was another. Naser slowly released the man's balls. He didn't soften. It was Naser's words that made his desire throb, not his touch alone.

"As long as it involves me fucking the cum out of you until you can't breathe at some point, I'm all in."

"You're a bad man, Mason Worther."

"I'm a bad man who's trying to be a better man," Mason whispered. "That means I'm going to be as bad as you want me to be."

*I'm fucking done for,* Naser thought.

"Bedroom," Naser said.

Throughout the week, as he'd speared himself with increasing vigor using his favorite toys, as his mind worked to imagine a night with Mason that ended with more than one drunken kiss, Naser had done his best to recreate this bedroom in his mind. Now that he was back, he could see he'd done a pretty good job. The walls and carpet were as white as he remembered; the bedspread and the space-age style TV chairs the same shade of sky blue, along with the ripple fold drapes that had danced on the ocean wind that night.

They stumbled away from the bathroom door together, Mason holding him from behind, moaning the word "naked" over and over again into the nape of his neck with increasing insistence. Powerful hands shoved his gym shorts down over his ass. His briefs followed in several sharp tugs that left cool air tickling his cock and balls. "I thought I was making the rules," Naser said.

"You are, but you gotta do it naked."

It was cute. It was sweet.

It was not what Naser wanted.

In the bathroom, Mason had promised him something edgier and sharper, and Naser was determined to collect.

Mason reached for Naser's cock, but he batted his hand away.

He backed up, staring into Mason's eyes, kicking his briefs and shorts down off his feet. Tugging his T-shirt over his head, revealing the downy black hair across his chest, the hair so many men had pressured him to wax or shave because it didn't fit with their porn-driven conception of what a pocket-gay sized twink should be—porpoise smooth, more cartoon than man. He'd never caved to that pressure, and now Mason Worther, the last man in the world he would have expected to admire his natural body, was staring at him—all of him—with open-mouthed desire.

Slowly, Naser sank to his knees on the carpet.

Mason smiled, expecting another blow job, he was sure.

*Fat chance, golden boy.*

Naser beckoned for him to close the distance.

Mason started forward, proud cock bobbing in the air in front of him.

Naser ignored it, slid his hands around the back of one of Mason's hard thighs, and licked the front of his quad, nibbling it. Kept going down the leg, down his hair-dusted shin. The effort forced him to poke his ass out further behind him as he went, which made him feel delightfully exposed. He couldn't see Mason's reactions, but he could hear them. Grunts of surprise that turned to gasps of pleasure as Naser's hands squeezed and caressed in search of the most sensitive spots along the arch, the ankles, the sides of the heels.

Then, a long, wet lick from one big toe and across the veiny arch of his giant right foot.

At the base of the ankle, a little nip. Hard enough to leave rosy marks, but light enough for them to quickly fade.

Same thing on the other, kneading, listening for the tell-tale responses from above. Then once he'd made an assessment of both feet—both big, beautiful, veiny feet—Naser sat back onto his haunches, gazing up. He saw anticipation and confusion on Mason's face, but mostly hunger.

*Perfect.*

Bambi eyes was Connor's term for the pleading and submissive expression Naser gave off when trying to get his way with a single look. In this moment, it meant submission by design.

Slowly, Naser sank back onto the carpet, shifting so that he lay parallel to Mason's feet, gazing up at the man now like a tourist sprawled on his back to better study a fresco on the museum ceiling above. Then, Naser gripped Mason Worther's left ankle and used it to gently place the man's foot on his throat.

*Jesus fuck,* was Mason's first thought.

This was a test. A test he was desperate to pass.

One careless shift of weight, one wild, uncontrolled spasm of desire and Naser could get hurt. Badly hurt. No way would Mason have ever attempted something this aggressive without an explicit invite. But Naser had positioned him this way as if he were a mannequin, and his two-handed grip on his calf remained confident. A safety valve if anything went wrong.

And then came a tap.

A single tap.

A tap that meant *keep going.*

Slowly, gently, Mason pressed his foot down on Naser's throat. He had no frame of reference for how much pressure to apply. And that was part of it, he realized. He was forced to move like molasses, follow Naser's cues. Forced to read every flicker in Naser's eyes, which stared up at him with hunger and challenge and anger glazed in lust. Forced to closely read every inch of Naser's body for a response, a sign that it was not enough or too much or just enough or heaven.

He stopped, assuming he was in danger of choking off Naser's air flow.

One tap.

*Keep going.*

Naser's cock glistened, rock hard and bouncing against his stomach, brown shaft slicked with pre-cum. An undeniable testament to how badly he wanted this.

Mason applied more pressure, pressure that made Naser's eyes roll back into his head as he bit his lower lip. Mason had been with guys who seemed to go limp as soon as Mason had their way with them. He'd never seen an act of submission light up a body like it was lighting up Naser Kazemi's now. It was the first time he'd seen surrender make a man writhe.

"Is this what you want?" Someone else had spoken these words, some growling animal Naser had drawn forth from Mason's soul.

One tap.

More. Naser wanted more.

Mason felt power, pure power. But it came in a surge, then crested.

Because Naser's grip on Mason's calf was a reminder this power could be taken away in an instant. It had been given. Not an entitlement, not an inheritance, but a blessing and a gift.

*A test*, Mason reminded himself.

Naser was pushing them close to the edge. Seeing if Mason could be yanked back at just the right moment. No other explanation made sense. If Mason couldn't maintain the perfect balance, if he overshot the mark, left even the slightest bruise or lost himself in some fit of uncontrolled passion—if the bully he'd been all those years ago seized too much control—he would never have this again, never have the mouthwatering sight of Naser Kazemi, heaving and sweaty and beneath him. And that was out of the fucking question. Inconceivable.

"Is this what you want? My fucking foot on your throat?"

"Yes," Naser whispered.

"Is this what you want, you little fa…"

*Woah, woah. No, no.* He was about to blow this whole thing, and in the wrong way. It wasn't his first time doing role play like this. For willing partners, male and female, he'd acted out fantasies involving brutish and punishing doctors and teachers, and yes, even bullies like the one he'd been in high school. But this was Naser! Invoking that old slur, the very one he'd coughed and muttered under his breath when they'd passed Naser in those cinderblock hallways, would be too far. Way too far. But Naser didn't bat Mason's punishing foot away, didn't roll to one side, sputtering angry, lust-free curses. Rather, the fear in Mason's expression brought a smile to Naser's face.

"Say it," Naser whispered. A taunt, a dare. Mason realized he'd instinctively lightened the pressure he was placing on Naser's throat. Naser tightened his two-handed grip on Mason's calf. "Say it," he whispered again.

"Is this what you want, you little faggot?"

Naser bit his lower lip, then gave a lazy grin that said satisfaction.

Mason felt both shamed and purged, and it was all Naser's doing. By making him repeat the old slur when his voice was thick with desire, his cock half hard and throbbing from the sight of Naser naked and pinned underfoot, he'd made a mockery of that hateful word. Exposed it as Mason's gruff and childish attempt to dismiss his own desires. An attempt that had, a decade later, spectacularly failed. Together, they'd tossed that vile word into the simmering brew of their desire, melting down everything inside of it that had once seemed solid, rigid.

The contradiction of it all made Mason's head spin.

He was desperate to please the man below him, but to do it, he'd have to drag the bully he'd been from his cage and set him free.

Not free, he realized.

Leashed.

On a leash Naser held in both hands.

"Answer me," Mason said, but what he thought was, *Tell me I'm doing it right. Tell me I'm giving you what you want.* "Answer me, you little faggot."

Naser lifted Mason's foot an inch from his throat and swallowed his big toe. A hard, mean, angry suck that started with pain, then turned into something wetter and wilder. Insane, really, that Mason should be surprised by this response, but the unexpected pleasure of it arced up his leg. In an instant, he'd gone from pretending he was about to crush

Naser's voice box to struggling to keep his balance as Naser unleashed a wild, slick assault on Mason's entire foot. Long, wet licks down the center, from ball to heel, followed by another, another, and another. Little nips like the one he'd left on Mason's ankle a few seconds before.

Now it was Mason's turn to draw wicked pleasure from the contrast between their old versions and the men they'd become. Naser, once so prim and proper. Naser, who walked with an unassailably upright posture and spoke the King's English, had been reduced to a slobbering little beast who could only manage to growl the words "big fucking feet" over and over again as he worked.

"Dirty boy." Mason wanted it to be a growl, but it came out filled with wonder and awe. "Such a dirty, fucking *boy*."

In response, Naser bit the ball of Mason's foot, hard enough to sting. Then he licked toward the center and swirled. Mason had never realized how sensitive the spot was. Once Naser realized this, his tongue did a wild flicker as he tightened his grip on Mason's calf. It was a struggle to stay standing now, and the gasping breaths that came from him put the growling bully he'd just released back inside his cage. What had seemed like a powerful weapon a second before—his big left foot and all of the weight he could have shifted onto it in a second—had been exposed as a bundle of sensitive and easily manipulated nerves, capable of reducing alpha dog Mason to a giggling, gasping mess.

Finally, Mason's eruptions had Naser laughing under his breath. He returned Mason's foot to the carpet, sucking in a long, deep breath that left his nostrils flaring and chest heaving. His lips were slick with his own spit, and between that and his sparkling eyes, he looked as if Mason's foot had been covered in some glaze of sugar and caffeine that had left him both satiated and wild.

For a while, they just stared at each other, as if they needed a beat to process what they'd turned into, what they'd become. What they'd always hungered to be.

Naser reached up and slapped Mason across the back of his calf.

Once for keep going.

Suddenly, Naser felt himself go airborne. The bedding let out a soft woosh as he landed, Mason's hot palms releasing his armpits.

The man had hoisted him to his feet and thrown him onto the bed in the blink of an eye.

He rolled onto his back, mouth meeting Mason's as the guy came down on him like a giant breaking wave, forcing him back into the pillows. Suddenly it was the all-consuming embrace of last Friday, but this time it was sustained, and their cocks were no longer confined, rubbing against each other in a slick, hot tumble.

Naser felt a deep ache in his center, a desperate desire to be filled that bordered on frenzy, as if any barrier between him and Mason's entry needed to be swiped away with one bat of the hand, one swipe of the tongue. And that scared him suddenly. Tempted him to ignore safe sex boundaries, just throw his legs back and let Mason shove it in. Also, he hadn't exactly prepped himself for a full invasion, which entailed its own kind of risk.

But when Mason pressed up on the undersides of Naser's thighs, exposing his crack, his hole, obscenely, to the open air, it wasn't to invade. It was to see. To stroke, to graze. To lightly circle the entrance with three fingers working together, blue eyes finding Naser's again and again, only to get distracted by sights that had been walled off from him for too long by shame. Naser wished he was a painter so he could capture this sight forever. Gorgeous Mason Worther—former golden boy turned reformed mess—studying Naser's upturned ass with languid, loving attention. Mason bit his lower lip, lost in thought—filthy thoughts, it looked like. He dove forward, spread Naser's cheeks and licked the heat within, making Naser's breath stutter like automatic gunfire. He finished off the move by taking one of Naser's balls into his mouth, releasing it with a slick pop.

When his eyes met Naser's, they were wild. "Never done that before," he gasped.

"Never done what?"

"With a guy, I mean. Never tasted a guy like this."

Before Naser could ask the obvious question—did you *like* it, you filthy, beautiful son of a bitch?—Mason did it again, and again. And again. Long, determined wet sweeps that started to put Naser's foot work to shame. Then he took Naser's cock down his throat, his now messy, beautiful blond hair draping his face as his head bobbed. Naser's entire body spasmed. Mason pulled off quickly, sensing an eruption. He gripped the shaft and studied the head, smiling at it.

*Mason Worther is smiling at my goddamn cock.*

"You're close, aren't you, Nas?" Mason stroked.

"Mason, if you—"

"Better not tell you all the places in our high school where I dreamed about fucking you, huh?"

"Mason. Mason, I'm—"

"Better not tell you about the janitor's closet outside the gym where I wanted to grab you by your arm and pull you inside one day so we could—"

*"Mason!"*

Mason stroked harder at the first signs of eruption. If there was such a thing as a joyful growl, that's what Mason was doing as Naser buckled, bellowed, and erupted. Never before had Naser experienced a release this powerful under the force of someone else's madly stroking hand. There'd always been that awkward moment he'd have to take over, bring himself over the edge with his own practiced grip. Mason's fist had opened something inside of him, and now Naser's soul was emptying through it.

Then it was like he was melting into a puddle of something that could live off shallow breaths until the bed swallowed him entirely. Mason's weight shifted. He was crawling up Naser's body, their lips suddenly inches apart. Too crazed with lust to care about how wild and messy his hair was, how the long bangs he usually pushed back and styled were draping his face now. Naser reached up and brushed them back from his forehead.

"Got a thing for janitor's closets, huh?" Mason's voice was raspy.

"You know good and well that's not what my thing's for."

"Yeah, it's feet, apparently."

"And boys who call me bad names."

"On cue."

"And only on cue. Now."

"Feel like you might have set the stage for that one on purpose."

Naser smiled and waggled his eyebrows. "Maybe. It was still a bold choice. Given our history."

"Giving you three hours to do whatever you wanted to me was a bold choice. But it's paid off rather nicely, as far as I'm concerned."

"Has it? You still haven't finished." Naser reached down and gripped the base of Mason's shaft. "How can I help you there, sir?"

"Like this." He brought their mouths together, stroking himself as they kissed.

*Me. Mason Worther needs* me *to come.*

Then Mason's eyebrows arched, his mouth popping open into a gasping *O*, and as much as Naser wanted to maintain eye contact, he couldn't help but look down, couldn't help but watch the thick jets that shot from Mason's cock. They glazed Naser's stomach and the dusting of black hair around his freshly emptied balls. It was more than cum. It was more than an orgasm.

It was a confession. It was proof laid out all over Naser's ravaged body.

Mason crumpled down onto Naser like a sleeping bear, taking him into a slick and sweaty embrace.

And Naser, struggling to breathe deeply, waited for the delirious fever to break. Waited for the cold, reckless reality of what they'd done to press in on all sides, for Mason's embrace to turn sweaty and oppressive. Instead, the deep hunger inside him had only intensified in the wake of his orgasm, as if nothing could vent it. Submission and a desire to be fucked often tailed each other, but they were different animals with varying appetites. The second could turn you into a growling beast to rival the most aggressive top. That's how he felt now, and at the very moment when he should have felt spent.

"What happened to fucking the cum out of me?" Naser whispered.

"That's next."

*Next.* Three hours and then some and still going, apparently. Maybe the minute the clothes had come off, Mason had reset the clock.

Silence fell, and when Naser turned his head, Mason was staring back at him with one uncovered eye. "Beautiful," he whispered.

"Excuse me?"

"This morning, when I was out for a run, I was wondering what your face would look like right before I kissed you, and the answer is beautiful."

A kiss in this position would be an awkward misfire, so Naser crawled up onto Mason and pressed their mouths together, hoping their lip lock channeled every tremor of still-quaking and unaddressed hunger inside of him.

They finally broke, Mason's hands gently gripping the sides of Naser's face.

"Shower," Mason said, "together this time." And then they were stumbling toward the bathroom together, much like they'd stumbled across the threshold to the bedroom earlier. Mason's hands were silky and warm and powerful. He soaped the crack of Naser's ass by running one hand after the other through it from top to bottom, his fingers moving like the long bristles of a brush. Naser kissed the stone wall as he groaned.

Then a high, sharp chime sounded from the bedroom. "Shit," Mason whispered.

Suddenly, Naser was alone. Behind him, Mason was grasping for a towel, leaving Naser under the spray, wondering if the awkward, frosty post-sex moment he'd been fearing had finally arrived.

## 19

**Cookies**, the reminder said.

Mason had phrased it simply, worried the alert might pop up when he was in the presence of his father or Chadwick, or anyone else for that matter. He sure as hell didn't want the words **Remember to bring cookies to the AA meeting** flashing across his home screen in public.

"Shit," he whispered again.

Forty-five minutes until the meeting, and it was a twenty-minute drive from his house. And he'd forgotten about it entirely, even after Shirley's reminder that morning.

The cookies were baked, from a recipe he'd downloaded off the Internet that week and managed not to ruin. It was maybe the second thing he'd baked in his life, and the first not in partnership with a girl he was dating. It helped that the directions called for covering almost the entirety of each cookie's surface with M&Ms.

Already, he was thinking of excuses. Then he saw the look Shirley would give him the next time she saw him if he bailed.

An idea occurred to him. A desperate idea, but maybe it was worth a shot. He opened the app he'd been using all week to find meetings. Earlier that week, he'd memorized the codes that appeared next to each meeting name. Next to the listing, the letter *C* indicated the type of meeting it was.

"Dammit."

It meant closed to non-alcoholics. The idea of bringing Naser with him wasn't just nuts, it was out of the question.

Feeling as if there was a great weight pressing down on his neck and shoulders, Mason wandered back into the bathroom, staring at the phone in his hand. When he finally looked up from the screen, he found Naser staring at him from under the spray, eyes vacant, arms crossed protectively over his chest. The pose of someone trying to relax but failing. Trying not to betray how jarring it had been to be left in the shower so abruptly. "Everything okay?" he asked warily.

"I forgot I have to do something tonight."

"Oh. Okay."

Ice in his tone, just a sliver of it, but it was there.

Mason could feel Naser's desire to be offended losing out to some internal monologue telling him his feelings weren't justified, that none of this had been planned—not the last part, anyway.

As he stood there, paralyzed by awkwardness that felt tinged by hurt, Mason craved a drink for the first time in a week—an Arctic blast of Absolut that would blow these fears out both ears. This mile-a-minute thinking, this trying to read deeply into every silence, had always been a part of his life, and he could see now how effectively vodka had shut it down. Obliterated—temporarily, of course—the constant sense that one misstep could destroy everything good in his life. That was his fear now. If he left, it was over. He'd never see Naser Kazemi again. Except for in his dreams. And that fear was boiling over because what they'd just done had knocked the lid off the pot. Not just the role play and the sex, but the intensity of it all.

*Sober sex.* He'd heard the term used at meetings, and the truth was, he couldn't remember the last time he'd had sex sober.

"Stay here," Mason said.

"The shower?"

"My house. Until I'm back. It'll be about an hour."

"An hour. Wow. All right. Is everything okay?"

"It's fine. I just... I forgot I made a promise to somebody."

*Himself.* The promise he'd made was to himself. The meeting would survive without cookies. The commitment was so that Mason had an obligation to be in the presence of people who could help him survive his worst impulses.

"Seriously. Stay here. I'll come back and we'll grill."

There was hesitation in Naser's eyes, and his next thought came to him so fully formed, it was impossible to ignore. *He's going to leave. This was too sudden and new and weird, and the minute he has some time alone to think about it, he's out the door and never coming back.* Mason had to explain more fully, lay even more of his cards on the table. But then he remembered what the second *A* stood for—anonymous. Meaning you didn't blab about meetings to people who didn't go to meetings.

It looked like Naser was going to rinse the shampoo out of his hair, but instead his hands traveled to the back of his neck and stayed there, as if he'd been paralyzed by thoughts.

*Doubts. Not thoughts. Doubts.*

"You sure you don't want to do it another night?" Naser asked.

"I want you to stay." At the intensity in Mason's voice, Naser's eyes shot to his. "I've wanted this for years, and I want you to stay."

Naser nodded, lips parted as if to speak, but instead of saying anything aloud, he nodded with greater emphasis.

Mason nodded confidently, feeling anything but sure. "I'm gonna get dressed and then…" But he was back in the bedroom before he could finish the sentence, desperate to put every moment he had to spend away from Naser on fast forward. By the time Naser emerged from the bathroom, toweling himself off, Mason had slid into old jeans and a fraternity T-shirt. Mason could only think of one way to make the moment less awkward. He found his key ring on the nightstand, pulled the house key off it, and handed it to Naser.

"In case you want to take a walk on the beach or anything."

"Sure."

Naser smiled politely—*politely,* after everything they'd just done to each other. Mason wanted to die—then closed his fingers around the key even though he didn't have a pocket to put it in.

"An hour," Mason said.

Naser nodded.

Mason was halfway down the steps when the argument raging in his head resolved itself with sudden clarity. The anonymous in Alcoholics Anonymous was about other people, other people's names and stories and attendance. Not his. And goddammit, if today wasn't about being honest.

*Baring it all.*

When he sprang back into the bedroom, he could already feel the lump in his throat. He felt a rising tide of sadness and fear out of scale to everything around him. Sober sex had done this, he suspected. And the wild ride leading up to it. For years now, he'd done his best to drown uncomfortable feelings. Now he'd gorged on a buffet table of them in a day's time.

"It's an AA meeting." It came out like a shout instead of a confession. Naser looked up like a gun had gone off. "It's not just some random thing... It's... I went for the first time a week ago. My—" Any mention of Shirley, or a reference to a neighbor would violate anonymity, so he stopped. Readjusted. His tone was too harsh. He wanted to explain, not to accuse. "A friend took me a week ago and... Um... It's changing things. Changing *me*." Softening his tone had softened the dam inside of him.

"Mason."

The gentle tone of Naser's voice alerted Mason to his coming tears before his vision blurred.

"And it's the only thing I would walk out on this for. You see, I agreed to bring cookies. But it's not just about cookies. It's about being accountable and consistent. Being connected to something bigger, bigger than..." A dozen ways he wanted to finish that thought. Something bigger than Ferraris and your dad's money and all the abusive conditions that came with it, and houses that impressed people you didn't like, and a never-ending wheel of parties that were supposed to seem cool and edgy but where you were too numbed out to feel them because inside you felt like you didn't belong there or anywhere.

To escape all that, he needed to connect to something bigger than who'd he been, bigger than all the shitty things he'd done.

"Mason."

There was a frog in his throat now, but he could feel Naser gently gripping his elbows. "And it feels like...a really good thing that's made better things happen. The meetings, I mean. And it's only been a week, but I just wanted you to know that... I want you to know that I've wanted this for years—you, here. Like this. For years I've wanted this, and the only thing, the *only* thing that would make me walk out on it even for an hour is this. Something this serious. Because...because what's wrong with me is very serious, Naser."

"Mason..."

Their foreheads were touching. Naser sounded quietly astonished by Mason's display. And maybe his words, too. Maybe he wasn't used to grown men breaking down into tears in front of him. As for Mason, he felt more naked now then he had during sex.

"I'd take you with me, but it's a closed meeting and so it's only alcoholics and I... Please don't leave. It would mean the world to me if you stayed."

Begging. Mason had never begged for anything in his life.

He'd never *had* to. But his life was changing.

"I'll stay."

Naser's whisper sounded rushed and lacking in conviction, a Band-Aid slapped on a cut.

A gentle kiss came next. Mason kissed him back. Hard, forceful. Probably sloppy in the wrong way thanks to his salty tears, and like everything else he'd just done, too much.

Then he was headed down the stairs, feeling like a child and a fool. By the time he was backing out of his garage, whatever voices had spent years convincing him vodka was the solution to his problems had managed to convince him that Naser was lying and that the house would be empty when he came back.

The meeting was in a bland, brick Methodist church on a suburban side street. The windows were dark, save for the bright light coming from an open side door. He'd learned to recognize this signature—a huddle of smokers standing a State of California mandated distance from a welcoming rectangle of yellow. It meant twelve-step recovery was being spoken somewhere within.

Meeting folks had mentioned God and higher powers a bunch during the past week. Some of it had intrigued him; some of it had rankled. But when he saw Shirley pulling into the church parking lot ahead of him, he thought it was divine providence. She smiled as he approached, then she saw the expression on his face and hurriedly closed the distance.

It poured out in a frantic rush. The whole time, he sounded like a little boy trying to make his dad care about a minor playground injury. But Shirley stood close, listening to every word, and only when he was finished did he realize he'd just come out to her too.

"You did the right thing, coming to the meeting," she said.

"I know, but what if he leaves?"

"Then maybe he comes back later. Or another night." When she saw these answers failed to calm him, she gripped his elbow. "Look, Mason, this thing that you're feeling right now, this sense that if you like something you've got to lock it up and never let it go, that's alcoholism, sweetie. It twists the mind into this kind of binary thinking. All is lost or all is won. Everything's bliss or it's hell. It takes control of us through fear and tells us there's no in between. But the world's more complicated than our appetites. And right now, since you're not feeding the beast inside you, it's going to try to kick the shit out of you so you'll pour it a drink. Don't let it. It's fine to hear the crazy thoughts, but don't *listen* to them, sweetie. I want you to think of a name."

The sudden command at the end startled him. "A name?"

"For the voice in your head. For the one that tells you there's no point, that nothing will work out and why try and why leave the house, and why don't I just drink? Some people call it the committee. But I find it easier to think of as one person. That way, it's easier to tell it to shut the fuck up."

Mason was stumped. They'd gone from swimming in a swamp of feelings to trying to think of nicknames for self-destructive thoughts.

Shirley seemed to tire of the silence after a minute or two. "Mine's Ms. Cartwright. She was my third-grade teacher. Total bitch. Her mission in life was to destroy the self-esteem of anyone under nine. So when Ms. Cartwright comes at me first thing in the morning, telling me I'm too old and fat to try for anything I want, that I was wrong to divorce my abusive, shitbag of an ex-husband just because I've never been able to replace him, that I wasted my life on that damn soap opera when I should have been trying for an Oscar, I say, 'Thank you for playing, Ms. Cartwright. But I'm not a little girl anymore and I have things to get accomplished today. Also, I think the rumor you killed your husband is true, you nasty old witch.'"

Mason laughed and wiped tears away with the back of one hand. "Banjo."

"Like the instrument?"

"Like our neighbor's dog when I was little. Mean little dude. Barked all the time. Used to chase me whenever he got loose. And that's what this feels like. Somebody barking at me in my head."

"Banjo it is then." Shirley bent forward and pecked him on the cheek. "Don't listen to Banjo. He's just a dog. Dogs are great. But we don't take life advice from them. All they do is eat and sniff things. I'll let them boss me around when they can engage in witty conversations about good books."

He laughed, nodding.

Shirley patted him on the shoulder. "You're a sweet boy, Mason. You've spent your whole life trying to cover it up, and untangling that's going to be your story. But you are. I need to warn you right here, right now. People like us can turn other people into vodka. They deserve more, and so do we. So I'm glad you're here."

Had she just accused him of using Naser like a drug? He'd need some time to process that one. Luckily, he had some. An hour, at least, during which he'd try his best to listen to the speaker and the shares, while fighting worries that Naser was already headed home.

*Fighting Banjo.*

She looped one arm through his and walked them toward the side door.

Before he could respond, they'd stepped inside the corridor, where several eager, hungry sober alcoholics moved toward the meeting room's door when they saw the tray of Saran wrapped cookies Mason carried. Apparently, some folks were more than happy to live the life of a dog.

On the way home, Mason resigned himself to the idea he'd be returning to an empty house. Had already started scripting the apology texts he'd send Naser, all with the aim of getting him to come back another day, and to come again in his bed. Or maybe multiple rooms this time.

But the fact was, Mason's breakdown had been too much, too intense. He'd overloaded the guy. Or worse, Naser had gotten all he wanted out of him, and that was that. Three hours of office work that edged on manual labor and an orgasm loud enough to scare seagulls.

And if that's how Naser wanted his amends, there was little Mason could say about it.

Then he pulled through the guard gate to his street and saw the guy's white Volvo still parked across from Mason's garage. His first deep breath in hours made him sag.

Curled up on one of the big white sofas in the living room, Naser dozed in the television's flicker as the happy chatter of a home renovation show filled the house.

*Here.*

A single word, swelling inside of Mason because it meant so many other things. Things like hope.

He hadn't left, but also he was *here,* after a decade's worth of distance and separation during which he'd rarely left Mason's thoughts. And dreams.

He wanted to pull him into his arms and devour him with passionate kisses, but Shirley's caution about not using people as vodka whispered to him. Gently, Mason settled into the sofa a few feet away, then lifted Naser's bare feet onto his lap. Naser stirred, dark eyelashes fluttering. Mason watched him. Once his heart rate had slowed and the adrenaline released by unreasonable panic dissolved into something that felt less terrifyingly potent, he ran one finger lightly along the ball of Naser's bare foot, hoping to rouse him with a teasing reminder of their session a few hours earlier.

It worked. Naser laughed gently and shifted. When his eyes opened, he looked drowsy and content, not frightened and concerned like he'd been when Mason had blubbered in front of him like some pussy.

*I'm not a pussy, Banjo. Shut up. You're a bad dog.*

"Hey," Naser whispered.

"Hey, there."

"How was your meeting? Oh, wait. You can't say. Sorry."

"I can say it was good."

"Good."

Mason kept running his finger up and down the ball of Naser's foot, and while Naser was smiling, his eyes weren't exactly rolling back in his head the way they'd done during their bedroom session. "This does nothing for you right now, does it?"

Naser pouted and shook his head.

"So it's a one-way foot fetish?" Mason asked.

"Afraid so."

"That seems unfair. For you, I mean."

"Sometimes it's better to give than to receive." Mason raised an eyebrow, wondering if Naser was referring to penetrative acts. "Not *all* the time," he added with a wicked smile.

"I'm glad you stayed."

And Naser didn't say *Of course* or *I'd never leave after sex like that* or *Don't be ridiculous,* which said to Mason that he'd considered making a run for it the second Mason drove off.

Mason brought Naser's foot to his lips and kissed the arch gently.

"Mason?"

Was there actually a note of wariness in Naser's voice or was that just Banjo barking in his ear? Either way, Mason steeled himself, thinking maybe Naser had stayed only long enough so he could call it a night in person.

It took all the courage he had, but he turned and looked into Naser's eyes.

"I'm hungry," Naser said.

And Mason smiled, feeling like he'd been rescued from the executioner's blade.

# 20

It had taken all of Naser's strength not to bolt from Mason's house before the guy returned from his AA meeting.

Instead, he'd paced Mason's bedroom after the man drove off. Mason's tears had frightened him, and that was saying something, given the seriously scary shit the man had done in his presence over the years.

It wasn't the crying, he'd finally decided. It was the wild swing from sexual aggression to total vulnerability, the speed of it.

Drunk or sober, Mason Worther was a man in whom powerful emotions roiled with storm-like force.

Hadn't some of these feelings once knocked Naser into lockers and chased him down hallways?

Had it been wrong—dangerous even—to go fast and hard with someone like that as soon as the clothes came off?

Had he awakened a violent beast—a violent beast who was going to cry at the drop of a hat and rush off to AA meetings carrying trays full of cookies?

Maybe Naser's fears were off base. If violence was Mason's chosen mode of self-expression—drunk or sober—the guy would have reacted to the forgotten AA meeting with anger and balled fists, not sputtering tears. Naser was no therapist, but he'd always thought the people who resorted to abuse were trying to vault over their fear, only to get burned by its flames during the flight, so that they ended up punching and roaring when they landed on what they'd foolishly hoped would be the other side. Fists were raised, he'd always assumed, when tears were suppressed, not the other way around. In those final, startling moments before Mason had driven off, he'd suppressed nothing, it seemed.

Now the two of them were outside on the house's concrete beachfront patio, bathed in brisk ocean winds as Mason grilled. Smoke billowed across the house's ocean-facing glass walls before blowing south. On the patio's sofa, Naser snuggled deeper into the oversized UCLA sweater Mason had lent him. Far out in the night-dark sea, beyond the crashing waves, anchored ships sparkled like little jewels as the houses lining the beach threw a latticework of light across the powdery sand. A postcard perfect moment, if not for the heaviness of fatigue—the hangover left by sudden and powerful emotions. So many of them at once.

He studied Mason's movements as he worked. They seemed significant, and he wasn't sure why. The more he thought about it, the more he realized this was why most guys ran out after the dirty deed was done. Because if you stuck around and watched the man who'd just kneaded and stroked you into bliss do things like flip a steak or suck a bit of seasoning off his fingertip or bring a glass to his mouth, it drove home the intimacy and gravity of what he'd just done to you with those very hands, those very lips. A blissful feeling if the guy meant something to you; a little gross and weird if he didn't. Mason had always meant *something* to him, whether he liked it or not, and right now, Naser felt caught between the sense that he'd done something perfectly right—preordained, even—but also absolutely reckless.

"It's fine if you were going to leave," Mason said.

They'd been chatting mostly about the beach, the neighbors, how long Mason had lived on this idyllic stretch of sand—less than a year, it turned out—and then, after a silence that had grown pregnant with Naser's ruminations, Mason delivered this sudden right turn.

"It was a lot, I know." He worked the spatula under one giant, sizzling piece of meat, flipping it with a force he probably wanted to give his words. "Honestly, I kind of expected you to."

Sensing a gentle challenge, Naser rose, walked past the patio table Mason had already set for them both, and hovered next to the grill, safely out of the smoke plumes. "I couldn't come up with a good enough reason to."

"But you were looking for one." Mason glanced at him, then returned his attention to the grill.

"No. I found one, but it was shitty."

"Let me guess. Too intense, too fast."

"Not really."

"Oh, so it was worse, then." Mason's smile seemed forced.

"You stopped being a fantasy."

Mason worked the spatula under the steaks to make sure they weren't sticking, which was clear after the first few seconds of effort. He kept doing it anyway, which told Naser he was trying to distract himself. The answer had stung him. "So that's why you wanted to jet, or that's why you're still here?"

"A little of both, maybe." Naser took a long swallow of sparkling water, wishing it were something stronger. Knowing it shouldn't be.

"Interesting."

"One minute you were groveling and trying to earn my forgiveness. The next you were this incredible sex god and then, suddenly, you were…"

"Crazy."

"Emotional."

"A mess."

"Honest. I stayed because you were honest."

"I'm still Messy Mason, I guess," he said. "Probably will be for a while." A note of warning there, Naser could tell.

"The meetings will help, right?"

"Oh, I know they'll help. But the way everybody talks about it, it's slow. One day at a time. Basically, you start acting like the person you want to be, little by little, and your thoughts and feelings follow."

"Sounds like cognitive behavioral therapy."

Mason nodded. "I wouldn't know. I mean, along the way you talk about the real shit, the dark shit, with people you can trust. People who feel the things you do. But they keep saying it like this." He paused his work on the grill, as if he was summoning his next words with the raised spatula. "I can't *think* my way into right actions, but I can *act* my way into right thinking." He shrugged. "It feels phony at first, but it's like you turn yourself into the kind of person you can feel good about at the end of the day. You start with not taking the drink no matter what. Then, when the good feeling spreads, you start doing the opposite of what you used to do in other areas too. Contrary action, they call it."

"Interesting." Naser sipped his drink.

"Bringing you here, that was about being the person I want to be."

"And everything we did once I got here?"

"*Everything* we did once you got here." Mason hooked the waistband of Naser's shorts with one finger, drew him close, and curved his non-grilling arm around Naser's shoulders. Save for Mason's foot teasing on the sofa, they'd been nervously distant since he got home. Now, wilting into the man's bulk felt like a delicious return to his natural state. A natural state a few hours old.

"Spend the night." When Naser hesitated, Mason spoke again. "Too soon?"

Naser shook his head before realizing Mason couldn't see it. "Not too soon."

"But?"

"There's something I need to tell you first."

Only once the words were out of his mouth did he realize there were really two somethings, but the second was pounding against the other side of a door he'd prefer to keep locked. It was less immediate, and in the end, it wasn't about Mason. If whatever this was kept going, if one night became several, maybe he'd unlock that door. But not now.

"Let me guess. You snore?" Mason asked.

"No, amazingly. It runs in the family, but with me, it skipped a generation."

"You're married to a nice guy from West Hollywood?"

"Very much not so. Never even had a really serious boyfriend."

"Phew, then. So what's this terrible thing you've got to tell me?"

"So Friday night, you left your phone with me at the hotel. And you gave me the code because you wanted me to call you an Uber, and then Fareena came and whisked you off Fareena-style."

"Immediately and on her own schedule, you mean."

"Correct. And there I was, with your phone."

"Which you brought back."

"Yes, but…"

"*But?* Ooo, this is getting good."

"I kind of went through it a little first."

Mason seemed nonplussed. When it came to Naser, maybe he thought he didn't have many secrets left. "A little, huh?"

"You see, I was… Well, I was going to try to get you back for the Coach Harris email. Maybe send a…" Just the thought of Chadwick's name brought him dangerously close to the second thing he wasn't ready to discuss. "You know, embarrass you with a text or an email pretending to be you. But I couldn't."

"Crafty. What changed your mind?"

"Oh, I don't know." He sighed.

"Yeah, I think you do."

Naser turned into their half embrace, forcing the guy to set his spatula down to one side of the grill and stare down at him. "I saw texts from your dad."

Mason's half smile flickered, turned into something that looked more like a wince. A secret had been exposed, after all, or maybe he always reacted to the mere mention of his dad's name like it was a splash of cold water in the face.

"They were mean."

"My dad's a tough customer. That's for sure."

Naser told himself to hold his tongue. He failed. "Your dad's mean, Mason. And he's a homophobe."

Mason didn't drop his arm from Naser's shoulders, and he didn't look away, but Naser could feel the tension coursing through every inch of the man's body, and it made Naser's heart race for the wrong reasons.

"All right, well, I've only been at this whole cleaning up my life thing a week, so maybe give me some time before I work on my relationship with the only family I've got."

"I'm sorry. That's not why I said it. I'm not trying to pressure you. I'm just...has he always been like that? I mean, was he like that when we were in high school?"

Mason nodded. "Pretty much, yeah."

"So if that's how you were being treated at home, maybe it's no wonder why you were..."

Silence now except for the sputtering of the grill and the pounding surf.

He'd gone too far. Another few moments and Mason would ask him to leave, which would be epically unfair given his earlier tears and the fact that Naser had stuck around. And a bad sign that, like Naser's foot fetish, authenticity was a one-way street in Mason Worther's new and improving life. Or it would mean Naser, once again, had phrased his concern for another person in a sweeping manner that gathered up too many sharp judgments along the way—which is what his sister accused him of weekly.

"He never raised a fist to me," Mason finally said. "Never spanked me when I was a kid. Never touched me, really. But I guess that's why I always put up with it. Because I was afraid if I didn't, the fist was next."

"I'm pretty sure you could take him now."

Mason's laugh was a quiet little huff. "And where would that leave us? We're the only family the other's got. Apparently his dad was a real son of a bitch. Died when he was young. I think he *did* get hit a bunch. He doesn't want to talk about it. But every now and then he'll say, *You should feel lucky I'm not your grandfather.* Never met the guy so I can't say. Steaks are ready." The announcement at the end sounded deliberately abrupt, a rushed attempt to close off this painful line of inquiry.

Even though he didn't want to, Naser withdrew, sat in an empty chair, and watched Mason's every move as the man headed back inside to fetch the vegetables he'd stir-fried earlier then set to warm in the electric wok on the kitchen counter.

A few minutes later, they were eating, the only sounds between them the clinks of silverware and ocean waves.

"And your mom?" Naser finally asked. "Is she in the picture?"

"Try Greece. Or Dubai. Last text I got, I think she was in Rome. She's always cruising the world with the boyfriend of the moment. They were only together for a hot minute. As long as it took them to figure out I was too much pressure on a Vegas wedding that already wasn't working. My mothers were nannies and housekeepers. And then later, my friends' moms."

Naser bit back a comment about how he hoped Chadwick Brody's mother wasn't evil like her son.

Things got quiet.

Naser wanted to pretend it was a relaxed silence, a comfortable one, but it wasn't.

The topic of Pete Worther had plunged Mason into deep, dark reflection.

When he was done, Mason leaned back from his plate and suppressed a belch, and Naser was surprised to find no judgment or coldness in his eyes. And something about this casual moment seemed more momentous than the other things they'd done—the two of them sitting together on this intimate patio that felt like it was perched at the edge of the world. How was this possible? How was this his life? How had they become these people, these men? The answer seemed to lie in the fact that they'd always been these people deep down, and the hands of fate had decided to start jostling them loose.

"It was too far, wasn't it?" Naser finally asked.

"Searching my phone?"

"What I said about your dad."

"I made your life a living hell for three years. I'm not sure I'm in a place to start demanding apologies yet."

"Okay, let's not go crazy. My life wasn't a *living hell* back then."

Mason took a slug of sparkling water, as if Naser's refusal to accept the assessment was a challenge he had no choice but to meet. "Fine. I took the way I felt about you and turned it into something wrong. Something hurtful. How's that?"

It was a description so perfect, Naser wasn't sure what to say. He could only nod.

Mason rose, moved to him, and extended one hand. "Let's walk. On the beach."

Naser looked out at the dark expanse of sand and thought, *This is the part where he drowns me and I end up on* Dateline.

He shook off thoughts of Connor and Logan giving tearful on-camera interviews to Andrea Canning, kicked off his shoes, then peeled off his socks, one after the other, and the next thing he knew, Mason had taken his hand again. The cold, soft sand suckled his bare feet as they walked away from the house's blaze of light. The beach felt like it belonged to them.

"Maybe we even the scales a bit, though," Mason said.

"How's that?"

"Share one uncomfortable fact with me about your dad."

"Well, he's been dead for about thirteen years, so there's that."

"Oh, man. I had no idea. I'm sorry, Nas."

"Heart attack. Happened my freshman year. It's why I transferred to Laguna Mesa. My mom had to drive me to school, and Pari was already up in LA at Otis College of Art and Design, so she needed me somewhere closer to the hospital where she worked."

"Don't sell yourself short. You were also wicked smart, and Laguna Mesa's hard as hell to get into. Unless you buy your way in like my dad did me."

"You were plenty smart. You were just trying to hide it."

"Second time I've heard that tonight."

"Oh, yeah?"

"Sweet, actually. My friend, from the meeting, she told me I was a sweet boy, but I've worked all my life to cover it up. Anyway, we're talking about you."

Being jealous of a woman he didn't know for calling Mason a sweet boy was a reaction so ridiculous he had no choice but to turn his face to the sea so Mason wouldn't see a trace of it in his expression. He stared out at the night-dark ocean then closed his eyes against the wind, hoping it might sand off some of the hard edges of his past.

"I never got the chance to come out to my dad. I'm not sure he could see it. If he did, he ignored it. I mean, I felt loved. I felt like I mattered to him, but one night when I was twelve…" He closed his eyes and saw the same glittering chandeliers that had haunted him the night of his sister's event, saw the jeweled walls of the mirrored mosque rising above him as they never had in real life. Only in pictures he'd enlarged in his mind. In his daydreams. In his fantasies of what could have been. He and his dad, traveling Iran together. The missing pieces of the puzzle that was his family sliding into place. Assembled in full, if not exactly healed.

But too much of that history—of his family, of Iran—seemed tangled up in one story, one confession, and he wasn't sure where to begin.

"Hey," Mason said softly. "It's fine if you don't want to, Nas. We can talk about somet—"

"One night when I was like twelve, my dad talked about the idea of the family making a trip back to Iran, and my mother heard him and she got this look on her face and called him into the kitchen. I overheard her saying they could never bring me because of the way I talked, the way I walked. I was twelve, but already I was too gay to meet the rest of the family without bringing shame down on everyone." Naser brought his sparkling water to his mouth, but he couldn't bring himself to take a sip. "He died without ever going back."

"They were protecting you," Mason finally said.

"Maybe. But so many things come between the diaspora and the country they knew, the country they loved. I've never really been able to get over the fact that I was their barrier to reentry."

"Nas." He pulled him close, as if whatever tone he heard in Naser's voice had hurt him deeply. "Nas, no."

"I mean, I was twelve. Did they really think the family would have run screaming from me because I wasn't ready to throw a football?"

"Look, I'm no foreign policy expert, but did your parents leave because of the revolution in '79?"

"Oh, yeah."

"It kinda sounds like you're blaming yourself for world events here. You weren't the thing standing between your parents and Iran. The ayatollah was."

It was a good point. One Connor had made various times whenever Naser showed the wound.

Never in all his life had he expected to hear it out of Mason Worther's mouth.

"Too much?"

Naser brought him close by one hand, resting his head against his chest. "More like just perfect."

They were two hours into a home renovation show marathon when Mason realized this was another first for him—a man he'd slept with staying in his home hours after they'd had sex. No scurrying out the door as soon as the deed was done, no false promises of another hook-up to speed the guy's departure along. Instead, said guy was snuggled up to him on the sofa while they occasionally blurted judgmental comments about the cabinet selections being made by the people on television.

"I feel like every episode of this show turns into this woman giving a lecture on the virtues of putting a brass hood in the kitchen," Naser finally said.

"True, but she seems like she'd be fun at parties," Mason answered.

Soon after, Mason was slipping in and out of consciousness, occasionally getting lost in strange little dreams that played with his sense of time. But in each one, Naser's warmth and weight stayed steady. Finally, he was roused by the gentle caress of the man's fingers and found himself staring right into his eyes, which were inches away. "Someone's sleepy," Naser whispered.

Mason stood up too fast, head spinning from drowsiness, only one eye open against the weight of a coming food coma. He put out a hand and Naser took it, and the next thing he knew, they were in the bedroom, stripping down to their briefs, sliding into his bed from opposite sides.

*Turning in for the night with another man next to me. Sober. So many firsts...*

A few seconds later, they were spooning.

His sleep was deep and dreamless. For a while. Then his eyes popped open on a dark bedroom. The clock on the nightstand told him it was only 3:46 a.m. He thought maybe a bad dream had roused him, but he couldn't remember any, and Naser was still next to him. But one word was on his mind, on the tip of his tongue, even though he'd never say it aloud again.

*Prancer.*

Moonlight spilled through the open curtains, falling in a soft, white line across Naser's upturned shoulder. Their entwined bodies had heated things up under the covers, and one of them had pushed the top sheet and comforter down far enough to reveal Naser's hip. He traced fingers along the edge of Naser's briefs, tempted to draw them down, rouse him. Stroke him, suck him. Bite him. But the sight of his hip inspired memories of the sassy, swaying walk it had always played part in back in high school.

*Prancer.*

Who'd thought up the nickname? He couldn't remember, just remembered that every time he spoke it, his unwanted desire for Naser contorted into something that had made him feel safe even as it wounded the man lying next to him now.

And earlier that night, when Naser had confided in him about the reason his mother thought she couldn't take her young gay son to Iran, she'd cited that walk as one of them. The one that had earned him their shitty brand.

The scope of the nickname's insult hit Mason all at once, dropping something that felt like a big, cold rock in the middle of his stomach. Heavy, indigestible. His fingers froze. Suddenly, it felt like he had no right to touch Naser at all, no right to enjoy the sight of his nearly naked body.

He could feel the full injustice of it for the first time, the way words you intend to wound only on the surface strike deeper than you realize, sending shockwaves beyond the campus of Laguna Mesa, into Naser's home, his family, his father's memories of the country that was torn from him. Like throwing a rock through one window only to watch it crash through five more you didn't realize were stacked up right behind it.

He fought the urge to wake Naser up right there, spill out this realization on a tide of guilty tears. But who would that serve?

He'd just be unburdening himself and disturbing Naser's peaceful sleep.

Instead, what he needed to do was accept the magnitude of what he'd done, make that acceptance a part of the person he was becoming. Remind himself that he hadn't just been insulting a guy who made him feel feelings he hadn't liked at that time—he'd been injuring a guy who was struggling to find a place in his family, his culture, the world.

If this is what accountability and self-awareness felt like, no wonder so many people ran screaming from it.

And yeah, it would be easy to blame his dad for his behavior back then. As much as he'd like to, it felt like a cheat. That's why he'd gradually changed the subject when Naser brought it up. Maybe he should come clean about that. To Naser. As soon as he was awake.

The heaviness didn't leave his chest, but sleep finally returned.

He woke to a sun-filled bedroom and Naser's fingers gently stroking his chest, and he knew, for the first time in a while, what perfect contentment felt like. Then Naser bit down gently on one of his nipples and sucked hard enough to make Mason gasp.

"Sorry. I've wanted to do that since last Friday."

"Don't apologize. Just give the other one some love next time."

"Deal." Naser lifted his head from Mason's chest and smiled—boyish, carefree, and bright-eyed. It felt like the first time he'd seen the man's face free of the intensity of worry. "I like music in the mornings. Is that cool?"

"I'm open."

"But my phone's downstairs." Naser pouted.

"All right, well, mine's right there."

"Seriously? I'm going to be allowed phone access after what I admitted to last night?"

"iTunes access. How about that?"

"Deal."

Still under the covers, Naser took his time wriggling across Mason's body, an act that involved him gripping and caressing Mason's thighs in ways that caused a hungry stirring in his balls. Once he'd reached his destination, Naser picked up Mason's phone and gave him a questioning look.

"Go ahead. I'm sure you remember the code."

Naser bit his bottom lip, tapped the code in, and started swiping through Mason's playlists. A few seconds later, he looked up at Mason again, his brow furrowed. "You have a prom playlist?"

"I loved prom. You know, except for the part where…"

The heavy memory settled over them both.

*Kiss from a Rose* had been the theme, the décor a sparkling enchanted garden that had filled an entire ballroom at the Disneyland Hotel. In the weeks leading up to the dance, all three of them had pissed off the closest thing they had to regular girlfriends, so the three golden boys of Laguna Mesa had decided to go stag, with plans to get wasted and hit up a strip club after. They'd gotten a jump on the getting wasted part thanks to

Chadwick's flask.

Mason hadn't expected Naser to show, but he looked for him anyway and soon spotted him in similar circumstances. Dateless, the third wheel to his math club buddy Kenny Yang and Kenny's girlfriend, Jessie, both of whom had been accepted early to Harvard. He'd been checking the time on his phone so often, Mason wondered if his family had forced him to attend the dance for at least an hour and he was counting down the minutes until he could jet.

Then Naser had gotten up to leave, and Mason, emboldened by several swallows of Stoli and the fact that his buddies were already too buzzed to know what he was doing, gathered the courage to follow Naser out—alone.

"You followed me out. You never used to come for me alone. What were you after?"

"I wasn't coming for you, but I…" Mason's hungry smile filled the awkward silence.

Naser cocked his head to one side, still holding Mason's phone in his hands. "You were *not* actually going to try to hook up with me at prom."

"I was open to all possibilities."

"You were wasted. I saw the flask."

"We were about to graduate. I didn't know if I'd ever see you again. Freedom was on the horizon. I don't know. Everything seemed possible."

"Also, you were wasted."

"True. But you sure as hell shut me down."

Naser averted his eyes, looking sheepish and chastened. On prom night he'd done anything but. As soon as Mason had called out the words, "Hey, Nas," Naser had whirled, jaw tense, eyes blazing from a blend of anger and fear set to boil by the sound of Mason's voice. And Mason realized immediately the injuries they'd inflicted upon the guy couldn't be healed in a moment, not with a single kiss, or even several. That he'd been an idiot to think the heady mix of booze, sparkling décor, and their imminent graduation could offer up a special moment on par with the love songs being played in the ballroom they'd both left.

"I can't even remember what I said," Naser muttered.

"I do. You said, *Go fuck yourself, Mason Worther.*"

Naser flinched. "Sorry. But you can't blame me for thinking it was going to be some kind of Carrie White pig's blood situation."

"I can't, and you don't need to apologize." Mason caressed the side of Naser's face with his knuckles. "But that's not what it would have been."

"What would it have been?"

"I don't know, but for a moment, I was willing to find out."

Naser looked to the screen of Mason's phone. "Just for a moment, though. So, it's probably better we didn't do anything if it was just going to be...you know, a moment."

Mason could feel it in his gut—Naser wasn't talking about the past, he was talking about the present.

"Yeah," Mason said. "So it's a good thing we waited until it could be more than that."

Naser's eyes flashed to his—desire and expectation, without any of the reserve or hesitations of the day before, the years before.

"Are you asking me to go steady, Mason?"

"Something like that, I guess."

Naser nodded as if it were little more than a polite request, but the way he moistened his lips as he made a show of scrolling through Mason's prom playlist suggested he was trying not to giggle. "I will consider it, for sure."

"Okay, well, maybe you shouldn't leave my house until you've made up your mind."

"Are you threatening to hold me prisoner?"

"Only if that's your kink too."

"Depends on the restraints."

"Take your pick. My designer filled this house with stupid trendy shit I can't stand. I wouldn't mind getting your cum all over most of it."

Naser slapped him playfully on the chest, then returned his attention to Mason's playlist. "*Bed of Roses* by Bon Jovi. This wasn't our prom song."

"It should have been!"

"Wow. Clearly I've touched an open wound."

"Well, I was friends with Katie Kramer, who was on the prom committee, and she was totally down, but then she told me the faculty complained because there was a line in it about a vodka bottle, so they had to go with that stupid Seal song."

"*Kiss from a Rose* is a great song."

"It's no *Bed of Roses,* okay?"

Naser rolled his eyes. "Whatever, white boy."

"Anyway, later I found out Katie was lying. She thought the song was too retro and the theme wasn't nineties, but she didn't want to say it to my face. Traitor."

"And you were too much of a big manly man to actually serve on the prom committee yourself, where you could have had some sway."

"True, but…"

Before Mason could gather his response, Naser had hit play, and suddenly his favorite Bon Jovi song was coming through the speakers set inside the bedroom's walls.

"We going to have our own prom?" Mason asked.

"Sure." Naser grinned.

"We gonna slow dance?"

"Maybe. But first…"

The next thing he knew, Naser's head had disappeared under the covers, and Mason's briefs had been tugged down over his crotch in a single, hungry jerk. Bliss coated his body as Naser went to work with more languid patience than he'd had the night before, slowly drawing the blanket down as he suckled and stroked. The song surged around them, the kind of melodic, soaring hair band ballad that opened up big, weepy parts of Mason's soul he'd too often kept locked. When he went to grip Naser's head encouragingly, the man pressed Mason's hands to the side of the bed—he planned to work Mason to the edge on his own time, at his own pace.

And Mason, having forgotten about slow dancing altogether, couldn't complain.

# 21

"Who's Mason Worther?" Pari asked.

No questions about the deal she'd just read over.

*Had* she read it over?

Naser had emailed her a scan a few minutes before calling, making it clear nothing was definite until she signed and that she shouldn't feel obligated if she didn't like the terms. Apparently, his sister had gone right to the signature page as he'd recited the agreement's broad strokes.

He was struggling to answer her question as surgically as possible when a burst of laughter came from the other side of his closed and locked office door. After giving them a tour of the grounds, Jonas had thoroughly charmed the representatives of a writer's association that wanted to have their annual conference at Sapphire Cove next year. Naser had hoped for a similar level of excitement from his sister. So far, she sounded tight-lipped and wary.

"Someone I went to high school with. He's done well for himself."

*If that version of the story was any more surface level, it would be a rug.* He wasn't being dishonest, he told himself. Just minimalist.

"Didn't you hate high school?" she asked.

"I wouldn't repeat the experience if given the opportunity, no."

Pari grunted.

*That was close,* Naser thought.

"And you're sure this guy's good for it?" She sounded distracted, like she was reading.

"I've seen proof of funds."

On the other end of the line, Pari flipped pages. "A two percent rate of return? Is he crazy?"

"Not quite, no."

"This deal is…amazing. Did he write this up?"

"No, I did. But he agreed. As you can see from his signature."

"You did this for *me*?"

"I did."

Naser prepared himself for an uncharacteristic show of gratitude. His sister rarely thanked him for anything. How would he respond? It seemed like a challenge—a welcome one.

"All so you wouldn't have to hear Maman and I scream at each other."

A challenge for another day, apparently.

"That's one way of putting it," Naser said.

There was a long silence. Had she seen something in the deal she didn't like? How was that possible? It was beyond lopsided and entirely in her favor.

"Pari?"

"*Merci*, Naser-*joon*," she whispered.

And then she hung up.

He'd heard a catch in her voice before the line went dead.

She'd hung up on him because she'd been about to cry.

Had she been embarrassed to accept a bailout by way of her little brother?

There was a loud and familiar knock on his office door.

"Shit," he whispered.

The knob rattled against the lock.

Knowing he had no other choice, Naser opened the door. "Are you avoiding me?" Connor wailed once he'd thrown his arms around him.

"Never," Naser lied. He'd been avoiding Connor all morning.

To his hotel-branded blazer and white dress shirt, Sapphire Cove's general manager had added a bright blue tie, a rare occurrence. Together with the excessive amount of product that had darkened his hair from its usual sunny blond, it was a sign he had a meeting later that day with the manager of the trust that owned Sapphire Cove, an event which always put him a little on edge.

"How did everything go?" Connor asked.

"With what?"

"Your sister's event, silly."

"Oh, it was fine. Everything's fine. She's fine. We're fine."

Connor frowned. "That can't be true. You and Pari are never fine."

"She violated her contract a little, but I let Jonas take the lead on it."

"That's probably for the best. He hasn't said anything to me, so I'm sure it's no big deal. You want to have lunch later?"

Naser tried to swallow and failed. "I have plans, actually," he managed.

"Oh, with who? Jonas? Oh, please say it's with Jonas." Connor dropped his voice to a whisper. "It would be so cute if you guys hooked up."

Naser gently shut the door behind Connor. "Um, first of all, Jonas and I can have lunch together without hooking up, and second of all, it wouldn't be cute at all if we did because we work across the hall from each other and we're both wound like tops."

"Well, not those kinds of tops. In your case, anyway."

"Is this an appropriate workplace conversation?" Naser snapped.

Connor took a step back, one blond eyebrow raised. "Well! Someone is very much an employee today and not a best friend."

He felt terrible. Connor was right. They chatted about boy stuff all the time at work, just not in mixed company. But Naser needed another day or two to figure out a way to tell Connor he'd hooked up with one of his old bullies from high school. Right now, he was too busy sleeping with his old bully from high school. So what he needed was out of this conversation and quick.

"Look, I just…we have some catching up to do, but I've got a lot on my mind right now. I'm helping my sister with some things, and my mom too. That's who I'm having lunch with. My mom."

"Your mom's a workaholic who hasn't left the hospital for lunch in twenty years."

"Well, that should tell you how bad it is."

"Okay, give her my love and tell her I hope it works out, and maybe work in the fact that I didn't convert you to homosexuality when we were in college."

"She only said that once, and she'd had wine."

Connor nodded. "Uh huh. Enjoy your lunch, Nas."

Naser checked the time on his phone.

He wasn't having lunch with his mother. He was having lunch with Mason, and he was supposed to meet him in twenty minutes.

# 22

There was something both exhilarating and terrifying about being in his father's presence so soon after waking up in Naser's arms. Like it was the ultimate act of defiance. As if, even though several hours and a long, hot shower separated Mason from the moment he'd shared a goodbye kiss with the man who'd made it hard to get out of bed that morning, Pete Worther might detect the scent of another man on Mason's body.

Save for the hour and a half on Sunday when Mason had stepped out to attend his AA meeting, he and Naser hadn't spent any time apart since Saturday. Now the work week had begun. Their departures that morning as they'd headed off to their respective jobs had felt absurdly dramatic, like they were each leaving to start new semesters at different colleges, even though the plan was for Naser to return to Mason's house that evening after he fetched some more things from his condo. After they had lunch together that afternoon.

They'd yet to do the deed. The full mile. The thing he'd dreamed about doing to Naser for years. The thought filled him with delicious anticipation. But given their history, simply spending time in each other's company—affectionate, unhurried time—carried its own sustaining, erotic charge. He'd kissed plenty of men, but he'd never made out with one for hours. Long symphonies with crescendos and decrescendos, and snippets of giggly chatter thrown in.

Suddenly the design team members were rising from around the mahogany conference table and Mason was sitting up straighter, nodding and pretending he'd been impressed by their presentation of the first landscaping designs for Vistana's community pool. The meeting was ending the way so many at Worther Properties did, with employees scurrying from the room, grateful not to have incurred Pete Worther's wrath over some small infraction.

"You drunk?" Pete took a sip of the coffee his assistant had brought him before the meeting started. His salt and pepper hair glistened with product, his side part 1950s straight.

"No."

"Hung over?"

"Not in the slightest."

Unless Naser Kazemi's smell counted as a controlled substance. Maybe it should.

"Well, something's up. You usually love this faggoty gardening shit."

"Could you not?"

The words popped out before he could think twice. His tone combined irritation and injury, a combo he'd rarely, if ever, used on his dad.

The man sat back in his chair as if his son was growing another head in front of his eyes. "Not *what?*"

"That word. What's up with that word? Why do you use it all the time?"

"Gardening?"

"Faggot."

His dad flinched. Mason couldn't tell if it was from the anger in his tone or the fact that when the word was said back to him, it sounded like a denigrating accusation.

"I don't use it all the time."

*Let it go,* Mason thought. *You made your point.*

"Actually, you do," he said instead.

"Oh, okay, MSNBC. I'll be sure to tone it down so I don't offend anybody."

"Good, 'cause you could say it in front of the wrong person and they could take it the wrong way and—"

"I don't say it in front of the wrong people."

"That's right. You just say it in front of me. So maybe start thinking of me as the wrong person."

Jesus Christ. Was he about to come out to his dad? This was a mistake, going at the issue this quick and hard. But discussing the man's constant insults with Naser on Saturday had left Mason with a sense of embarrassment and shame. Knowing that someone he cared about had glimpsed Pete Worther's relentless, furious texts had made Mason feel strangely exposed. Which seemed kind of nuts. The one who should have been embarrassed by it was his dad.

Now the expression on his old man's face had more anger than shock. "Well, you're real high and mighty all of a sudden. It's been what, two years since I bailed you out of that mess in LA?"

Mason felt his cheeks bloom. "There was no *bail*. I didn't go to jail. I slept through a listing appointment."

"You slept through three, not one. You were at one of the top brokerages in Los Angeles. You were working two different listings priced over seventy million. The Conyers brothers both called me because they didn't want to fire you out of deference to my relationship with them. And I lied for you, remember? I said you'd had minor surgery and the medication messed with you. But thanks to me, you got a commission off that listing when it finally sold. Without you. I negotiated all that, remember?"

Of course, Mason remembered. He remembered the whole embarrassing incident so well his dad usually only had to reference it with a simple phrase, like *your mess in LA* or *your LA nightmare* to bring the blood roaring to Mason's cheeks. The fact that Pete Worther was going into excruciating detail now was proof of how angry Mason's comment had made him.

*Because it hadn't just been a comment. It had been a request, and Pete Worther doesn't take requests.*

"Then I set you up here where you've got a whole staff to clean up after your messes. So if you don't like my choice of words now and then...well, tough shit."

Mason opened his hands. It was better than following his instincts and saying something like *fine*. It wasn't fine. None of this was fine, and Mason didn't feel like pretending it was.

"You were kissing ass all over the office last week. That can only mean one of two things. One. You made some drunken mess out there that I'm going to have to clean up any minute now. Or two, you're getting ready to do something real stupid and you're already managing the fallout. Which is it, brainless?"

"Neither. I'm trying to make a positive contribution."

"Yeah, I know, why?"

"I'm getting sober."

Shock and something that looked like pain flashed in his father's expression. Mason was surprised by the combo. He'd expected a dismissal. This was something else. There was concern in there somewhere, but it couldn't work its way through the stone walls inside the man's soul. Then a frosty veil fell, and his dad looked down at the table as if he didn't want his son to see the look in his eyes. And for a second—a brief, fleeting second—his dad looked...what? Mason struggled to put a name to it. Happy? Eager? Hopeful?

"Getting?" his dad asked.

"It's been a week and some change."

Pete nodded. Mason couldn't tell if the figure impressed or disappointed him. "Yeah, well, I'll believe it when I see it."

"You are seeing it. Right now."

Pete studied him, angry mask softening into something that seemed more introspective, maybe a little puzzled. "Oh, okay. So *you* dealing with *your* shit means *I'm* going to have to talk differently? What? 'Cause you might get triggered and pour yourself a drink. Is that it?"

"The opposite, actually. I'm *not* going to pour myself a drink. And you're going to have to deal with what I say back when I don't."

Pete's mouth popped open. He sat back in his chair. His laugh seemed late to the party, and when it came, it sounded forced, a little breathless. "All right, then. Good. Sounds like fun. Anything'll be better than you rolling in here two hours late with one eye open, pretending like nobody notices when you close the door and sleep on the floor of your office."

"Yeah, we'll see." Mason got to his feet, collecting his file folders. "I'm meeting someone for lunch, and then I'm going to spin by Vistana. They were supposed to pour the slab for the guardhouse foundation this morning. I'll make sure everything went in okay."

His dad grunted and started scrolling through his calendar on his iPad. Mason doubted he was worried about his next appointment. The calendar routine seemed like it was for show.

Mason rose and headed for the door.

"How about pillow biter?" Mason turned and found his dad looking up from the iPad on his lap with a raised eyebrow. "You know," his father added, "instead of faggot? Kind of old school. But I don't know. Maybe it's trendy now. Like *queer.*"

When Mason started back toward the table, his father sat up straight suddenly, as if his quick, short advance was a show of aggression for which he was utterly unprepared. As if they were about to finally have the fist fight that had been brewing between them for years.

"Why are you so damn angry all the time? I know what my deal is. I'm an alcoholic. I've screwed things up. I'm trying to do better. I've accepted that. But you've gotten everything you've wanted in life and you always act like somebody just crapped on your shoes. So what's your excuse, *sir*?"

The mirth left his father's expression. The seconds seemed to turn to minutes as they stared at each other. For a brief, teasing second, Mason thought the man might lay down some truth, maybe even a little insight. Instead, he set his iPad on the table and leaned back in his chair, nostrils flaring.

"You know what," his dad finally said, "do whatever hand-holding, hippy-dippy bullshit you gotta do in your meetings or your therapy or however it is you're going to deal with this. But leave me out of it, son. I'm a grown-up."

Mason nodded and had one foot out the door.

"Mason?"

He turned, bracing for another blow.

"Good luck," his father said.

Mason studied him, trying to see if it was an insult or a genuine sentiment. It seemed like a toxic mix of both, so he nodded at his father without thanking him and got out of the office as soon as he could.

As much as he'd tried to hide it, Pete Worther had been knocked off balance by Mason's response, and that put a skip in Mason's step as he headed back to his office. It had felt good—damn good—taking those steps back toward the conference table that had made his father's eyes widen. Everything that had come out of his mouth after had been gravy.

Anger, it seemed, was as powerful a drug as any other.

Maybe that's why his dad used it so often.

# 23

When Mason texted him the directions to what looked like a desolate stretch of hills not too far from Naser's condo, Naser had anticipated either a picnic or an attempted murder. So when he saw the tall, blond, no longer drunk Viking walking through a dirt parking lot crowded with construction vehicles, carrying a wicker basket in both arms, he smiled as he slowed his Volvo to keep pace with him.

"Any of that for me?" Naser asked, powering his window down.

"Half of it, in fact." Mason transferred the basket to one arm and approached the car. Behind him, inland Orange County stretched east, a bright, mostly bone-white checkerboard beneath a dome of hard blue. The parking area wasn't for a lookout or a trailhead, he realized. It was for the construction site a little way uphill. There, the first shells of contemporary-looking homes were taking shape along asphalt streets that looked pitch black and brand new.

"So did you bring me out here to disappear me?" Naser asked.

"Only if you eat all the turkey wraps. Turkey's my favorite."

"They're all yours. I'd actually like to stay awake through the second half of the workday."

"Overrated." Mason did a quick dive through the window and gave Naser a hard, brief kiss on the lips. His eyes were hidden behind aviator-style sunglasses, but Naser was pretty sure they'd cut to the construction site uphill during their brief lip lock. A giant wooden sign proclaimed the property as *More Dream Homes on the Way from WORTHER PROPERTIES.* Behind it were the first makings of a guard gate entrance—lone columns of brown brick, still missing the metal gates that would probably close the gaps between them. The prospect that Mason's dad might be hanging out somewhere nearby sent chills through him—the wrong kind.

"Park and follow me," Mason said.

When Naser stepped from his parked Volvo, he looked for the Ferrari but saw the used Lexus Mason had driven to work that morning. When was the Ferrari coming back from the shop, he wondered? He followed the guy to a spot where he'd already laid out a blanket on a patch of dry grass.

As Naser carefully took a seat, there was a subtle woosh, and suddenly he was sitting in comfortable shade. Mason speared the umbrella's pole into the hard, packed dirt next to the blanket. "Don't worry. I already checked for snakes." He smiled like an explorer having just planted his flag on a newly discovered island. "They probably won't be out for another month or two. The bad ones, anyway." He sank to his knees.

"Wow. You really thought this through."

"I thought it might be a little too hot given we don't have ocean winds here. But it's pretty cool, right?"

"Very cool. I mean, I'm not the biggest outdoors person unless it's, like, *Sizdah Be-dar.*"

Mason removed two paper plates from inside the picnic basket and set about assembling their lunches. "And that would be?"

"The thirteenth day of Nowruz. Technically, it marks the end of the holiday, but it's when everybody gets together and picnics outside and talks smack about what everybody wore for all the other events."

"No offense, but what *is* Nowruz? I've asked Persian people over the years, and they get cagey on the subject."

"Cagey?"

"Oh, you know. They'll just compare it to other things. Like they'll say, 'Oh, it's like Persian New Year's, or Persian Christmas. Or Persian Nascar.'"

"*Nascar?*"

"Okay, I made that one up, but you know what I mean."

"There's no car racing involved."

"Sure, but what *is* involved?"

"Well, it's a new year's holiday that marks the first month on the Iranian solar calendar, but it's about new growth. New life. The first event is usually a gathering at somebody's house. Most Persians will set up something called a haft-sin table in their living room. It's got seven items on it, and in Persian, the name of each one starts with an S. Typically they all have something to do with rebirth and renewal."

"Nice."

"And then you eat dinner at four in the morning."

Mason stopped loading the plate in his hand. *"What?"*

"Okay, it's not *always* four in the morning, but you're supposed to gather and do something formal at the exact moment when the sun crosses the equator during the vernal equinox. Which means here in the US, it can be four in the morning. And not everyone eats dinner. Sometimes you just stand over the table and read Persian poetry at the exact moment the equinox happens. But my mom's a great cook, so usually there's a meal involved."

"That sounds intense."

"It's not really. You just have to schedule accordingly. And you're just eating. It's not like you finish it all off with a round of lawn bowling."

Mason went back to preparing a plate. "That's a shame. I haven't lawn bowled since I was a *wee bairn.*"

"You've lawn bowled?"

"No. I have no idea what you're even talking about. What's lawn bowling?"

"I don't know. I was just trying to say something that sounded like the worst idea ever on a full stomach at five in the morning after you've been up most of the night with your family. The point is, my mother's dinner is always casual and lovely, the food is amazing, and as long as my mother and sister don't end up screaming at each other, everyone has a great time. Then we spend the rest of the season paying visits to elders, but most of our family's elders are still in Iran, so my mother would take us to visit her older friends. The intense part is actually *chaharshanbe suri.*"

"What's that made with?" Mason handed him a plate with enough food on it to last him several days. Naser smiled and set it down on the blanket next to him.

"It's not a dish, handsome. It's fire jumping. It's a purification ceremony we do the last Wednesday before Nowruz."

"Cool. I didn't realize jumping over fires was a Muslim tradition."

Naser threw his hands over his heart as if he'd been speared and rolled to one side with dramatic moans. "Oh, and you were doing so well, white boy."

"What? Don't make fun of my Dutch ancestry."

"Yeah, the historical oppression of the *Dutch* really keeps me up nights."

Mason set down the plate he'd been preparing for himself. "All right, all right. What did I do wrong?"

"Nowruz is not a Muslim holiday. It's Zoroastrian, which is the more ancient religion the Persian Empire practiced prior to the Muslim Conquest. Fire is central to a lot of Zoroastrian religious observances. They believe it represents God's light or wisdom. And it's also the religion my sister is into because she thinks it's less homophobic, but she's not really sure and neither am I, and I don't care. It's fine. I'm just not religious."

"But you like Nowruz?"

"I *live* for Nowruz. It's so fun. It always feels…hopeful."

But now his memories of it felt tinged by his sister's accusation that he never let his mother get to know the real him—the *gay* him.

The lead-up, along with the celebrations themselves, entailed a flurry of activity, all of which he'd done side by side with his mother ever since his father's death. His mother took the spring-cleaning part very seriously, and throughout those hours of labor, he would match her step for step, lifting up furniture legs when he could, running out to buy extra vacuum bags, emptying dust pails and the trash so she could keep attacking already immaculate surfaces like a robot fueled by meth.

For years now, these things had seemed like bonding activities, but in light of Pari's recent indictment and his own case of clamp mouth when his mother asked him about Mason's drunken antics at Pari's event, he wondered if they were just a set of distractions he and his mother used to be near to each other without actually being close. It was easier not to discuss Naser's sexuality when you had little bonfires to assemble and hours of cleaning to do and pounds of braised beef to stew.

Naser took a bite to distract himself. "This is really good."

"Thanks. I got up early this morning and made it."

"Really?"

"No. I woke up with you, remember?"

"That's what I thought. Either way, it tastes great."

Mason raised an eyebrow and set about attacking his own plate. From the homesites just up the slope, construction noises echoed. Naser looked back to the parking area uphill from where they now sat in the comfortable shade. Aside from Mason's loaner Lexus, most of the vehicles were construction trucks and vans. "When's the Ferrari coming back from the shop?" Naser asked.

"It isn't." Mason took much time positioning his turkey wrap for his next bite.

"What happened to it?"

Mason took a healthy bite and chewed methodically. "I sold it," he finally said, licking mayonnaise off his fingers.

"When?"

"Last week."

"Why?" Naser asked.

"Meh, it was my drunk car. I needed a sober car. Fresh start, and all that."

But Mason was staring down the canyon as he slowly chewed. When he felt Naser staring at him, he swallowed and looked his way.

"Mason..."

He shrugged. "A new investment opportunity came along."

"Mason, you sold a Ferrari so you could invest in my sister's line?"

"I sold a Ferrari so I could spend three hours with you."

"It was a really nice car."

"Yeah. I'm sure it looked great like a beached whale out on the sand."

"You know what I mean."

Mason looked back at Naser, as if trying to gauge whether or not he was upset. Naser wasn't upset. He was moved.

"It was nicer waking up in bed with you this morning," Mason said with a smile that made Naser want to melt into his arms.

"I'd kiss you right now, but you have food on your face."

Mason grinned, then chewed his lower lip in a way that reminded Naser how good it felt to kiss Mason Worther. "With a construction crew right up the hill? Pretty kinky. You an exhibitionist too?"

"No, I'm not. Also, the idea of outdoor sex in general always sounds better than it is, so if that was part of today's plan, let's cancel that right off."

Mason shrugged. "Oh, I don't know. Outdoor sex can be fun."

"That's right. You don't know. Because you're not a woman and you've clearly never bottomed."

"Beach sex. What about beach sex?"

"Once again, you've never had a mix of sand and God knows what else up your naughty bits."

"That's what blankets are for."

"And the fact that you think that's enough to protect one's privates against the all-powerful force of beach sand further proves my argument."

"All right, tonight's festivities are off the menu then."

"I'll take you any way I can get you. Inside."

Mason gave him a cocky grin. "Actually, *inside* is exactly where I'd like to go with you."

Naser was surprised by the cascade of responses that ricocheted through him. A bolt of desire so powerful he wanted to pin Mason to the blanket right there. Then, right on its heels, fear that seemed so sudden and total it encased his entire body in something cold as metal.

The wildness of their Saturday night session had made for a complicated memory ever since. He felt partly responsible for having triggered Mason's breakdown, felt like their role play might have been too much, too soon. Their make-out sessions since had only occasionally resulted in nudity and orgasms, and then they were easy, relaxed. Mellow. A comedown, or a buildup to something bigger, he wasn't sure. The thought of accelerating their tempo again frightened him.

More specifically, the thought of letting Mason inside him returned him to that moment of frenzy in bed on Saturday when he'd felt a desire so potent it seemed capable of wiping away all good sense.

"Hey, no rush," Mason said.

Naser smiled, his thoughts forming a logjam.

"Eat up!" Mason said, then he reached over, gripped the back of Naser's neck, and gave him another hard peck on the lips. It was like the kiss he'd given him through the car window, and there was something Naser loved about it. A man learning how to show semipublic affection with another man. It was quick and confident—like he was trying to outrun his own doubt—but it was also strained in a way that reminded him this was all new. For both of them.

When they were done eating, Mason packed up the basket, the blanket, and the umbrella and carried them back to his car as Naser followed. Then he asked Naser to follow him to the construction site where he introduced him to the foreman and several members of the crew. The prospect of meeting the infamous Pete Worther put Naser's heart in his throat, but Mason's father wasn't among the introductions.

Mason listened and nodded while the guys gave him a long lecture on their plans for the guardhouse's foundation.

Naser stepped aside to check some work emails. When he looked up again, he saw Mason had drifted over to where a man and woman in matching dark green polo shirts were examining two rows of concrete planters that had been installed in a line leading from the first brick walls of the entrance gate to where the guardhouse would soon rise. On their shirts were logos for something Naser figured was a landscaping company. Mason seemed excited to see them both.

Odd, given there weren't any actual plants in view, just the empty receptables for them. After a while, Naser got concerned about making it back to work in time for his next meeting, so he gave Mason's sleeve a little tug.

"Oh, hey. Sorry, Nas. This here's Paula and her husband Jim. They're with Green Mountain, our landscapers for the project."

Naser shook their hands, and they gave him bright smiles.

"I'm trying to make a case for Douglas Iris in the planters, but they're coming down hard on the side of Canyon Liveforevers."

With no idea what either thing was, Naser just smiled.

"All drought tolerant, of course," Mason added quickly, as if Naser had been on the verge of filing a report with the water authority. "You have no idea what we're talking about, do you?"

"None."

Paula spoke next. "I know what you're saying about the color, Mason, but the shape of the succulents in these planters is going to have more of an impact as people drive up even if they don't rise as high."

"What about a mix of both?" Mason asked.

"Crowded," Paula answered with a wince.

Mason shook both of their hands. "All right, we should head out. Thanks, guys."

The landscapers both smiled and waved goodbye.

Mason started back toward their cars. "Those guys are really amazing. Dirty little secret of Southern California is it can be really hard to get good landscaping out here, when it comes to the fine tuning and the details. Honestly, I think it's 'cause everything here grows so quickly and easy, you usually find guys who just plant and then trim like hell once or twice a year. Finding a crew that's really artful about how they position and shape things over time..." When he noticed Naser's stunned look, he fell silent. "What?"

"You're into plants?"

"I'm *crazy* about plants."

"Seriously?"

They stopped at the tail end of Mason's Lexus. "Why do you say it like that?" he asked.

"Mason, there is not a leaf of green anywhere in your house."

He seemed so shocked by Naser's words, Naser was worried he'd accidentally insulted him.

For a while, they just stood there.

"Damn," he finally said. "You're right. I guess we'll have to plant some then."

Then came another one of those quick, hard kisses on the lips.

He was pretty sure some of the guys from the site must have seen, but Mason skipped back to his car as if he didn't care. Naser cared, but for all the right reasons.

The phrase *not a leaf of green* seemed to follow Mason around for the rest of the day.

An hour after lunch, Naser texted to say he'd be at Mason's house by six-thirty—with a surprise. Mason hoped the surprise was Naser on all fours, buck naked, with a gift bow on the back of his neck Mason could pull off with his teeth. But he hadn't told the guy about the secret key hidden in the little bed of crushed stone by the front door, so no point in getting his hopes up. As he headed home around five, Mason wondered if it was time to give Naser access.

If Chadwick could enter his house unannounced, why not the guy Mason had been slow-motion falling for since they were teenagers?

The interior of Mason's home seemed not just stark, but barren. Naser was right—impossible for anyone to believe the guy who lived here nursed a love of green things.

The house wasn't truly his. Maybe that's why he'd never personalized it.

Mason was bound for his laptop, planning to research plant types that could stand up to the salty ocean winds out on the patio, when there was a harsh knock on his front door.

It was way too early to be Naser. His next thought was *Chadwick*, and his breath caught.

He needed to move the key. Letting Chadwick have unrestricted access to his home right now was a terrible idea for a lot of reasons.

Mason checked the security camera over the front door and saw two handsome white guys he didn't recognize standing on the other side. Despite their comical size difference, their dark blue blazers seemed to match. More intrigued than frightened, Mason opened the door.

Both men stared back at him blankly. The shorter one had a cherubic face and big blue eyes. Along with a military bearing, the taller one had dark, heavy eyebrows that gave him an automatically menacing stare.

"Can I help you gentlemen?" Mason saw the gold logo on the lapel of the smaller guy's blazer—the logo for Sapphire Cove. "Oh my God. Is Nas okay?"

Both men seemed surprised by Mason's concern, then the blond one looked down at his jacket and shook his head. The hotel's logo, it seemed, had given him away. Did Sapphire Cove dispatch people to notify the loved ones and friends of their employees if they were injured? A bit much for a beach resort.

The little blond guy raised an eyebrow that said this wasn't a bereavement call. "We *think* he's okay, but that's part of why we're here. May we come in, Mr. Worther?" He brushed past Mason without waiting for a response. His large companion followed, eyes locked on Mason's with a look that said, *Stop us at your own peril, buddy.* Suddenly the three of them were standing awkwardly in Mason's kitchen as the little blond scanned their surroundings with a raised eyebrow and pursed lips. The bigger guy looked way more impressed.

"What do you mean you *think* Naser is okay?" Mason asked.

"Well, we understand you two have been spending some time together, and that has us intrigued. My name is Connor Harcourt, and this is my security director, Logan Murdoch."

The guy named Logan ran his finger along the kitchen island's marble waterfall edge. "This place is *sick*," he whispered.

"Babe, focus," Connor whispered back.

Logan turned and extended his hand to Mason. Mason was about to take it when Connor batted Logan's arm down.

"Do you always hit your security director?" Mason asked.

Connor pursed his lips. "Let's not be dramatic. That was more like a tap."

"Do you always call him *babe*?" Mason asked.

"He's also my fiancé. But if he doesn't stay on message, he will not stay my fiancé either."

"Sorry, this is just a really cool house," Logan muttered.

"Did Naser mention me at all?" Connor asked.

Mason nodded enthusiastically. "He did say his best friend was like a carbon copy of him, only mayonnaise-colored, entitled, and not great at math."

Logan sputtered with laughter.

Connor crossed his arms over his chest. "Look, I'm here for a very simple reason."

Mason opened his arms. "I'm all ears."

"I'm aware of the complicated history between you and Naser. So complicated, in fact, that my closest friend in the world saw fit to keep his lunchtime assignation with you a secret, so, please, be aware that if you do anything to hurt Naser Kazemi..." Connor paused for emphasis, took another step toward him. "Logan will kill you."

"Wait, what?" Logan muttered.

"He will. He's a trained killer."

Logan cleared his throat. "Veteran of the United States Marine Corps is more like it, but I do have extensive training. That said, I think the purpose of this visit is more to say..." Logan cleared his throat again, then met his fiancé's glare. "What's the purpose of this visit again, babe?"

Connor rolled his eyes. "To scare him. Great job, Staff Sergeant Murdoch."

"I'm terrified," Mason said, "promise. You guys want something to drink? I've got juice, juice, and more juice. And sparkling water. And Diet Coke. And then juice."

Logan closed in on the fridge alongside him. "Ever thought about adding sparkling water to the juice?"

"Damn. That's actually a great idea. Let's do it."

The refrigerator door jerked out of Mason's grip. Connor Harcourt had pushed it shut from the other side. Suddenly, he and Mason were eye to eye. "The point of this visit," Connor said softly, "is to let you know that Naser didn't have a lot of friends in high school, which means he didn't have a lot of people who had his back. Now he does. Got it?"

Despite his size, the guy had spunk. He also had a giant fiancé standing a few feet away, but Mason figured Connor Harcourt didn't suffer fools even when Logan Murdoch was nowhere around. Mason was no fool, and only a fool would consider pissing off the best friend of the guy he was trying to make things right with. A guy whose imminent arrival would be the best part of his day.

"Loud and clear," Mason said softly.

But Connor didn't move or break eye contact.

"I think the point's been made, babe," Logan finally said. "Let's have some juice."

"With bubbles," Mason added to try to lighten the mood.

It seemed like it might work, then he heard the front door open.

*This should be interesting,* Mason thought.

Naser knew something was wrong when he saw the front door was unlocked. Then he saw Connor and Logan standing in Mason's kitchen, and he thought the problem was in his head and that it was a massive stroke.

Had the stress of rushing through traffic to Mason's house brought it on?

He'd picked up a ton of food from Hatam, his favorite Persian restaurant in Orange County when it came to takeout, and he'd been desperate to get there before any of it got cold.

"Smells good," Logan said.

"What's happening right now?" Naser asked.

Mason gave him a wide-eyed grin and waggled his eyebrows as if to say he knew and didn't know but thought it would be exciting either way.

Connor stepped forward. "Since my best friend has suddenly decided to start keeping secrets from me, I decided he deserved a surprise of his own."

He was about to set the bags down when Mason stepped forward and carefully removed them from his arms. "Is this *my* surprise?" Mason asked gleefully.

"Yes, but Connor ruined it. Because he ruins everything."

"We're not staying. Don't worry," Connor said.

Naser glared at him. "I wasn't. Other room, please."

Logan pointed to his own chest. "Both of us?"

Naser turned his glare on Logan. "I'm going to assume you were just along for the ride?"

Logan nodded emphatically.

Mason set the bags onto the kitchen's island and took a big whiff of one that left him smiling like a delighted eight-year-old. "Is this Persian food?"

Naser smiled and nodded. "It is." He dropped his smile and pointed an accusing finger at Connor. "Other room, now."

Connor threw up his hands. "What *other room*? It's an open floor plan!"

Mason gave Connor a pat on the upper back. "I think he's talking about the half bath just inside the front door."

"I am." Naser pointed to it with an arm so stiff he could have balanced plates on it.

"Should I serve this?" Mason asked, lifting one of the containers of food from the bag.

"*No!* There is enough there for two people and two people only. Connor. Bathroom. Now."

Connor huffed and followed Naser a few paces to the tiny bathroom in question. Once they were sandwiched like sardines between a frosted green glass sink and a toilet that looked like an ivory box, Naser pulled the door shut and whirled.

"Have you lost your mind? This is boundaryless and crazy."

Connor raised a warning finger. "This is what happens when you lie to your best friend."

"You followed me to lunch?"

"Of course, I did. I could tell you were lying through your teeth, and then I realized it must have something to do with the party, so I went back and reviewed the footage, and I pulled the release from his cannonball into the pool incident, and there was his name in black and white. Mason Friggin' Worther? Seriously? Nas, come on. Some of the stories you tell about what you went through in high school still make me cry. You had it way worse than I ever did. Partly because of *him*. And now you're hooking up with him and bringing him Persian food."

"I'm sorry I lied to you."

Connor dropped his voice. "Is Mason Bleachers Guy?"

*Bleachers Guy.* How was it possible he'd come up with such an innocuous nickname for someone who'd hurt him so badly?

"No, no, no. That was someone else."

Naser's face felt hot. He was scanning the tiny bathroom for an escape hatch.

"Was he friends with Bleachers Guy?" Connor whispered.

"Yes, he was."

"Is he still?" Connor asked.

"It's complicated," Naser muttered.

"Does he know what Bleachers Guy did?"

"Okay, look. I'm sorry I lied to you. But Mason is turning over a new leaf. He's getting sober. He's trying to make up for who he's been in the past, and apparently…I an…duh, *this* is all part of that, I guess."

"So is *this* dating?" Connor asked.

"I don't know, okay? And as soon as I do, I will tell you what it is, and if I know what I'm doing. But until then… Rest assured. I *don't* know what I'm doing. I'm just going with it."

Connor sighed. "Well, if this has any sort of relationship potential at all, you should only have to do one thing, and that's be yourself. And I say this with love, Nas." He placed one hand over his heart to emphasize the point. "That is not always your strong suit."

"Seriously?"

"With love, Nas. And yes, seriously. You're the most important person in my life next to Logan, and you deserve someone who accepts you exactly as you are. And I'm not exaggerating when I say I will lose sleep tonight over the prospect that you might get treated less than you deserve by this guy just because he represents something complicated out of your past. A guy who might use that over you in ways he shouldn't."

"He's treating me like a prince. I barely know how to deal with it."

"You're buying him Persian food, which is a sign you're getting serious."

"Blondie, look. I'm sorry, but I just wanted a beat to figure all this out before I told you about it."

Connor nodded, but his eyes were moist. "Don't keep secrets from me just because I'm getting married. Logan is the love of my life, but you will *always* be my best friend. I'm sorry I invaded your privacy, but I got afraid."

"Of what?"

Connor's rounded chin quivered. "That you forgot how important you are to me."

"Oh, Blondie." Naser hugged him, hard. "It's not that at all. Don't worry. But I'm a big boy now, and you have to trust me about some things."

"True, but when you and I team up, we're an even bigger boy. We're almost six feet tall."

For a while, they hugged.

"Just ask, size queen," Naser finally whispered.

"Okay," Connor whispered, "how big is it?"

"I'm going to need a lot of Imodium. And maybe a bottle of wine."

"God bless us every one," Connor whispered, then patted Naser on the back.

When the two of them stepped out of the bathroom, Mason was giving Logan a tour of the living room and explaining the renovations with a lot of hand gestures.

"All right, babe," Connor barked. "Time to go."

Logan shook Mason's hand, then hurriedly set his drink down on the island as he rushed to join Connor.

"It was nice to meet you, Mason," Connor said.

"Stay longer next time," Mason said.

"And call first," Naser added.

Then Logan and Connor were gone, and Naser was standing inside the closed front door listening to their chatter as they departed.

Naser couldn't manage a deep breath until he heard what he thought was either Logan's truck or Connor's Mercedes. Whichever car they'd brought, they must have parked it outside the guard gate, maybe as far away as the public lot, and he'd cruised right past it on his way in.

From one of the counter stools, Mason watched Naser's every move with an amused smile on his face. "That was fun."

"One way of putting it." Trying—and failing—to steady his hands, Naser put all the cartons of food out on the counter, then he fetched plates and bowls from the cabinets. Three days in Mason's house and he already knew the kitchen like the back of his hand.

"You're embarrassed?"

"Mortified." Naser removed more utensils than he needed from the drawers in front of him, avoiding Mason's stare.

"Want to talk about it?"

"What did they say? Before I got here, I mean."

"Nothing I wouldn't expect them to given…our history." Mason was looking down at the little steeple he was unmaking and remaking with his fingers. "I guess it won't be the last, either."

"The last? What do you mean?" Naser's hands froze where he'd just removed a plastic lid from a carton of ghormeh sabzi. He knew exactly what Mason meant but didn't want to say it himself.

"You know…" Mason was struggling now. "If we keep doing this, I guess that won't be the last meeting that goes kind of like that."

They were already talking about meeting friends and family? This was all Connor's fault. Connor was the reason the words *Bleachers Guy* were still ringing in his ears. "Connor shouldn't have done that. I'm sorry."

"Don't worry. I'm not going to rush you into a sit-down with my dad."

Feeling his own smile like he might a plastic mask, Naser returned his attention to the food, started plating, and was about to launch into some distracting lecture on the intricacies of Persian cuisine when Mason rose and started toward him around the island. But he stopped short, worried, it seemed, about getting in the way of Naser's increasingly frenzied work. "You shouldn't be embarrassed."

"I'm not embarrassed."

*I'm afraid. Afraid the reality of your personal life will eventually destroy this blissful, lustful fantasy we've been living for seventy-two hours.*

"Nothing wrong with having protective friends," Mason said.

*Ah ha, an opening,* Naser thought. "What about your friends?" A thread of rice snaked along the counter in front of him. He must have dribbled it while ladling the stew into one of the serving bowls. He was about to clean it up when Mason suddenly did the job for him, with a paper towel he'd swiped in record time.

"What about them?" Mason's tightly coiled voice didn't match his generous, split-second act of assistance.

"Are they protective too?"

Mason tossed the waded-up paper towel into the trash. "Why would they need to be? I don't need protecting. I need improving, remember?"

"Did I say that? I didn't say that."

Mason turned, gripping the counter on either side of his butt. If Mason played poker, he probably lost every game—disappointment and a desire to please had given him puppy dog eyes and a not-so-subtle pout. "You don't need to say it. It's the truth. It's *my* truth. It's what I'm living right now. I didn't mean it to sound like I was...pissed about it."

"Okay, I just... I don't know."

"Nas, I feel like there's a moment here that I missed."

*We're both trying like hell not to talk about Chadwick Brody,* Naser thought. *That's the moment.*

"Nas, could you stop with the food for a second and maybe look at me?"

His tone was gentle and cautious, and still Naser froze as if a gun had gone off right behind his head. He set down the serving spoon, summoned all the courage he had, and looked Mason in the eye.

"Okay, so, um... I guess that when you talked about meeting friends my head immediately went to the fact that..." Naser stood up straighter, but it didn't help. No way could he get through what he had to say next and maintain eye contact with Mason at the same time. "Mason, I've been out of the closet since I was eighteen. And before that, my closet door was made of Lucite, apparently. So I guess when you talked about us meeting each other's friends, it was weird because I felt like I was caught between two things. On the one hand, I don't want to be introduced as just another friend. But on the other, this is all so new that I'm not sure I have the right to ask to be anything else."

"Is it new, though?"

"Mason, we hadn't seen each other since high school."

"But you thought about me, right? 'Cause God knows I thought about you."

"Yeah, but not always kindly."

Mason held up both hands. "Fair."

For a while, neither one of them spoke.

"No matter what happens, I don't want to be anyone's secret," Naser finally said.

Mason's tongue made a lump under his upper lip. He studied the fridge off to Naser's right. Better than looking at the floor, which Naser had learned was what the man did when fighting feelings that made him deeply uncomfortable. "When the time comes, I'll introduce you to the people in my life however you'd like. But give me just a little time on that one."

"Exactly. That's what I'm saying. Let's not rush. I don't want Connor's little case of Rich Boy Saves the World syndrome to force us into anything here. The only schedule we should be following is our own."

"Agreed. Totally." Mason started for him.

Naser felt immensely proud of himself. He'd spoken his true feelings, been honest and candid despite the fear.

*And he hadn't mentioned Chadwick once. So how honest had he been, really?*

Naser went back to plating food. Suddenly Mason was right behind him, sliding his arms around him, taking advantage of their height difference to rest his chin on the top of Naser's head.

For a second or two, Naser thought the man would be content to watch him, hold him, while he worked.

And it felt good.

"Just like I'm not going to rush you into giving me this sweet, beautiful ass either."

Mason made his point by slowly grinding his bulge into Naser's ass cheeks.

This felt better.

Naser didn't drop the spoon, which in this particular moment would have felt the same as dropping the soap. Instead, he lowered it gently into the bowl full of stew, then he brought his hands to the edge of the counter so he could stay upright as he struggled for breath.

"Not rushing," Mason whispered into Naser's ear. "Just feeling. Promise."

They hadn't had a fight—technically—but they'd stared down a fearful topic together and managed to take a step back from the edge, thanks to a courageous bit of candor and a mutual agreement.

As a result, they both seemed filled with the kind of white-hot charge that ignites the best kind of make-up sex.

"No pressure," Mason whispered.

Mason's embrace felt gentle and affectionate, but it was spiced with the lustful yearning of the man's slow grind against his ass. His hands traveled underneath Naser's polo. His fingers knew their destination, but they were true to his word—no rush. They traced a path right to Naser's nipples, tweaking each one lightly on arrival, pulling them out just the right little bit from his chest before rolling them slowly between thumb and forefinger. In seventy-two hours' time, Mason had learned the perfect amount of pressure, the perfect degree of tug, and as a result, Naser struggled now to keep his eyes open, struggled not to drive his ass back against Mason's bulge in a way that swept aside the boundary he'd set for himself.

"This isn't pressure?" Naser asked, voice thick with lust.

"Just a reminder. Of my interest."

"Interest?"

"Given our complicated history, as your best friend put it, I feel an obligation to constantly remind you of how badly I want to fuck you. Just in case you forget and assume the old version of Mason has taken over."

Naser turned his head as far as he could and found Mason's lips inches from his. "Rumor has it the old Mason wanted to fuck me too."

"Yeah, but he had a lousy way of showing it."

"This is better," Naser whispered. "This is a much better way of showing it."

"Good. But you know…" Mason managed to give Naser a light kiss on the lips given their contorted pose. "No pressure."

Mason unsnapped all four of the buttons on Naser's jeans, released Naser's engorged cock, and started a leisurely stroke that said Naser's pleasure was his priority, but in this moment, penetration was not. Which was a good thing because Naser hadn't properly prepared. And the truth was, until his head was ready, he didn't feel like braving the rituals required to prepare his body.

"Can I play instead?" Mason whispered into Naser's ear, then followed it up with a little bite on Naser's earlobe.

"Surface level only, please," Naser whispered back.

"Of course."

Mason tugged Naser's jeans down to his thighs. His briefs followed, then he started to move his fingers the same way he did when he'd lavished Naser with sudsy ministrations in the shower. Ten fingers working constantly and in succession, kneading and stroking and grazing, traveling from Naser's cock, along his taint and up the crack of his ass, seeking out the most sensitive nerves until the effect was like being licked and kissed by several mouths at once. It was as comprehensive and obsessive as everything else Mason had done for him since their reunion.

Again and again, Mason grazed his entrance without poking it or prodding at it or crossing the boundary. Instead, he showed love for the boundary, slicked his fingers with his own spit and moistened the boundary, drew a white-hot line across the boundary that seemed to say, *If it feels this good now, imagine what crossing the boundary will feel like when it's time.*

There was one element that had yet to be added to Mason's little round of play, and it was up to Naser to include it. Naser reached behind him, found the drawstring of Mason's sweatpants, and tugged at it until the knot came loose. Mason withdrew the hand with which he'd been caressing Naser's balls. In the next second, Mason's cock sprung free from its confines before it was stopped by the cheeks of Naser's ass with a little slap.

The whole scenario—their location, their hurried, tangled pose—had the trappings of a stolen, forbidden moment, like they were two naughty servants trying not to be caught by the master of the house. Years of being told his desires were deviant and wrong had left Naser with a taste for the forbidden. Mason, he figured, was the same, which was why they were both epically hard.

With one hand, Mason stroked the length of Naser's crack, occasionally lingering and circling his entrance. With the other, he stroked Naser's achingly hard cock, all with his lips pressed against Naser's neck.

Time went fluid. His bones went molten.

"Take over," Mason whispered.

Naser was too dazed by desire to comply, so Mason took one of Naser's hands and moved it to Naser's cock.

Startled, Naser began to stroke himself, wondering if Mason needed a bathroom break or something. That would be a mood killer. But then the man's fingers found Naser's nipples again, and he realized he was trying to maximize the pleasure he could give Naser's most sensitive body part. And it worked.

God, did it work.

Combined with the hungry mix of licks and suckling Mason was giving his neck, Naser turned incandescent with desire.

"Mason..."

That was the only word of warning he could manage. One whisper of the man's name and Naser was coming so fast and hard it was like he'd been shot out of a rocket, maybe because Mason kept up his steady work even as Naser bucked and jerked and bellowed. With each second, he thought the rush of pleasure would end, and then another staccato round of bliss shot through him. The whole time Mason grunted with delight, as if the sight of Naser's pleasure were as gratifying as a bite of ice cream.

As soon as Naser caught his breath, Mason pressed down on the center of his spine with one hand. The next thing he knew, his cheek was pressed to the counter right next to the plates of food, his ass out and exposed.

Mason steadied himself with the same hand he'd used to bend Naser over the counter. That's when Naser realized what he was doing. Mason was pleasuring himself at the sight of Naser's exposed ass. He'd loved the boundary, slickened the boundary, now he was going to coat it and mark it, and the idea made Naser shudder with lust, threatened to fill his deflating cock again.

Next came the delicious barrage of teeth-clenched profanity Mason always unleashed when he came—a display that sounded both angry and hungry, a combination Naser had longed to draw out of Mason for years. "Fuck." Right on cue, Mason's cum painted his hole, the firm press of his hand holding him in place, rooting him in place as he slicked his ass with little jets so hot Naser wouldn't have been surprised to hear them sizzle against his skin. "*Fuck,* Naser. Fuck!"

*My name. Coming hard while he says my name.*

The eruption was replaced by the slow and steady slide of Mason's slick cock along his ass, as if he was trying to drive home the point.

*Feel it. Feel what you did to me.*

Mason wilted against Naser's back, curving his arms around him. Then slowly, still sliding his cock back and forth along Naser's crack, he brought Naser to an upright position, nibbled his earlobe, and planted several long, hard kisses along his neck.

"You have a filthy mouth when you come, Mason Worther," Naser whispered, "and I love it."

# 24

The next day, Naser had finished a quick lunch at his desk and was still working his way through the morning's emails when his phone chimed with a text from his mother.

*Khahareto peyda kon.*

*Find your sister.*

Mahin Kazemi texted infrequently and succinctly, and only when she considered the matter to be of great importance. During the work week, this was doubly true. Her messages often combined a nightmare scenario—*Your sister might be dead!*—with a directive—*Find her now!* The goal was to conceal a truth more unpleasant than disturbing. In this case, that Pari was ignoring her calls.

He knew better than to argue.

He also knew better than to ask follow-up questions.

Naser typed a text to his sister—**Stop ignoring Maman**—and figured that would be the end of it. No doubt, Pari would text back in twenty minutes with a cover story she wanted him to pass on. In turn, he'd respond to their mother with the slimmed-down, one-line version he was willing to share—the one that made him feel less like a liar.

An hour later, there was no text from his sister.

Another hour, silence from his sister.

Three texts later, still nothing. So he texted Fareena. She hadn't heard from her best friend in two days, and she wrote back a few minutes later to say she wasn't getting a response either. Then, with a little jolt, he remembered the choke in Pari's voice when she'd abruptly ended their last call. His worry turned into fear.

He checked his emails to make sure he hadn't missed any from her. Nothing.

That meant she still hadn't returned a signed copy of the contract.

So she was brushing off the lifeline that would save her business?

That was impossible. Something was wrong.

At four-thirty, about an hour before he usually left work, he called Mason. "So I think I might have to postpone our first restaurant dinner. Something's up with my sister."

"*Up?* Uh-oh."

"Yeah, she's not responding to calls or texts. I'm going to drive up to LA, make sure she's okay."

Mason's desk chair squeaked.

"You want company?"

He did and he didn't, and he wasn't quite sure how to say it. Mason sensed his wariness. "Sorry. Family thing. Got it." But he sounded a little petulant, like a kid who'd been caught reaching for an extra cookie from the jar. The truth was, this unexpected change in their immersive schedule made Naser feel weird too. A last-minute trip to LA might have him coming back late. Would it make sense for him to spend the night at Mason's house—for the fourth night in a row? Or did his discomfort have more to do with his hesitancy to explain his new—meetings? Assignations? Regular booty calls? *Relationship?*—to his opinionated sister.

Better to let Mason be an old classmate, a shadowy investor. For now.

Which made Naser feel like a hypocrite given his speech the night before.

He didn't want to be Mason's dirty secret, and now he was turning Mason into one.

"It's just...my sister can be kind of a drama queen, and I'm not sure I want to inflict that on you. Yet."

"Got it."

"You sure?"

"It's a family thing. I understand. Still coming over later or will you..." Mason's voice trailed off.

"Let me call once I figure out what's going on with her."

"Sounds good."

If it sounded good, why did it feel so weird? Would the smallest bit of distance between them cause this whole thing to fall apart? If they stepped back for even one night, would they realize the craziness of what they were doing and come to their senses?

Traffic was stop and go for most of the drive north, another reminder of why he preferred living in Orange County, where most streets had four lanes in both directions and there was a left turn light at every intersection.

Naser knew Los Angeles well. He'd visited West Hollywood plenty during his college years, usually to hit crowded gay bars with Connor and their college crew. But his sister's home was in Silver Lake, a good ways east. Despite being heavily gentrified, it was still considered an artsier, funkier alternative to the more affluent neighborhoods of LA's West Side. The terraced hillside houses sported stunning views, but they sat on smaller lots and lacked the eye-popping infinity pools of the celebrity mansions perched throughout the Hollywood Hills.

Pari rented the lower unit of a two-story, paint-peeling wooden house that tumbled down a leafy hillside and looked out over the Silver Lake Reservoir and the rolling green hills beyond. Mostly he visited here to attend her wild parties, so it was the first time in a while he'd encountered her narrow street when it wasn't fully clogged with parked cars. Her guests were always a blend of starving artists and funky Hollywood types who dressed like starving artists even though they made seven figures a year, to whom his sister would introduce him as if he were some alien from another planet. "This is my brother. He is an accountant. Forgive him, please." Her friends would in turn ask him concerned questions about why he still lived in Orange County, as if some form of systemic oppression had prevented him from being granted political asylum in Los Angeles. When he told them he loved his peaceful condo and that his favorite thing was to watch planes take off from John Wayne Airport, they'd pinch his cheek and call him "adorkable," and he'd head back home the following morning, reminded again that he and his sister inhabited different worlds.

The black Prius at the curb was definitely Pari's, but LA was such a dry city he couldn't tell if the dusty windshield meant she'd returned home the day before or an hour before.

Hell of a detective he'd make.

He raced down the rickety set of outdoor steps that led to the porch outside her front door and saw the curtains on her windows were pulled shut.

He didn't knock. He banged, his bottled-up fear spilling out through his arm and fist.

"It's open!" his sister yelled back.

"Wait! *Seriously?*"

He stepped inside, taking care not to slam the door behind him, which is exactly what he wanted to do.

Pari's apartment was mostly open space, the bedroom cordoned off with some tapestries she'd dyed herself. The furniture in the seating area was made up of precisely arranged stacks of beaded pillows that required guests to sink to their knees before taking a seat. His sister lay across a mound of them with her arms thrown out, as if she'd been dropped from a great height. Smoke rose toward the ceiling from her right hand.

Persian rugs covered the hardwood floor. Piled just inside the front door were plastic tubs full of fabric rolls, bags of sequins and beads, and several sewing machines. She'd either cleared out her studio space or she'd started to after the Bliss Network dropped her.

A noxious odor hit him in a suffocating wave. He coughed and waved a hand in front of his face. "Weed? Seriously?"

"I know. It's terrible. Why is this a thing?" Even as she asked this question, she brought the joint to her mouth and inhaled.

"You tell me. You're smoking it."

She exhaled dragon style. "I had to try something. I'm off sugar, and mushrooms seemed extreme."

"Celebrating your new investor?" He knew good and well this wasn't a celebration.

"So you drove up to gloat, is that it?"

"More like Maman's worried sick. I had to cancel a date tonight."

Pari's eyebrows shot up like rockets. "A date? *You?* With who?"

"I'm the one who just sat in traffic for three and a half hours. I get to ask the questions."

Pari shrugged. "No phone."

Naser knew his sister wasn't going to offer him anything to drink, so he made a beeline for the fridge. "Since when?"

"Since I threw it."

"Threw it where?"

Pari gestured over one shoulder. "Out the window. It's down the hill, I think. Or a coyote got it. I don't know."

Naser took a long slug of caffeinated soda, knowing he'd need it. "Why are you feeding phones to coyotes?"

She stubbed out her joint and gave him a heavy look. "Feelings," she answered, as if he'd never had one and she was too tired to explain how they worked.

Naser dashed off a text to their mother informing her Pari was alive and there was something wrong with her phone. Covering for his sister was reflexive. The little fib only stung after he'd sent the text. He pocketed the phone. "Should I call someone you actually feel like talking to?"

"I don't feel like talking. That's why I threw my phone."

"Are you sure? I mean, there's lots of reasons to throw a phone. Anger's usually at the top."

Pari leveled him in a penetrating gaze that offered no hint of sarcasm or amusement. "I know who he is, Naser."

His hand froze halfway to his mouth. "Who?" he asked, even though he didn't need to.

"Mason Worther. I know who he is. And what he did. To you." Pari let that sink in and slouched back, her hair fanned out on all sides of her head like a lustrous, black halo. Her chest rose and fell with deep, labored breaths.

*Goddammit, Connor.* "Who told you about Mason?"

"Maman."

Naser slammed his Diet Coke can down on the counter. "You talked to Maman about your new investor? Are you crazy?"

"Hell, no. She told me about Mason when you guys were in high school."

"What? How did she even know who he was?"

"Your journals."

Before he could stop himself, Naser made a sound like he'd been whacked across the back of the head. "My journals? I hid them in the attic."

"So she searched the attic for your journals," Pari said, her hands out as if this were obvious. "Naser, don't play dumb. A Persian son is allowed no privacy from his mother. You know this."

"I thought she was different. She was always busy. She didn't have the time to butt into my business."

"She didn't, so she saved time by reading your journals."

As the enormity of this revelation swept over him, Naser brought his hands to his face. The things he'd written in those journals—private thoughts, sexual fantasies. It was an epic invasion, but it also made a mockery of his lifelong strategy to only share edited versions of himself with the most important woman in his life. The whole time, she'd had access to his private inner self.

During high school, anyway.

*And she loved me anyway.*

*Or it's why she was always busy. My truth repelled her.*

Naser spotted a copy of the investment agreement sitting on the counter, moved to it, and flipped to the signature page. She'd printed it out, but she hadn't signed it.

"Did you think I wouldn't care?" Pari asked. "Did you think I wouldn't care the lifeline you threw me came from a man who tortured you in high school? Did you think I wouldn't have any feelings about that? Is your opinion of me that low, Naser-*joon*?"

"No."

"Liar," she whispered.

"I didn't know, Pari. I didn't know Mom read my journals. I sure as hell didn't know she told you about it. And I didn't expect any of this to be a thing when I hooked you up with Mason."

"Now you do, and now you know why I fed my phone to a coyote."

He also knew better than to talk back. Anything he said when his sister was this deeply in her feelings would be construed as an attack. So he stayed silent, stayed in the kitchen, and nursed his soda like it contained a life-giving force. But nothing could lower the volume on the cry that rung through his head every few seconds—*Mom read my journals! Shit!*

Finally, Naser found his voice. "Mason Worther came to me. He wanted to make things right between us. I told him this was how to do it. Invest in your line, on these terms. I did this because you are my sister and I love you."

Tears glistened in her eyes. Her chin quivered the way it always did when she was about to cry. "Well, maybe I don't want his damn money because you are my brother and I love you. Did you ever think about that?" Naser's answer was in his silence. "And there it is. You both think I'm this weird monster of ambition and you hate me because I won't lead a normal life like you two."

"No, *no*, Pari. What I think is that your business is hard and full of risk, and I can't pretend to understand how it works. I also know that you're weird enough that no matter what life you attempt, it will never be normal by virtue of the fact that you're the one attempting it. And that's as it should be. I don't want you normal. I want you...*you*."

Pari looked unconvinced.

"Also, Mason and I are sleeping together."

Pari sat up as if a gun had gone off, eyes wide, mouth agape. This wasn't the shock of anger—it was the shock of fascination and delight. "Seriously? You're dating Mason Worther?"

"Dating? Hmmm. Maybe. More like I've been spending the night at his house a lot. I don't know what to call it. It's a thing, it keeps happening, and Connor's already threatened the guy's life if he hurts me. Oh, and I brought him Persian food. So it's clearly...a thing, I think."

Pari gasped. Naser wondered if *It's a Thing, I Think* would make a suitable title for a pop song about love. After a second or two, he couldn't imagine it coming out of the mouth of Harry Styles, so he let the idea go.

"What I'm saying is that even though I don't know what it is, it's moving very fast."

"You must tell me everything." Pari patted the cushions next to her.

"Tell Maman and I'll throw you out a window after your phone."

"I won't. But only if you tell me everything."

And so he did. It felt strange but also good, pouring out his heart to his sister. He'd never done it before on the topic of men. Had always assumed she wouldn't have the patience for any story about his life that lasted longer than thirty seconds. Maybe she only had the patience for it now because it made her feel better about accepting Mason's money—if she *did* finally accept Mason's money. But it felt good to be listened to, close to her, good to be able to pull her back from the brink of self-destructive fantasies with a story about himself.

A story that was true. And complete.

When he was done, she was beaming, her tears an afterthought. She reached across the little distance between them, cupping one of his cheeks in her hand. "Oh, I'm so happy for you." He braced himself for a gooey platitude about finding love. "You are finally doing something interesting. My perfect little brother might make a complete mess of his perfect little life." She clapped her hands together. "This is growth! I am proud of you, Naser-*joon*."

"So you're going to take Mason's money?"

Pari sat up straight and slapped her knees with her hands. "Absolutely. Now I have the perfect cover story. If Maman finds out, I can just say you were blinded by lust, and I went along for the ride. You'll be the one she yells at for a change. I can't wait. I'll make us some food." And like that, his sister was on her feet and headed for the kitchen, her tearful monologue forgotten.

"You really are special, you know that, Pari?"

"I do," she replied somberly, pulling pots and pans from the kitchen cabinets. "It's just a matter of securing the right distributor so everyone else knows too." She opened her fridge. "I have no food! We'll have to go out."

# 25

When it became clear his evening plans had been delayed, Shirley enlisted Mason to visit a nearby hospital with a small group of sober folks. An old friend of hers had relapsed the previous weekend and driven his car into a telephone pole. Physically, the guy was recovering nicely, but according to Shirley, his wife, who'd been pacing nervously outside his room when they showed up, was poised to pack up and leave if the guy didn't clean up his act for good. Their little impromptu AA meeting—which consisted of them gathering in a small circle around the man's bed and saying the Serenity Prayer before they read various passages from the *Big Book*—had ended with the man in tears, clutching his wife's hand and vowing to get back in the program.

As they'd filed out of the hospital, Mason had felt that special kind of joy that came from linking hands with other sober people and pushing back against the darkness that plagued them all.

And according to his last text, Naser was on his way south again, which made Mason feel like he was flying.

Life was good.

He felt like a paragon of mental health.

Then he saw Chadwick's bright orange Maserati parked outside his garage, and in an instant his heart was thundering and his palms had greased the steering wheel.

Mason parked and got out.

"What the fuck, man?" was Chadwick's greeting.

"Chadwick, I told you I—"

"You moved my key! Where's my key?"

"It's actually *my* key, C."

"Wait, where's the Ferrari?"

"I sold it."

"Sold it? For this piece of shit? Did you hit your head or something?"

"It's late, man. Seriously. I'm not up for a party tonight."

"You see a party? I've been texting you all week. I'm here to find out if my best friend's rocking back and forth in a corner, picking at scabs and shit."

Despite his claim, Chadwick was dressed for a wild night out—designer, quad-hugging jeans and a tailored bright purple dress shirt unbuttoned midway down the hard chest he always kept perfectly waxed. Mason had grown into his body after high school, but somehow Chadwick had managed to keep his almost exactly the same. His face was another story. It was loaded up with fillers and injections in an attempt to give it contours his natural-born skull barely allowed.

Mason had avoided this moment for as long as he could. "I'm sober now, C."

"All right, well, we can fix that." He patted his front pocket, suggesting it had a nice fat eight ball of coke sitting in it. As always.

"No. I quit, Chadwick."

The guy flinched, swallowed. "Wait...*quit?* Quit what?"

"Everything."

"Everything." Chadwick nodded in dumb shock. "Like...for how long?"

"Forever."

"*Forever?* What the fuck, dude? Why?"

"Because I was a mess."

And here it was, one of the major reasons he'd been ducking this conversation for so long. If Mason was a mess, what did that make Chadwick, his partner in crime?

The guy sputtered, batting his hands through the air in front of him. "You were late to work a few times. What's the big—"

"I was late to work for five years."

Chadwick studied the pavement.

"And I lost a job in LA most people would kill for," Mason added.

"So that's why you hid the key? 'Cause you were afraid I was going to bust into your house and start partying?"

"Isn't that why you're here?"

"The girls are at Lenny's, waiting for us."

"I don't feel like hanging out with random girls tonight."

"They're not random. Starla was a Playboy Playmate, and Jennifer sells vitamins based on your astrological sign or something." Chadwick winced suddenly as if Mason's denial of access had leveled a second blow. "You took my key away, dude. What the fuck?"

"Look, I can't have you just doing whatever you want in my house. Not right now. It's a transitional period for me and it's...it's about respecting boundaries, okay?"

"Boundaries? Jesus, fag. What, are we *girls* now?"

"I don't know what we are, okay?" Mason's shout echoed across the railroad tracks behind his house, up the palisade that towered over the beach. Chadwick jerked like a gun had gone off. It was the slur that had set Mason off. Chadwick said it just like Mason's dad did, all venomous contempt—a single syllable designed to shame and silence in an instant. "I don't know what you and I are when we aren't blasting lines off my kitchen counter until three in the morning or going so hard on the weekend we wake up at a house in Malibu with a bunch of people we don't fucking know. And clearly you don't either, which is why you're freaking out because I don't want to party 'till dawn on a *Tuesday.*" Chadwick was stunned silent. "I just...need a breath here, okay? So would you relax and back off and maybe take no for an answer for the first time in your life?"

Headlights bounced across Chadwick's stunned, horrified expression. Mason heard the gate lift behind him.

A car slowed next to them, Shirley's Tesla. He'd left her chatting in the hospital parking lot with two of her AA friends. Now she'd caught up. She powered the passenger side window down, leaning sideways over the armrest to get them both within view. "Everything all right here, boys?"

Chadwick stepped up to the car and gripped the edge of the open window with both hands. "Everything's fine, Grandma Moses. Run along now before you miss the nightly news."

Shirley's jaw tensed, and her eyes blazed. "I wasn't asking you, *squirt.*" Her eyes met Mason's.

"I'm good," he answered. "I'll check in."

Shirley nodded, then looked at Chadwick. "Get your hands off my car, *kid.*"

Chadwick drew back as if his fingers had been burned and turned to face Mason as Shirley drove away at a crawl. "Jesus. What is it, Asshole

Day at Capo Beach? You banging that old prune?"

"She's a friend. Don't talk about her like that."

Chadwick grimaced, lifting his hands in a sarcastic gesture of surrender. "So…what? Some new therapist told you I was a bad influence or something?"

"We can talk about this later. Go hook up with the girls before Lenny tries to attach them to a drone. Have fun. Enjoy your night. I'm going to bed."

Chadwick snorted and started for his car. For a second, Mason thought that might be the end of it. The end, perhaps, of a lot of other things too. But as soon as he gripped the door handle of his Maserati, Chadwick froze. "You joined a cult, didn't you?"

"AA's not a cult," Mason answered.

"Oh, shit, man," he groaned. "The Jesus People with the tokens? No fucking thanks." When Chadwick swung one leg inside the car, something inside of Mason seized up.

"There's no Jesus in AA. Unless you want there to be. It's a higher power of your own understanding."

*And I haven't found mine, yet.*

*Or I have and his name's Naser.*

"Yeah, well, mine's Maserati. Over and out."

As Chadwick went to shut the door, a nagging voice told Mason he'd played this moment wrong, and his new sober friends would encourage him to be more spiritual in his approach.

"Chadwick." His friend—possibly his former friend—froze. "We could have lunch."

Chadwick stared at him for a while. "Lunch?" he finally said, as if he'd never heard the word before. "Will there be *tea* too? We're fucking warriors. We don't have *lunch*. Fuck off, dude."

Mason watched the Maserati make a loud U-turn before it headed off into the night.

He heard footsteps approaching and caught a draft of Shirley's sweet floral perfume. They stood there in silence for a while. Shirley broke it. "Dreadful best friend got your tongue?"

Mason grunted in the affirmative.

"Want to tell me what happened?" she asked.

"Well, there's what I did, and then there's what I *really* did."

"Let's hear both."

"I hid the key so he couldn't get into my house unannounced and start partying."

"Sensible. Which version is that?"

"What I *really* did is pick a fight with my best friend because I was too afraid to tell him I'm falling for a guy."

Shirley nodded.

"What should I do?" Mason finally asked.

"Yeah, I'm not the right one to ask on this one. I'm too biased. It's been a hell of a lot quieter around these parts since he stopped visiting. And if that little shit calls me Grandma again, I'll hand him his balls in a brown paper bag." She rubbed his upper back gently. "Sleep on it. Maybe there's something to clean up there. But I wouldn't rush to bring all that energy back into your life. You did a good thing for my friend Hugh tonight. Let that be the note you end your day on."

"We all did a good thing."

"You helped." She gave him a quick peck on the cheek, then headed for her house.

By the time he reached his kitchen, his hands had started to shake. But he didn't feel queasy or even anxious. Instead, he felt elated. It had felt good to shout Chadwick down. Damn good. Good to meet his slur with a burst of authentic anger and the volume it demanded.

Adrenaline. That's what he was feeling.

He and Chadwick had fought before but usually when they were both wasted, and over superficial things—mostly drugs and girls that hadn't been shared to Chadwick's liking. This was different. This was Mason dropping his mask and Chadwick sneering and attacking what he saw underneath. And Mason striking back. It wasn't fear that was making his hands shake, it was energy that wanted to be put to use.

Put to use grabbing Chadwick by the back of his neck and slamming him face first into the street.

*Woah.* The image of it—the *fantasy* of it—was so vivid and clear, he felt like he'd left his body. Traveled back in time. Lived out an alternate version of the moment he'd just finished outside.

He knew sobriety was to blame. In the same way it had sharpened the edges of his lustful fantasies about Naser until they were impossible to ignore, here it stoked the flames of his rage toward the guy he hated to call his best friend. He didn't regret giving in to the fantasy when it came to Naser. Would he regret pounding Chadwick into the pavement if it came to that?

It didn't feel like it. It felt like he'd enjoy every minute of it.

And that scared him suddenly. A blow leveled against Chadwick was really a blow leveled against the parts of himself he was trying to leave behind, a version of Mason that somehow felt old even though it had been in full force until about two weeks before.

Anger, he realized, could be a high as potent as cocaine.

Suddenly, he was afraid Chadwick's visit had unleashed something in him he couldn't control.

His phone rang before he could chew over the comparison. It was Nas. *Thank you, God.*

"Hey." He'd tried to sound normal, but his voice came out as a husky growl.

"Jesus. That voice," Nas said. Mason felt instantly ashamed. His rage had crept into his tone. "That voice makes me want to come over." Apparently, there was no need to worry about sounding angry on the phone when you were sleeping with a guy who liked it rough.

"Aren't you?"

"See, that's why I'm calling. It's pretty late and I just…I mean, I want to come over, but I feel like I'll be in better shape tomorrow if maybe I go back to my place and get some rest. But…"

"But?"

"I guess I'm…scared not to. Does that make sense?"

"Scared not to come over?"

"Yeah. Which sounds stupid."

"It's not stupid." *Please come over,* he wanted to say, *please come over and save me from myself. Take this anger from me in the kind of inches and thrusts you like.*

"It is, though," Naser said. "I just…I really…"

Feeling a blend of hunger and disappointment he was determined not to inflict on the man who'd made his life so much better in such a short time, Mason started upstairs. "I'm listening." The answer from the other end was a steady rush of freeway sounds.

"I've got this thought in my head," Naser finally said, "that if we take a night off, that might be it, you know?"

"*It?*"

"You know, that if I don't come over tonight, there might not be another night. Ever."

"Well, that's *definitely* not the case. I'd be banging on your door, boner in hand, in no time."

"Wow, that's vivid. And kind of hot. Yet goofy." Naser groaned. "I know. It's crazy. But I just had to say it out loud."

"It's not crazy. It's just not true. I'll tell you what is true, though." Mason sat down on the edge of his bed, the side he'd come to think of as Naser's after only three nights. "As much as I'd love to save up for you tomorrow night, I probably will resort to smelling your side of the bed while I stroke my cock. Maybe driving myself into the sheets a little like you're still here."

"Also kind of hot," Nas whispered.

"Is it?" Mason stood, unbuttoned his jeans and lowered his zipper, hoping Naser could hear.

He sprung free, achingly hard, as hard as if Naser was gripping his shaft instead of him. The fear of Chadwick and Naser meeting, the catharsis of shouting Chadwick into silence for the first time in his life, the heady drug of Naser's sweet, soft voice in his ear. It had him worked up like crazy.

"I might have to do it now then," Mason said.

Mason sank to his knees next to the bed, pushed the comforter away from the spot where Naser had slept the night before, and took in a whiff so loud he was pretty sure Naser could hear it. His smell was there, just as he'd hoped. His sweet, spicy cologne, a hint of what the nape of his neck tasted like. Before he could stop himself, he was stroking himself, on his knees, a slave to scent and memory.

"Are you...?" Naser couldn't finish the sentence. Maybe because he was afraid of driving off the road.

"Can't help it. Your smell makes me hard."

"Oh, God. You're trying to make me come over, aren't you?"

"No time. Don't bother. Now that I've smelled you, I can't stop."

It was the truth. A little sheen of pre-cum was slicked along his shaft now. He took another whiff of the sheets. "Need a taste," he growled.

"Oh my God. Are you actually *licking*...?"

Mason gave an affirmative grunt. He wasn't technically licking the sheets, but it was damn close. He'd sucked a little patch between his lips and was suckling it gently, like he might one of Naser's nipples.

"Screw this. I'm coming over," Naser said.

"Unh-uh. No time. Won't last much longer. And you need your rest."

"Mason..."

"I'm not playing with you, Nas. I'm stroking my cock while your smell turns me inside out and your voice feels like someone's kissing my ear."

"I thought you were just teasing about smelling the sheets."

"I was. Then I did it and I lost control."

"You're seriously jerking off right now and I'm not there?"

"I'm *epically* jerking off right now. And you're going to have to sit there, driving, listening to every curse word that flies out of my mouth when the smell of you makes me come. Did you leave any underwear here?"

"Maybe."

"Good. I'm going to eat them."

"Jesus. I'm pulling over at least. No way can I—"

"No, you're not. Drive that damn car. You had a long night. You need to get home, get some rest. Keep that pretty dick of yours in your pants so you don't wreck. Meanwhile, get ready to listen to every dirty word I'm going to yell when you finally let me find out what it's like to come inside you."

"Mason...Jesus."

His hand was flying now, and the sound of soft, astonished hunger in Naser's voice only made his balls churn harder. The speed of it, the slightly degraded position of being on his knees next to his own bed, the sound of desire and good sense warring inside Naser's gentle voice—it was a potent blend. Combined with Naser's announcement the night before that he loved how dirty Mason's mouth got when he came, it had Mason gritting his teeth, his thighs feeling molten, a tell-tale flutter in his chest that told him eruptive bliss was near.

"Mason?"

"Coming." A choked cry, but a truthful one. "*Fuck,* Nas. Fuck! Gonna come like this when you let me inside you. Gonna fucking wreck you the way you want. Make it hurt just like you want. Awwwww, *fuck.* Jesus! Look into those fucking eyes while I make it hurt the way you want." He collapsed against the side of the bed, head buried in the crook of one arm, gasping for breath.

The rush of freeway sounds in his ear had never stopped.

"Are you there?" Mason asked.

"You're an animal," Naser whispered. "A filthy fucking animal."

"And you love it."

"I do," Naser said quietly. "I do love that you're a filthy animal."

"Don't worry. You can take the pressure off as soon as you get home," Mason said.

"Not me. I'm a good boy. I'm going to wait until I see you again. I've got patience. Unlike some men on this call."

"Is that so?" Mason asked, pulling himself up into bed.

"It is. Goodnight, Mason Worther. Sweet dreams."

The call ended. He thought for a second Naser might actually be pissed, but there'd been a devilish lilt to his tone before he'd hung up.

He crawled up onto the bed, rolled over onto his back, and lay there staring at the ceiling, gasping for breath. Seeing Naser, smelling Naser, hearing Naser. He'd blown his load across the carpet, but some of it was drying on his cock, which still felt stubbornly thick. He felt spent, but not purged. He was suddenly grateful he didn't know where Naser lived because he might have driven straight to his place and banged on the door until Naser let him in, and that would have been too much.

He lost track of time, felt drowsiness tugging at the edge of his thoughts, then the phone rang.

Naser.

He'd never answered a call so fast in his life.

"Hey." Naser's voice sounded quiet, a little strained.

No freeway sounds in the background.

"Where are you?" Mason asked.

"Home. That's where you told me to go, right?"

"Yeah, but..."

"But?"

"Can I come over?"

"No time." Naser's little gasps, his breathlessness told Mason he was doing what Mason had just done.

"Oh, I see. This is my punishment."

"Not really. More like my confession."

"What do you have to confess, Nas?"

"I'm not a good boy," he whispered, then he let out a sharp little grunt that sounded like he was doing more than jerking off. Maybe a little something that hurt just the way he liked. "I couldn't wait."

"Are you jerking off to the sound of my voice, Naser?"

"More than that..."

"My winning smile?"

Naser sputtered with laughter. "Stop it."

"My connections in real estate?"

"No."

"So what's the more?"

"Don't get jealous."

"You don't want to make a man like me jealous, Nas. I might break down your door and lay claim to you on your kitchen floor."

"Promise?"

"Dirty boy," Mason whispered.

"*Your* dirty boy," Naser whispered back.

The simple three words carried an electrical charge, sending the word *Mine mine mine* rocketing through Mason's brain. Mason's cock was rising again.

"So, uh, what should I not be jealous of?"

"Something inside me," Naser said between sharp little gasps. "A toy. But I'm pretending it's you... It's almost as big. Not quite."

Breathless suddenly, Mason rose to his feet. The thought that his own voice had turned Naser on so much the guy was now working a fat dildo into himself had Mason stroking his own cock again as it filled.

"Yeah?" Mason asked. "Are you fucking yourself while you think about me?"

"So many times... Done it so many times, thinking about you."

"You're going to get the real thing as soon as you're ready."

Silence followed, then more gasps. For a second, he thought Naser might be about to come, then he broke the silence.

"Want your hands on my throat." There was desire in Naser's voice, but his words also had the tense energy of a quick confession, one that was easier to make when they weren't face to face. One that made the phone call somehow more intimate, safer. "When you fuck me, I want your hands on my throat."

Mason felt hunger and elation, as if he was being entrusted with the keys to Naser's body.

"Yeah? You want me to squeeze?" He'd tried to make it sound porny and hot, but the question was a serious one, and he fought the urge to grab a pen and paper and start taking notes. He kept languidly stroking his cock instead, his balls jerking every time Naser let out a high, sharp gasp that indicated the toy he was using had passed over some inner pleasure zone.

"Not too hard," Naser answered. "It's not... Not about choking. It's about holding me. Making me be still. *Seeing* me while you...fuck me. Not letting me get away."

"I'll never let you get away. If that's what you want."

"I want you. Inside me. Want you inside me. Don't think...just 'cause I'm afraid that I don't want you inside me." He'd needed to hear this.

Desperately. Every few hours since Saturday, he'd fallen prey to the fear that Naser's wariness about giving his body entirely concealed a gulf they might never cross.

"I only want to hurt you the way you want to be hurt," Mason whispered.

Naser's orgasms were the opposite of Mason's—nonverbal, primal wails that seemed to come from the core of his soul. They sounded like pleas for mercy, as if they contained more pleasure than Naser could bear. This one was the loudest, by far. The purity of it—so unrefined and unedited compared to everything else that came out of such a constantly poised man—had Mason rocketing toward a second orgasm faster than he'd ever expected. And this time, his eruption was silent save for a few sharp grunts that were lost to Naser's wail. Like his bliss was tangled up in the sound of Naser's.

How was it possible that physical distance, the inability to see each other, could somehow produce a connection that felt deeper?

"Jesus," Naser whispered. "Sorry."

"What are you sorry for?"

"That was loud."

"It was perfect. You made me come again."

"Seriously?" Naser was gasping for breath. "Oh, hold on…" Naser let out a sharp grunt. No doubt, he was easing the toy out of himself, and somehow this routine little bit of business felt as delightfully debauched as everything else they'd done that evening.

"So maybe some of that was easier to say on the phone," Mason offered.

"The hands on my throat thing, you mean."

"Yeah."

"Yeah. I'm still…"

"I'm listening."

"I still worry maybe the first night was too much, too soon."

"It wasn't for me," Mason said.

"But you got…emotional."

"Yeah, that was about not wanting to leave, though. You know, like, not wanting to do something I knew was good for me because it might take me away from you. It was about being afraid you wouldn't stay."

"So kind of like what I was afraid of tonight. That it would all be over if I didn't sleep over."

"Yeah. Sounds like it."

"Why are we both afraid the other's going to bolt if it still feels like we can't get enough of each other?" Naser asked.

At first, Mason didn't seem to have an answer, then he saw Chadwick's horrified expression after he'd yelled at him, saw the contempt in his father's eyes as he'd practically lunged at him the other day in the office. It wasn't the fear that he was going to run, or that Naser was going to run. He feared the specters that stalked the perimeter of the little world they'd built together. Deeper than that, he was afraid he wouldn't be strong enough to stand up to them if they ever truly encroached. Yeah, he'd shouted Chadwick down that night. But he hadn't come out to the guy and wasn't prepared for what might happen when he did.

"I don't have an answer," Naser finally said. "I guess I just wanted to put that out there."

Mason did have an answer, but it scared him. And the thought of saying it aloud shamed him.

"Maybe we're both afraid because it's…real." At first, the words filled Mason with pride. They were truthful, but truthful and the whole truth were two different things. The former was like the first blush of light on the horizon; the second was a full-on dawn.

"Like…dating real?" Naser asked. His tone had the same breathy quality that had entered it right before he'd come, which somehow made this simple question feel just as full of sensation.

"More than that…I think."

Silence followed. Silence that teemed with implications and fears.

"Tomorrow," Naser finally said.

"What's tomorrow?"

"You're going to be inside me."

Mason wanted to curse, but he was too breathless to attempt it.

"Sweet dreams, Mason Worther."

"Goodnight, Naser Kazemi."

Mason hung up, convinced he wouldn't be able to sleep a wink, but the word *tomorrow* ushered him into dreams of Naser that were becoming reality day by day.

# 26

When Mason's eyes popped open the next morning, he felt like a kid on Christmas Day.

He hadn't been this excited for a planned sexual event since he was a teenager. It felt tantamount to losing his virginity—the prospect of being inside a man he'd slept next to, made food for, snuggled with for hours, talked with late into the night. On top of that, he'd be doing it stone-cold sober, feeling every inch, hearing every gasp. Fully present for the bliss.

After his shower, he made the mistake of trying to help plan the evening, texting Naser various ideas for romantic restaurants before Naser had texted back.

**Dinner after. Don't make me explain why. It'll ruin the mood.**

That's when he got the message. For Naser to fully surrender, he'd have to control the schedule.

He beat his father to the office and was still reading through a detailed and increasingly contentious email thread between the Vistana foreman and the landscapers at Green Mountain when the man appeared in his door. He wasn't sure what had captured his dad's attention. Maybe Mason's brow had furrowed during the long read. Or his dad still wasn't used to finding him at his desk bright and early and with no hangover to hide.

"Problem?" Pete asked.

"Shipping delay on some of the river rocks they're going to put around the guardhouse at Vistana. The landscapers think the vendor's explanations are fishy, and the foreman's digging in. It's the third delivery date this vendor's busted by weeks."

"Fishy?"

"The foreman's got history with this vendor. Green Mountain thinks it might be clouding his judgment."

"Kickbacks?"

"Not sure. I'll probably head over there to mediate later today."

"All right, figure it out, but don't make a federal case over a bunch of rocks."

Mason nodded and went back to reading.

Pete hovered. "You hanging with Chadwick later?"

"No."

Mason figured that would be the end of it. Instead, his dad lingered. Mason had dressed that morning in a hurry. One of his old LA outfits—lightweight Italian dress pants the color of café au lait and a white linen dress shirt he'd left unbuttoned down to the center of his chest. As if his spirit had been brightened by his lustful fantasies about Naser.

"Plans with someone else?" Pete Worther asked.

There were a dozen questions hiding behind his stare, and none jumped to the front.

Mason stared back thinking, *Maybe this is the moment. Am I ready?*

"Yes," Mason answered.

"Crybaby meeting?"

"No."

He waited for his dad to ask for a name, vowed he'd be ready to share it when he did.

Pete didn't say a word. Was he afraid too?

Then he was gone, and Mason sat there, heart rate slowing gradually, wondering if he'd just missed an opportunity or if his father had somehow managed to figure out his sexuality from a subtle and unintentional shift in office wear.

His phone chimed on the drive to the Vistana site. Sober Mason was trying to be a good, conscientious driver, so he didn't read the text until he'd pulled into the parking area. It was from Chadwick, and it was a picture. An old photo of the two of them from high school. The guy had taken a snap of the glossy yearbook page with his phone, possibly that day. They were seventeen and on the sidelines after a homecoming game win, their arms loped around each other's bulging shoulder pads, youthful faces flushed, their hair sweat-tousled. No words accompanied it, but the message was clear. *This is us. This is what you're giving up on.* The picture was over a decade old, but apparently, this didn't seem to strike Chadwick as ironic.

A few hours later, after a mediation session between the landscapers and the foreman that felt mildly productive, he was on his way back to the office. His phone lit up with another text. This one was accompanied by the Klaxon siren alert he'd attached to his dad's incoming calls and messages.

> **Avis Cooper flew in a day early from Dallas. Brought his daughter with him. We're meeting them at the Montage in Laguna at seven. Go home and change after work, then meet me there.**

"Goddamit," he cursed.

Was his big night with Naser about to be delayed by one of their biggest investors? Avis Cooper was an oil billionaire who traveled by private plane. Mason knew about the visit, but their dinner plans with the man were two nights from now in Newport Beach. And the more he thought about it on the drive back to his office, the more suspicious it seemed.

Mason would rather act like a spoiled brat—possibly an unprofessional one—on the down low, so he hatched a plan to fact-check his father's story without confronting his father directly.

Cooper's assistant was a perpetually caffeinated jack of all trades who'd taken a flirty shine to Mason during their last visit, and he was able to get through to her room at the Montage on the first try. Yes, the team had arrived a day early, and she'd notified Pete of this, but she knew nothing about dinner or drinks at the resort that evening.

Mason gave the assistant some excuse about crossed wires, but when he ended the call, his hands had tightened around the steering wheel.

His father was up to something.

Mason pulled into the office lot, making sure to roll to a stop before he typed out his text. But before he could type, he saw another message from Chadwick. Another photo. This one was more recent and direct from Chadwick's phone. The two of them on the deck of Lenny Victor's yacht in Newport Harbor, splashed with setting sun, surrounded by bikini-clad women who probably hadn't eaten a full meal in days. Mason couldn't remember any of the women's names or how the excursion had ended. Could Chadwick?

But he didn't have time for Chadwick right now. The title Headache of the Day had already been claimed by his old man.

Mason responded to his father's text.

> **As I told you, I have plans tonight.**

He tucked the phone in his pocket so he couldn't check it second by second for his old man's response. This time when he entered his office, he closed the door. The response he dreaded most was, *With who?* But if his father couldn't bring himself to ask that morning, why would he be able to ask now? Maybe the distance of texting would give his old man the courage.

An hour and a half went by before the response came:

> **Cancel them.**

*He knows. Son of a bitch, he knows.*
Another text came through:

> **After dinner tonight, you're taking Avis's daughter out and showing her a good time. The kind you're good at.**

He'd never met Avis's daughter Marva, but he'd heard rumors she was one of Dallas's premiere party girls, a fact that wasn't sitting so well with her new husband. The Paris Hilton of the Big D, as her father had called her during their last meeting, and with an expression on his face like he'd tasted something bitter.

> **I'm two weeks sober. Taking a party girl on a night club tour isn't advisable for me right now.**

The response was quick this time:

> **Fuck her brains out sober then. She's your type. Unless your type has changed.**

Mason winced.

How was this his life? How had he gone so long with a best friend and a father who talked about people, especially women, as nothing more than opportunities to either get off or make money? The answer—he'd been too drunk or hungover most of the time to care. Too caught up in feeding his own dangerous appetites to take stock of the moral fiber of those close to him. In fact, he was starting to suspect he'd used their lack of character to feel better about his own reckless life choices.

Mason stared at the text. Where the hell was his old man anyway? It was well past lunch, and there were no meetings on the calendar. Was he just sitting in his office, stewing? And texting?

> **Has your type changed?**

Mason's fingers were shaking when he raised the phone again.

> I am not having sex with a married woman to keep an investor happy.

> And I'm not attending any dinner where that's the expectation. Sorry.

A few breathless seconds later came his father's response.

> **Seven o'clock.**
> **The Montage in Laguna.**

> **Sorry. I have plans.**

Silence. And no answering dots on his phone.

Then he heard it—footsteps brushing the carpet outside. And if it hadn't been for the carpet, they would have pounded, thundered, echoed. The next thing he knew, his office door had flown open and Pete Worther was standing there, red-faced. The veins in his neck bulged, and the skin on his throat flushed a bright red that outlined every razor bump he'd left that morning.

Mason stared back, wondering if he should be ready to defend himself with his fists. He'd never had to fight off blows from his father. His father had never deigned to touch him at all. But something felt different now. A line had been crossed. Mason had told him something his father wasn't used to hearing—no.

"What's his name?"

Mason stared at him.

"The man you have *plans* with this evening. What is his name?"

Mason shouldn't have been surprised, but a part of him was. Maybe his father had always known and that's what the constant verbal abuse had been about, making sure Mason never displayed his alleged sin in his father's presence. Or maybe someone had reported back that he'd taken a certain special someone picnicking a stone's throw from the Vistana site.

Hell, Mason's blackouts had been so severe, for all he knew he'd come out to his father and forgotten about it. But now, by refusing to bend to his father's manipulation, by prioritizing a man he was falling for over his father's constant control, Mason had committed an unforgivable sin. In Pete's eyes, at least.

*Showtime*, Mason thought.

"Naser. And if you ever say it with anything less than kindness and respect, if you *ever* say it with the contempt and the anger you use to talk to me and everyone here, I will flatten you."

Pete flinched, but he held his ground. Through the open office door, Mason saw heads turn, wide eyes staring.

"You better watch your fucking mouth, *son,*" Pete growled.

"Or else what?" Mason was suddenly eye level with his father—he'd stood up from behind his desk without planning to. "Or else *what?* I'm not the one who clings to you like an old blanket I can't stand the smell of but won't throw away. Three weeks in to those *crybaby meetings* and I've already got more people in my life, more people I can trust, than you've racked up in a lifetime. You want to kick me to the curb for being bi? Go ahead. I'll land. You think I'm going to miss this plum gig? Being subjected to your abuse every day?"

"You might miss your house," Pete snarled.

"It's not my house. It's an old fuck pad where you took women you were paying not to have an honest opinion about you."

Pete whirled and slammed the door to Mason's office so hard the window rattled in its frame.

"No son of mine is—"

There was a fierce crash that made Pete jump and whirl, and that's when Mason realized he'd picked up a glass picture frame housing a baby picture of him and his mother and thrown it at the wall a few feet from where his father stood. Thrown it hard enough to dent the wood and shatter the glass into several chunky fragments and a diamond-like spray of smaller ones across the carpet. The stunned look in his father's eyes, the singing pain in Mason's throwing arm, these things might have silenced another man. But a rage coursed through Mason's veins that felt powerful. Delicious. Intoxicating.

"Don't you even," Mason growled. "Don't even start with some bullshit speech from some pamphlet for a church you've never attended in your goddamn life. You can kick me out of that house. You can kick me out of a job. But you can't shame me. I don't respect you enough for that. So take your pick, *Dad*. Fire me or get out of my office."

The last time Pete Worther had looked like this, Mason had been ten. They'd been on a rare bike ride through the mountains together. Pete's front tire had slammed into a rock in the middle of the path, hurling him to the ground. The wind had been knocked out of the man, and there'd been several panicked seconds of young Mason watching his big, burly dad, down on all fours, white-faced and wheezing. But in that long-ago moment, he'd shouted questions at his dad about how he could help, convinced the man was having a heart attack, and his dad had waved him away with one hand. Even when his body was singing with pain, the prospect of his son's touch repulsed him.

This time Mason didn't say a word.

This time he wasn't afraid. He was relieved.

He'd done it, finally. Cut the cord. Said too much, lost his shit, served the man more truth than he could handle.

His dad would fire him, for sure. The short-term results would be gnarly and complicated, but the long-term result would be something he'd craved for years—his dad would finally let him go. And there would be no glittering temptation for Mason to come back to. No house, no cash, no cars. No hate-tinged gifts.

Just freedom.

But his dad didn't even give him that. He turned and left Mason's office instead.

*Call Shirley,* he thought as he reached his car. *Your hands are shaking. Call Shirley.* But he didn't want to slow down. Sitting in the feelings would only make them worse.

*Naser,* he thought, as he sped home. *All I need is Nas.*

But as soon as he walked through his front door, he started a perpetual swipe, refreshing his emails and texts, braced for some official-sounding termination letter from his dad or a gussied-up eviction letter from his dad's lawyer. Something official sounding and especially dickish.

Hours passed. The sun sank into the ocean, painting the sand orange and pink as it went. His phone stayed silent.

If his furious words hadn't done the job, should he drop the ax himself and quit?

He lost track of time until he heard a car engine outside, followed by a light, familiar knock on the front door, and when he opened it, there was Naser, redolent of the same spicy cologne that had turned Mason's bedsheets into a passport to bliss the night before, dressed in tantalizingly tight dark jeans and a dark blue band-collar tee that exposed the inviting brown expanse of his neck.

When Mason looked into his beautiful eyes, his first instinct was to tell him everything. Tell him how he might have just fucked his life up royally, but he'd loved every damn minute of it. And that he'd done it for him. For *them*. But Naser's expression was a mixture of vulnerable and hungry that joined up with all of Mason's fantasies of the moment to come. Fantasies of what Naser would look like writhing beneath him. What it would feel like to grab his luscious, meaty hips with fingers slick with lube as he drove himself into him from behind. What it would feel like to close his hands around Naser's throat with just the amount of pressure he craved.

So instead of spilling out his truth, Mason grabbed Naser by one hand and pulled him inside.

"Waited long enough," he managed to get out before he brought their mouths together. Naser let out a surprised grunt as their lips met, then he was lost to the kiss. The kitchen had played host to enough of their hurried pleasure. It was time to return to the bedroom, the site of their original undoing.

When Mason threw Naser to the bed, his eyes brightened as fiercely as they had when he'd guided Mason's foot to his throat. And then Mason was on top of him thinking, *Finally. Tonight I finally make him mine.*

And then a car horn started blaring.

A familiar car horn.

He knew full well it was coming from a bright orange Maserati that had to be parked right outside his front door. Because stupid, messy Mason hadn't given Chadwick the guest code for the gate when he first moved in: he'd given his own. Now, if he wanted Chadwick barred from their private drive, he'd have to petition the HOA to change the code for all the residents.

But maybe this was perfect. Maybe this was how it was supposed to be. Maybe there was a twisted kind of justice in ignoring Chadwick's latest plea for attention while joining his body with Naser's.

The horn continued to blare.

Naser stiffened, lips leaving Mason's. "Who is that?"

"Just ignore him."

"*Him?* Wait, who?"

"Seriously, it's fine. He'll go away."

"It's kind of ruining the mood."

"Don't let it."

Naser's hands pressed against Mason's chest, a small move that shifted things from a green light to a red one. Mason went still, opening his eyes to see Naser staring up at him.

"Mason..."

"It's just Chadwick. He'll go away."

A pounding knock against the front door. The name, Mason could see, lanced through Naser like a hot sword.

*This is probably how he used to look when people said my name,* Mason thought.

The anger was back. As white hot as it had been in his father's office. No way could Chadwick or his father steal this moment from them. But Mason could channel his anger, he was sure. Redirect it. Turn it into something positive.

He started for the stairs. "Come on."

Naser didn't follow. "Wait, come on *where*? What's happening?"

"I'm going to deal with him. *We're* going to deal with him. Together."

At the top of the stairs, Mason turned. Naser looked paralyzed, legs dangling off the side of the bed, resting back on his elbows, black hair still mussed from their burst of passion.

"If he wants to force his damn way into my house, then he gets to meet my boyfriend," Mason said. "I mean, that's what you are, right?"

"Mason, I..." The words left him on a sigh that sounded both happy and confused. And afraid.

He figured Naser would follow if he made the first move, so he did, taking the stairs two at a time. When he threw the front door open, Chadwick reared back a step. "Figured if I gave you a day to sleep off your PMS you'd realize what a dick you were being, but you're ignoring my texts so..."

Mason gestured for the guy to cross the threshold. But once he'd closed the door behind Chadwick, he didn't see any sign of Naser on the stairs, which made his stomach feel cold.

"Naser?" he called out.

Wide eyed, Chadwick looked from Mason to the empty stairs. "Na*whut*?"

A few seconds later, footsteps sounded, as slow and cautious as the ones Naser had sometimes taken to avoid them in high school.

When Chadwick and Naser's eyes met, Mason struggled to put words to the current that seemed to pass between the two men.

Naser looked dead inside and cold on the outside. Chadwick, on the other hand, looked caught. Mason would have expected the dynamic to be reversed, but maybe this was how Naser had looked at Mason when he'd crossed the pool deck at Sapphire Cove two weeks before. Mason had been too drunk to remember. After all, Chadwick had been the worst out of the three of them. The aggressor. The ringleader. The one whose rage always had to be dialed back. Mason hadn't done nearly enough to put a stop to him in high school. It was time to make up for that, right here, right now.

"There's something else I need to tell you," Mason said, "something I didn't say last night, something I don't think you're going to be able to handle, to be frank." Chadwick couldn't take his eyes off Naser. "Chadwick, are you listening to me?"

Chadwick turned, giving Mason a stunned look.

"I'm bisexual. And Naser and I are in a relationship. I think he's my boyfriend, but I might've sprung that one on him too fast. We'll see. That's fine. I'll give him all the time he needs. But the deal is this. If you want any part in my life, you have to accept that. Both of those things. You have to accept *him*."

No quick response. No shitty retort. No slur. The news had shocked the man across from him, and when Chadwick was shocked, he went blank. Then, slowly, he started to nod.

For an instant, he felt pride. Chadwick looked speechless and repentant, and that meant Mason had handled this perfectly.

Then he saw the look on Naser's face.

Naser felt like he'd had no choice but to come downstairs, to answer Mason's call.

He blamed himself for not putting up more of a stand in the bedroom, not saying something about Chadwick sooner. And now, as he studied the man he'd only referred to as Bleachers Guy since graduating high school, there was a chance the bastard's extensive face work might make this whole thing bearable—the implants and fillers rendered him unfamiliar.

Almost.

But the look in his eyes was the same—all challenge and hate. The same look Chadwick had given him that day senior year when he'd finally managed to roll over onto his back, head roaring with pain, coughing dirt.

That was the part that had haunted him the most.

Chadwick hadn't taken off running after his assault. He'd lingered, stood over him to make his point, as if to say, *I gave you what you want and then punished you for it.* But the worst had always been his memory of the pain in his throat, of how it had left him hoarse for days, and how every time his mother had asked him about it, he'd lied and told her he thought he was getting a cold. And the lie only made the memories come roaring back. One minute he'd been down on his knees, thinking *finally*. Finally I get to do a secret, dirty, sexy thing like I read about in those stories on the Internet. The next he'd slammed headfirst into a post.

"Sure," Chadwick said.

Mason looked stunned. *"Sure?"*

Chadwick nodded more emphatically, chewing his lower lip in a way that made him look thoughtful, which Naser suspected was an act. "Yeah, I mean, can't say I blame you." Chadwick stared into his friend's eyes. "Kid sucks a mean dick, doesn't he?"

Mason looked like he'd been punched in the stomach.

Naser's vision blurred, and he felt his jaw quiver. Somehow the idea that Chadwick, all these years later, would talk about that long ago moment as if it had been nothing more than a hookup made Naser want to scream. And then there was Mason's desperate, pleading look, a look that seemed to say, *What's happening? What's Chadwick saying?*

"Tell him the whole story." Naser's voice was a cross between a whisper and a gasp.

Chadwick huffed with laughter, as if he thought Naser was about to embarrass himself.

Quaking inside, Naser took another step down the stairs. "Tell him what you did to me before I could get up off my knees, after you forced me to swallow. Tell him how you grabbed me and threw me headfirst into a post, so hard I could barely breathe, so that it felt like my skull was on fire. Tell him how you grabbed me by the back of the neck and shoved a handful of dirt down my throat so far I choked, and said, *This is what you'll be breathing if you ever tell anyone about this, fag.* Tell him that part, *Chadwick.*"

The only sound that came next was Mason's breaths. Breaths he was struggling to take in. Naser's breaths felt too small to make a sound.

Chadwick turned and looked at him. There was no shame in his eyes. "What can I say? A mouth's a mouth, Prancer."

The next thing Naser knew, Chadwick was flying.

Because Mason had grabbed him by the front of his shirt and thrown him.

*So fast,* was all Naser could think.

First, they crashed to the floor just past the dining table, then they were up and scrumming into the living room area, spinning dangerously close to the coffee table before a roundhouse punch from Mason slammed Chadwick into the wall just shy of the television.

Chadwick rushed Mason with enough force to send them crashing into the side of the coffee table, knocking the glass surface sideways off its seashell base before they flew over the top in a tangle of limbs, landing on the sofa behind it hard enough to tip it back against the wall.

Then it was a tussle on the cushions, each man struggling to pin the other, neither man succeeding. It would have looked comic if they hadn't both been spotting the white cushions with blood.

Two men fighting without regard for any of the physical objects in their presence.

Even though Mason had thrown the first blow, it had erupted as quickly as Chadwick's assault that long ago afternoon behind the bleachers, when it had become clear, too late, that his response to the furtive pleasure Naser had given him would be furious, shame-filled silence.

They crashed to the floor just shy of the sliding glass door. When they rose, Chadwick tried to make a run for it, realizing what Naser could see. A volcano of rage inside of Mason had erupted, and Chadwick would be lucky not to drown in lava.

But Mason grabbed him and turned him and landed an uppercut against the man's jaw, sending him backward into the glass door, stunning him enough for Mason to grab him by his shirt and toss him back in the other direction.

This time, the glass coffee table did shatter.

"Is that what you did?" Mason roared.

Chadwick groaned and slid off the giant carved seashell and onto a bed of shattered glass.

"Is this what you fucking did to him?"

Pulse roaring in his ears, arms tingling as if they'd become more raw energy than flesh and bone, Mason saw real fear enter Chadwick's expression for the first time since he'd crossed the threshold. But it did nothing to quell his rage. His skin was aflame, his injuries an afterthought. Every cell in his body felt flushed with fresh oxygen.

*I did it too,* Mason thought. *I'm just as guilty as he is.* He hadn't been there, hadn't shoved a fistful of dirt down Naser's throat, but he'd opened the door, made Naser a target. Set the stage for a moment that sounded a hell of a lot like rape. Sex turned brutally violent without warning, without consent, without Naser's system of taps to indicate yes, harder, stop. What else could you call it? Mason felt as guilty now as if he'd shoved that dirt down Naser's throat himself.

Chadwick had to be punished.

Chadwick had to be crushed.

The guy rolled sideways off the broken glass, onto all fours, blood spotting the back of his shirt from where he'd landed. He started crawling for the nearest wall, one hand searching blindly for it. He was in bad shape. His gym time had always been vanity driven, and his drug use hadn't contributed to his cardiovascular health.

A spare dining room chair was pushed against the wall next to the sliding glass door. It was high-backed, with a heavy wooden frame and upholstered seat. It was heavy, but Mason's rage felt like it could overcome gravity. When he picked the chair up by two of its heavy wooden legs, he heard Naser call his name, sounding breathless and terrified.

*Scaring Nas,* a quiet voice in his head said. It didn't sound like Banjo, the voice of his fears. It sounded gentle and more encouraging. Like Shirley.

*You're scaring Nas.* But it was a quiet underscore to the roaring voices of guilt and anger that told him Chadwick had to be demolished right there on his living room floor.

Gripping the edges of its upturned seat, Mason raised the chair over one shoulder.

*"Mason!"* Naser cried.

Chadwick spun, but he couldn't get to his feet. His eyes widened.

"Apologize," Mason growled. "Apologize to my boyfriend."

Chadwick's laugh started as a wheeze and became a wet cackle.

"I'm sorry." He let lose a wet, fluid-sounding cough. "I'm so, so sorry I won't be on the guest list for your faggy little fag wedding."

Mason raised the chair. Then Naser was in front of him, eyes wide and streaming tears, hand out in front of him, fingers on his raised hand trembling. "Put it down. *Please.*"

Impossible to say he was defending Naser—*avenging* Naser—when the man was terrified and trying to stop him.

A dam was getting ready to collapse inside Mason. Behind it was a lake of shame that would swamp the fires of rage that had been fueling him for hours now.

He lowered the chair without turning it right side up again, lowered it until the upturned seat was resting against the floor. When he released his grip, it fell over to one side with a loud *thwack*. Naser lowered his arm, then he turned to Chadwick. "Get out," he said.

As if every muscle in his body hurt, Chadwick slowly hoisted himself to his feet, one hand pressed against the wall next to him. He coughed—a miserable sound that suggested one of Mason's blows had done serious damage to his throat or maybe his chest. Then he turned for the front door, hunched over and shuffling.

Once he was gone, once he and Naser were standing there, chests heaving with breaths as they listened to the Maserati fire up and then peel off into the night, Mason suddenly felt the pain of every blow Chadwick had managed to inflict. He wanted to find salvation and comfort in Naser's eyes, but all he saw when the man looked back at him was fear, as if he'd been dragged around the room with them.

"Nas," he whispered.

He reached for Naser's face. Naser flinched, then grimaced as if the reaction made him ashamed. The sight leveled another blow against the dam inside Mason, leaving another, longer crack. *I scared him. On the night I was supposed to claim him, I scared him.* Maybe it was the blood on his hands that had done it. No choice but to lower them to his side.

"Do you have a first aid kit?" Naser had tried for a businesslike tone, but his voice was shaking.

"I'm fine."

"Band-Aids?"

"I don't know. Maybe the cabinet above the sink."

When Naser started for the kitchen, it felt like he'd done so just as an excuse to turn his back on Mason. The adrenaline rush now made Mason feel unsteady. He righted the chair he'd almost used to kill Chadwick and sank down into it. After he managed to lift his head from his hands, he saw Naser searching the cabinet above the sink, coming up short.

"How could you not tell me?" Mason asked.

Naser froze and bowed his head, gripping an open cabinet door in each hand. "Seriously? You think I had some big, passionate affair with your best friend? Is that what it sounded like to you?"

"That's not what I meant."

Naser slammed the cabinet doors, turned on the faucet, and started wetting a rag.

Mason couldn't bear the silence. "If you'd said something upstairs, I never would have brought him into the house."

"You didn't ask. You just announced. It was like everything else with you. It was so fast and intense I was afraid of what would happen if I didn't go along. I mean, did you really need to know *that* story to know how much I wouldn't want to see him again? He was always the worst one. Always."

Head bowed, avoiding eye contact, Naser crossed the room, sank to his knees in front of Mason, and started dabbing at his bloody hands with the wet rag, trying, it seemed, to see how shallow the wounds were. To see which blood was Mason's.

"Tell me what happened," Mason whispered. "Please."

Naser dabbed. "Why?"

"So I can—"

"You can't make up for what *he* did."

"Says who?"

Naser threw the rag to one side and dropped back onto his haunches. "Me!"

It hurt, Naser's anger. Hurt the way he rose to his feet and turned his back on him, but Mason told himself this was Chadwick's doing, what he was seeing—this pain that coursed through Naser like a poison. For a terrifying few seconds, Mason thought Naser was going for the front door. Instead he wilted into one of the dining room chairs, resting his elbow next to a stack of unopened mail.

"He flirted with me. Beginning of senior year. I didn't know what to make of it. It was like Jekyll and Hyde. No guy had ever flirted with me. Especially not him. But after school one day, he came up to my locker and started asking me all kinds of questions. He even told me not to be nervous. He said, *We're getting too old for that bullshit.*

"The longer he talked, the more real it felt. Then he asked me if I wanted to hang out with him, and I just stared at him, like I couldn't believe what he was saying. And he actually reached up and tousled my hair. It was…tender. Another guy had never touched me like that. I got chills all over my body. And he noticed and he smiled like some hero out of a romcom and said, *Do I give you chills, Nas?*

"I knew it was dangerous. The whole time he was walking me back to the bleachers I thought you and Tim might pop out from behind something and beat the shit out of me. But I was starving, and so it felt worth the risk. Everyone around me was dating and going to dances, and I'd never been with anyone.

"So yeah, I knew. I knew it was dangerous as hell, but I did it anyway because it was *him*. Because it was one of you. And I wasn't exactly drowning in other offers. And to be honest, he went so far with it, I thought it was real. But then when it was over, when he was gone and I was lying there coughing up dirt and trying to breathe again, I realized it was more of the same. He'd just used his dick this time."

"I'm sorry," Mason whispered.

"It's not your fault."

"They targeted you…*we* targeted you because of me. Your first day of school, I went right for you and put my arm around you before I knew what I was doing, and when I saw the looks on their faces, I tried to turn it into something else because I was too afraid."

Naser nodded.

"Prom," Mason said quietly. "At prom, when I followed you, were you afraid it was going to be like that?"

Naser nodded, tears spilling from his eyes.

In the silence that followed, he could hear the echoes of their crashes and their furious grunts.

"I hate him," Mason finally whispered. "I've hated him for so long."

Naser wiped his cheeks with the back of one hand. "Then why is he still in your life?"

"After this? He's not. Trust me."

But Naser didn't look convinced. Mason wanted to rush to him, wanted to hit his knees and plead his case. But the memory of how Naser had flinched when he'd reached for his face held him in his place. The chair he'd almost used as a murder weapon now felt like his prison. "What?"

Naser shook his head, as if his thoughts were nothing. But his thoughts had silenced him and quickened his breaths, so Mason knew they were far more than nothing.

"What, Nas?"

"It's just… It's been ten years, Mason. He's got the code to the gate. How did he manage to hold on for so long?"

"Why did I hold on to him, you mean?"

Naser shrugged, studying the fingers he'd clasped in his lap.

Mason sat up, feeling fresh tension around every aching injury. "You just said what he did to you wasn't my fault. Now it sounds like you're accusing me of something."

"I'm just asking why you were so ready to kill your best friend."

"For you. I did all of that for you. You're the one who stood in my kitchen yesterday and lectured me on how you didn't want to be anybody's secret."

Naser shot to his feet. "*When the time comes*, you said. Those were your words, Mason. When the time comes. And I agreed and said let's not rush. Let's do it on our own schedule and no one else's, and that included Chadwick Fucking Brody.

"I'm sorry I didn't mention him specifically, but I have trouble saying his name, okay? I mean, you just made the decision for both of us. He blares the horn and you're suddenly coming out to him in the foyer and shoving me in his face. Even if you didn't know what he did to me that day, you knew about everything else. But you didn't stop to ask yourself if I wanted to ever lay eyes on him again.

"I swear, Mason, sometimes it's like you woke up one day and suddenly decided you want this life that you've spent no time building, and now I'm this accessory you're tugging along on your journey of recovery."

Mason shot to his feet. "That's not fair! You know that's not how I see you. You know how I've always—"

"*Always?* Mason! You have to stop. You have to stop talking about high school like we had this great long-distance romance. Because that's not really how it played for me, okay? You may have had all these big, secret feelings while you lived the life of a golden boy. But I had my room, and Math Club, and one afternoon behind the bleachers with your best friend. There's how you see me and then there's how well you know me, and you've been getting to know me for a week, Mason. A week, that's all, and this is where we are."

Naser gestured to the ruined living room around them, but Mason couldn't bring himself to look at any of the debris. He didn't need to.

"What are you saying?" Mason asked. "Are you…are you *ending* this?"

Naser shook his head. "I don't… I don't know."

Mason rose to his feet. "I did this for *you*. I did that to him because of what he did to you."

"There's no way all of that anger was because of me, Mason. You've been waiting to do that to him for years. I don't know why you haven't before now, and it's not for me to figure out. But what it feels like is that you dragged me downstairs and threw me in his face because you thought it would get him out of your life forever. And that's not how I want to be treated by my *boyfriend*."

Naser said the word *boyfriend* with as much hate as Mason's father said the word *fag*, and suddenly he was dizzy and his breaths were shallow. He'd made it sound as if Mason had been a fool to apply the label at all. As if Mason could never measure up to the title in Naser's world.

"Everything I've done since I saw you again has been about wanting to make things right with you. Everything, Naser."

"Everything you've done has been about wanting to feel better about who you were by fucking me."

The words hurt worse than any of his best friend's blows.

"Well, sorry. Guess I misread the signals when you put my foot on your damn throat, Prancer."

Naser flinched from head to toe this time, took a step back, then raised his chin as if he thought Mason might be prepared to strike him—physically, this time—and he was prepared to accept the blow. His eyes were hooded, distant. He wasn't seeing the Mason of right now. He was seeing the Mason of ten years ago. Or worse, he was deciding they were the same person after all. And Mason had just given him permission to—with a single word.

"Nas."

Naser turned his back and started for the door.

"Nas…"

He didn't slam the door, which somehow made it worse. The quiet click made for a more determined and thoughtful end, and then Naser was gone, having left the house as easily and quietly as if he were following a preordained schedule of which Mason should have been well aware.

"*Nas!*"

The Volvo's engine answered.

Mason's vision wobbled, the destruction surrounding him veiled by tears. He felt the chair's seat touch his butt before he realized he'd sunk into it. And then his face was in his hands, and he was hearing a voice in his head he didn't quite recognize. It sounded small and quiet and reasonable.

*Just one,* it said, *just one drink. That's all. Just one.*

Another Mason got behind the wheel of his car, another Mason drove to the gas station closest to his house and nodded at the night clerk behind the counter. They'd never said much to each other, but it had been two weeks since Mason had stopped off to grab some vodka bottles, so the clerk looked up from his magazine to indicate his version of surprise—a raised eyebrow and a longer nod than usual.

Then Mason was standing at the liquor case, hearing the buzz of the fluorescent lights for the first time, fingers resting against the chilled glass. His stomach contorted into what he figured was his body's best attempt at rebellion, best attempt to tell him to stop.

Then he heard a gentle, familiar sound. Designer clogs clapping linoleum floor, the swish of a long sundress.

Then he smelled the sweet floral perfume that had come to mean hard truths would be told. Shirley was standing next to him at the case.

"Thought you were an ice cream guy," she said. "Freezer's on that wall."

If he looked her in the eye, that dam inside would finally give. And sure enough, it did. When he met her gaze, his vision blurred, and he was blinking back tears.

"That's going to be a helluva shiner," Shirley said.

"Did you follow me here?" Mason croaked.

Shirley nodded.

"How much did you hear?"

She rested her back against the liquor case. Her pose looked casual, but she was blocking the vodka, he realized. "I heard the Godzilla versus Douchebag part. Then, once Naser left, I figured you might be headed someplace like this." When he didn't say anything further, she added, "You're Godzilla, by the way."

"I screwed up, Shirley."

"Have you had a drink?"

He shook his head.

"Then it's fixable. Take a drink and it won't be."

He told her the whole story, starting with his fight with his dad that day, trying to keep his voice low, hating how it made him sound like a pouting little boy.

"I was working so hard to be different and then one word comes out of my mouth. And it was like I ruined everything."

"Why'd you say it?"

"I don't know."

"Well, you should do the work to figure that out."

"All I've been doing is working on myself."

"Oh, sweetie. Please."

"How many damn meetings have I been to? How many apologies have I made? I mean, all of that means nothing now because I said one word?"

Shirley stood up straight. "You almost killed someone tonight. And you lashed out at the man you claim to care about with the most hurtful word you can think of. And no offense, Mason, but you *haven't* been doing all the work. You've been popping into meetings for two weeks and getting to know people, but you haven't cracked the spine on the copy of the *Twelve Steps and Twelve Traditions* I gave you, and you haven't put a pen to paper to do a single writing exercise I've suggested. And all of them are about getting down to the root of this rage that made you throw something at your father and almost beat your best friend half to death.

"From day one, you fast-forwarded to the first step out of the twelve that you thought would put Naser in your bed fastest. And it worked. For this long. And in that time, you made him your higher power, and now that you think you've lost his approval, you're six inches from a vodka bottle. That's not love. Not for him, not for you. What I heard in your house tonight sounded louder and worse than any of your drunken parties. Look, Mason, there's chemical sobriety and then there's emotional sobriety. You've had one and not the other. Now you're about to lose both."

He was too shamed to fight, too tired to argue.

Too exhausted to admit she was anything other than right.

"What do you think I should do?" he asked.

She sucked in a long, deep breath, as dramatic as any she'd performed on television over the years. "Are you sure you want to ask me that question?"

He nodded.

"All right, then. Strap yourself in."

# 27

Sometimes losing was a blessing. Falling just short of a prize could be its own reward. Naser had learned this early in life, and he suspected his acceptance of this cold truth formed the basis of his sister's judgment of him as someone who constantly avoided risk.

The truth was more complicated.

When the interview for a job that seemed like your dream gig didn't result in a hire, when the response from the Northeastern university of your choice took the form of a polite but dismissive paragraph, or—more recently—when the man who'd haunted your fantasies for years erupted into a fit of terrifying violence and capped it off by using the cruelest nickname for you he could think of, you were freed. Freed from having to upend an orderly and fairly enjoyable life to make room for something that might bring you the occasional moment of joy, but at the cost of being humbled and degraded while you struggled to keep it.

Naser had spent most of his adult life working around the very rich. Very few of them lived stress-free lives. Indeed, it seemed the more you had, the more you worried about losing it. And so, after he left Mason's house, ears ringing as if he'd been thrown headfirst into a post all over again, he returned to his condo the way he might after a long and stressful trip, as if the place were a warm and welcoming cocoon, and he'd been a fool to leave it for so long.

His job had always been to break bad news to people, to tether their dreams to cold, hard realities.

He had no trouble performing this service for himself.

He was home, and he was free. Free from worrying about his mother finding out about him and Mason. Free from the worry that Mason was so extraordinarily good looking, with an ocean of family money behind him, he might throw Naser over for a better offer as soon as the taboo wildness of their reunion faded.

He was also free to pour himself a glass of wine.

He finished half of it before falling into bed. The rapid approach of sleep seemed like another sign he'd done the right thing. Released a big—and beautiful—but terrible weight. With inevitable speed, the night's events had made clear there was no real future for him and Mason Worther. Chadwick would be just the first of many violent roadblocks. Mason's abusive father, Naser was sure, would have been much worse. It was time for Naser to move on, grateful he'd been able to live out some extended version of a gay porn fantasy—closeted bully bangs gay boy. It was hot, it was fun, it was over.

His sleep was dreamless and deep.

For two hours.

Then he woke in darkness and rose with some vague notion of going to the bathroom. Instead, he opened the door to his closet, sank to the floor inside and wrapped his arms around his knees, reverting to his old habit for concealing the sound of his nocturnal tears, even though he now lived alone. This was the price he had to pay. He'd accepted Mason's invitation and been dragged into some funhouse mirror version of their past, been forced to relive one of his worst moments without warning.

Hours later, he woke with a start and a terrible crick in his neck from where he'd been resting his head against the closet wall. Sunlight poured through the slatted closet door.

He was scheduled to sit in on a lunch meeting that afternoon with Connor and two representatives from a health and wellness company who'd flown in to discuss a possible branding partnership with Sapphire Cove's soon to be renovated spa. Connor was putting them up at the hotel, and Naser's job was to keep his ears open and see if anything sounded fishy about the numbers in their pitch.

He told himself not to, but he checked his phone.

Nothing from Mason.

Again, the first stab of pain was accompanied by a wash of relief.

But there was an email from his sister—she'd signed the investment agreement.

Fighting tears, he showered, dressed, and plotted a strategy for keeping a professional demeanor all day. Deep breaths. Mantras. And, when absolutely necessary, remembering the anger in Mason's eyes when he'd said the word *Prancer.*

Twice as he drove to the resort, he was tempted to pull over and catch his breath.

As soon as he reached the hotel, he made a beeline for his office and closed the door.

Jonas called out to him, but Naser seemed to hear the man's voice on a delay.

He was leaning against the front of his desk, fighting tears, when he heard Jonas enter the office behind him. "Everything all right?"

"Not really, no."

"Well, why don't we have a seat in my office and—"

Naser spun. The sight of whatever wild expression was on Naser's face set Jonas back a step. "Why don't you tell me the name of *one* corporation you worked at between college and the Four Seasons in DC?"

Jonas flinched and took a step back. "Naser..."

"Just one. That's all. I'll wait."

"Okay, clearly, I've done something—"

"You know what, let's just not bother. The answer is I'm not all right. I had one of the worst days of my life yesterday, and I don't feel like talking about it with someone who can't be authentic with me in return. I know nothing about you, Jonas. Nothing. And I sit here all the time spilling my guts to you so..."

Jonas looked around the room as if he thought Naser must be talking to someone else. When he could no longer deny that they were alone, the man swallowed and wet his lips with his tongue. "Well...I apologize for getting in your line of fire today."

"Or you could apologize for brushing off my attempts to actually get to know you with patronizing lines like that."

Jonas's eyes blazed. "You do know me," he whispered. "You know who I am, *here*, every day."

He knew he was lashing out at someone who didn't quite deserve it, but inside he felt as vulnerable and exposed and violated as he had behind the bleachers at Laguna Mesa High that awful afternoon. "I'm sorry, Jonas, but if you think I'm someone who would judge you for whatever's in your past, then I don't feel comfortable talking about what I'm dealing with right now."

Jonas nodded, but his expression was tense and angry. "Sometimes when someone doesn't want to share something, it has nothing to do with who the other person is or isn't." Jonas gazed at Naser as if he wanted to say more, then he bowed his head and took a step back. "I apologize for intruding."

Naser was about to call out to him when Connor appeared in his doorway, eyes wide, clearly having heard the last moments of their exchange. Seeing the distress on Naser's face, he closed the door behind him, moved to him, and gripped his shoulders gently. "You have a visitor," he said. "In the motor court."

"Who?"

"Mason. I didn't tell him you're here, and apparently, he had them call my office instead of yours. Which says he's not sure how he's going to be received. So…is this a meeting you want to have right now, Nas? Or would you like me to get rid of him?"

"What time is it? When's our lunch?"

"Forty minutes. I can handle the Dawn Blossom folks on my own."

Naser shook his head. "No, I can deal." But he sounded drowsy and disoriented and incapable of dealing with pretty much anything.

"Nas, is this safe?"

"I don't know what that word means anymore."

"Yeah. I need a more direct answer than that before you go to talk to this guy alone."

Naser swallowed. "I told him his friend Chadwick was Bleachers Guy and he beat him within an inch of his life in front of me. I thought he was going to kill him."

Connor nodded slowly, obviously fighting dozens of questions and even more opinions. Instead, he gently patted Naser's shoulders. "I see. Well, later you can explain to me how that's a problem. Meanwhile, I'm going to go get Mason Worther a gold medal. I'll be close by if you need me."

Averting his eyes, Naser headed for the door.

The motor court was relatively quiet. On his first sweep, Naser looked over Mason without recognizing him. He was standing on the other side of the gurgling French fountain, and it was the first time he'd seen him out of the house with no product in his hair. Unstyled, his blond bangs draped his forehead, making him look years younger. Sunglasses concealed his eyes, but they weren't big enough to hide the bruise on his right cheek and the long, scabbed cut on the right side of his jaw.

As Naser approached, Mason removed his glasses, revealing a vicious black eye.

In an instant, Naser lost the surefootedness of the night before, lost his belief that turning on his heel and walking out of Mason's house would spare him all the complicated discussions the fallout of that night might beg for. His heart was racing.

A white Tesla idled close by. Naser recognized the car. Behind the wheel was a well-put-together woman who looked like the woman he'd seen watching them from her porch the night he'd fetched Mason from his beached Ferrari.

"Is that your neighbor?" Naser asked.

"Shirley, yeah. She drove me."

The bottom dropped out of Naser's stomach.

Had Mason wrecked his car? Did the bruises from his fight with Chadwick include further damage from some drunken accident? Naser had felt so weakened and small when he'd left the house, it had never occurred to him that Mason might drink over it. When Mason saw Naser's expression, he put his hands out.

"Wait. No. *No*, I didn't drink last night." Mason steadied himself with a deep breath. "I mean, I was close. Like liquor store close. But, um... I'm not supposed to say that because it's manipulative and I'm responsible for my own choices, so..."

An SUV nosed around the fountain behind him, forcing Naser to take several steps closer to Mason. When he looked up, he saw Mason extending an envelope in his direction. He took it.

"The check," he finally said. "I made it out to you. I figured that would be easier."

"For Pari." Naser heard his own voice as if he were underwater. "This is the check for Pari?"

Mason nodded.

*This is goodbye,* Naser thought, and it felt like his lungs had turned to stone.

"Listen," Mason finally said, "I don't know if it's cool, me dropping by like this. I was trying to give you space after what I said. But things are happening kind of fast and... I'm going somewhere, Nas. And I'm not going to be able to have a phone, and if you did try to get in touch with me at some point, I didn't want you to think I was ignoring you."

"Where are you going?"

"It's a rehab. It's in the mountains not too far from here. But I'm going to be there for a while."

"How long?"

"Thirty days."

The number hit Naser like an anvil. Suddenly walking out of Mason's house felt like a luxury he hadn't been able to afford. "Thirty days? That's a month."

"Last time I checked, yeah."

"And they take your phone away?"

"Some of these places are like health spas, but this one's pretty hardcore. You can have your phone back at any time, but as soon as you ask for it, they take away your bed and you have to leave. I might be able to have visitors at some point and I'd..." A tear slipped down Mason's cheek. He huffed a quick breath through his nostrils to clear them of the first threat of tears. "I'd love it if you came. If you can forgive me for last night."

In the course of one surprise announcement, he'd gone from letting Mason go to wanting to hang on to him for dear life. The latter urge shamed him.

Had he stubbornly nursed some small hope that after a few days of alienation, Mason would return, hat in hand, more sober apologies coming fast and furious? This was like that, only different. Much different.

*Thirty days.*

Mason nodded grimly, as if accepting the reality that Naser was too overwhelmed to agree to a visit. The truth was, Naser felt trapped between his comforting belief that he'd been done with Mason since the night before and his new and spreading terror that he might never see him again.

He was that thing he hated more than anything, that thing he'd fought being his entire life with numbers and plans and projections—he was confused.

"So you didn't drink but you're going to rehab anyway?" The question came out sounding peevish and strained, which wasn't what he'd intended. But somehow, he and Mason had ended up in some frightening zone where actions and intentions were dangerously out of whack.

Mason grunted as if he were struggling with the concept too. "Apparently I'm running on rage. And it's a family trait. Not one I'm interested in inheriting. And you're not the only one who thinks it was wrong to bring Chadwick into the house last night without talking to you about it first. *Really* talking to you about it."

Naser nodded. "So you're going there right now? This...mountain rehab?"

"I managed to score a bed last minute, so I gotta jump on it."

"No email? No social media? No anything?"

Mason shook his head, as if the prospect frightened him too. Was it the prospect of being cut off from the world or the prospect of being cut off from Naser?

"It is cool. That you stopped off to tell me. It is cool, and I'm glad you did." Naser's eyes flooded. But when he tried to stop his tears, his cough turned into a choke. Crying in front of Mason still felt like crying in front of his bully—especially after the night before—and the resulting shame paralyzed him.

"I never should have said it, Nas. I never should have said that—"

Naser waved his hands through the air. "Don't. Don't leave feeling guilty. I don't want you to go wherever this place is feeling guilty, okay?"

"You're talking like we're never going to see each other again."

*We won't.* Naser was stunned by the clarity and force of the thought. *You'll get your head put on straight, clean up your act, and realize I was just a wild phase. Just a way to avoid what you're doing now.* He tried to keep his expression neutral, but some flicker of these thoughts must have flashed in his eyes because Mason took a step toward him and whispered his name under his breath.

Naser struggled to find his words. "'I...I want you to know that whatever happens, you don't need to feel guilty about me anymore. This past week, except for the last part, has been amazing, and it more than makes up for, you know, our past." He wasn't sure he believed it. But it seemed like the only thing that could draw this painful moment to a close in a way that wouldn't scar them both forever.

Mason stared at him. He clearly wanted Naser to keep talking, wanted him to say more. Part of Naser wanted to, but it was the same part of him that felt locked inside his closet, sobbing into the shadows. And Mason didn't seem to have the energy to coax that boy out into the light. Or the time, given the Tesla idling nearby.

So he nodded and turned and started for the car, and that narcotizing, confusing mix of anguish and relief flushed Naser head to toe again, an invitation to return to his natural, accustomed state of sexual frustration and isolation and not hoping for very much when it came to his love life.

Mason was almost to the car when he turned and started for Naser again.

"No," he said as he closed the distance between them. "No." When his hands gripped Naser's shoulders, chills swept outward from their warmth, as if he'd been forced to go without the man's comforting touch for eons instead of hours.

"I don't want to be done with you. I'm not going to this place so that I can be done with you, Naser. I'm going so I can *start* something with you. Something I've never had. Something it sounds like you've never had. But I have to be the man who's worthy of it, and I'm not there yet. But I want to be. I'm scared, and I don't know what I'm doing. But I know sure as hell, I am not trying to be *done* with you."

The kiss was hard and forceful, not furtive and boyish and tentative like the others Mason had given him in public. But Naser, for the first time, resisted it despite himself. And when he realized how rigid he'd gone, Mason had already turned and started for his neighbor's car. He wasn't sure how to interpret Mason's sudden burst of speed—did he feel rejected by Naser's resistance or was he trying to get out of there before Naser could say anything else that made the goodbye sound permanent?

He refused to torture himself by watching the Tesla depart. Instead, he steeled himself and marched back into the lobby. It felt like there was a bird beating its wings inside of his chest, the same feeling he'd get in high school when he pretended to ignore a coughed or hissed comment from Mason and his crew because to let the other students know it was getting to him seemed like the ultimate defeat.

In a daze, he walked back to his office and locked the check for Pari in his desk drawer. But he didn't linger there. Connor would find him and pelt him with questions. Instead, he headed to the stairs to the beach and walked halfway down them so he could pretend like he was enjoying the view of the sparkling sea from behind his sunglasses. Then he texted Connor.

**All good. See you at Camilla's in thirty.**

*All good.*

As if.

Then, in a daze, he put on his bravest and most professional face as he sat next to Connor and nodded his way through a meeting with the representatives from Dawn Blossom, who were so coiffed, so slathered in their own facial products and so doggedly cheerful, Naser thought he might scream and run from the table. Connor asked a ton of questions. Naser didn't hear most of them. He did pick up on the trend line, though. Connor wanted to know more about what they'd do to the spa's infrastructure and less about their product line.

Then the meeting was over and they were all standing and shaking hands and saying goodbye. As he and Connor watched the brightly dressed Dawn Blossom reps make their way back into the lobby, Naser felt like some security blanket had suddenly been yanked from them. The obligation that had been keeping him relatively on his game had departed. He feared his composure was about to flee with it.

"Nas." The soft concern in Connor's voice coupled with the gentle way Connor closed a hand around Naser's arm threatened to undo him.

He started walking, holding one hand up as if he needed a few seconds to figure out what he was going to say. Instead, he quickened his steps, and by the time he was outside, his hand had drifted down to his waist, and the next thing he knew he was making his way to one of the more secret corners of the property—a paved walkway that ran just below the lowest terrace of villas and looked south down the coast.

That's where Connor found him sobbing into one arm he'd bent and rested against the balustrade.

# 28

They took Mason's phone just like Shirley said they would.

They searched his one suitcase for pills, bags of powder, and hidden bottles. The guy who did it wore plastic gloves and had hints of tattoo sleeves spilling out from under the cuffs of his long-sleeved T-shirt. Despite its fullness, his long, salt and pepper ponytail looked freshly washed and neatly tied back, and he had an electricity and liveliness in his eyes Mason had come to associate with sober people. He'd introduced himself, of course, but in his nervousness, Mason had already forgotten the man's name.

While he worked, Mr. Ponytail gave Mason a speech that sounded like it had been crafted by a lawyer.

No one was a prisoner at Pine Rise.

There was a little town with a few motels about ten minutes away by car—half an hour if you set out on foot. The van could take him there anytime he wanted. But it would be a one-way trip.

Same deal if he demanded his phone back: he'd lose his bed and be out on his behind—house rules. To emphasize this point, the guy pointed to the wall behind his desk and explained that inside the little cubbyholes designed to receive mail—thirty of them, Mason counted—sat the abandoned cell phones of the current residents, each one tucked inside a little brown manila envelope with a first name written on it. The fact that they weren't locked up seemed deliberate, a form of display on par with some reality television contest. Or that bell on Coronado Island that Navy SEAL trainees rang when they couldn't go another brutal day.

The intake process went down in a clean office that filled one of the single-story cabins spread across a clearing shaded by tall pines.

He'd been so overcome with emotion on the ride away from Sapphire Cove he wasn't sure if he could pinpoint their final location on a map. He knew they'd driven across the smoggy Inland Empire before snaking up into the pine-forested mountains but wasn't sure if they'd ended up closer to Lake Arrowhead or Big Bear. The place had the look of one of those summer camps he'd avoided attending in high school because he was usually on expensive trips with Chadwick and his family or at some sports training clinic trying to beef up for the next season.

Shirley hovered nearby.

By the time Mr. Ponytail had finished, he'd removed a bottle of mouthwash Mason had included with his toiletry kit. "Enough alcohol in there to catch a buzz off of if you swallow," he'd said with a smile and a wink, and he'd also taken Mason's Gillette. "We give every new guy an electric razor. Don't worry."

*Suicide risk.* He didn't say it, but Mason felt the words in his gut. He hadn't even considered the razor blades in those terms. Their confiscation frightened him, suggested the feelings he'd be forced to deal with in this mountain hideaway might force him into some dark places. Places where guys like Mr. Ponytail wanted to ensure he wouldn't be armed with easy instruments of self-harm.

Then Mr. Ponytail was handing him his bag and Mason was rising to his feet. And when he turned to Shirley, he realized it was goodbye. And the look on her face told him she still didn't have an answer to the question that had been circling over their heads since the night before.

Their first calls to Pine Rise had made clear the health insurance plan Mason had through his father's company required the boss to approve expenses like rehab. Mason was considering footing the bill himself using what he'd made from the sale of the Ferrari, but if things with his dad continued on the course he'd started the day before, he'd need every penny of that money to live off of when he got out. Shirley had volunteered to call Pete, leaving the request on his voicemail.

"Nothing?" Mason asked.

Shirley shook her head. She was afraid Mason would use the uncertainty as an excuse to bail, but Pine Rise had made it clear they never gave someone the boot over a bill. Sometimes they worked out liberal repayment options with patients that went on for months, years even, after they graduated the program. Still, it felt like making the request of

Pete Worther had given the man power over one of Mason's lowest moments. For her willingness to make the call on his behalf, Mason would owe Shirley for the rest of his life.

"We'll figure it out," Mason finally said.

"All right, kid." She was fighting a catch in her voice. "Say yes where you want to say no, like you did with me." She pulled him close and kissed him on the cheek. The enormity of it all closed over him again. No phone, no visitors until something called Family Week, and that was two weeks off. And the word *family* didn't exactly give him a warm, fuzzy feeling right now.

"Thanks for saving my life," Mason whispered.

"If I could, I would in a heartbeat, but that's going to be on you. Here." Her second hug was fiercer, then she pulled away, head bowed, starting for the dirt parking lot nearby.

Suddenly he was alone with the guy whose name he couldn't remember and the vast quiet of the woods all around them.

A few minutes later, they were walking through the clearing toward one of the cabins.

When they stepped inside, the threadbare accommodations gave new meaning to Shirley's description of the place as *hardcore*. Several bunks in a single room, a window unit AC in the far corner that looked moldy from years of disuse—the colder mountain temperatures probably meant it never got turned on. At least there were two private bathrooms—for five guys. And all the beds looked occupied.

On the nightstand next to his bed, like a spartan welcome package, was a new copy of the *Big Book of Alcoholics Anonymous*, several workbooks of some sort, and a fresh new Mead spiral notebook with an unopened package of felt-tip pens resting on top. And most importantly, a paperback copy of *Twelve Steps and Twelve Traditions*, the very text Shirley had accused him of ignoring the night before. The work he'd avoided doing for days now was waiting for him.

Of the two other guys who rose to their feet when they entered, one looked like he should be managing a small regional bank in the Midwest; the other was a long-haired rocker type whose shoulder-length hair was several different colors of fading neon hues.

When they shook hands, Rock Star apologized for the fact that the colors in his hair were fading. "Fresh dye jobs aren't exactly the priority here," he added with a sheepish grin. They were friendly enough, and after the guy who'd admitted him left—Tony, he'd reminded Mason after it became clear he'd forgotten—Mason sat there, feeling like it was another version of himself making polite conversation. The guys kept their questions simple and not too invasive and gave him plenty of time to respond, their long, patient looks telling him they'd been where Mason was just a few weeks or maybe a few days prior.

"Car accident?" Mr. Midwest said, while pointing to his face to indicate Mason's injuries.

"Best friend," Mason answered.

They both nodded, as if a fistfight with one's best friend was a regular weekend where they came from, and for the first time, Mason thought he'd ended up in the right place.

Then he remembered the stunned and wounded look in Naser's eyes as he'd left Sapphire Cove, the way he'd gone rigid under Mason's kiss, and he sank down onto his bed as if his bones weighed five times as much as they had the day before. Remembered that when he'd asked Naser if he'd come visit, Naser hadn't said yes.

# 29

The only thing Naser loved as much as his best friend was the comfortable, suburban house his best friend shared with Logan Murdoch. It was in a hilly section of Mission Viejo, a comfortable distance from Sapphire Cove, and in the year since the two men moved in, it had become Naser's favorite refuge.

Several months of renovations had turned it into a delightful jumble of Connor and Logan's contrasting tastes. The kitchen, with its brightly tiled backsplashes and dusty gold drawer pulls, was all Connor. In the grassy backyard, the fire pit and stark stone fountain might as well have had Logan's name carved into their bases.

The yard also sported a serene view of the wooded canyon beyond. There, underneath a pergola threaded with string lights, Naser and Connor sat by the sputtering flames, wine glasses in hand.

Logan remained inside, puttering around the kitchen and watching television, giving them a respectful distance.

Nobody knew him better than Connor Harcourt. The reverse was true as well. And that's why, a year before, in the midst of the endless drama that had marked Connor's return to Sapphire Cove, Naser had barged into the hotel room where Connor had been staying and told him in no uncertain terms how he thought he was about to blow it with Logan. He didn't want to take credit for keeping them together. He liked to think he'd helped, though. A little bit.

Whatever the case, ever since that night, Naser knew that he'd laid himself open to a similar lecture should their roles ever be reversed.

And now they were.

Having finished the entire tale, Naser took a long, fortifying sip of rosé. "Speak, Blondie."

Connor cleared his throat and set his glass on the rim of the fire pit. "So when Mason asked you why you hadn't told him, you really thought he was accusing you of having some affair?"

"It felt like an accusation. Like he thought he had a right to know. But..."

"But what?"

"You think I should have told him before?"

Connor nodded. "Not because he had some right to know. So you could see how he would react. Because you have a right not to be involved with someone who doesn't think what Chadwick did to you was a big deal. Because it was a big deal."

Naser rolled his eyes before he could stop himself. "I was bullied in high school. It's part of my story, that's all. A week with Mason, now everyone's acting like it's the whole story. I'm not interested in letting Chadwick Brody take over my life."

"It was beyond bullying, Nas, what Chadwick did to you." Connor's gaze was so suddenly direct, his blue eyes so full of intensity, Naser's wine hand froze halfway to his mouth. "Look, it means a lot to me that you would trust me with this story, and I've done my best to hold my tongue about it over the years. Really, I have. But this wasn't some tryst that went wrong. That man used sex to get you alone, vulnerable, and on your knees. Then he violently attacked you. That's sexual assault, and it's a crime. Last night, Mason saw that, and he reacted like someone who really cares about you. And it's the first time I haven't wanted to push him off a cliff."

"So you think I should have let Mason kill him with a chair?"

"No, I think you were right to stop him, and I think Mason's right to go someplace where he can get his emotions in check. And yeah, he was totally wrong to bring that skeeze into the house without talking to you about it first. Obviously, things got out of control. What I'm saying is maybe you got so upset with Mason because he reacted to what really happened to you. He reacted like it's a big deal. Because it is."

Naser stared into the fire. Connor didn't rush to fill the silence.

"What did Dr. Kelley think?" Connor finally asked.

Naser tensed up from head to toe. "I haven't seen her in years."

"Yeah, but when you were seeing her, what did she..." Connor read

Naser's stony expression instantly. "Nas, you didn't tell her about what happened with Chadwick?"

"I didn't want her to kink shame me."

Connor swallowed, clearly biting his tongue. It was a lousy excuse. Naser's reason for going to therapy in the first place was that he'd been kink shaming himself for years.

"I had concerns about my kinks turning into self-harm, but I don't like what I like because of Chadwick."

"Nas, you like it when guys step on your throat and Chadwick—"

"I know what Chadwick did. It's not the same. What I like is about..." He took a thirsty sip of wine to fortify himself. "Everything Chadwick did that day was about throwing me away. What gets me off is about being...held down, seen. Being a guy's sole focus. It's the *opposite* of what Chadwick did. He threw me out like trash. I like it when a guy doesn't want me to get away."

"It's about control too, right?"

"*My* control," Naser corrected him. "I turn it on and off. The tap system, remember?"

Connor nodded, sipping wine. "I don't disagree, but I'd be a shitty friend if I didn't tell you I think all of that's worth unpacking with a professional. Especially in light of recent developments."

"Fair," Naser responded.

Connor nodded and looked to the flames. "I'm ashamed," Naser finally whispered. "I'm ashamed I didn't tell him. I'm ashamed I didn't say anything even though I'd friggin' hidden from Chadwick right there in his house. I'm ashamed I didn't say anything because of how badly I wanted him. How badly I've always wanted him."

"If you think there's something wrong with you being attracted to Mason Worther even after all this, then you *are* letting Chadwick Brody take over your life."

"Bitch," Naser whispered.

Connor took a sip of wine then held up his hands in a gesture of surrender. "I call it like I see it because I love you more than Logan's ball sack."

"That's disgusting," Naser whispered.

Connor smiled and toasted him with his glass. Naser returned the gesture, then a silence settled over them, interrupted by the guttering sounds of the gas-fueled fire pit.

Connor's assessment felt true, and he couldn't deny it. Maybe it hadn't been that old nickname that had driven him from Mason's house the night before.

Maybe, by beating the crap out of Chadwick Brody, Mason had shined a fierce spotlight on something Naser had relegated to the shadows for most of his adult life. By punishing Chadwick for his crime, Mason had made clear the depths to which Naser's secrecy and shame had allowed Chadwick to get away with it for years.

"He'll move on." Naser heard his voice as if from a distance.

Connor frowned. "Mason?"

Naser nodded. "He'll meet some guy or some girl in rehab. It'll be all intense like it was with me, and they'll have a life together."

"That would be easier for you, wouldn't it?"

Naser glared. Connor glared back.

"Excuse me?" Naser finally asked.

"You know, you've got a life that's kind of built for one. It would have been challenging to involve someone else in it. They might interrupt your reading time."

"Are you deliberately trying to provoke me, Blondie?"

Connor nodded. "Yes."

"Why?"

"Because I love you, but you're kind of full of it right now."

"Care to explain?"

"Naser, this is the closest to love at first sight I've ever heard. The problem was, the one who fell felt like he lived in a world where he couldn't be honest about how he felt, and so it turned into this contorted, twisted thing that has to be healed."

"I did not spend my high school years in love with Mason Worther."

"I'm not talking about you. I'm talking about him." Connor got to his feet. "You're staying for dinner. I'm cooking."

Then he headed toward the house before Naser could disagree.

# 30

Mason's first dinner at Pine Rise was served in a larger cabin than the one in which he was supposed to sleep. It wasn't as terrible as he'd feared. The other new residents he'd fallen in with were all a different version of humbled and embarrassed about where they'd ended up, and that made for a quiet meal, a version of relaxed that felt close to shell-shocked.

Then all the men on site—about thirty of them, total—formed a procession to the fire pit in the center of the clearing where they took their seats on folding chairs. Tony handed out big, woolen blankets for them to wrap themselves in as the temperatures fell. A dome of stars appeared beyond the interlocking branches overhead. And in that moment, Mason felt as if he had finally come to rest inside of his bones, as if he'd stopped moving through his life at warp speed for the first time in years.

Then they opened the meeting by asking all of the new arrivals to introduce themselves and share for three minutes. And Mason thought he might barf.

But when his turn came, the words tumbled out of him without pause. He gazed into the flames as he spoke so that he could tune out any reactions from the strangers around him. He talked about being a closeted bisexual for most of his life, about the type of man he'd been in high school, the way he'd tried to make it up to Naser, how badly he'd beaten his best friend the night before. When the timer went off, he was amazed at how much of it he'd managed to get through. Maybe because he hadn't edited or held back or even paused, and his truth had come pouring out of him in a determined but gentle rush.

He'd been himself with strangers for the first time in his life.

And when he found the courage to look up, he saw only understanding in the fire-lit eyes of the men around him. Then the other newcomers shared, and his story fell into place beside theirs. Tales of broken homes and kids who wouldn't return phone calls and partners who'd finally left for good.

Back home, on Shirley's arm, he'd still felt like the new kid, the odd man out who might bolt at any minute, the special project for the old timers. Now he felt like one of the survivors of the shipwreck, which also meant he wasn't alone on the shore.

A few hours later, they were all back in their cabins when Tony knocked on the door as a warning, then entered without waiting for a response. He made a beeline for Mason's bunk. "We heard from your old man," he said, and extended a slip of paper in one hand.

Mason hesitated, even though he doubted Tony would be sharing the message if it were abusive crap.

### DO WHAT YOU NEED TO DO. I'LL GET THE BILL.

His eyes filled.

Coming from his dad, it was practically a Christmas carol about love of family.

Coming on the heels of their last conversation, it might as well have had a heart emoji at the end.

Never in his life had his dad told him *not* to worry about something, but that's what he was saying now.

Mason had gone his entire life without showing anger to his father. Now that he had, something had shifted. Was it permanent? Only time would tell.

Mason went to hand the paper back, but Tony held up one palm. "Keep it. See if it helps."

Mason opened the drawer on his nightstand and placed the note inside. When he looked up, Tony was gone and other guys in the cabin were looking at him as if they were curious about what had gone down but too polite to ask.

He pulled back the sheets, settled into bed, opened the workbooks that had been waiting for him on his nightstand when he'd arrived that day, and flipped through pages with various exercises asking him to make a list of his resentments—the people, places, and things that made him angry on a regular basis. Worksheets with entry blanks, interview questions. Lots of them. He'd been hearing some version of the ideas within for weeks, but he'd been listening out of one ear, like an airplane passenger watching the preflight safety video with one eye.

He'd do it. All of it. But he knew he'd never get through it all unless he gave himself an incentive. A reward.

Mason opened the spiral notebook and brought his knees up under the sheet to make a writing surface. They hadn't said anything about mailing letters, and maybe they wouldn't let him, but they couldn't stop him from writing one.

The words *big, secret feelings* had been ringing in his head ever since Naser had shouted them the night before, reminding him again and again of Naser's accusations that theirs hadn't been a long-distance romance. There was truth to what Naser had said, lots of it. But it was also true that Naser might not appreciate the depth of those so-called secret feelings. And so Mason was determined to put them on paper, to give them as much detail, as much history as he could.

He'd finished a paragraph when something shifted and changed, and he realized he was writing something altogether different. He'd gone back to that moment in the hallway at Laguna Mesa High when he'd slid his arm around Naser. Only instead of looking back to see how Chadwick and Tim reacted, he kept walking, kept his arm around Naser's shoulders, kept asking him questions about who he was and how he'd ended up in their school.

He realized he'd gone from revisiting the past to rewriting it, and that's when he decided these letters he planned to write would need a title. So at the top of the page, he wrote one—**Who I Could Have Been**.

# 31

Seventy-two hours. That's how long Naser thought he'd need before Mason stopped occupying his every other thought. His reasons for this projection were simple—forty-eight hours seemed rushed, and a week seemed absurdly self-indulgent. He shouldn't spend longer grieving Mason's abrupt departure than he'd spent in the guy's actual presence after their reunion.

He was almost on target.

After three days, his every other thought stopped being of his former bully.

His every fourth or fifth, however, was still a painful freeze-frame from those final moments in the motor court of Sapphire Cove, when only a thin stream of Naser's true feelings had managed to bubble to the surface. That's when he found himself googling Southern California rehabs, making a list of all the ones located in mountainous or even relatively rugged areas. He figured he'd narrow it down to three, then send Mason an email through the main contact address for each facility. But when he tried to draft something succinct and powerful, something that would both convey how badly he missed him while not embarrassing him to the office administrator sure to read it first, his fingers froze, and his face got hot.

The fifth day after Mason's departure, Naser did the unthinkable, something that made clear to all who knew him that his mental health was in a perilous state—he canceled on his mother.

She was scheduled to have her eyes dilated during her visit to the optometrist, and it was common knowledge in their family that as long as Mahin Kazemi had adult children with cars, she would never take an Uber anywhere she couldn't drive herself. So Naser called his sister and guilted her into being chauffeur. To this end, he offered Pari a semi-tearful CliffsNotes version of his fight with Mason, leaving out the detail that Mason had gone off to rehab. Pari's persistent delight over the sudden messiness in her perfect brother's life—which she masked in dramatic sympathy, of course—seemed to trump her annoyance at having to drive south from LA on a weekday.

He hung up, grateful she hadn't seen through to his real motives. Now that he knew the woman had read his secret high school journals, Naser was too freaked out to be alone with his mother, especially with the stress of Mason's departure added to the mix.

The fact that he didn't hear from either woman after the doctor's visit should have been a red flag. A red flag consumed in flames that spelled out, *Depart California immediately*. But he was too exhausted and upset to monitor the situation closely, and that's why, when his mother showed up unannounced at his townhouse the next morning, he was buck naked and trying to masturbate his feelings away.

Mahin Kazemi thought doorbells were for other people—common people—which meant she always knocked with great verve, as if whoever was on the other side was awaiting not just her arrival, but the lively cadence of her signature announcement. When he saw her on the Ring cam, he cursed, frantically wiped lube off himself with a handful of Kleenex from beside the bed, spritzed himself with enough cologne to tranquilize a cat, then threw on an outfit that would barely pass muster at the gym. As he hurried downstairs, he hoped to die somewhere around the fifth step.

Instead, he found himself opening the front door, wearing a smile that felt like a grimace.

For the first time, Naser saw that she hadn't come alone. Standing behind her was a startlingly attractive man in nurse's scrubs holding some sort of medical bag. He looked eerily like one of the porn stars Naser had just been watching upstairs—olive-skinned, muscular, with a jet black buzz cut, bedroom eyes, and a bright silver stud in his right ear.

His mother stepped forward, cupped his chin in her hands, and squeezed. Hard. "Stick out your tongue, Naser-*joon*."

"Why?"

"If you are canceling on your mother, then you must be very sick and you must be examined."

Rather than refute this misdiagnosis, Naser stuck out his tongue.

Mahin tapped his chin, an indication he should close his mouth. "This is Randy. He is going to take your blood." She moved past him into his townhouse. "Say hello, Randy."

Randy complied.

Another son might have objected to an unannounced blood draw orchestrated by his mother, but Naser had been enduring surprise blood draws since he was a little boy, mostly in the middle of the night and never for an urgent or compelling reason. The thermometer, however, was a surprise, and he jumped when she popped it in his mouth before he could sit down at the breakfast table. After a few seconds, it beeped.

"Ninety-nine. You are high!" Mahin proclaimed.

"That's actually normal for me, Mom."

*Especially when I'm jerking off,* he thought.

"There is no normal for *you*. There is only normal, and you are high. What have you been eating?"

"Pita chips."

*And porn,* he thought.

"That is not real food. What are you eating for real food?" Mahin headed for his pantry.

"I don't know. The only meals I ever remember are the ones you cook for me, Maman-*joon*." She rejected this obsequious compliment with a grunt and started rifling through his fridge.

Suddenly, Randy was sitting next to him, setting empty blood tubes on the table between them. Naser didn't protest as the studly nurse attached one to a vein in Naser's upturned forearm. "What are you testing me for?" Naser whispered.

Randy shook his head. "Well, she said *everything,* which isn't really a thing in our line of work, so I'm sort of winging it here." He looked Naser in the eye and dropped his voice. "Anything you *don't* want me to test for?"

Mahin opened the refrigerator and plopped several cans of diet soda onto the counter. "*Marg bar aspartame,* Naser-*joon*."

"Sugar is worse, Mom."

Mahin threw the diet soda cans into the trash without emptying them first, then she went for the cabinets and removed several boxes of crackers and cookies.

"How come I don't have one of those Persian mothers who's always trying to get me to eat rice? Instead she comes into my house chanting death to artificial sweeteners," Naser whispered. Randy shook with silent laughter.

"Randy is very attractive, no?" Mahin opened a box of crackers, popped one in her mouth, then tossed the box into the trash as she chewed.

"He is. Are you guys dating?" Naser asked.

"We are not. Because Randy is a gay." Mahin announced this as if it came with a cash prize.

"Not *a* gay. Gay. Just gay. Do you work for my mother, Randy?"

Randy didn't look up from the latest blood tube. "Not directly. I work at the hospital. Everyone there just does what your mother says no matter what department we're in. It's easier that way."

Naser understood perfectly. "I see. Is the goal here to take *all* of my blood?"

Mahin stood over him now. "I don't know. You are clearly very sick, and this is why you didn't drive me to the doctor yesterday."

"I wasn't sick. I was upset."

"Okay. We'll test your blood for things that upset people then. Maybe we'll find traces of me because according to your sister, I am a very upsetting mother."

"Oh, dear. What did Pari say yesterday?"

Mahin took a seat at the table. "Oh, what does your sister not say? Because at some point your sister says everything, especially if it is about how other people are doing it wrong."

"I wonder where she got that," Naser whispered. "Randy, that's enough blood, sweetie."

"Got it." Randy capped the last vial and laid it next to the other five.

"Randy, how would you like to do gay things with my son?"

*"Mom!"*

Randy gave her a sheepish smile. "I'm actually married, Mahin."

"To who? What does he do?"

"Well, um, to *two* whos actually, and they both farm goats while I—"

"Okay, well marry Naser too and then you'll have at least one husband with a real job."

*"Mom, toro khodo, nakon. Koshti mano!"* Sometimes accusing his mother of murdering him with words was the only way to get the woman to change subjects.

"What? Is this wrong too? I spent all of yesterday being told I am a terrible mother to my gay son, and so I brought the most attractive gay from the hospital to meet you and touch you. This is not supportive?"

"Yeah, nothing like getting five vials of blood taken for no reason to get me in the marrying mood."

Randy sputtered with laughter.

"See? He is funny, Randy. You should add him to your marriage of many goats."

"Randy," Naser said, "did you bring your own car, sweetie?"

Randy nodded.

"Why don't you head out? I'll handle this."

The man looked between the two of them with puppy dog eyes. "This is kind of fun, though. I mean, no offense. My marriage is capped at three, but—"

"It's fine. I just think my mom and I need some alone time."

"Sure, should I…" He gestured to the vials.

"Take the blood, Randy," Mahin said, then she rose from her chair and returned to the kitchen. Randy rose, too, and hurried out the door, waving as he went. "Test him for loyalty to his mother. His levels seem low."

Then they were alone, and suddenly she was digging in the tote bag she'd brought in on one arm and set on the counter. There was a rustling from inside. "I brought you a gift. Because you are sick or upset, or I don't know which thing. With your sister, I never know what to believe. She's better with colors than facts."

She pulled out a bright blue paper bag. Naser took it. "Where is it from?"

"The gay store."

Naser froze, suddenly afraid of its contents. "The what?"

"The *gay* store."

"Mom, what gay store? What are you talking about?"

"I went on the Internet and I searched for *gay store,* and it sent me to this place in Santa Ana called books for adults."

"You went to a porn shop alone?"

"No, I took Fatemeh with me. It was fine. We did not stay long. I went up to the counter and I said to the clerk I have a son who has always been very…*gentle* and what gift should I give him, and she gave me this lotion."

Fatemeh was his mother's oldest Persian female friend, the kind of woman whose money probably went back to Darius the Great and who never stayed in a hotel that didn't have the word Ritz in the name. The image of the two of them cruising like grand and stylish ocean liners through a flotsam of dildos and butt plugs in what was probably one of the rougher neighborhoods of Santa Ana was one he needed a minute to process. Suddenly, he was desperate to know if Fatemeh had ever removed her Gucci sunglasses at all during the visit.

He'd drawn the alleged lotion bottle only an inch out of the bag before he saw what it actually was—a giant plastic tube full of anal lube. He dropped it back inside the bag and fought the urge to throw the entire thing in the trash.

"My God, what did Pari say to you yesterday?" he managed.

"What? That's not lotion?"

"A very specific kind. What did she say, Maman?"

Mahin took the bag from his hand so quickly he was forced to drop the lube back inside. She set it on the counter, made as if to go to the fridge, then her thoughts overtook her and she sucked in a deep, pained-sounding breath. "She says I am a terrible mother to my gay son. That you are struggling. With a man. And that you won't tell me about it because I don't...*see* you. That's what she says to me. And I'm on the way to the eye doctor when she says it, so it was very rude. What kind of thing is that?"

"Wasn't it a routine checkup?" Naser asked.

Mahin grunted and waved a hand through the air. "I wear contacts, so we never know."

"Is that all Pari said?" At the thought that his sister might have mentioned Mason by name—a name his mother had read in Naser's journals years ago—Naser's skin felt tight and prickly from head to toe.

"No. No, of course not. That would have been too easy. She said if I wanted to know more, I had to ask you. That I should ask you about your *whole* life for a change, and not just the parts of it I want to see."

This was his fault. He shouldn't have thrown them together in a car under semi-false pretenses. And he should probably muster some gratitude that his sister had found a way to acknowledge the conversation he'd had with her the morning after her event. But he would have appreciated at least a word or two of warning that she'd yanked the rug out from under the delicate balance he'd maintained with his mother for most of his adult life.

"That's a lot for a pretty short car ride, Mom. Did you say anything to her first?"

Mahin hissed and closed her hand in the air beside her head as if he'd just clasped a bell pull and tugged. "Why do you always say this? Where is the wine?"

"It's eleven in the morning, Mom."

Mahin started searching cabinets again. "Oh, it was nothing. I told her she was clearly a failure of a fashion designer and should go to a real school." When she saw Naser's expression, she stopped and shrugged. "What? I said I'd pay for the school. What, with the look?"

"She's talented, Mom. She's talented, and her business is hard, and when you say critical things to her, it hurts her."

"And when she tells me I am a terrible mother to you, the son who looks so much like the husband I loved and lost? Am I allowed to be hurt by this too?"

"Of course."

Mahin nodded slowly, as if she was trying to summon more gratitude for this answer than she possessed. "Do you think this is true?" she asked finally. "I am a terrible mother to you?"

"No."

She found an unopened bottle of red in the cabinet. "Are you lying?"

"Mom, it's too early for wine. You drove."

"Then you drive me home." There was a challenge in her eyes. Was it the only reason she'd dropped by unannounced? To make him square the debt for not having driven her to the doctor the day before? He could work with that.

"Fine," Naser said.

Mahin gave him a thin smile and started to hunt for a corkscrew. Naser sidled up to her, opened the right drawer, and set it onto the counter next to her hand. She patted his hand gently in thanks, then her fingers closed over his.

"Are you struggling, Naser-*joon*?" she asked.

A lump formed in his throat. "It's been a rough week," he managed.

"Because of a man?"

"It started fast. Maybe too fast. And it might not work out. He's gone away for a while. It'll give me time to think things through."

The quick kiss he gave her on the cheek was supposed to serve as a period on the sentence and the topic in general. But she was studying him closely—curiously—as he backed away. The matter wasn't closed and wouldn't be until she said it was. He'd secretly wanted her to initiate a conversation about his personal life for years now. The moment had finally arrived, but in the wrong package.

"Who is this man?" The protective tone in her voice warmed something deep inside of him. Then he was struck by an image of her crouched in the attic of their house in Fullerton, reading through the pages of his high school journals, where Mason's name appeared again and again and again. And never in a flattering light.

He sank back into the chair he'd just abandoned a moment before. "He's in real estate," he answered, feeling like a liar. And a hypocrite.

Mahin nodded. A tense silence settled. She pulled a wine glass from a cabinet, filling it carefully as if she thought her hand might start shaking at any moment. "Well, clearly your sister is wrong."

"About what?"

"You don't want to talk about this man, and I was stupid to ask."

"Can I ask you something?" Naser asked. His mother nodded, but she looked wary as she brought the glass to her lips. "In high school, did you read my journals?"

"Pari told you this?"

Naser nodded.

"That's it. We no longer speak to your sister. It's too dangerous."

"That's not going to be a thing."

Mahin stared down into her wine as she swirled it, a tense set to her jaw. "I knew something was wrong. After the email with the coach, that whole thing, the fake one where someone pretended to be you, I knew more was going on, but you wouldn't talk about it. And I felt guilty."

"Why?"

"Because I worked."

"You supported us."

"It wasn't just for that. I worked because I had lost so many things. Your father, Iran. And your father, he was the heart and the soul, the one who felt things. Who cried over songs. When I felt things I didn't like, I worked. I still do. And when that happened with the email and the coach, I worried that I lost you to something I didn't see. Because I was working. Instead of feeling."

"So you read my journals?" he asked.

She nodded and took a long drink of wine.

"And then?"

"I wrote letters. To the parents of all those boys. Threatening them."

"Wait, what?"

She fluttered one manicured hand through the air. "I never sent them. Because every time I wrote them, I would threaten them with torture and execution and not…you know, the law."

"What boys, Mom?"

"Don't play dumb. I got one of your yearbooks and I looked them up. There was, what…Morris, I think? With the yellow hair like a pillow?"

"Mason."

"Right. And then the one with the stupid name like a candle."

"Chadwick."

"Right. And what was the other one, with the scary eyes. Tim, I think?"

"He's dead."

"Good. I wish they were all dead."

"Mom."

Mahin's eyes flared, and the wine glass froze halfway to her mouth. "They hurt my son. They hurt my son, and I did not do anything about it because I talked to all my Persian friends and they said, 'We don't do this here, Mahin. Here we are supposed to give our children their privacy even when we are trying to keep them alive.' Child death has always been more acceptable in America, I guess. Besides, Naser-*joon*, you stopped writing in them so I figured you knew I had read them."

Naser's stomach went cold. He'd forgotten this detail, forgotten what had brought his secret musings to a halt. "That's not why I stopped," he whispered. "I didn't know you'd read them."

"Why did you stop then?"

Suddenly Naser was blinking back tears and trying to keep his chin from quivering. "One of them did something that was pretty bad, and I didn't want to write about it."

His mother was stone still, but her eyes were blazing. She cleared her throat. "Do you want to talk about this thing that he did?" The question sounded like a struggle.

"I might need a little time for that. This is happening pretty fast. This new mother-son honesty thing."

"We have always been honest."

"Mostly about other people, though."

Mahin nodded, but her expression seemed frozen, and when she lifted her wine glass back to her mouth, she used both hands. "I don't want to blame your father for this, but I blame your father for this," she said.

"How?" Naser asked.

"He knew."

"Knew what?"

"He came to me when you were very young and he said, 'Mahin, you need to prepare yourself. He is different. And we must never take his pride over it.' And I thought he would understand better because he was a man. He was not like you. He was not a man who loved other men. But I thought he would know. And so in my eyes, your pride became the most important thing. Why are you crying, Naser-*joon*?"

"I always thought you knew first."

"That you were gay?"

Naser nodded.

"Why?"

"There was this night when I was, like...I don't know, twelve, I think. Dad was showing me pictures of the mirrored mosque in Shiraz and saying how he wanted to take me there. And then you took him into the kitchen and...I heard what you said."

For a second, he thought his mother might play dumb or that she didn't remember the incident. Then, eyes glazed and vacant looking, she rose to her feet and turned from him, as if it were too painful to look directly at her son while she recalled the night in question. She braced herself against the kitchen counter, struggling for breath.

Had Naser taken their new honesty too far?

Did he have the right, given he was staying tight lipped about Mason?

"I didn't know this." She sounded breathless, exhausted. "I didn't know you heard us."

In the silence that followed, his mother drank the last of her wine in several swallows.

"I'm sorry to bring it up, Mom. I'm just... I've always hated that I was the reason we couldn't go back."

"You weren't. I was." His mother stared down into her now empty glass. "You were my excuse. I used you. Your father..." She went to take another drink, realized the glass was empty, then set it down so firmly Naser made a mental note to check it for cracks later. "Your father had a gift. He could always see what he wanted to see in everything. And I knew if we went back, for him it would be like nothing had changed. He would see only what he had loved that was still there. But for me, I would only see what was lost. And so what you heard that night was me denying him something he wanted because I did not know how little time I had left with him. That you would take this on yourself breaks my heart."

"Mom..." Naser rose to his feet and closed the distance between them, and when he slid his arms around his mother's waist, she crumpled into him.

After a minute of wilting, she pulled back, cupping his face in her hands. "This is my only fear for you, Naser. My only one. I fear that I did not work hard enough to hide my grief from you, and you saw how badly I was hurt by losing your father. And you are afraid of being hurt yourself like this, and that is why you are alone today."

He'd never heard her say these words, or anything to their effect, and he needed a minute to process this revelation. The idea was so new to him, he wasn't sure if it was true. He certainly didn't want to dismiss it out of hand. He feared doing so might shut his mother down, wall off this honesty from him forever.

"I'm possibly single, Mom. Not alone. There's a difference."

"That's not what it's about. It's about being able to love something you won't be able to keep forever. This was your father's gift. That he could love so much without fear. He loved you, Naser-*joon*. We did not carry you and your sister across the sea as dreams to let you go because you were different. But I used the fact that you were different to get out of doing something I did not want to do, and this is my shame."

"I absolve you of this shame."

She ran her hands through his hair and kissed him on both cheeks. "For this, I love you, Naser. But in the end, a mother absolves herself or no one does."

For a while, he held her, then he steered her to a chair.

The conversation flowed more easily after that. She let him take a quick shower, and then they were off to lunch, and the air between them felt more relaxed than it had been in years.

Hours later, after he'd chauffeured her home in her own car and taken an Uber back home, he slipped through the front door of his house feeling more relaxed and at ease than he had in days. Then he realized that somehow, he'd managed to get through the entire day with his mother without giving her the name of the man he was pretty sure he wouldn't be able to let go of anytime soon.

# 32

At night, Pine Rise was dark as a tomb, so as Mason followed Tony into the man's office in the administrative cabin, the only lights outside came from the dim flicker of the smoldering fire pit in the center of the clearing and some floating squares of warm gold that marked the windows of the residential cabins beyond.

"All right," the counselor said. "Ready to dive in or you want to check in with me first?"

"Hitchhiking to Mexico isn't an option?"

"Always, but it won't change the terms of our deal."

With a grunt, Mason sank into Tony's empty desk chair and stared at the corded phone on the guy's desk as if it might bite him if he reached for it too fast.

The Family Week portion of the program happened after a resident completed two weeks. It was several days of workshops and group activities designed to restore and improve communications with their loved ones upon release. They were all required to invite at least one relative.

Mason was dying to invite Naser. But after listening to most of Mason's life story, Tony had decided Pete Worther was a better candidate, despite Mason's six hundred or so reminders that his father was an angry, verbally abusive bully. Better to deal with a guy like that in a structured environment where immediate support was available, Tony had countered. And by immediate support, he meant a trained staff ready to kick Pete's ass off the property if he broke the rules.

Despite Shirley's exhortation to say yes where he wanted to say no, Mason had proposed a compromise. If his dad rejected the invitation, he could immediately invite Naser. Tony had agreed, and the deal had been struck.

Now it was showtime, and Mason wanted to run screaming into the woods.

"Okay. Remember the script. He can toss the rope at you, but if you don't pick it up, there's no tug of war. If he uses a slur or he gets crazy angry, ask him to stop once politely, then hang up if he does it again. This is about giving your father an opportunity to be a better man by asking for what you need."

"And he agreed to this time?"

"He said he'd be waiting by the phone," Tony answered.

He doubted his father had used those words.

All Mason had to do was get through this. Once Pete said no, his next call would be with Naser, and the guy's voice would pour into his ear like sweet music after two weeks of radio silence.

Mason picked the phone up off its cradle. "This is a waste of time, Tony."

"No such thing when we're being rigorously honest." Tony stepped outside the office to give him privacy, and Mason dialed.

His dad answered after the first ring. "What's wrong? Are you coming home?"

"No," Mason said. "Everything's fine."

"*Fine?* You're in rehab, genius."

"Uh huh. Okay, there's…this thing they're going to do here. It's called Family Week."

Silence.

"Figured something like this was coming," Pete finally grumbled. "You call your mother?"

"Why would I call her?"

"I don't know. I figured you guys were close."

"She walked out when I was three."

"I'm sure she's got her own version of that story."

"Well, she's not around to tell me. I don't even have a number for her. Look, I'm not calling to talk about Mom."

"I gotta go up there for a whole damn week?"

"You don't, actually." And just like that, Mason had gone off the script he'd agreed to with Tony. "If you don't want to do it, I've got somebody else lined up."

More silence.

"Who?" His father sounded offended. "Chadwick?"

"God, no. He's a mess. He should be a resident here, not a visitor."

"Who then?"

"Someone you don't know."

"This Nazar guy?"

"*Naser.*"

Mason braced for a homophobic attack that would have him throwing the phone across the room and telling Tony to screw their deal.

Finally, his father broke the silence. "How long you been seeing him?"

"I've known him a long time."

"Yeah, but how long have you been *seeing* him?"

"A few weeks." Which felt like a lie because the second and third week had been spent apart, and his attempt to formalize their relationship before he'd left had been an unmitigated, bloody disaster.

Pete Worther grunted. It sounded like he was shifting in his chair. "A few weeks. And he gets the number one spot? Jesus."

"It's rehab, Dad. Not a competition."

Another silence fell, and in it, Mason's fear bloomed. Had he accidentally insulted his father into coming by denting his ego?

"Okay," Pete finally said.

*Oh, fucking goddammit to hell,* Mason thought.

"I'll be there. But don't throw anything. I never raised a hand to you in my life. You can at least show me the respect of not throwing shit at my head."

His father hung up.

When the door to the office opened and Tony returned, Mason was resting his forehead on the desk and trying to remember how to breathe.

Family Week, it turned out, wasn't actually a week. It was three days. But this news didn't help Mason sleep any easier as his father's arrival drew near.

The residents of Pine Rise spent the Tuesday before start day meeting with counselors and preparing the statements they were supposed to make during the one-on-one sessions that would close out their loved one's visit.

*One on one.*

Never in such a short time had a single phrase come to embody so much dread in Mason's mind. He'd seen a version of it in movies and TV shows—two chairs facing each other in the center of the room, two relatives struggling to look each other in the eye as they bared their messy souls, the onlookers appearing quietly grateful it wasn't them in the ring.

His instructions from Tony were clear—they hadn't invited his dad so Mason could validate the man's verbal abuse. Instead, Mason's job was to tell his father how much the man's words had hurt over the years and how they'd given Mason a paralyzing fear of revealing his true self.

But it was time for Mason to own the fact—out loud and to his father's face—that he'd accepted his father's financial assistance when he hadn't wanted to, and that he'd done so because it was easier than coming clean with his firm in LA about his substance abuse problems.

And then, of course, there was the all-important goal of being completely honest about his sexuality outside the angry theater of their office confrontation.

This all sounded good, Mason told Tony again and again, but odds were the whole thing would end his relationship with his father once and for all, so why go to all the trouble? Tony's response was, "If your old man's gonna walk, he should walk away from the real you. Then you know you did everything you could to fix the relationship."

Honesty, Tony reminded him again, was a gift you gave yourself, the ability to be comfortable in your own skin. If you were doing it for any other reason, it probably wasn't all that honest. Either way, even if his father rejected him, Mason would be permanently liberated from the false version of himself that had served like a cumbersome suit of armor in a battle that had raged for too long.

In other words, Tony had a response for everything.

It was all a moot point, Mason figured.

No way would Pete Worther last all three days. One, tops, Mason figured, before the man lost his temper and was asked to leave. Would that be so bad? Mason would be vindicated in the eyes of Pine Rise's staff, and hell, maybe they could bring Naser in for the last few days of activities and workshops.

Tuesday night before Judgment Day, he barely slept a wink. Instead, he tossed and turned and scripted and rehearsed all the things he'd say during the awkward-to-agonizing reunion they were sure to have first thing in the morning.

There was no reunion first thing in the morning.

The first bell rang early, and the residents were rushed through their showers and a quick breakfast, then they were escorted on a long and sweaty hike to one of the worksites they'd been visiting since their arrival—a wooden staircase cut into one of the steeper dirt slopes on the property. The family members, he realized, all of whom were staying at motels just down the road, would arrive to a fairly empty property where the staff would have them all to themselves.

Nerves aflame, he worked alongside the other men, offloading logs from the flatbed before pounding them into the remaining stairs that had been carved in the dirt in the days prior.

Had his dad shown up?

Would he last until Mason got back, or would someone ask him to hug a tree first and he'd blow his stack?

For the next few hours, he'd have no way of knowing.

Finally, they were escorted back to their cabins and allowed to shower before lunch.

Lunch with their families.

His father was there, sitting by himself in the clearing, dressed in his usual work outfit of pressed chinos and a dress shirt. Had he ironed them himself at the motel? Something about this detail, the time and care it had taken his old man, struck him with unexpected force. Mason started for him, relieved to see that none of the reunions around them seemed all that warm or tearful. Instead, he saw the quiet evidence of strained marriages and children alienated from their parents. If he and Pete didn't exactly throw their arms around each other, they'd fit right in. This was not a Navy ship returning to port after months at sea.

His father stood, and for what felt like an eternity, they just stared at each other.

"We're going to eat lunch, I guess," his father said.

Mason nodded.

"How's the food?"

"Not terrible."

Pete grunted. "Stellar review. Where'd they keep you guys this morning?"

"Working."

His father grimaced. "You haven't been working."

"Not the firm, Dad. On a set of stairs we're building."

"Ah. So it's a labor camp too."

"More like we work on our mind-body connection through manual labor. And…you know, it's about contributing to something larger than ourselves."

"Getting paying customers to make improvements to the property, you mean? Slick operation they got here."

"That would be the dramatically nonspiritual way of looking at it."

Pete rolled his eyes and jerked his head in the direction of the meal hall. Some of the other residents and visitors had started shuffling through its propped-open double doors. Mason followed his dad inside. The shift in mood between breakfast and lunch was remarkable. The place felt like a library now. No smiles, all whispers and deep thoughts, everybody sitting a safe distance apart as if they were terrified of being overheard.

His dad started eating like a famished horse, a sign he was fighting nerves.

"That dude's in the NHL." Pete jerked his head in the direction of a giant bruiser of a guy Mason only knew as John C. The guy had shared tons of personal details about his marriage, but nothing about being a pro athlete. Most of the guys at Pine Rise didn't use last names, and Mason wasn't a hockey fan.

"All right, well, don't tell anyone you saw him here," Mason said.

"Yeah, I'm just dying to talk about my time at this place."

"Three days will be easier than thirty, I'm sure."

"They didn't have, like, a weekend package you could do?"

Mason shook his head. "What did *you* guys do this morning?"

"Some guy came in and talked to us about…" He twirled his fork in the air. "What you do here."

"Tony?"

"Ponytail?"

Mason nodded.

"That's the one."

Another long silence.

"What'd you think?" Mason asked.

His fathered chewed. "Look, I don't know about any of this stuff, okay? I'm here because you're my son and I don't want you to die drunk. Can't it be that simple?"

It was perhaps the most loving thing his dad had ever said to him, and he was shocked by what he saw in the man's eyes when he said it—need. And fear. In a man whose last name was Worther, they were often the same thing.

"It's new to me too, Dad. I guess the best thing we can do right now is just listen to what they have to say."

Pete looked to his plate.

They ate in silence.

And that's what they did in the hours that followed. Listened.

It seemed like no one had seen fit to mention anything to Pete about the one-on-ones, so Mason didn't either. Maybe the guy thought they'd be able to cruise through all three days by sitting still and staying quiet as guest speakers and visiting therapists lectured them about the dynamics that developed in families struck by addiction, the roles people played, the bad coping skills that didn't serve either the addict or their family. Later that afternoon, they were separated again, and according to Pete's terse reports when they were reunited, the family members had been broken down into smaller groups led by the therapist assigned to their relative.

That evening, they headed to Pine Rise's dirt parking lot where he saw his dad had declined the van service and driven his Mercedes the ten minutes from the motel.

"We're going to have to do a thing," he said. "Friday, they said. You and me. Like with chairs and stuff."

So they'd told his dad after all. "They're called one-on-ones. But it's kind of a misnomer because we won't be alone."

"You ready for this?"

"Not sure."

"That makes two of us then," his father grumbled, and then he was walking to his car.

*Thus ends my father's visit to Pine Rise Family Week*, Mason thought as he watched his father's taillights disappear into the evening dark.

During work hours the next morning, Mason felt more relaxed. He'd done his duty by inviting his father, been willing to do the awful work. When Pete didn't show up that day, Mason could be free of this whole messy affair and the stress of anticipating Friday.

No such luck.

His father was waiting for him in the clearing before lunch. Mason's heart raced. His palms started to sweat.

"How'd your morning go?" Mason asked once they were eating lunch.

"They had us work on what we're supposed to say in this one-on-one thing."

Mason nodded, but his throat had closed up.

"I guess you've been working on yours for a while." Pete shoveled a fork full of Salisbury steak into his mouth.

Mason nodded. That was all they said.

Then it was time for everyone to watch a hokey training film that was supposed to teach them about honest communication between addicts and their families, but Mason kept getting distracted by the fact that it was about forty years old, and several of the actors in it had gone on to have huge Hollywood careers. Break time was next, during which residents and family members were free to roam the property together. Mason walked them to the stairs they'd been building since he arrived. They were almost done now, a sinuous line of wooden logs leading to a bench-filled clearing down slope. Beyond was a stunning view of the dusty high deserts of Southern California that lay north of the forested mountains.

Silence settled.

"My dad drank," Pete finally said.

Mason was struck, once again, by how his dad never referred to his own dad as Mason's grandfather. Maybe because they'd never met. Or maybe because of this just revealed detail.

"As bad as me?" Mason asked.

Pete turned and looked him in the eye. Mason braced himself for an insult. "Worse." Pete lowered his eyes to the dirt.

It was a sign that something in his dad—something authentic—had been stirred up by this place. Mason thought he should lean into the moment, ask more questions. But there was too much of a chance his father would startle like a deer. And the truth was, when his father was startled, he acted more like a rampaging bear. Mason told himself to stay silent, listen, and wait for the two of them to end up in those dreaded, facing chairs.

On Friday morning, Tony drew the first set of names from a fishbowl: Johnny and Lana. Johnny was the hockey player Pete had pointed out on his first day. Lana was his petite beauty of a wife, whose long bright blonde hair always looked like it had been flat ironed against the back of her cardigans. For a few seconds after Tony read their names, the only answer was a rush of wind through the branches overhead and the squeaking sounds of the couple in question slowly rising from their folding chairs.

Mason felt like he'd been spared the executioner's blade.

For twenty minutes, at least.

He couldn't tell if the frosty look on Lana's face was proof of her disdain for the proceedings or simmering rage at her husband.

Then the two circles of attendees were enraptured by her eloquent and thoughtful description of what life had been like with her alcoholic husband for the past five years, how she'd woken most mornings believing she hadn't been loving enough, supportive enough, pretty enough to keep her husband from drinking the way he did. And as she described these feelings in raw detail, free from anger or hysterics, her husband slowly crumbled, his focus sinking from his wife to the dirt at his feet as the tears fell. Then she reached her account of what it had been like to discover him in bed with another woman, and his face was glued to his palms as his massive, muscular back shook with sobs. She finished by saying that she'd come to a decision—if he ever drank again, she would leave their marriage. If Johnny's shares all week were any indication, it was the first time he was hearing this.

Not every statement made in a one-on-one, the counselors had told them, needed to end with an ultimatum or a condition. The primary goal of the exercise was for the sober addict to experience the unvarnished truth about how their addiction had impacted their loved ones.

Then it was Johnny's turn. He described how he barely remembered being with the woman she'd caught him with—that's how drunk he'd been—how he'd regained consciousness the following morning remembering only the awful hurt on his wife's face, and that he'd woken up to that sight every day at Pine Rise. He explained that each time he'd taken a drink, it was because he'd managed to convince himself that this time, he wouldn't lose control. Now he'd come to the realization he'd never be able to control it, so he had to let it go altogether. And if he had to let drinking go just to keep her as his wife, that was more than a good enough reason by itself. It was her turn to break down. Clearly, she hadn't expected this promise.

As soon as Tony gave them the go ahead, they were in each other's arms. All told, the first session felt like an advertisement for how this sort of thing was supposed to go. Fearless honesty. An agreement. The promise of growth. Some of the guys around Mason were crying, and all Mason could think was, *How in the name of God am I going to do this with my old man?*

Tony stuck his hand into the bowl full of names, swished the little pieces of paper around, then drew one out. "Mason and Pete."

When Mason stood, his legs felt like rubber. Inside, a younger, childish version of him was running into the woods, screaming at the top of his lungs. He'd pass out before he got to one of the center chairs, he was sure. But he didn't, so now he was screwed. And his dad was taking a seat across from him as if he thought the chair might give way as soon as his butt touched metal.

Once they were seated, Tony spoke. "Pete, why don't you—"

"Mason goes first." There was a tense silence. "What? I mean, he's the reason we're here, so it's only fair, right?"

"Dad—"

"No, seriously. I mean, it's not my outfit, but I thought it was pretty shitty making that poor woman go first when the husband's the one who—"

"I'll go first," Mason said.

His dad fell silent.

Tony studied Mason.

In a few seconds, their dynamic had been laid bare for the group. Rushing into agreements he wasn't comfortable with, stuffing down how he really felt, all so he could douse the old man's latest flare of temper. If Mason was right, Tony was trying to figure out how the session would be best served—pressuring Pete Worther to conform to someone else's rules, or letting Mason take the lead. Finally, Tony nodded at Mason.

"My heart feels like it's going to burst out of my chest right now," Mason managed.

"Why? What have I ever—"

"Mason's going first Pete, remember?" Tony interjected.

"No, seriously. I mean, this kid has had every—"

*"Pete."* Tony's voice was like the crack of a whip, the voice of a man used to wrestling with addicts in all stages of recovery, anger, and sadness. "We do this one at a time. That's how this works. If you don't want to go first, that's fine, but that means we don't interrupt Mason until he's done. You'll have your chance to speak, like you just saw."

Pete's jaw tensed like he was chewing cud. His cheeks flamed. It had been a long time since anyone had batted him down like this, if ever. Instead of marching off, the man took in a long, pained-looking breath that flared his nostrils, then he stared at the dirt between their feet. Eventually, after what felt like an eternity, the man sensed his son's gaze and looked up at him, and Mason saw that same blend of fear and need in his old man's eyes he'd seen during their first lunch at Pine Rise.

"It never occurred to me what it was like for you to have a son who drank as much as I did."

Pete looked shocked. Mason was shocked too. He'd heard folks in meetings talking about having the sense that their higher power—their conceptions of God, or their sense of a greater force that governed the universe—was speaking through them. This was one of those moments. "I thought you were so tough that you didn't care...really. Or you were just embarrassed when I made a mess. And then the other day, your first day here, when you told me you didn't want me to die drunk. That meant a lot."

Pete was looking into his eyes now, but he looked wary. And embarrassed.

"I didn't think I had the power to hurt you, and I guess that's pretty childish of me. But the truth is, I'm afraid of you."

Pete flinched.

"I've always been afraid of you. I'm still afraid of you. For as long as I can remember, it feels like you've been angry, and it's been hard for me not to believe that I'm the reason. Because it's always been the two of us, so who else could it have been? But I realize now that's kind of self-centered of me. And it became my excuse to hide things from you. I hid how scared I was of you. How scared I was of losing your approval, which is crazy because to be perfectly honest, it doesn't feel like I ever had your approval." Mason cleared his throat. "But the point is, I wasn't honest with you about who I was, and I lied to you in college about how bad my drinking was. I told you a lot of lies. And that's on me. But one of those was that I never told you how badly it hurt..."

Mason felt his throat close up.

"What?" Pete asked. "What hurt?"

"The way you talked to me. The names you used to call me."

"What names?"

Tony cleared his throat and sat up. Mason shook his head at the man, hoping he wouldn't intervene.

"Well, faggot for one. Cocksucker was another."

"I never called you those things."

"You use the words all the time."

"Fine. Wash my mouth out with soap then. But I never called *you* those things."

"They're not just dirty words, Dad. They're slurs. They're...attacks on who I am."

"How the hell would *I* know who you were?"

Tony cleared his throat. "All right, guys. Maybe we should—"

"So I'm not going to get a turn?" Pete asked, face reddening.

Tony studied them both. "Mason, do you feel like you've said your piece for the moment?"

Mason nodded.

Now that he had the floor, Pete suddenly looked like he didn't want it. He stared at the dirt, shaking his head. "I mean, you sit here telling me how you've never told me who you really are, and then you get on my ass for not approving of you? How can I disapprove of someone I don't know? I mean, I didn't see you in high school, Mason. And I was like, okay. Fine. He's off playing sports. He's off with his friends. You were having a life. But before that, when I used to bring you to the beach house with the guys, you'd just... You'd get lost in space. You'd wander off in a corner, and it was like you weren't even there. And I'd try to talk to you, and you'd just look right through me like I was a stranger. I didn't even know how to deal with that. All right, fine. So I use words I shouldn't use sometime. All right, so—"

"It's more than that, Dad. You know it's more than that."

"How's it more than that?"

"You made up a work dinner to try to force me to cancel a date because you knew I was seeing a man."

"That's bullshit. I did that because you wouldn't tell me who you were going to see. I figured you were about to fall off the wagon."

Mason felt like ice water had been thrown in his face. Was this the truth or was his father lying? "No son of mine. That's what you said to me in my office. You were starting up some big speech about how no son of yours could ever be less than one hundred percent straight."

"No son of mine has a right to judge the type of woman I take to my own beach house. Which you had just done. *That's* what I was going to say to you before you threw a picture frame at my damn head. Because you were ready to dump shit on some version of me you made up."

"I didn't make up that you're a bully. You always have been. Always. If it felt like I was staring through you when I was a kid, maybe it's because I was afraid of you jumping down my damn throat."

"With *words?* Seriously, words? I spend how much bailing you out because of your messes, I bring you into my company when I don't know if I can trust you to even show up for work, and I get called up onto a mountain to talk about *words*."

"It's not just words!" Mason barked.

"Okay. Fine. *Fine*. I'm not crazy about guys who fuck with other dudes. You want to send me to another camp for that?"

Pete's rage sent a shockwave across the clearing, and Mason, for the first time, glimpsed something else writhing beneath the hate. Something that startled him silent. Something in the strange wording his father had just used—not fuck, fucked *with*. As if he felt he'd revealed too much, Pete ran his hands over his face and sucked in a deep breath.

"I know it's not PC or whatever, but how the hell was I supposed to know you weren't straight when you spent your whole life surrounded by bikini models? I swear to God, Mason. Honestly. I was ready to let you go. You went up to UCLA. And I thought, well, it's this big, liberal school, so he'll probably run off or become an artist or a Democrat or I don't know what. And I'll be down a son who talks to me like I'm supposed to park his car and I'm taking too long. No big loss, I guess. But then you came back. To me." He crooked a finger at his own chest. "*You* came back to *me*. Because you needed to be bailed out. Because you needed somebody to fund your nice cars and your all-night parties with Chadwick. And now I'm this son of a bitch who drowned you in all this crap when the truth is you used me for a check and a job, and now you want to punish me for it in front of all these people. You have any idea how shitty that makes me feel?"

"As shitty as it made me feel whenever you'd call a man you didn't like a faggot."

"I *never* called *you* a name—"

Mason could hear Tony trying to interject, could see the man coming toward them out of the corner of his eye. "You didn't have to! That's the point. Every day you made it crystal clear what would happen if I ever told you."

"I didn't know who you were! It wasn't about you!"

There was pressure on Mason's shoulder. It was Tony, standing next to his chair now, trying to put a stop to this. But Mason couldn't stop. "You'd never so much as give me a hug or pat me on the back. If you ever got hurt or I tried to help you, you'd bat me away like you thought I had a disease. You knew damn well who I was, and you thought I was so disgusting you couldn't touch me."

"*I was protecting you!*" Pete's roar would have terrified Mason if there hadn't been something else in it—something Mason had never seen before. Pete was crying. "The best *damn* thing I ever did for you was not touching you!" He'd pointed a finger at Mason, but his jaw was shaking. All of him, it seemed, was shaking, as if this admission was a gas vent that had burst through layers of bedrock.

Tony still gripped one of Mason's shoulders, but his other hand was open and extended toward Pete, as if to hold him in place. The group was stunned silent. It felt like they were doing the same thing Mason was—waiting to see if Pete was about to fall apart.

The next thing Mason knew the chair across from his was empty and they were listening to his father's Mercedes peeling out of the dirt parking lot.

They took a short break. The sympathetic hugs he got from the group implied they assumed he'd been rejected and cast aside. Mason didn't feel that way.

He felt drained, humbled, but his head felt clear.

A map to his father's anger was being shaken free of dust, and Mason wasn't the source.

His dad never wanted to talk about his own father.

Never wanted to refer to the man as Mason's grandfather.

Never wanted to draw a link between his son and his own dad. Mason had always assumed this meant Pete thought he and his own father occupied some special men's club, and Mason hadn't earned membership. But his father's parting words rang in his head, suggesting a distinctly different possibility—*I was protecting you.*

The day before Pete had admitted for the first time that his father drank. Drank worse than Mason which, given recent events, was saying something.

And then, in the one on one, the kicker. His belief that not touching his own son was the best thing he could have done for him. And he hadn't used the word hitting or throttling.

Touching.

Tony gave Mason the option of sitting out a few of the other sessions, but he stayed for all of them, did his best to pay attention.

The last scheduled event of Family Week was a s'mores-making session around the fire pit. As the afternoon darkened into evening, there was still no sign of his dad. Another family invited Mason to sit with them during dinner so he didn't feel abandoned. He was midway through his turkey casserole when Tony appeared over his shoulder. "Bring your food to my office," he said. Then Mason was taking a seat at the same desk where he'd called and asked Pete to come to Pine Rise. Tony picked up the receiver, took the call off hold, and handed it to Mason.

Mason listened, hearing faint country music in the background and a low clamor of conversation.

"Dad?"

"I went to a bar. Down the road." Pete's voice was slightly slurred. "That's why I didn't come back. I went to a bar, and I thought it wouldn't be right to... You know, my breath probably stinks, and I figured it wouldn't be right..." He didn't sound wasted, but he sounded fairly numbed out.

"It's fine," Mason said. "I'm glad you called."

"Are you?"

Mason closed his eyes and tried to summon all the gentleness he could. "What did he do to you, Dad?"

Silence.

"What did your dad do to you?"

He was prepared for the man to hang up. But the country music continued, the glasses clinked. A door opened and closed on greasy hinges. "The fucked-up part is I was so young I didn't know it was wrong at first. But part of me thought...maybe. So at school I kept listening to the other boys talk about their dads, and nobody ever talked about their dad doing stuff to them like mine was doing to me. That's when I knew it wasn't normal."

Mason felt something inside of him give way. He prayed for the perfect words and realized the best he might be able to offer his old man in this moment was his ability to listen.

"Whatever," Pete said. "Like that's the only fucked-up part of it."

"How long? How long did it go on?"

"He lost interest around the time I would have been big enough to shove him off. Not sure if one was connected to the other."

*Lost interest.* Two simple words that brought the enormity of what his dad had suffered down onto Mason. They implied years of abuse, years of a young Pete Worther feeling trapped and helpless and like he had no choices. Not hard to see how that torment produced the angry, defiant bully who'd raised Mason. And where had his grandmother been? Had she known about it and denied it? Or had Pete kept her in the dark too? There were so many questions he didn't have answers to. So many scars running through his father he'd never been aware of.

"Look, I don't want pity. That's not why I'm saying it. I just…wanted you to know when those words came out of my mouth, it wasn't always about you. It was about him. 'Cause when you're that young, you don't know it's wrong. And you don't know that you can say no. And so some days you think you wanted it…even though it doesn't feel like who you are."

"You couldn't say no," Mason answered. "It wasn't on you to say no. You were a child."

Silence except for the music.

"Dad?"

"Yeah. I'm here."

"Did you ever tell anyone?"

"Just you. And I sure as hell wasn't going to tell all those people."

"I understand."

There was a long pause, and Mason figured his father was sluggishly reaching for his drink and bringing it to his mouth. "I didn't ever cry to some therapist about it, but I tried to read some books, you know. About getting past it. Everyone said the same damn thing. The abused grow up to abuse. They made me think I couldn't even hold my own son without being, you know, like him. Like I was some sicko werewolf or something. Don't you get it? I was trying to protect you. I was trying not to…"

*Love me,* Mason thought. *You were afraid to love your own child because your father had polluted the concept.* The totality of it washed over Mason for the first time.

"Dad, come back to Pine Rise. We can talk about this here."

Silence.

"Dad, please."

"I can't face those people after what I…"

"Everybody's leaving in an hour. It'll just be the residents and the counselors, and we can—"

"Nah, son. I just…I wanted you to know I don't think you're disgusting. When you used to play on the field and I could watch you from the stands… Damn, you were good, son. Moments like that I could just sit there and be in awe of you. Because it felt safe to love you that way. You know, from a distance. I didn't… I mean, did I ever…"

"Ever what?"

His dad's voice was thick, the threat of tears evident through his drunken slur. "Did I ever...*do something* to you and forget?"

"No. Never. Not like that."

"You're sure?"

"Of course I'm sure. Dad, that's not how it works. I'm not bisexual because somebody abused me."

"But I'm a rotten son of a bitch because somebody abused me, right?"

"Somebody should have been there for you. Somebody should have helped you. Let me help you now. Come back, Dad. Come back to Pine Rise."

"I don't..." And then there was silence. No country music or bar sounds.

His father had hung up.

Mason shot to his feet as if it would somehow restore the connection. Tony was starting for him, and Mason was blinking madly to stop his tears. Mason slammed the phone down.

"Get him. Please. Go get him."

"Mason, he's been drinking. We really can't—"

"No. *No!* You wanted us to do this and we did, and this is what it looks like, okay? And now he's out there, and he's alone and we can't leave him like that. I've wasted most of my life hating that man instead of talking to him, and if I'd known any of this then I would... Just go get him, Tony. Please. We can't leave him out there all by himself in the dark on this goddamn mountain."

Tony gripped Mason by the shoulders, waiting for him to catch his breath.

"Okay," the man finally whispered. "I'll see what I can do. Stay here. And put some food in you."

Mason nodded and sank into Tony's desk chair.

He lost track of time until he heard the sounds of car doors closing, conversations between residents and their loved ones that sounded easier and more cheerful than the ones with which they'd greeted each other days before. Headlights popped on, engines revved. Family Week was ending.

And then, silence, and somewhere out there in the night on this dark mountain, his father was wounded and exposed and drinking, fighting a lonely battle with the ghost of his abuser.

Even though it had long gone cold, he was finishing up his dinner when a set of headlights sliced the now empty parking lot.

The driver's side door of a familiar pickup popped open. Tony jumped from the driver's seat and went to open the passenger door. His father dropped to the dirt as if his bones were heavier than when he'd left.

Mason walked toward them through the dark. He'd resolved to do what he planned to do next the second Tony had left in search of his dad. The results could be disastrous, but he didn't care. He had to do something, try something, and it had to be different from everything he'd done before.

When there was barely a few feet of distance between them, when his father finally lifted his head and gave him a hangdog expression visible in the truck's headlights in the instant before they snapped off, Mason threw his arms around him and held on. Held on even as he felt the brittle resistance of old wounds fill his father's muscles. He held on to his father because it had never occurred to him that the old man was the one out of the two of them who needed to be told he wasn't broken, wasn't tainted. And after a while, it became clear his father wasn't going to fight him off. Some of the resistance began to leave his body. Then they were two men holding each other up in the pine-fragrant dark because it seemed like the only way Mason could tell his father that if he put down his anger, Mason wouldn't be afraid to love him.

# 33

If it had been a normal year—a year in which his life hadn't been turned upside down by a man who'd made his heart and body sing in unison—Naser's only thoughts a week before Nowruz would have been of preparations for the holiday.

The spring cleaning required to get his mother's home in shape for their family gathering on the night of the spring equinox. The search for a brand-new outfit that would hang, unworn and untouched, in his closet until the family gathered. His frenzied and often ill-advised attempts to broker a peace between his mother and sister around whatever fresh sources of tension might threaten to flare up during the various celebrations and visits.

But his year hadn't been normal for weeks, and if Naser's day count was correct, Mason was due to be released from rehab two days before the spring equinox. This coincidence only drove home the absurdity of a secret fantasy he'd been nursing ever since they'd spoken of the holiday during their hillside picnic lunch.

No way, on any planet, under any sun, could Mason be his date for the first night of Nowruz. Now that he'd discovered how close his mother had come to threatening the man's life when they were in high school, it was even further out of the question. The fantasy wasn't simply absurd—it would be dangerous for everyone within a fifty-foot radius should it ever become reality.

And so, a more powerful fantasy—and a far darker one—had taken hold of his thoughts.

They were done.

Naser had been replaced by some fitter, richer hottie who had the added advantage of sharing in Mason's experience of addiction and recovery. Better to let Mason go now, meaning he should stop driving past his house every few nights and then speeding off before Mason's helpful Tesla-driving neighbor could spot him.

He kept reminding himself that he wasn't being ignored, wasn't being shut out. In fact, Mason had made a beeline for the hotel on the day of his departure to warn him explicitly that radio silence was about to descend and Naser shouldn't take it personally.

And yet, here he was, day in and day out, taking it personally.

Because imagining he'd already been rejected was easier than facing the unknown.

Who would Mason be after a month of being removed from his regular life, from Naser? The question seemed overwhelming, and sometimes the decisive nature of a worst-case scenario was easier to accept than a foggy and uncertain future.

And so he worked and he planned for the holiday and he dodged his mother's increasingly invasive questions about the man who'd stolen his heart and run off up a mountain with it.

Then, one morning, a week before Mason was due to be released, Naser froze in the middle of Sapphire Cove's lobby at the sight of a man who looked like an older version of Mason returned from the future, and suddenly it felt like his feet weren't making contact with the floor.

The man standing by himself in the center of the lobby, eyes hidden behind aviator sunglasses, slowly surveying his surroundings with a tense set to his stubbly, square jaw, was the same man Naser had seen on the website for Worther Properties the night he'd swiped Mason's cell phone.

"You Naser?"

"Mr. Worther, I'm at work right now. If you want to have a conversation about your son, we can schedule a time to talk. On the phone. When I'm not busy."

The man's eyes, as deep blue as his son's, widened. His nostrils flared. For a second, Naser thought the guy might clock him right there. But if he did so, he risked releasing the spiral Mead notebook he'd clamped in one armpit. The notebook seemed a little ragged and youthful given the rest of his appearance. Pete Worther looked so groomed and put together Naser wondered if the guy ironed his briefs.

Pete cleared his throat. "My reputation precedes me, I guess."

"It does."

Pete studied him, nodding. "All right, well, guess I better get right to it then. I saw Mason."

"Where?"

"You know…at the place where he went."

Naser nodded. "How is he?"

"Pretty good. Wish I could say the same for myself." When he saw Naser's baffled expression, Pete gave a nervous glance in both directions. "We did a…family thing. Like, I don't know, a workshop or something. It was for a few days and…it was nuts. But you know, the kind of nuts that's supposedly healthy, I guess. Anyway, you were actually his first choice, so…"

"For what?"

Pete studied Naser like he thought he was baiting him, then he swallowed—hard. "He didn't want me to come, but he made a deal with the counselors that he'd ask me first, and if I said no, then he could ask you. But I got so pissed when he told me that, I said yes. Serves me right, I guess."

"You feel punished by spending time with your son?"

"Look, I don't know what he's told you about me—"

"He didn't have to. I've seen text messages on his phone. From you. They spoke for themselves, Mr. Worther."

Pete blew out a long breath between pursed lips, nodded at the gleaming marble floor, then he went still.

Suddenly it was like they were both dock piles in the roiling waters of the lobby's midday crowd. "Mason and I are going to be doing a lot of work on our relationship," Pete finally said.

It sounded like he'd been uttering these words constantly under his breath in an attempt to turn them into a comfortable mantra.

He had a ways to go in that regard.

"But I'm going to be doing a lot of the *a lot,* if that makes sense. So I'm starting by bringing you this." He tugged the spiral notebook from his armpit and handed it to Naser. "That's something he wrote for you. We kind of smuggled it out. He's not supposed to send letters or anything, so you know, keep it to yourself, I guess. He's got another week before he's home."

Naser turned the notebook over in his hands, his best method to avoid giving in to temptation and popping it open in the middle of the crowded lobby. "He wrote this for me? While he was there?"

"Yeah. And he told me about what he was trying to do with you. Making things right, I mean. So it gave me an idea. What could I do to start making things right with him? He said I could bring you this. Makes sense, right? Making up for the kind of dad I've been by showing respect for the man he's fallen in love with."

*"What?"* The word ripped from Naser in a startled whisper before he could stop it.

"What? I'm not doing this right. I thought I was doing this right. Was I supposed to wear a rainbow shirt or something?"

"He said that? That he…"

"That he's fallen in love with you? Oh, yeah. Like ten times."

"Oh."

Pete cleared his throat and stared at the floor. "I guess he hasn't told you yet."

Naser shook his head, blinking madly to hold his tears at bay.

"Well, I guess that's kinda weird I told you first, but weird is on the menu lately so…"

"Thank you. For bringing this to me."

"Maybe you should read it before you thank me. I mean, I don't know what kind of writer my son is. Some of his proposals these past few months have been for shit, but I think that's 'cause he was so wasted that he—"

"Okay, you know what, Mr. Worther—"

"Sorry. I know. Like I said, I'm working on stuff, but I just started two days ago, so give me a minute here." Pete raised a hand and started backing up in the direction of the lobby doors. "And call me Pete. I prefer it to asshole."

"I didn't call you an asshole."

"Your eyes did."

"Thank you for bringing this to me, Pete Who Is Working On Not Being An Asshole."

"Thanks for, you know, being the reason my son started cleaning up his act."

"I'm not sure I'm the reason he went to rehab."

"Maybe not. But he's sure as hell excited to see you when he gets out."

Then Pete Worther was gone, and Naser gave in to temptation and opened the notebook's front cover. His eyes went to the title of whatever this was. The words **Who I Could Have Been** were crossed out with a single line, and above them, written in the same handwriting were the words **Who We Could Be**.

Dear Nas,

I guess this is going to be a letter, but it's going to be a long one because I'm going to be here for a while. Calling it an essay doesn't feel right.

It's Day #1 at Pine Rise, and right now I'm writing this because I can't stop seeing the look in your eyes when I left you at Sapphire Cove. It's haunting me because I know you were already saying goodbye forever. Maybe that's what you need to do. I'm not sure.

I'm only sure of one thing right now.

I haven't done enough.

I haven't done enough to make up for what I really did back in high school. And I'm not just talking about being a jackass to you and not doing enough to stop He who Shall Not Be Named (HWSNBN for short) and Tim. when I say I still haven't done enough I mean I haven't done enough to show you the depth of my feelings for you then, and how hard I worked to shove them down into deep and dark places.

It all started the first time I laid eyes on you. It was a day that changed me. When you entered my life, you brought true beauty into it for the first time, and in such a new and unexpected package I realized what I had called beautiful before was really just appealing. Your walk. The way you looked at me with that flash of interest before you tried to cover it up with a furrowed brow that made you look like a grown-up. I even laughed a little under my breath when you did it because I thought it was so cute.

I don't think I've told you this yet, but when I walked up and put my arm around you in the hallway that day, I didn't do it because I was planning to hurt you or embarrass you. I literally lost control. I had a need to be near you I couldn't hold back. For thirty seconds, I stopped thinking about what everyone else thought. And what I can't stop thinking about now is what would have happened if it had been longer than thirty seconds? What if

I'd gone a week or a month or maybe the rest of high school without listening to my fear? Who could I have been for you then?

What if I'd never looked back to see how Tim and HWSNBN were reacting to what I'd done? What if we'd kept walking down the hall together and I'd left my arm looped around your shoulders so you could feel that what I felt was serious? What if instead of pushing you into that locker, I'd asked you some of the questions that haunted my sleep in the days after? You weren't the first guy I'd had the hots for, but my desire for anyone, male or female, had never come with that much curiosity before.

I wanted to know if you slept in pajamas or boxers. I wanted to know if you ate sushi with chopsticks. I wanted to know if you laughed out loud at the funny parts of a movie. I wanted to know if you snored. I wanted to know what your neck smelled like and tasted like. I wanted to know how you kissed.

You're right. Ours wasn't a long-distance romance. Still, you might be surprised to know I learned as much about you back then as I could. But I did it from the shadows and without ever showing you my true face, and that's on me, and now there's a price to pay.

It could have been this.

In the hallway at school that day, I ask you what you like to do for fun and you tell me how you love to go to the Back Bay and watch airplanes take off from John Wayne Airport. You tell me how you're obsessed with airplanes, but sometimes it feels unfair because most plane nerds on the Internet are all about military aviation and what you love is commercial planes, but everyone on the message boards wants to talk about bombers and fighter planes and not the advantages of the 777 over the A350. (I heard you and Melony Chen laughing about this one day at lunch while I was pretending to listen to whatever bullshit HWSNBN was saying at the time.)

Then I ask you if one day soon you'll take me to your favorite place and you say yes.

Dinner time. Back soon.

Okay. It's Day #2, and I just found out I can't send letters apparently, so I'm going to have to hold on to this until I'm out.

Let's talk about the first date we never had.

Here's the thing.

I love to think I'd be all sweet and lovey-dovey on our walk, but I think there's a good chance I try to get your pants off, even if it's awkward and I do a bad job of it and you eventually ask me to stop. But the truth is, I used to drive myself into the mattress some mornings thinking about how bad I wanted you. But maybe not. Maybe as we walk side by side through the sunset, I realize I've only pushed through the layers of fear that might cause me to be a bully in denial, and going the rest of the distance still feels scary. I'm humbled. I'm in the presence of feelings so significant and monumental I'm suddenly cautious. And nervous. Maybe my heart roars as I reach out for your hand and interlace my fingers in yours so all your suspicions about my intentions can be confirmed. I do my best to watch you as you watch the planes rise into the sky, and it's the most intimate thing in the world, seeing someone else's joy and not saying or doing anything to interrupt it.

But when we get back to the car, I definitely kiss you.

All right, off to another happy fun day of rehab...

It's Day #5. I had to skip a few days of writing because there's a lot of intense work we do here. But this letter is my reward for doing all their 12-step worksheets that are sometimes like having your teeth pulled. Finding "your own part in it" is what they call it, and it's not exactly fun. I'm learning a lot. About myself. Which is apparently the idea.

So since our imaginary first date over ten years ago went so well, it's time for me to take you to one of my favorite spots, the bluffs down in San Onofre. It's all open beach and endless ocean, and it's one of the few places I can go where my head is completely quiet. With you, it's something even better, something both peaceful and exciting. When I try to take my friends there, they talk the whole time or they want to drink beer or they just want to talk about the military helicopters flying overhead to Camp

Pendleton. But when you and I reach the bluffs above Trails Head Beach, it'll just be the two of us and the world below. Maybe it will feel like we're flying. Which is the perfect metaphor for what we're doing. Flying above fear and other people's expectations for us, their judgments.

And then maybe I try to get your pants off again and you make some joke about how our first time being naked together isn't going to be on a frigging bluff.

Time for bed. I brought an extra pillow and I sleep with it against my chest and imagine it's you.

Day #14. Big time jump, I know.

The truth is, I was starting to regret this letter. I was thinking I might not even give it to you. I was starting to feel like writing out some imaginary vision of what we could have been was missing the point, a distraction from what I really need to do to make this work between us.

But then the guy who spoke at one of our meetings today said something I'd never heard before, and suddenly this little writing exercise made sense. He said that people like me, people who have a problem with drugs and alcohol, we stop maturing emotionally at the moment we start abusing substances. We begin avoiding our true selves and as the addiction takes hold, we abandon our true selves altogether and they start to dry out inside of us. Recovering from that isn't just about removing the sources of our addictions from our lives. It's about returning to the fundamental truth of who we are, the one we tried to drown.

For me, the moment I abandoned my true self wasn't the moment I took my first drink. It was the first time I lied about how you truly made me feel. It was the moment I made what my friends thought about the fact that I'd put my arm around you more important than what you thought. That's the moment I betrayed myself—and you. Every wrong thing I did to you flowed from that.

I know you think I'm going to move on, forget about you. That all I did for you was about my guilt and not my love.

Maybe you're afraid this whole sobriety and rehab thing will turn me into a different person, a person who forgets you. But don't you see? The person who fell in love with you at first sight is the person I need to be again to live because that's who I really am.

I love you, Naser Kazemi.

I'll see you soon.

If my dad and I don't kill each other at Family Week.

He read it three more times after he got home from work, then he fell asleep on top of his covers with the notebook open across his chest, and when he woke the next morning, it felt to Naser like he'd spent the night in Mason's arms.

At first, he vowed to keep it to himself.

That lasted about eight hours into the following day.

By that night, he'd called Connor and read him the whole thing, and over the days that followed, they were taking time out from their days to quote their favorite lines to each other.

As the final week of Mason's stay in rehab wound down, Naser read the letter again every night before bed, hoping it would inspire his dreams.

Then, on Saturday morning as he was making breakfast, a full four weeks after Mason had said goodbye, Naser woke to his first text message from Mason in a month.

**I'm free!!! I have to see you, Naser.**

Giddy, Naser abandoned his eggs.

**Want me to come and get you??**

**I'll come to you. Want to see one of my favorite spots?**

**The bluffs at San Onofre??**

Mason answered with three thumbs up in a row, his token signature for enthusiastic agreement. Naser wrote back.

**We're long overdue for a date there.**

**We are.**

**Give me two hours.**

The response was a Google map pin drop. It looked like a section of trail that had amazing views of the Pacific. Shifting from one foot to the other with excitement, he tapped out a response.

**It will feel like we're flying.**

Mason wrote back with a blushing smile emoji.
Naser typed.

**Your letter was...**

Naser typed out five heart emoji in a row.

**Can't wait to see you. Kiss you. Get my hands on you**, came Mason's response.

The L word was on the tip of Naser's tongue, but he held it there. Some things were better said in person.

# 34

When Mason had imagined the day of his release, he'd pictured himself making the return trip in Shirley's Tesla, downloading all of his experiences and personal revelations in a frantic, caffeinated rush. He never imagined he'd be making this ride with his old man.

But here he was in the passenger seat of his dad's Mercedes after a morning spent gathering his belongings and saying goodbye to the counselors while his dad hovered nearby the whole time, hands in his pockets.

They'd been riding in silence for a good half hour before his dad broke it. "So, um, Chadwick… He called the office two days ago. He was a mess, son."

Mason grimaced. "We had a fight before I left. A bad one. It's part of why I went to Pine Rise."

"Yeah, well, he barely mentioned that. Apparently, the shit's really hitting the fan. Did you know he's about to lose his license?"

"Why?"

"He was talking a mile a minute, but it sounds like he's being accused of paralyzing some woman's face with the wrong injection."

Mason went cold from head to toe. "Jesus," he whispered. "He said something about an investigation a while ago. He wanted a statement from me or something, but he wanted me to lie and say he was with me when he was accused of intimidating a witness against him. When it came to Chadwick's work life, there were a lot of questions I didn't ask. I didn't want the answers, I guess. But he's out of my life now. The fight was bad, Dad."

"All right, well I fucked up then."

"How?"

His dad cleared his throat, clenching the steering wheel at ten and two. "I told him you were at Pine Rise. I thought it would shut him up. He kept saying he needed you, but he sounded high. I thought if I mentioned rehab he'd shut up and go away. Given how messed up he sounded, I didn't want him anywhere near you when you got out."

Mason was genuinely touched by his father's protectiveness. "Thanks, Dad."

Another silence.

"So…Naser?" his dad asked.

"I'm going to call him when I'm home. I don't want the first time he hears from me to be a text message."

"That sounds…you know…sweet, I guess."

"Sweet? Pete Worther thinks something is sweet?"

"Okay, fine, *romantic*. Jesus. What are you trying to do to me?"

"Just give you a little shit, I guess."

Pete shook with silent, restrained laughter.

Silence descended again.

Handing over his phone a month before had felt like getting a hand cut off. But now, after four weeks without it, the thought of wedding himself to it again made him feel clammy all over. The envelope into which Tony had placed it on day one was now stuffed inside a larger one containing pamphlets and helpline numbers and a bunch of resources Pine Rise gave all its graduates upon departure. He couldn't bring himself to pull it free just yet. For one, it would be out of juice. Now he was pretty sure there'd be a dozen psycho voicemails from Chadwick on it.

Shirley met him on the steps of his house with a giant, perfumed hug that made his throat catch.

"So proud of you," she whispered into his ear. Then she made halting, awkward conversation with his dad as the three of them moved inside.

On his kitchen counter was a giant gift basket filled with bottles of his favorite sparkling water and some of his favorite snack foods.

But only one word pulsed through his mind again and again.

*Naser.*

Suddenly he was terrified.

He had no way of knowing how the guy had reacted to his letter. He wanted to stay hopeful, but if there was one thing he'd learned about

Naser during their time together, it was that past events sometimes caused the guy to swiftly withdraw from anything he found overwhelming. Even something that might be overwhelmingly good. Of course, Mason had given him his fair share of bad along with the good this past month.

Time to tip the scales in a positive direction.

When he told Shirley and his dad he needed some time alone, they both nodded, but neither one of them made a move to leave the house, a sign they both wanted to keep an eye on him as he transitioned back to normal life.

He grabbed the bulging envelope that contained his departure package and headed upstairs.

He'd need to get Naser's number up from his contacts. It shamed him a little that he hadn't memorized it.

After finding a charger in his nightstand drawer, he tore open the envelope and shook its contents free onto his bed. Pamphlets and stapled pieces of paper slid out along with the small, familiar envelope that had his first name written on it. The one he'd passed on a regular basis where it had sat tucked into a cubbyhole for all to see—an invitation to quit Pine Rise or a token of his persistence, depending on whatever mood he'd been in at the time. The sight of it now filled him with a vivid memory of that first terrifying day.

The envelope was the wrong shape.

He picked it up. Something blockier and heavier than his phone shifted inside. Then he saw the flap had been opened and taped shut.

Heart thundering, he tore the entire envelope in half. A little box of business cards thudded to his comforter. Tony's business cards.

*Replaced.*

His phone wasn't just missing. It hadn't just been stolen. It had been replaced so that nobody would know it was gone until...until...

He ran for his bedroom closet and tore the laptop off the top shelf where he'd left it. His pounding footsteps drew Shirley and his dad upstairs. The questions started flying, but he waved them off as he tapped keys. He was about to open the app that would locate his phone when he saw the big red number next to the Messages tab. Hundreds of texts had come in while he'd been at Pine Rise. When he clicked on the tab, he saw Naser's name at the top of the list.

A conversation between him and Nas.

It had been happening all morning.

Only Naser was talking to whoever had stolen Mason's phone.

# 35

The minute Naser left San Clemente in his wake and crossed into San Diego County, the dry, rugged mountains of Camp Pendleton charged east from Interstate 5. To the west, dramatic bluffs plunged to rugged, isolated beaches popular with intrepid surfers and campers. Somewhere out there, in the wind and the sun, Mason was waiting for him.

He parked in a lot that also serviced the campgrounds to the north, then he started walking south on the trail that should lead him to the pin drop Mason had sent that morning. He tried to send a few texts updating Mason, but they all had red dots next to them indicating they'd gone unsent. Cell service cratered out here by the sea.

Up ahead, the trail traveled a gently sinuous line along the top of the bluffs. Most of the brush was low scrub, perfect for offering endless vistas on all sides.

An empty bench waited for him next to a bend in the trail.

When he reached it, there was no sign of Mason. He turned, looking out at the sparkling sea. Over a hundred feet below, the beach was mostly empty, save for a few lone sunbathers and surfers bobbing farther out in the sparkling swells.

A branch crunched behind him. Naser turned.

The smell hit him first, the kind of body odor and booze stench he'd associated with someone living on the streets. Chadwick Brody's eyes were wild and bloodshot. When he saw the terror on Naser's face, his leering grin was replaced by something harder, meaner.

Then he lifted the gun he was holding in one hand and pointed it at

Naser's chest.

"Jump, Prancer."

Naser had never had a gun pointed at him before. He'd always assumed you wouldn't be able to take your eyes off it. Instead, even though the weapon was black and oily, the sight of it struck him like a wall of bright and blinding flame, and his first instinct was to bow his head and throw himself to the dirt.

But everything inside of him coiled at the thought. A tremor moved through his muscles. At first, he thought it was terror. It was something else. Something more powerful, something he might be able to use. It was a resistance that bordered on rage.

*Look up,* he thought. *You spent years looking away from this asshole. If this is really the end, buck a trend and don't give him the satisfaction.*

Suddenly he was staring into Chadwick Brody's eyes. Eyes that looked like they hadn't seen sleep in days.

"Go ahead," Chadwick said, wetting his lips with his tongue. "Don't worry. I wrote you a note."

"A note?"

"A goodbye note. From you. To the world. What? Like it's such a fucking stretch? Little homos like you take a flying leap all the time."

"How long have you been awake, Chadwick?" Naser couldn't believe the preternatural calm in his voice.

"No, don't even try that shit." Chadwick shook his head like he was trying to rid himself of a cap he wasn't wearing. "Don't try that distraction bullshit. I want you gone, Prancer. Gone. I thought I'd never fucking see you again, and then suddenly you're back in his goddamn house and presto change-o, everything's shit again. What? I'm supposed to think that's a coincidence? You're probably some kind of Persian witch doctor or something."

"If Persian witch doctors were a thing, you wouldn't have survived high school."

Chadwick raised the gun another inch.

"What did I ever do to you, really?"

"What do you think? You brought up all that old shit. In front of him. And then he…then he…"

"*You* brought it up. You're the one who told him I suck a mean dick, remember?"

"You changed him. You always *changed* him. Every time he was near you, you changed him."

"Oh, okay. I get it now. You didn't do that to me behind the bleachers because of how I looked at you. You did it because of how *he* looked at *me*."

Chadwick took a step forward, gun raised. "Jump, Prancer. Go head first. It'll make it quicker. Trust me. I'm a doctor."

The wind blowing against his back suddenly felt like an invitation to oblivion.

In his head, he was imagining running. To the right or to the left. To the right would force Chadwick to turn into the sun. Maybe he'd get blinded as he tried to take aim. Or maybe he'd fire the second before and Naser would get a bullet in the chest.

What if he taunted Chadwick into coming closer?

The closer the gun, the closer Chadwick's gun hand, the better Naser's chances of grabbing either and shoving them skyward so the shot went over their heads. But the resulting tussle might send them both dancing off the cliff.

Then he realized he was missing the most obvious point.

Chadwick Brody didn't want him to jump so he could torture him. He wanted him to jump because he was too scared to kill him. There was only five or so feet behind Naser and the cliff's edge, and Chadwick hadn't shoved him over the side. A cold-blooded killer would have knocked him to his death while his back was turned, dropped the fake suicide note, and gotten the hell out of there. Instead, Chadwick was wasting time by running his mouth, holding a gun on him out in the open when someone could come running by at any second.

And that's what happened.

Naser heard the bike whiz to a stop off to his left. *"Hey!"* A man's voice, like the crack of a whip.

Chadwick spun, firing in the direction of the cry.

The crack of the gunshot drove knives into Naser's ears. The guy's bike went over. He dove into the low brush beside the trail.

Was he hit? No time to tell.

Naser hurled himself at Chadwick with all his strength. Chadwick slammed to the earth and rolled onto his back. As soon as he took aim, Naser brought his foot down on the man's crotch with enough force to crush everything underneath.

Chadwick yowled like a dying dog, loud enough for Naser to hear over the terrible ringing in his ears. The gun didn't fire.

Lungs burning, Naser ran. Ran in the direction of the parking lot, the direction of help.

Heard a dull crack behind him, another shot.

Nothing struck him.

What felt like a breathless eternity later, there was another crack. Something zipped right past his shoulder, close enough to make his entire body seize against his will—a bullet missing him by inches.

He lost his footing on a rock, slamming face first into the dirt.

The wind knocked out of him, he jumped to his feet. Dizzy and wheezing, he turned back in Chadwick's direction by mistake.

One hand clamped over his crotch, roaring from the complete destruction of his balls, Chadwick raised the gun to fire. That's when a ton of navy blue chrome exploded from the brush next to him. Naser had been too deafened to hear the car's approach. Mason's Lexus was going so fast the tires had left the ground as it crested a rise in the earth. The car slammed into Chadwick broadside. His entire body bent at an impossible angle, then he was a dusty tumble of limbs beneath the tires.

There was a moment of elation when he realized the gun hadn't gone off.

But the Lexus kept going.

And it only had eight feet of stopping distance before the cliff's edge.

It wasn't enough.

When the taillights disappeared over the side of the cliff, Naser let out a scream he could barely hear even as it set fire to his throat.

# 36

Shock warped Naser's memory, upending his sense of time.

He was on a stretcher being wheeled through the ER as doctors shouted questions at him over the ringing in his ears.

Then he was back on the cliff's edge, screaming into the wind as the hikers who'd come running at the sound of Chadwick's last gunshots held him back by both arms. And there, far below him, the Lexus had landed on exploded tires, nose decimated, air bags bulging so hard against the windows they crowded out any view of Mason within.

Then his sister was next to him, holding his trembling wrists, kissing him gently on the forehead. Were they in the hospital or had they brought him home? The temporary deafness made time harder to track.

Then he was being wheeled into some sort of machine. A scan, someone told him.

Then hospital lights whizzed by overhead, and the ringing in his ears was finally fading, replaced by the beeps and clamor of a crowded ER. And by the time he was back behind the curtain, the grip on his hand now was firm, a man's grip. He looked up. The hand was Connor's, and he was doing that thing he always did when he was trying not to cry—pursing his lips together in what looked like a pout, his eyes wide and glazed. Logan stood behind him, holding his shoulders, eager for Naser to see that he was there.

*Where's Mason?* He wanted to ask, but he couldn't find the words. Couldn't find any words at all. His lungs felt small and dry.

Then he was back at the cliff's edge, staring down at the ruined Lexus sedan, one question screaming inside his head again and again.

*Where's Mason?*

He heard the curtain pushed back on its rod, felt the energy around him tense. He blinked, feeling like he was back inside his body for the first time. As soon as they introduced themselves as detectives, he heard his mother tell them to get lost—his mother was there? When had she shown up? Come back once I've managed to get the results of Naser's cat scan and a lawyer, she told them. They weren't questioning her son without either. Male grumbles followed, then his mother made the high chirping sound she'd used to use while corralling their dog out of the kitchen, and the detectives were gone.

"Where's Mason?" he whispered.

There was a tense silence. He felt a grip on his shoulder, his mother's manicured hand. And he looked up into her dark, welcoming eyes. "Surgery, Naser-*joon*. He's in surgery." He wanted to ask her why she'd hesitated before answering.

Next he heard his mother interrogating the attending physician.

Normal cat scan results, a few scrapes and bruises, but nothing physical.

Then the curtain was pushed back again, and this time it was a familiar face, but a new one to this ER. Jason Maleki, his bald brown head gleaming and his eyes full of alert sympathy. He was one of his mother's oldest friends, and a lawyer. Mahin cleared out their room, and Naser gave his account, describing it all like something he'd witnessed from a distance. Because that's how it felt.

He told them everything that had happened that morning.

Everything Chadwick had done to him in high school.

And when he described the instance of sexual assault behind the bleachers, his mother's hand closed over his and held to his tightly, and he heard her let out a small, choking gasp. But she stuffed it down quickly, determined not to center herself in this awful moment.

Then they were leaving the ER, their whole entourage walking in a kind of formation, with Naser flanked by his mother and sister, and Connor, Logan, and Jason Maleki tailing. The corridors seemed endless and administrative—they didn't pass any gurneys or wheelchair-bound patients. Then he saw two men he assumed were the detectives he'd heard earlier outside the door to a small conference room.

Connor, Logan, his sister, and his mother, they all peeled away, and then Jason was showing him to a chair across from the detectives and they were around a wooden conference table. He told them everything he'd told Jason and his mother in the ER. They listened attentively, asked a question here and there.

And then they were gone, and that's when Jason told him that several witnesses had captured the worst parts of the incident on their camera phones. That Chadwick Brody's life had completely fallen apart in the days before he tried to kill Naser—he'd lost his license that Tuesday, threatened his own mother with a gun the day before, and spun out into a spiral of addiction and paranoia before he'd driven to Pine Rise and stolen Mason's cell phone so he could lure Naser to the bluffs. In other words, nobody was doubting Naser's story in the slightest, or that Mason had acted only to save Naser's life.

Once he was in the hall outside again, he asked the only question he could give voice to. "Where's Mason?"

He figured shock, or the residue of it, would carry him through the worst of what was to come, but when he saw Pete Worther, sitting all by himself in the surgical waiting room, hunched over, his face in his hands like he'd been struck across the spine, Naser's knees felt molten, and his eyes filled. The man looked up and saw the assemblage headed toward him. Seated a chair away was the red-headed woman who had driven Mason to rehab, but she looked at Naser warmly, as if they were old friends and she'd been waiting for him.

"He's...uh...he's still in surgery," Pete managed.

Naser sank into the seat next to Pete's.

"We will wait for him then," Mahin said quietly and sank into the chair next to Naser's.

A silence settled. His mother and sister had linked hands across the arm rest of their chairs, and this pleased him.

"He's all I got," Pete finally said into the tense silence, voice wavering. "I might be a mean son of a bitch, but he's all I got."

For the first time in Naser's life, he could draw no comfort from accepting the worst-case scenario. It was one thing to accept the idea that you might be rejected by someone you really wanted. But the death of the man you loved, the one who'd saved your life, might shatter him into a million pieces. His mother had lost her husband. Maybe she would know how to put him back together if Mason didn't make it.

What felt like hours later, a woman in surgical scrubs entered the waiting room. Everyone sat up ramrod straight.

"Are you Mason's family?" she asked.

Pete rose to his feet and started toward her, then he stopped and looked back at Naser. "What are you doing?" Pete asked. "Step up, kid. It's showtime."

Stunned by the invitation to join him, Naser followed Pete and the surgeon to one side of the waiting room, doing his best to focus on the surgeon's stoic expression as she rattled off a dizzying litany of details.

Mason had made it through surgery.

There were no detectible spinal injuries, which was excellent news, but they were dealing with multiple broken bones—both arms and a thigh bone—and a serious head injury that had required immediate decompression surgery to reduce bleeding in the brain. They'd hoped to do simple aspiration—which meant drilling a hole in Mason's skull—but the bleeding was too extensive, and a craniotomy with open surgery had been required. This was a very serious and often risky procedure, and the next few hours of recovery would be critical. They were confident they'd managed to stop the bleeding, but it would take some time to see if the surgical repairs to the blood vessels in his brain would fully mend.

At the sound of medical terms being delivered rapidly, his mother drew near. He risked a look back at her and saw from the fixed expression on her face how serious all these terms were, how serious Mason's condition was.

"Can we see him?" Naser asked.

The surgeon nodded. "Two at a time. He's in ICU recovery now. He's not responsive, and I wouldn't expect him to respond soon. Some of that's the anesthesia, but some of it's the time he's going to need to come back."

"But he is coming back, right?" Naser asked.

The surgeon looked him in the eye and took a breath. "The brain has miraculous ways of repairing itself. We're going to do everything we can for him. But Mason had a very bad fall, and this was a very serious intracerebral hemorrhage."

"So you're saying he needs a miracle," Pete croaked.

"He's had a miracle. He survived the crash. What he needs now is excellent care, and we're going to give it to him. And he needs people he's familiar with around him. We often hear from brain injury victims that even if they're not responsive they're hearing what's said in the room with them. So two at a time in ICU for now."

Naser looked to his mother again. She nodded to indicate she agreed with everything the surgeon had just said.

Then suddenly he was alone with Pete as a hospital volunteer led them deeper into the hospital, around corners and through automatic doors before the letters *ICU* loomed over them, following a swift-moving nurse who guided them through a suite of recovery rooms where most of the curtains were pushed back and the patients inside looked as much like machines as they did people.

At first, it made it easier. The fact that Mason's broken arms were both wrapped in casts and elevated above his head, that most of his head was bandaged, and the only visible parts of it were his sleeping eyes and his bruised lips.

"Hey, handsome," Naser whispered. "Well, looks like you've *more* than made up for our past. What do you think?"

Beeps and distant chimes were the only answer.

He wanted desperately to take Mason's hand in his, but the casts made it impossible. So Naser pulled the closest chair next to the bed and sank down into it, threading his forearms through the bed's guardrail until he could rest one hand on Mason's shoulder.

Save for a few bathroom breaks, that's where Naser stayed for twenty-four hours.

Pete came and went, but he never left.

Occasionally he traded shifts with Mason's neighbor Shirley.

Throughout the night, Naser dozed, dreaming fitful dreams of walking hand in hand with Mason through the Back Bay as they watched planes from John Wayne Airport climbing toward a dome of cornflower blue.

When Mahin showed up the following morning, thermos of coffee in hand, she insisted Naser come home with her for a shower and a change of clothes. Pete said he'd stay, then head home for the same once they were back.

During the brief trip, she gave him details.

The Lexus had killed Chadwick instantly.

His mother, who he'd threatened with a gun the day before, was now in hiding from the media, who wanted to know why she hadn't reported her son to the police the day before he'd opened fire in a public park. Chadwick's disastrous professional life had been laid bare before the world. The patient who claimed he'd partially paralyzed her face through drunken incompetence had expressed her sympathy for Mason's loved ones and made clear this was not how she'd wanted to receive justice.

Then it was back to the hospital and time to relieve Pete of his vigil.

Mahin stayed for a while, then Pari came to relieve her, bearing bags of food for them both.

When Pete came back an hour later, he was holding a tattered hardcover in one hand. The cover was adorned with fading illustrations of bright, pastel-colored flowers, *A Natural History of English Gardening*. "He loved this when he was in high school, but I made fun of him for it so…" Pete pulled his chair close to the bed and began to read aloud about the pioneering naturalist Gilbert White.

His voice sounded stilted and strained, but Naser wasn't sure he would have given a better performance while reading about soil samples.

But still, Mason didn't stir.

Again, Naser lost track of time and dozed in the chair.

Shirley woke him next and explained that one of her friends from AA, a man named Hugh, was there with several of his other sober friends, and they'd gotten permission from the nurses to bring Mason an AA meeting. Apparently, Mason had done the same for Hugh the month before when he'd been laid up in the hospital for injuries he'd suffered during a relapse.

Naser stepped outside to give them privacy and watched as they linked hands over Mason's comatose body and said the Serenity Prayer.

Night fell outside.

The end of their second day.

Then he was waking up to the smell of his mother's perfume, felt her hand caress the side of his face, and when he opened his eyes, he saw she was beautifully dressed and there were others in the ICU suite with them. His sister, his cousin Shaya, who'd driven up from San Diego, and her husband Pasha, and their teenage daughter Tara. "Wake up, Naser-*joon*. It is time for Nowruz."

He'd forgotten the holiday entirely.

His family hadn't.

He blinked and saw Mason still unresponsive in the bed.

They'd brought a low table into the room and covered it with a shimmering cloth bearing one of his sister's designs. A goldfish swam in a small bowl. The barley looked fresh. The bottle of oil gleamed. It was the *haft-sin* table Pari always set up in the living room of their mother's house. They'd transported it here along with cartons of food that covered over all the hospital smells with scents fragrant with memory and warmth.

He checked the time—almost four in the morning. The spring equinox would arrive in minutes. At the same moment all across the world, in Iran and Turkey and countries throughout the West, Persians would gather and dine together and read Hafez together and mark the arrival of a new spring, a new year.

His mother had brought his Nowruz outfit from home. He'd had alterations done, and it was still in the plastic covering from the dry cleaner. Never worn, as was the custom. He changed in the tiny bathroom, and when he emerged, his sister was standing at the room's single window, the curtain pushed back in one hand. "Nas, come here."

He could see them before he reached the windowsill. Candles, a sea of them. They seemed to be floating, but he realized people were holding them and they were standing on the roof of the nearby parking structure. He recognized Shirley and Pete. He saw Connor and Logan and even Jonas and Gloria, along with others he didn't recognize.

"They are from his meetings," Pari whispered. "And rehab. So many people."

"They all came for him?"

"They came for both of you. Both of you, together." She curved an arm around his shoulders.

He and Mason were going to spend Nowruz together after all.

He assumed they'd use paper plates, but his mother had brought her best china inside giant Ziploc bags, and they ate off their laps. The delicious smells drew the attention of the nurses, who'd allowed them to break the rules regarding the number of visitors. Quickly, his mother doled out plates of *sabzi polo mahi* to all of them, taking care to scoop the rice across the fish, reminding them to bring her good china back when they were finished.

And for the first time in hours, Naser laughed.

After the sun rose, they left one by one, and after he refused to leave with them, he curled up in the chair again and drifted off.

Hours later, someone whispered his name. He opened his eyes and saw the room was empty. Pete was outside, in quiet conversation with one of the nurses.

"Nas."

He spun to the bed and saw Mason's blue eyes staring back at his. There was recognition in them.

"I thought we said no broken bones," Mason whispered.

Weeping, Naser brought their lips together.

When Mason managed to gently return the kiss, he cried even harder.

# 37

Four days after his surgery, Mason was surrounded by a garden.

Orchids were lined up like spindly soldiers along the windowsill, and each corner of his room sported several potted ferns. Among the expected *Get Well* balloons and basic flower arrangements, Naser had worked with Mason's friends at Green Mountain to fill the room with plantings, heavy and moist. When he gazed at them, he could briefly forget that he was trapped in a hospital and would be for another week or so.

Every day they reduced his pain meds a little bit more. This pleased him.

He'd insisted Shirley come in to talk over the medication protocol with the doctors. She wasn't a medical professional, but pills had been more of her poison, and she had a good grasp of which prescriptions were the most addictive.

So far, so good.

The hospital controlled the dosages, and after the two of them made Mason's addiction issues clear, the doctors promised to employ more anti-inflammatories than narcotics, so long as Mason's stomach could tolerate it.

There'd been plenty of visitors since he'd been moved to his private room. The hardest had been Tony at Pine Rise, who blamed himself for the theft and assured Mason they were formulating a new commitment ritual that didn't involve leaving resident's phones unsecured for most of the day. Tony's guilt was so palpable, his sense that he'd betrayed Mason so great, it had taken Mason an hour to calm the man down.

His surprise visit from his mother paled in comparison. He hadn't seen her since he was a teenager, and even then, it had been a one-day drop in following years of absence. She looked so different now as to be almost unrecognizable, and when she'd first entered his room, he'd thought she was a consulting doctor he'd yet to meet. As always, she was gentle and sweet. But she talked to him like they were both passengers on a long plane flight who'd just met. There was no sign of her man of the moment. When she left, she didn't say when she'd be back. And he knew better than to ask.

Above all, there was one visitor who commanded his full attention. She'd been a regular. But as Mason's condition had improved, she'd grown progressively more distant—Naser's mother.

She was, no doubt, the parent from which Naser had inherited his crisp, businesslike manner, his focus on efficiency. Mahin did not leave a room without straightening at least three or four things in it first. In her world, everything seemed to have its perfect place, and if her increasing coldness was any indicator, she wasn't quite sure where Mason belonged in hers.

Every day, he and Naser tried to figure out a way for Naser to crawl up into bed with him, but they still hadn't come up with a method that didn't involve knocking the wind out of Mason or injuring his crotch. Sometimes Connor helped. But today they were on their own. Naser had slid under one of Mason's plaster-encased arms like a limbo player before gently rolling over, ending up face down on Mason's chest as if he'd dropped down from the center of the ceiling.

"Is this working?" Naser asked into Mason's hospital gown. "I mean, are we snuggling or do you feel attacked?"

"You're lucky I got bathed earlier."

Naser lifted his head up from Mason's chest. "I'm sorry, who's bathing you?"

"Relax. It was Nancy."

"How's that supposed to make me relax? You're bisexual."

"Nancy's not, and she's been married to her wife Glynis for six years."

"Okay. I feel better. But my arm's asleep."

"Mine are both broken, so you're not going to get any sympathy from me."

Naser brought his lips inches from Mason's, and Mason felt a frustrated, ravenous hunger for the man rise in him, a hunger held down by casts and persistent aches throughout his body and the general inconvenience of being hospitalized on a long-term basis.

"Ten bucks says if we start making out right now, my mom will walk in."

"Safe bet. Isn't this when she gets off work?"

"Fair."

"Also, I haven't touched my wallet in a month, so if you want ten bucks, you can probably just take it."

His mother's voice came from the doorway. "Naser, what is this? You are on him like a worm."

"I'm stuck! It took twenty minutes to get in this position, and now I don't know how to get out."

Mahin exhaled loudly and started for the bed. "I will help then."

"Fine," Naser said, "but don't judge me. If a man ever saved your life, you'd be on him like a worm too."

She lowered the guardrail on the side of Mason's bed with a loud clack. "I do not get on men like worms. This is a terrible way to talk to your mother. Hold my arm." Naser did, and a few seconds later, she'd helped him wiggle out from under.

Once he got to his feet, she began brushing the shoulders and lapels of his shirt.

"Seriously, though, didn't Dad ever do anything that made it impossible for you to keep your hands off him?"

"Yes. His recliner would get stuck, and it would take me an hour to get him out. I need some time alone with Mason. Go and get a coffee or something."

Naser's smile faded, and he looked to Mason. "Well, that was an abrupt transition."

"Go," Mahin said, and patted her son on the backside like he was three.

Naser complied. Sort of.

Out of the corner of his eye, Mason saw his boyfriend draw the door almost all the way shut, save for a few inches. He took up a hiding place on the other side.

Mahin walked to the windowsill and made a show of fluffing the flowers lined up there. "How are you feeling?"

"Better. You?"

Mahin waggled a hand in the air, and a silence descended.

"If he had told me about you before you saved his life, I would have done everything I could have to destroy this relationship."

Mason was shocked silent.

"But then you went and drove off a cliff for my Naser, so now I cannot say this without seeming terrible."

"You actually did just say it, Mahin."

"Well, don't get me wrong. It's not because you are a man."

"I know why it is. But I did, you know, drive off a cliff for him and all."

"This is true, and that is why I did not say it."

"You did actually say it, but okay."

"It's why I did not *do* it. It's why I'm giving this my blessing even though I haven't been asked. But you must tell me, what is it I am blessing? What are your intentions with my Naser?"

"To love him. To love him the way I've wanted to from the moment I first saw him."

Mahin studied him, nodding slowly. "That is a good answer," she whispered. "But I am not done. What do you know about what happened in my country in 1979?"

Behind the door, Naser threw his hands out and made an expression of astonishment. Mason was pretty startled too.

"The Iranian Revolution?" Mason asked.

Apparently, that was the wrong answer because Naser started shaking his head and waving his hands like Mason was about to step into flames by mistake.

Mahin's frosty expression and slow approach suggested the same thing. "It was a populist uprising that was stolen by the clerics. It was not a revolution."

"My mistake."

"Don't worry. I long ago stopped expecting anyone in this country to know anything about Iran they did not see in a movie with Arnold Schwarzenegger or Ben Affleck. Anyway, my point is this…"

Her hand was still raised, but it looked as if painful thoughts had claimed her. Not just thoughts, Mason realized when he saw the way she was studying the floor—memories.

"When the first tanks rolled, we did not know what would happen. Some people thought the Shah would hold fast. Some people thought if he fell, the ayatollah would never come back. And some people thought the progressives would prevail and we would get a real democracy at the end of the day. Naser's father, he was in the last group. I was not. I made us leave before many of the others left. I let him believe it would only be weeks or months before we went back. But in my heart, I knew this was not the truth.

"I don't regret my decision to make us come here. I would not have had a life for my daughter where she was forced to wear the hijab. I am grateful I did not raise my son in a place where he could be put to death for loving you."

She seemed to remember how close her son had come to death and looked to the floor.

"By the state, at least," she added. "No, what I regret is the guilt I felt over insisting we leave. Because it was the guilt that kept me from talking about Iran with my husband late at night. That made me shut him down every time he brought up taking a trip back there to say goodbye to all the things he thought we would see again a few months after we left. He was a soft, sensitive man, and I loved these things about him very much. But when it came down to it, I did not let him grieve. And I worry each night that this destroyed his heart before it was his time. And so this is what I ask of you, Mason Worther. You let my Naser show the world his heart so that he might live a long and happy life."

"I wouldn't dream of doing anything else," Mason answered.

"Good. Come back in, Naser. I know you are behind the door."

Naser was wiping tears from his face as he reentered the room. Mahin curved an arm around his back, and he pulled her into a tight embrace. For a while they hugged, then she crossed to Mason's bed and did her best to curve her fingers around the ones that emerged from the cast on his left arm. He saw she was holding Naser's hand as well, forming a link between them.

"But when the time comes, you are going to have a big, expensive wedding to impress all my friends because that is what we do. You're not getting out of it just because you're both men, and that is final."

Then she left the room before either one of them could protest or point out that they weren't engaged.

# 38

**Three Months Later**

Naser had resumed a cordial and respectful relationship with Jonas since returning to work, but their dustup on the day Mason left for Pine Rise had yet to be addressed. So when Jonas knocked on his open office door holding a bright floral bouquet in one hand, Naser assumed it was a belated apology, one well past the point of being necessary.

"To celebrate." Jonas set the flowers on the edge of Naser's desk. "Mason's getting his casts off today, right?"

"That's so thoughtful of you." Jonas must have learned the news from someone else. While he'd given the man general updates on Mason's recovery from his injuries, he still wasn't comfortable getting specific and personal with someone who could never be specific and personal with him.

"A summer bouquet, given the season. But around the border here, that's freesia. It symbolizes trust."

Naser wasn't sure who was supposed to be trusting who in this scenario, and he didn't want to ruin the moment by asking—even though he wasn't sure what moment he would be ruining. "Thank you, Jonas. I know Mason will appreciate it too."

Jonas nodded and went to leave. Naser had restarted treatment with Dr. Kelley soon after the terrible events in San Onofre, filling her in on all the events he'd omitted from his story during their last sessions. So far, they'd remained focused on how Chadwick's attack had churned up memories of Naser's past abuse, but he'd also broached the subject of his alienation from Jonas several times because it weighed on him.

"Jonas, I—"

"We don't..." The man turned, one hand raised, head bowed. "That's not why I did it. It really was just to celebrate the occasion, Nas."

"I know you gave me a pass on the whole thing because of everything that happened with Mason, but the day I snapped at you, I was dealing with something very painful, and I took it out on you, and I'm sorry."

"You made a valid series of points, and I can't blame you. Like that old Bible verse."

"Sorry, I'm bigger on Hafez than the Bible."

Jonas looked directly into his eyes. "John 8:32. And ye shall know the truth and the truth shall make you free."

"Never took you for a religious man, Jonas."

"I'm not. But there are advantages in being who you truly are, as you and Mr. Worther have proven. Enjoy having Mason's arms back."

Jonas smiled and left. Naser stared at the door for a while, wondering if this new Bible-quoting side of Jonas was a sign of more intimate disclosures to come.

Orange County was baking in an early summer heat wave, and Mason had turned off the AC in Naser's townhouse before he'd left for the doctor's office. Even though this made for a warmer than comfortable condo when Naser returned home, it was another delightful sign of Mason's residency that put a skip in Naser's step.

In the three months since Mason had moved in, the potpourri on the console table had been changed from cinnamon to a new scent that combined Naser's love of rich spices with Mason's affection for green things.

In the living room, a stack of glossy real estate magazines sat piled next to Naser's old copies of *Scientific American.*

In the closet in his bedroom where he'd once cried himself to sleep over the man, Mason's lightweight, cream-colored work attire now hung next to Naser's more conservative slacks and dark dress shirts. There, Naser stripped off his work clothes and headed for the shower, heart racing with excitement.

After twelve weeks of being virtually housebound, cared for by a home nurse during the hours Naser was at work, Mason's arms would be liberated from the plaster prisons in which they'd resided since he'd saved

Naser's life. The man was so excited by his imminent freedom he'd refused to wait until Naser got off work to go with him to the doctor's office.

The truth was everyone was excited.

Until Mason's path through recovery was clear, Connor and Logan had been waiting to set the date of their wedding. They were determined to have him there and wanted to be sure they picked a venue where accessibility wouldn't be an issue for him if his injuries proved slow to heal.

After working out a deal where Mason would get a significant chunk of proceeds from the transaction, Pete Worther was planning to put the beach house up for sale. Before he listed the place, he wanted to be sure Mason could participate in the move-out process so none of his valuables were lost. During Mason's lengthy hospitalization, Pete and Shirley had done their best to clean up after Mason and Chadwick's brawl. But there was no sweeping up the echoes of that terrible night, and no keeping those echoes from stirring up memories of the afternoon Naser had almost lost his life.

And so, as soon as the hospital released him, Naser had decided to move Mason into his place.

For the time being, they'd said.

So far, the *time being* didn't have an end date, and neither man seemed interested in giving it one.

And while there had been plenty of physical intimacy in the past three months, all spiced with a fair share of naughty sponge baths and nurse-on-patient roleplay, it had been limited by Mason's dual casts. But the deed, once delayed by Naser's hesitancy, had been further delayed by medical realities.

Was it too optimistic to assume today would finally be the day?

Naser prepared himself anyway, which also involved stripping down to a pair of skimpy white briefs that drove Mason wild and lying face down on the bed in a pose that had made the man growl more than once.

When he heard a car engine outside, followed by the low voices of Mason and his dad telling each other goodbye, he felt a hungry gnawing in his stomach. Then he was listening to Mason's footsteps on the stairs. Confident footsteps, the footsteps of a man newly freed from several pounds of plaster. The bedroom door creaked on its hinges easily, a sign Mason had opened it with his hand and not by pressing one cast against it as he'd had to do for months.

"Oh." Mason's voice had a soft note of delight in it.

Naser didn't roll over, but he smiled into the pillow.

And then came the blissful feeling of Mason's fingers moving up his lower back with grips that were strong and powerful—healed. His other hand joined, kneading and massaging Naser's back before moving to his neck with such gentle but determined force, gooseflesh swept him from head to toe, and he felt himself start to thicken in his briefs.

"I was going to ask how your mobility is, but it looks like it's pretty good," Naser said.

"*Feels* like it's pretty good, you mean."

Naser rolled over. Mason was chewing his bottom lip as he smiled, eyes twinkling with a mixture of hunger and relief.

"Everything went okay?" Naser asked.

Mason nodded, and then swiftly and without breaking eye contact, tugged the front of Naser's briefs down so his hard cock popped free. Then he gripped its base and began to stroke. "Grip strength seems to have returned quite nicely. Do you agree?"

Naser nodded and gasped as Mason stroked. Mason's other hand roamed across Naser's chest, kneading, pinching. Naser brought it to his mouth and nibbled, then sucked.

"Is someone getting a hand fetish as well as a foot fetish?" Mason asked.

"Can you blame me? I've been denied their full power for three months. Four, if we count your stay at Pine Rise."

"True." Mason stood, pulled his shirt off over his head, and kicked himself out of his jeans, all without breaking eye contact. There were scars from the accident, but mostly he was sheepish about what three months of no gym time had done to his body. Naser couldn't have cared less. Some of the hard angles were gone, but the thickness that had replaced them ignited Naser's desire. There was more weight to his chest, more manly bulk to hold on to, get lost in, bear down on him with delicious force. That's what Mason was doing now, kisses joined by caresses and grips they'd both gone without for too long.

Mason paused. "I wasn't sure…after what happened that you'd still want it the way you used to want it. Know what I mean?"

"The only good thing about that day is that Chadwick didn't manage to lay a hand on me." Naser kissed him gently. "Well, that and the fact that you saved my life."

Mason smiled, then gently reached up and gathered a handful of

Naser's hair in one hand. "So this is still…" Mason tightened his grip and pulled. Delicious chills raced to his fingers and toes. A warm and welcoming heat caressed the base of his neck as Mason pulled tight enough to cause a light sprinkle of pain across his scalp. He wasn't sure if it was the pleasure of having a kink satisfied or the absence of shame that filled his bones with warmth. Maybe it was both.

"Good?" Mason asked.

"Very," Naser whispered.

Mason sank his teeth into the base of Naser's neck—a quick, hard bite, the exact speed and pressure Naser had taught him after he'd moved in.

Then they were a frenzied, liberated tangle, and the next thing Naser knew, Mason had one hand around the front of his throat while he used the other to yank Naser's briefs down his thighs, then over his shins. Then Mason was reaching into the nightstand drawer, slicking himself with lube, all without breaking fierce eye contact, all without releasing his hand from the front of Naser's throat. All without muddying the message that Naser was the center of his desire, the center of his world.

"Feels like I've waited my whole fucking life for this," Mason growled.

"I'm done waiting," Naser whispered. "Are you?"

Mason answered by sliding two lube-slick fingers into Naser's entrance, watching Naser's face as he explored. The eye contact was as arousing as Mason's expert finger-work, and so when Mason hit Naser's prostate, when everything inside of Naser went soft and pliant, he fought the urge to throw his head back and gasp, forced himself to gaze up into Mason's eyes, which only made Mason probe harder and with greater determination, desperate to undo him.

"You're so open," he whispered. "You're so fucking open, Nas."

"Like I said, wait's over."

Their noses were almost touching suddenly, Mason's breath bathing Naser's lips. "For both of us," Mason said.

Then Naser felt the pressure he'd been craving for years, felt himself yielding to it, the first sense that it wouldn't be as formidable as he thought, followed by a sudden wall of resistance. And then, the release— the physical release coupled with the knowledge that Mason was entering him, inch after inch, sliding deeper into him. And for a moment, there was no bottom, no top. Just two bodies joined in a way that an instant before hadn't seemed possible but now seemed irreversible.

Mason's hand had left his throat.

The familiar shudder of surrender moved up his spine. He laced his ankles over Mason's lower back the way he'd wanted to that first messy night in Mason's bed.

"Nas…" A whisper, but it also sounded like a question. "Do you still…" Mason didn't have to finish the question. This feeling of union was new for them both.

Did it demand its own new lazy rhythm, or did Naser still crave rough with flashes of pain?

Slowly, Mason fucked him, building up speed, pulling back slightly so he could watch Naser's body, read the music of pain and pleasure on his face.

Naser answered Mason's unfinished question by bringing the man's hand back to the front of his throat. "Hard," Naser whispered. "Fuck me *hard*."

With thrusts alone, Mason learned him, building from long and hard to fast and hard, adjusting and varying based on Naser's grunts, whines, and pleas. And the taps—the single tap on his back that said *more*. Naser felt like a warm bath under Mason's sweaty, thrusting bulk, more energy and heat than sweat and skin. Mason fucked like something once caged inside of him had been set free to devour. And Naser delighted in the knowledge that he'd emancipated this beast by being willing to receive it.

"You're mine," Mason growled. "You're *mine*."

Naser could hear the pleading undertone to the proclamation, the sense that Mason was close to eruption and trying to coat the imminent loss of control in aggression.

"Yours to fuck," Naser whispered in his ear. "Yours to own."

Mason erupted. It was a delicious combination—the profanity Mason always unleashed when he came was accompanied for the first time by a burst of wet heat inside of him.

"I need…" Mason gasped. "Just give me a minute and then I can, you know, finish you off."

"I'll give you ten minutes, and then we're going again. We've got a lot of time to make up for."

He laughed, lifted his head from the pillows beside Naser's, and gave him a wet and sloppy kiss.

For a while after Mason slowly pulled himself from Naser's heat, they lay in a sweaty tangle, catching their breath. And it was perfect that they'd waited this long, that it had happened this way. Not in the strange, glossy stage set of Mason's father's beach house, but here in Naser's homey, lived-in condo. Perfect that he'd been forced to make space for another in the very place where he'd one convinced himself he'd be content to live a life of solitude and fantasy.

Mason's body against his was intact, healed. Warm and healthy.

And Naser still felt filled by him even though he'd withdrawn.

"How was work?" Mason finally asked.

"You mean the part I didn't spend thinking about finally doing this?"

Mason laughed. "Yeah, how did those thirty seconds go?"

Naser tightened his embrace around Mason's back. "Well, Jonas got kind of religious on me, which was a little weird."

"Wait, like, *bad* religious?"

"No, he was talking about you and me actually, and he quoted this Bible verse. John 8:32, I think."

"Oh, I know that one. People say it in meetings a lot. The truth shall set you free, right? So he thinks we set ourselves free by living our truth. That's pretty nice, actually." Mason reared up, kissing Naser gently on the tip of his nose. "And accurate."

"Absolutely. But Jonas never quotes the Bible."

Mason extracted himself from Naser's limbs and swung his legs to the floor. "I doubt he was trying to convert you. That verse is really common. I think it's even the motto for the Central Intelligence Agency."

When Mason felt Naser go rigid behind him, he turned and looked over his shoulder. "What?"

"Nothing," Naser whispered.

He forced himself to smile, but he was thinking of the bouquet from Jonas currently resting on the kitchen counter downstairs.

Freesia, flowers that meant trust.

In the moment, it had seemed like an odd choice, since Jonas hadn't chosen to trust Naser with any information about his past.

Or had he?

"How about a shower before our next round?" Mason asked.

"Deal," Naser answered, letting Mason pull him up off the bed by one hand, but all he could think as he followed Mason into the bathroom was, *Oh my God. Jonas was in the CIA!*

# Epilogue

**Four Months Later**

"Ladies and gentlemen!" Pari Kazemi's shout turned heads in a conference room thick with hairspray fumes and the humid smell of steam irons. "I would like to introduce you all to Mason Worther, the man who saves everything I love."

Pari took his hand and raised it skyward. Mason's face got hot as the applause from the runway models and their dressers surged. Then Pari looped an arm around her brother's shoulders and pulled him close.

"*Everything* I love," she added, which made Naser bow his head and chew his bottom lip.

There was another smattering of applause and cheers.

Naser's near murder and Mason's heroic cliff dive had been splashed all over the news for weeks, so even the folks who weren't regular members of Pari's staff understood the significance of Pari's declaration.

Then Pari flipped the switch back to stressed-out diva. "Out, both of you. We've got work to do."

"God forbid more than a minute of this night should be about something other than you," Naser grumbled.

"Correct. Now go make sure Maman doesn't walk out halfway through."

Mason took Naser's hand and led him into the main corridor of Sapphire Cove's conference center, where other formally dressed guests were processing through the open doors to the Dolphin Ballroom.

Pari's introduction had given Mason a burst of pride that would fuel him for the rest of the night. Hopefully, it would also propel him through his nervousness over how he planned to end the evening.

With his investment money, she'd put together a new ball gown collection that was entirely her vision. The first few dresses had caught the attention of a Persian venture capitalist who'd previously dismissed her work for the Bliss Network as too corporatized and bland.

Tonight, Pari would be given the fashion show she deserved, without the jerry-rigging and subterfuge of her poolside event almost a year before.

Tonight, the main event would be inside the Dolphin Ballroom, which she'd transformed into a stark white landscape of minimalist curtains and taffeta screens designed to rival the biggest runway shows in Paris and Milan.

Tonight, Pari wouldn't be forced to improvise a catwalk with whirling dervishes as crowd control and a spotlight snuck onto the hotel's roof.

And this time, Mason, sober for almost eight months, would remember every last detail.

Mason took his seat next to Mahin, Pete, and Shirley. But when Naser saw only one empty chair, he remained standing and scanned the room. "What about Connor and Logan and Jonas?"

Mason averted his eyes and pretended to dust lint off his lap. "They're working. It's fine. Take a seat."

"Pari doesn't want them working, she wants them watching."

Mason reached out and took Naser's hand. "Don't worry. There's something they need to take care of." Mason cursed his loose tongue as soon as the words left his mouth.

"What something? Pari brought in her own team."

Mahin reached out, took her son's other hand, and yanked him down into his chair. "Naser-*joon*, maybe give up control somewhere besides the bedroom, huh?"

"*Maman!*"

Pete and Shirley laughed into their fists.

Persian pop music pumped through the speakers.

The show began.

Mason didn't know the first thing about women's fashion, but it gave him a deep sense of pride that he'd been able to make this colorful parade possible. That no matter the pain and twisted motives that led up to it, a choice he'd made had allowed Pari Kazemi to give life to a pure, strutting, and glittering version of her aesthetic and vision.

When the show was over, Pari took the stage to a standing ovation. As soon as she finished a few words of thanks, she extended one hand in the direction of their seats. Mahin nudged Mason with her elbow. No doubt she assumed Pari wanted to thank him for his investment. But Mason had been briefed about this part of the evening. When Mason shook his head and gestured for her to accept her daughter's invitation, Mahin Kazemi blinked and looked from Mason to her daughter and back again.

For a few seconds, the woman pretended to be overwhelmed by the request, then she burst up onto the catwalk and began smiling and nodding at friends in the audience with a politician's poise that made clear Pari had inherited her love of the spotlight from her mother.

"As many of you know, we are members of an immigrant community, and the circumstances by which many of us came to America are painful and complicated. But what happens in communities like ours is that our elders become the keepers of our history, and sometimes those of us who are younger, we forget the value in this, and we mistake what they try to share with us as confining or limiting."

Pari took her mother's hand, and for a second, the two women stared at each other as if seeing each other for the first time. "I have never seen Iran," Pari said, with a catch in her voice. "But I have seen what lives of it inside my mother, and I do the work that I do so that you all will see that too. So that you will see her the way that I see her. And so tonight, the show, my new collection, it is dedicated to you, Maman-*joon.*"

Mahin Kazemi did what she always did when she was about to cry—she turned her head to one side and waved her hands quickly in front of her face as if trying to rid herself of an irksome fly. Pari brought her into a fierce, tight hug.

As the applause surged, Mason caught sight of Jonas staring at him through the cracked doors across the ballroom. A short nod indicated everything was ready.

Mason's heart raced.

After they'd congratulated Pari and left her to a crowd of admirers, Mason took Naser's hand and started pulling him toward the ballroom doors. "Where are we going?" Naser asked.

"The afterparty."

When they started down the hallway toward the double doors leading to the ocean-facing lawn, Naser said, "The afterparty's out by the pool."

"This one's just for us."

At the top of the wooden steps that descended to the little crescent of beach far below, Mason saw the tent had gone up right where they'd planned it, and a soft glow within was pushing at the cracks in the flaps. "Mason…"

"Come on."

At the base of the steps, he made them take off their dress shoes and socks, then they plodded barefoot across the sand.

When they were within a stone's throw of the tent, Mason heard a rustling sound, followed by a curse, which suggested either Connor or Logan had tripped while trying to quickly evacuate out of the other side before their arrival. But when Mason pulled back the entrance flap, giving Naser a view of everything within, he saw it had all come together perfectly.

Naser gasped and froze.

Gently, Mason prodded him forward.

It was an enchanted garden just like the one that had filled a ballroom at the Disneyland Hotel the night of their senior prom. Dangling ferns composed of twinkling light strands, flowers fashioned out of Christmas light strands in which all the bulbs had been changed to purple and pink. Unlike that night, all of it shifted and jostled in the ocean breezes that managed to make their way inside the tent, making the plants look alive. And from the tent's ceiling hung one of the chandeliers Pari had placed atop her stilt walkers eight months before, a replica of the chandeliers from the Mirrored Mosque in Shiraz. Now it bathed Naser with the kind of light his father had dreamed of gifting to his son.

Tears in his eyes, Naser turned to Mason, trying to speak, but no words came.

And on the off chance the theme of the evening still wasn't clear, at that exact moment—thanks, no doubt, to the power of Bluetooth technology and the assistance of Connor, Logan, and Jonas, who were all standing somewhere outside—mournful electric guitar filled the tent, loud enough to drown out the surf. Suddenly they were being serenaded by Jon Bon Jovi.

"Prom," Naser whispered.

"Our prom, finally."

And then they were slow dancing to *Bed of Roses.*

Mason told himself to keep his eyes closed, to give himself over to the dance, the way Naser had done. He was marginally successful. Every few seconds, he opened his eyes to make sure everyone else had quietly filtered into the tent as planned.

When the song finished, when Naser lifted his head from Mason's chest, he saw that Connor, Logan, Jonas, Mahin, Pari, Pete, and Shirley had all joined them, standing close to the walls as if to give space to the energy coming off Naser and Mason in waves.

Mason sank to one knee, and Naser's hand traveled to his mouth as his eyes filled.

"Naser Kazemi, before you came back into my life, I used to think a second chance was something that came and went in a day, like a window you had to jump through before it closed. But with you, I feel like every day is a second chance to do better than the day before, and I never want to stop trying. Will you give me the chance to do right by you every day? Will you give me the chance to always do better? Will you give me you? Will you marry me?"

Naser answered with a nod and the humility to stop fighting his tears, and Mason rose and kissed him and took him in his arms.

And that's when Pari Kazemi said, "See? I was willing for, like, five minutes of this night not to be about me."

## THE END

*Keep reading for a sneak peek at C. Travis Rice's next steamy and emotional installment in the Sapphire Cove series...*

# SAPPHIRE STORM

Sapphire Cove, Book 3
Coming March 7, 2023

**Under his new pen name, C. Travis Rice, *New York Times* bestselling author Christopher Rice offers tales of passion, intrigue, and steamy romance between men. The third novel, SAPPHIRE STORM, once again transports you to a beautiful luxury resort on the sparkling Southern California coast where strong-willed heroes release the shame that blocks their hearts' desires.**

Ethan Blake has dedicated his life to satisfying other people's appetites. At forty-three, he's finally landed his dream job—head pastry chef at an exclusive resort. Now he's got a jet-setting career that's taken him to romantic locations all over the world. But years before, after his parents threw him out for being gay, Ethan supported himself in a manner he'd rather keep under the covers today.

Roman Walker is a twenty-five-year-old fitness celebrity awash in thirsty followers. But when he walks through the doors of Sapphire Cove, it's not just to oversee the menu for his celebrity client's wedding. Decades ago, Roman and Ethan crossed paths on a New York street corner during a terrible, life-changing moment that scarred them both. Now Roman's back for revenge.

But when his plan goes wildly off the rails, Roman suddenly finds himself at the center of an even stranger and darker plot concocted by his most famous client. Well-versed in the ways of the wealthy and the entitled, Roman's former target offers to be his strongest ally during a moment that might derail the young man's newfound career. But the experienced older man's offer also ignites an irresistible and forbidden attraction that threatens to consume them both, even as it exposes old secrets and incurs the wrath of the powerful and the famous.

\* \* \* \*

Ethan Blake had lived all over the world. He'd trained in some of the finest kitchens on the planet. At forty-three, he'd finally landed his dream job—head pastry chef at an exclusive resort. Under no circumstances should he allow a mean comment from some twenty-something on a dating app to torture him for days on end.

And yet three days after being shot down by BeachBoy24, he still found himself gritting his teeth whenever he thought of the young man's parting message, sent in response to Ethan finally honoring his repeated requests for a shirtless selfie.

*Yikes. No thanks, gramps! Over and out.*

While he was no stranger to the shallow cruelty gay men could show each other online, the young man's words had landed like a slap in the face. Maybe because Ethan had made no attempt to hide the weight around his midsection.

True, he'd been trying to shed it with regular workouts that were becoming increasingly exhausting and time-consuming now that he was in his forties. But while his morning gym sessions had kept his upper body brawny, down below was a different story. His abdomen had been following its own agenda since he turned thirty-five, and no amount of sits-up or crunches had been able to restore the washboard stomach of his youth.

Starvation, always fashionable in Southern California, was out. Ethan had dedicated his life to food—nutrition, sustenance, and the culinary arts. For him, a diet that required a level of deprivation that bordered on self-abuse would be more than unhealthy—it would be a form of hypocrisy.

And so, for the first few days of their correspondence, he'd tried to present himself to BeachBoy24—who'd claimed to be a registered nurse named Cody—as an older, stable professional. A nurturer. That's how his few close friends had always described him, even as they scratched their heads over the fact that the universe had yet to provide him with a romantic partner he could offer the same loyalty and support he gave them. But his character-first approach to Internet dating had been dashed to bits by an obligatory bathroom mirror selfie that made clear his chest hair was dappled with gray, and he hadn't sported a six-pack in years.

The truth was, there'd been a time in his life when he could stop a room just by entering it, when he'd had every muscle that might have sealed the deal with BeachBoy24. He'd also been BeachBoy24's age at the time. And considerably less focused on the career that eventually brought him happiness and fulfillment. But in the often merciless world of Internet dating—especially when the participants were male—all other metrics of success fell before the sword of body fat percentages. And the older he got, the less tolerant he became of the gladiatorial nature of it all.

Over the last few decades, he'd gone from being an Adonis to a daddy, a type that appealed to a certain subset of younger men. A subset that apparently didn't include BeachBoy24 after all, even though the young man had struck up their chat to begin with and had repeatedly asserted his wild desire for older men.

Right up until he saw what an older man looked like with his shirt off.

*Enough,* Ethan told himself.

He focused on the job at hand. It would fast become a dangerous one if his mind kept wandering. The work was loud enough to merit ear plugs, and it involved one of his favorite tools, one that rarely made an appearance in his pastry kitchen.

A chainsaw.

Perfect for venting his frustration and losing himself in the act of creation.

His junior chefs had covered the prep tables and equipment with plastic tarps, then cleared out so he'd have plenty of room to work.

He'd thank Chloe later.

They enjoyed a friendly version of the rivalry that existed between executive chefs and pastry chefs in hotels everywhere. Chloe's world was one where grease fires often bloomed, and banquet plating could become a frenzy of fast-paced argument. Ethan's pastry kitchen occupied a quieter, less sweaty corner of Sapphire Cove where precision was key and wedding cakes were carefully constructed over a period of days. But tonight, she'd given his crew space to pour molds in the main kitchen so Ethan could have room to carve this ice swan. And in about half the time he'd originally planned, given the surprise meeting his general manager had sprung on him a few hours before.

He was putting the finishing touches on the swan's beak when the door next to him swung open. Connor Harcourt stopped short. Another few steps and he might have knocked Ethan off his stepladder.

The hotel's general manager was about five foot four, with a shock of bright blond hair and round blue eyes. It amused Ethan to no end that the most powerful person on the property was also one of the shortest on staff, a *sparkly little shitkicker,* as Chloe often referred to him with an admiring smile. Behind Connor, the resort's special events director, Jonas Jacobs, cut a larger and more imposing figure, dark, bald head gleaming, the wire-rimmed spectacles he wore after dark giving him a studious air. Ethan adored both men, but he and Jonas had become especially close in the months since Ethan had started at Sapphire Cove. They were a few years apart in age, and like Ethan, Jonas wasn't very forthcoming about how he'd spent his twenties. Jonas Jacobs, it seemed, had secrets in his past as well.

He hopped down off the ladder, set the chainsaw on a prep table, and gestured to his handiwork with one arm. "Voilà!"

Connor and Jonas circled the swan, giving it admiring looks. Ethan was pleased. The sting of BeachBoy24's body-shaming dismissal suddenly felt further away. Tonight's event was personal. The hotel was throwing a giant going-away party for one of its most senior staff, the long-term assistant general manager, who was leaving to start her own business. The swan would be the centerpiece of one of several raw bars Sapphire Cove was footing at its own expense.

"Fabulous," Connor Harcourt said.

"Most extraordinary," Jonas added with a nod.

As they applauded, Ethan mimed a small bow before removing his earplugs and safety goggles.

Thanks to three other events that evening, in addition to the going-away party, his boss and supervisor were short on time, he was sure, so Ethan whipped his apron off and headed out into the main kitchen, confident they'd follow. In response, some of his junior chefs hurriedly replaced him in the pastry kitchen, preparing to transport the swan to its final destination.

"So this guy's a dietician, you say?"

From behind him, Connor answered. "Actually, his Instagram lists him as a fitness professional and nutrition expert."

He rolled his eyes, grateful his boss couldn't see. "Does it list any degrees? Or is he *self-taught*?"

This time, Jonas answered, his voice a bass counterpoint to Connor Harcourt's high-pitched one. "None listed on his profiles, but I did some digging and found a former website he had for personal training services. It mentioned some time studying kinesiology at Cal Poly San Luis Obispo. He was also a staff trainer at Apex in West Hollywood for a few years, which is probably where he met the Peytons."

Apex was one of the most exclusive gym chains in the world. Ethan had pumped iron at a couple of its locations in London and New York, but always as the guest of a friend who could afford it. Jonas's guess sounded correct. Over the years, he'd read a few magazine write-ups of the West Hollywood location, a two-story glass and chrome palace on the

Sunset Strip, depicting the place as a see-and-be-seen magnet for A-list celebrities looking to tone up before their next big role.

*Great. I'm about to be lectured on how to do my job by some pretentious Hollywood hanger-on.*

"But no degree?" Ethan asked.

"None," Connor and Jonas answered in unison. Their tone made it clear they were as annoyed about this meeting as Ethan was trying not to be.

Bound for the hallway of meeting rooms in the conference center, Ethan emerged into a lobby aswirl with smartly dressed guests. The only thing he loved more than the frenzied symphony of a professional kitchen firing on all cylinders was the surging foot traffic inside a popular hotel on a Saturday evening. Heels clacking on marble floors. Piano music drifting in from the bar in the hotel's main restaurant. Gatherings of the freshly made up and freshly perfumed, excitedly talking through their evening plans while standing in the glittering spray cast by the lobby's massive, three-tiered crystal chandelier. Outside the restaurant's soaring plate-glass windows, the last vestiges of an ocean sunset ignited explosions of blue and purple that looked like a celestial nod to the resort's name. After years spent working in elegant, five-star hotels where most of the guests in the lobby rarely spoke above an aristocratic whisper, the brassy energy of Sapphire Cove made for an invigorating change of pace.

"A trainer," Ethan said. "So the guy who wants to chuck my cake for the Peyton wedding is a *trainer*. Should I be offended?"

"You should stop walking, actually," Connor said.

Ethan obeyed and turned. "I had the sample slices sent over to Seal Rock I."

Connor nodded, eyes on the marble floor. "And *he* had them sent up to the penthouse suite."

"Well, that's an upgrade. Why the change?"

"I'm trying to find out," Connor answered.

Jonas cleared his throat. "Which is our boss's way of saying he didn't approve it."

"Correct, and I'm taking that up with registration and room service currently. Apparently, Roman Walker is a very persuasive young man."

Jonas chuckled. "Which is our boss's way of saying he's hot as a desert wildfire. Almost eight hundred thousand Instagram followers, over a million on TikTok, with views through the roof. Barely a shirt anywhere in sight on either of his profiles. And nobody's complaining in the comments. In fact, most of them are asking for more skin in ways that would make my grandmother slap their phones out of their hands."

"How'd he score the suite?" Ethan grinned. "Did he take his shirt off for room service?"

"I plan to find out," Connor answered, as if the prospect was both probable and infuriating.

"So I should head up to the penthouse?"

Connor shook his head. "I don't think it's appropriate for you to meet with this young man alone in a guest room."

"The hotel's a mob scene tonight. Far be it from me to add to your plates, every pun intended."

"One of us could sit in for part of the time," Jonas offered. "Or we could have security stand outside the door."

Ethan laughed, touched by their protectiveness. "Security? Oh, for God's sake. Guys, it's fine. Don't worry." He wanted to tell them he had ample experience handling himself in hotel rooms with strange— sometimes dangerous—men, but that would touch on parts of his life he'd worked hard to keep out of his personnel file. "Anything about the Peyton wedding, I'm happy to handle."

Connor grimaced. "It's a strange request and a bad precedent, Ethan. We're going to be working with these people for months."

"It's the Peyton wedding," he said again. "Diana Peyton's a household name, and her only daughter's getting married. Didn't she just win a Tony?"

"That's the daughter. Our bride. She was nominated, but the ceremony's not for a bit," Jonas answered. "Diana Peyton's never been nominated for an acting award in her life. And rightfully so, if you want my opinion."

Ethan didn't disagree. When he was a little boy, his mother had never missed an episode of *Santa Monica*, the trashy nighttime soap that had turned Ms. Peyton into a world-famous celebrity. For multiple seasons, she'd played the head of a powerful advertising firm whose workdays consisted of storming into conference rooms in dazzling sequined dresses and firing people, a fact that had once prompted young Ethan to ask his mother how the advertising firm could stay so successful when a senior employee was dramatically shown the door every week, and for infractions like attempted murder or kidnapping babies out of their cradles. She'd been beautiful, for sure, the kind of TV star whose hairstyles influenced young women all over the country, but she'd never been very good. Her Tony-nominated daughter was a different story, apparently.

"I'm not going to lie," Connor said. "It's a big event for us."

"Three different entertainment shows are scheduled to cover it," Jonas interjected.

Connor shook his head. "I don't care. Mr. TikTok does not have the right to make inappropriate requests. He's not footing the bill for the wedding and even if he was—"

"He lives with her." When Jonas felt their stares, he lifted his head and continued. "Roman Walker, the man you're scheduled to meet with, *lives* with Diana Peyton. He's her *live-in* trainer." Jonas mimed air quotes to the word *live-in*.

"So he's her boy toy." Connor sighed. "Great."

"Not necessarily," Jonas said. "He lives at Castle by the Sea, her enormous beach house up in Laguna. Oh, and he parked a Bentley with valet that's the cost of a house in any state that's not California. Make of that information what you will."

Ethan closed the distance between, setting a firm grip on both of their outside shoulders. "Gentlemen, I appreciate your protectiveness. Truly. I'm moved, to be frank. But I survived on the mean streets of New York City with barely a penny to my name. And today I'm senior staff at one of the *finest* and most well-run resorts on the face of this great planet where I'm honored to spend my days working alongside extraordinary men like the two of you."

Connor blushed. Jonas nodded deeply and smiled.

Ethan patted their shoulders and dropped his hands to his sides.

"In other words, I can handle some arrogant little *fitfluencer* who thinks he's hot shit 'cause he's got a rich sugar momma."

"All right," Connor said. "Well, if you charm Roman Walker the way you charm everyone else, things should be okay."

Ethan gave them a deep bow, then headed for the elevators, a skip in his step. Maybe it was the scandals the hotel had survived, or maybe it was the fact that queer men occupied positions of power throughout the resort, but there was a sense of camaraderie at Sapphire Cove that hadn't existed in any of his other places of employment. He'd had mentors during his career, but those relationships were usually one on one, little islands of refuge in environments of relentless competition and stress.

At Sapphire Cove, it felt like everyone had his back. A refreshing change of pace.

For most of his adult life, ever since his parents had banished him after finding him in bed with another guy, Ethan had been on his own. Some of the choices he'd made to support himself along the way haunted him. They'd also taught him never to count on anyone without first determining if their personal agenda aligned with yours. He considered this one of his great strengths, but when you added in widespread support from all your employees, it made him feel confident to the point of all powerful.

He knocked on the door to the penthouse suite. A male voice inside told him it was unlocked.

When he opened it and got a good look at the man waiting for him, all of Ethan's confidence crashed to the earth and shattered into a million pieces.

In Ethan's opinion, most people mistook the genetic advantages of youth for physical beauty. Baby smooth skin, bodies kept slender by youthful, humming metabolisms—these were not the same things as a facial structure that looked composed by the gods or a V-shaped torso that suggested hours of strenuous gym time. Roman Walker had both of these things.

Composed by the gods. It was a perfect description of the man who turned from the penthouse suite's open deck door as soon as Ethan stepped into the room. The social media star and trainer to one of the most famous actresses in the world regarded him with a penetrating, searching gaze, hazel eyes twinkling in the light of the pillar candles someone—probably a front desk clerk who'd been dazzled by his form-fitting, designer outfit—had lit throughout the expansive, two-room suite.

He stood on the other side of a dining table covered in sample cake slices resting on bone china plates. Night was minutes away from taking hold of the ocean horizon outside, and the flickering candlelight made it look as if the slices were all melting.

So were Ethan's insides, apparently.

The young man was six foot three, olive skinned, his black hair styled in a long, layered fringe with a low fade that highlighted his muscular neck. When he took a step away from the taffeta drape fluttering in the ocean breezes, the light from the chandelier over the dining table revealed subtle gold highlights in his brushed forward hair that matched the stud in his left ear and the thick choker around his throat that looked like a bronzed collection of little finger bones.

A choker Ethan suddenly wanted to grip like a dog collar as he forced the man to his knees and... *Bone down, Blake. You're at work.*

Studying Roman Walker's neck turned out to be dangerous business. The expanse of smooth, tan skin visible between the unzipped, upper portion of his jacket suggested that Ethan's joke of earlier might turn out to be correct—there was a distinct possibility the hottie had doffed his shirt. The jacket's design also did nothing to calm Ethan's bull-stomping-the-earth desire. It was some fashion designer's lustful take on a varsity letterman's jacket, snugger than any high school would allow. Despite its shiny leather, the black and white team number patches on the sleeves and the tell-tale fabric cuffs and collar triggered years of frustrated adolescent fantasies Ethan had cultivated while repressing his sexuality at a conservative Southern high school where football was king. His black jeans looked poured on, and Ethan knew if he let his eyes drop below the guy's waistline, he'd encounter a well-highlighted bulge. But when he stopped himself short, he ended up staring at a band of flat, tan stomach visible above the man's shining belt buckle.

Yes indeed, Roman Walker was shirtless under that jacket.

Or he was wearing a midriff.

And the man's eyes looked so familiar Ethan wondered if he'd scrolled through one of the guy's social media profiles without remembering it, maybe even relieved himself to the sight of the physical perfection on display there.

And now here.

When the young man smiled, his perfection was quickly tarnished.

Maybe because it was too contained, a smile that didn't quite take. A stiff and uncomfortable one. One he'd practiced in front of the mirror countless times so as not to let any expression of happiness disrupt the perfect symmetry of his face.

Suddenly, underneath the expensive, showy outfit, Roman seemed like a nervous kid trying to look like a painting of a fashion model. And the little flashes of bling seemed forced. Unnecessary.

Like wrapping paper.

Which was designed to be torn off.

*Probably by Diana Peyton, so knock it off and stay professional here.*

"I was starting to think you weren't going to come." The voice was a combination of low and lilting, but despite what looked like Italian ancestry, the accent was California vague.

"Apologies. The change of venue threw me off a bit."

"Is this okay?" he asked, as if there would be consequences for Ethan if it wasn't.

"It's your meeting, Mr. Walker. Your comfort's our priority. Have you had a chance to try any of the slices?" It was a foolish question. He could see they were all untouched.

"Well, someone's ready to get down to business."

"Apparently I kept you waiting, so…" Ethan smiled.

Roman chewed gently on his lower lip as he walked around the end of the dining table. Then he rested his butt against it, facing Ethan. The pose seemed like a deliberate attempt to show off his jeans-encased bulge.

It worked. This time, Ethan looked.

More impressed than he wanted to be, he cleared his throat and met the man's gaze. "I understand you have some concerns about the cake I proposed."

Roman stuck a finger in one of the slices and gently sucked the icing off with full wet lips that made Ethan want to groan under his breath. Once he swallowed, Roman said, "I have to protect my clients, and you deal in some very addictive substances, sir."

"Cake?"

"Among other things." Roman swallowed and let out a satisfied little groan.

Ethan gave him the same warm grin that had just charmed his boss and supervisor downstairs. "You wouldn't be calling me a drug dealer, would you, Mr. Walker?"

Roman licked more icing off his fingers as he locked eyes with Ethan. The message was clear—if Ethan was a dealer, the spectacular-looking young man before him could easily get hooked on his product.

Roman swallowed. "Sit," he whispered.

"That's very kind of you, but I work better on my feet."

"You're uncomfortable. With the room. Want to go somewhere else?"

"As I said, your comfort is the priority here."

Roman pouted. "What if I'm only comfortable if you're comfortable, Mr. Blake?"

Ethan wasn't prepared for what the sounds of the two words—Mr. Blake—out of this young man's mouth would do to him. The mix of deference and lustful invitation set loose pornified fantasies of professors and students breaking rules together. Or pastry chefs and live-in trainers endangering their jobs.

"Then letting me enjoy my comfortable shoes will keep us both comfortable," Ethan said.

"Sorry if it's too much. I kinda just wanted to get you alone. I'm a fan."

"Of mine?"

Roman nodded, smirking. "*Cake Face.*"

"Oh, dear." Ethan cleared his throat and studied the floor.

"No, it was awesome. You were too hard on that girl from Minnesota, though. Her cake totally looked like Eleanor Roosevelt."

"Eleanor Roosevelt in a tornado, perhaps."

Roman laughed. It was a startling, unrehearsed nasally sound that sent a little seizure through his upper body. As if he hadn't expected to laugh that evening and so he'd neglected to rehearse a version that was as poised and seductive as the rest of him. "Whatever. It was cool. I loved it," he added quickly.

"It's a dreadful show. I did it as a favor for a friend I used to work with. It was supposed to be a web series. I never expected Netflix to pick it up."

Roman gave him a patronizing nod and lifted one finger. "Hey, now. It was educational. For some of us, at least. I mean, I know way more about a bunch of our old presidents than I did before."

The show had required its contestants to make cakes that looked like famous dead people while baking and bickering and getting obnoxiously drunk inside a warehouse decked out like a cheap spaceship. Ethan had been a judge for the "Grand Old Pavlovas" episode, in which the players were required to capture the visages of famous pre-Eisenhower era political figures, and the season finale in which the winner had been declared. If Roman thought *Cake Face* was designed to inform, he'd probably skipped the "It's Buttercream, Bitch" episode, in which the entries had to be fashioned after '90s pop stars. Although, given his age, maybe that would have been an education for him too.

"I never thought about it that way."

"Also, you look good on TV." Another dollop of icing, another long, tender suck off his finger. "But you'd look good anywhere."

"For an older man, you mean."

Roman briefly nibbled his lower lip, leaving it a little wetter than before. "For a *real* man."

*I need to get out of here,* Ethan thought, but what he said was, "Thank you."

# Discover More Christopher Rice

## Sapphire Sunset
Sapphire Cove, Book 1
By Christopher Rice writing as C. Travis Rice

**For the first time *New York Times* bestselling author Christopher Rice writes as C. Travis Rice. Under his new pen name, Rice offers tales of passion, intrigue, and steamy romance between men. The first novel, SAPPHIRE SUNSET, transports you to a beautiful luxury resort on the sparkling Southern California coast where strong-willed heroes release the shame that blocks their heart's desires.**

Logan Murdoch is a fighter, a survivor, and a provider. When he leaves a distinguished career in the Marine Corps to work security at a luxury beachfront resort, he's got one objective: pay his father's mounting medical bills. That means Connor Harcourt, the irresistibly handsome scion of the wealthy family that owns Sapphire Cove, is strictly off limits, despite his sassy swagger and beautiful blue eyes. Logan's life is all about sacrifices; Connor is privilege personified. But temptation is a beast that demands to be fed, and a furtive kiss ignites instant passion, forcing Logan to slam the brakes. Hard.

Haunted by their frustrated attraction, the two men find themselves hurled back together when a headline-making scandal threatens to ruin the resort they both love. This time, there's no easy escape from the magnetic pull of their white hot desire. Will saving Sapphire Cove help forge the union they crave, or will it drive them apart once more?

\* \* \* \*

## Dance of Desire
By Christopher Rice

When Amber Watson walks in on her husband in the throes of extramarital passion with one of his employees, her comfortable, passion-free life is shattered in an instant. Worse, the fate of the successful country music bar that bears her family's name suddenly hangs in the balance. Her soon to be ex-husband is one of the bar's official owners; his mistress, one of its employees. Will her divorce destroy her late father's legacy?

Not if Amber's adopted brother Caleb has anything to do with it. The wandering cowboy has picked the perfect time for a homecoming. Better yet, he's determined to use his brains and his fists to put Amber's ex in his place and keep the family business intact. But Caleb's long absence has done nothing to dim the forbidden desire between him and the woman the State of Texas considers to be his sister.

Years ago, when they were just teenagers, Caleb and Amber shared a passionate first kiss beside a moonlit lake. But that same night, tragedy claimed the life of Caleb's parents and the handsome young man went from being a family friend to Amber's adopted brother. Has enough time passed for the two of them to throw off the roles Amber's father picked for them all those years ago? Will their desire for each other save the family business or put it in greater danger?

DANCE OF DESIRE is the first contemporary romance from award-winning, *New York Times* bestselling author Christopher Rice, told with the author's trademark humor and heart. It also introduces readers to a quirky and beautiful town in the Texas Hill Country called Chapel Springs.

READER ADVISORY. DANCE OF DESIRE contains fantasies of dubious consent, acted on by consenting adults. Readers with sensitivities to those issues should be advised.

\* \* \* \*

# Desire & Ice
## by Christopher Rice

Danny Patterson isn't a teenager anymore. He's the newest and youngest sheriff's deputy in Surrender, Montana. A chance encounter with his former schoolteacher on the eve of the biggest snowstorm to hit Surrender in years shows him that some schoolboy crushes never fade. Sometimes they mature into grown-up desire.

It's been years since Eliza Brightwell set foot in Surrender. So why is she back now? And why does she seem like she's running from something? To solve this mystery, Danny disobeys a direct order from Sheriff Cooper MacKenzie and sets out into a fierce blizzard, where his courage and his desire might be the only things capable of saving Eliza from a dark force out of her own past.

* * * *

# The Flame
## By Christopher Rice

IT ONLY TAKES A MOMENT...

Cassidy Burke has the best of both worlds, a driven and successful husband and a wild, impulsive best friend. But after a decadent Mardi Gras party, Cassidy finds both men pulling away from her. Did the three of them awaken secret desires during a split-second of alcohol-fueled passion? Or is Mardi Gras a time when rules are meant to be broken without consequence?

Only one thing is for certain—the chill that's descended over her marriage, and her most important friendship, will soon turn into a deep freeze if she doesn't do something. And soon.

LIGHT THIS FLAME AT THE SCENE OF YOUR GREATEST PASSION AND ALL YOUR DESIRES WILL BE YOURS.

The invitation stares out at her from the window of a French Quarter boutique. The store's owner claims to have no knowledge of the strange candle. But Cassidy can't resist its intoxicating scent or the challenge written across its label in elegant cursive. With the strike of a match and one tiny flame, she will call forth a supernatural being with the ultimate power—the power to unchain the heart, the power to remove the fear that stands between a person and their truest desires.

* * * *

# The Surrender Gate
## By Christopher Rice

Emily Blaine's life is about to change. Arthur Benoit, the kindly multimillionaire who has acted as her surrogate father for years, has just told her he's leaving her his entire estate, and he only has a few months to live. Soon Emily will go from being a restaurant manager with a useless English degree to the one of the richest and most powerful women in New Orleans. There's just one price. Arthur has written a letter to his estranged son Ryan he hopes will mend the rift between them, and he wants Emily to deliver the letter before it's too late. But finding Ryan won't be easy. He's been missing for years. He was recently linked to a mysterious organization called The Desire Exchange. But is The Desire Exchange just an urban legend? Or are the rumors true? Is it truly a secret club where the wealthy can live out their most private sexual fantasies?

It's a task Emily can't undertake alone. But there's only one man qualified to help her, her gorgeous and confident best friend, Jonathan Claiborne. She's suspected Jonathan of working as a high-priced escort for months now, and she's willing to bet that while giving pleasure to some of the most powerful men in New Orleans, Jonathan has uncovered some possible leads to The Desire Exchange—and to Ryan Benoit. But Emily's attempt to uncover Jonathan's secret life lands the two of them in hot water. Literally. In order to escape the clutches of one of Jonathan's most powerful and dangerous clients, they're forced to act on long buried desires—for each other.

When Emily's mission turns into an undercover operation, Jonathan insists on going with her. He also insists they continue to explore their impossible, reckless passion for each other. Enter Marcus Dylan, the hard-charging ex-Navy SEAL Arthur has hired to keep Emily safe. But Marcus has been hired for another reason. He, too, has a burning passion for Emily, a passion that might keep Emily from being distracted and confused by a best friend who claims he might be able to go straight just for her. But Marcus is as rough and controlling as Jonathan is sensual and reckless. As Emily searches for a place where the rich turn their fantasies into reality, she will be forced to decide which one of her own long-ignored fantasies should become her reality. But as Emily, Jonathan, and Marcus draw closer to The Desire Exchange itself, they find their destination isn't just shrouded in mystery, but in magic as well.

\* \* \* \*

# Kiss The Flame

By Christopher Rice

**Are some risks worth taking?**

Laney Foley is the first woman from her hard working family to attend college. That's why she can't act on her powerful attraction to one of the gorgeous teaching assistants in her Introduction to Art History course. Getting involved with a man who has control over her final grade is just too risky. But ever since he first laid eyes on her, Michael Brouchard seems to think about little else but the two of them together. And it's become harder for Laney to ignore his intelligence and his charm.

During a walk through the French Quarter, an intoxicating scent that reminds Laney of her not-so-secret admirer draws her into an elegant scented candle shop. The shop's charming and mysterious owner seems to have stepped out of another time, and he offers Laney a gift that could break down the walls of her fear in a way that can only be described as magic. But will she accept it?

**Light this flame at the scene of your greatest passion and all your desires will be yours...**

Lilliane Williams is a radiant, a supernatural being with the power to make your deepest sexual fantasy take shape around you with just a gentle press of her lips to yours. But her gifts came at a price. Decades ago, she set foot inside what she thought was an ordinary scented candle shop in the French Quarter. When she resisted the magical gift offered to her inside, Lilliane was endowed with eternal youth and startling supernatural powers, but the ability to experience and receive romantic love was removed from her forever. When Lilliane meets a young woman who seems poised to make the same mistake she did years before, she becomes determined to stop her, but that will mean revealing her truth to a stranger. Will Lilliane's story provide Laney with the courage she needs to open her heart to the kind of true love only magic can reveal?

# About Christopher Rice writing as C. Travis Rice

C. Travis Rice is the pen name New York Times bestselling novelist Christopher Rice devotes to steamy tales of passion, intrigue and romance between men. He has published multiple bestselling books in multiple genres and been the recipient of a Lambda Literary Award. He is an executive producer on the AMC Studios adaptations of the novels The Vampire Chronicles and The Lives of the Mayfair Witches by his late mother Anne Rice. Together with his best friend and producing partner, New York Times bestselling novelist, Eric Shaw Quinn, he runs the production company Dinner Partners. Among other projects, they produce the podcast and video network, TDPS, which you can find at www.TheDinnerPartyShow.com. Learn more about C. Travis Rice and Christopher Rice at www.christopherricebooks.com.

Sign up for the Blue Box Press/1001 Dark Nights Newsletter
and be entered to win a Tiffany Lock necklace.

There's a contest every quarter!

Go to www.TheBlueBoxPress.com to subscribe.

As a bonus, all subscribers can download
FIVE FREE exclusive books!

# Discover 1001 Dark Nights Collection Nine

DRAGON UNBOUND by Donna Grant
A Dark Kings Novella

NOTHING BUT INK by Carrie Ann Ryan
A Montgomery Ink: Fort Collins Novella

THE MASTERMIND by Dylan Allen
A Rivers Wilde Novella

JUST ONE WISH by Carly Phillips
A Kingston Family Novella

BEHIND CLOSED DOORS by Skye Warren
A Rochester Novella

GOSSAMER IN THE DARKNESS by Kristen Ashley
A Fantasyland Novella

THE CLOSE-UP by Kennedy Ryan
A Hollywood Renaissance Novella

DELIGHTED by Lexi Blake
A Masters and Mercenaries Novella

THE GRAVESIDE BAR AND GRILL by Darynda Jones
A Charley Davidson Novella

THE ANTI-FAN AND THE IDOL by Rachel Van Dyken
A My Summer In Seoul Novella

CHARMED BY YOU by J. Kenner
A Stark Security Novella

DESCEND TO DARKNESS by Heather Graham
A Krewe of Hunters Novella

BOND OF PASSION by Larissa Ione
A Demonica Novella

JUST WHAT I NEEDED by Kylie Scott
A Stage Dive Novella

*Also from Blue Box Press*

THE BAIT by C.W. Gortner and M.J. Rose

THE FASHION ORPHANS by Randy Susan Meyers and M.J. Rose

TAKING THE LEAP by Kristen Ashley
A River Rain Novel

SAPPHIRE SUNSET by Christopher Rice writing C. Travis Rice
A Sapphire Cove Novel

THE WAR OF TWO QUEENS by Jennifer L. Armentrout
A Blood and Ash Novel

THE MURDERS AT FLEAT HOUSE BY Lucinda Riley

THE HEIST by C.W. Gortner and M.J. Rose

SAPPHIRE SPRING by Christopher Rice writing as C. Travis Rice
A Sapphire Cove Novel

MAKING THE MATCH by Kristen Ashley
A River Rain Novel

A LIGHT IN THE FLAME by Jennifer L. Armentrout
A Flesh and Fire Novel

# On Behalf of Blue Box Press,

Liz Berry, M.J. Rose, and Jillian Stein would like to thank ~

Steve Berry
Doug Scofield
Benjamin Stein
Kim Guidroz
Social Butterfly PR
Kasi Alexander
Asha Hossain
Chris Graham
Jessica Johns
Dylan Stockton
Dina Williams
Kate Boggs
Richard Blake
and Simon Lipskar

Made in United States
Orlando, FL
24 October 2022

23799076R00221